TIMELESS

DIEGO AND THE RANGERS OF THE VASTLANTIC

ARMAND BALTAZAR

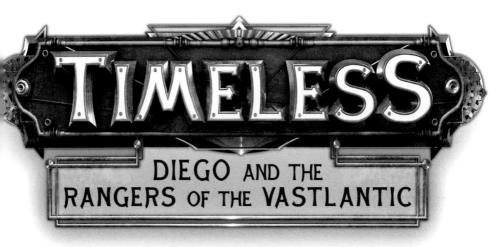

TIMELESS

DIEGO AND THE
RANGERS OF THE VASTLANTIC

Peachtree

KATHERINE TEGEN BOOKS
An Imprint of HarperCollins Publishers

Katherine Tegen Books is an imprint of HarperCollins Publishers.

Timeless: Diego and the Rangers of the Vastlantic
Copyright © 2017 by Armand Baltazar
All rights reserved. Manufactured in China.
Library of Congress Control Number: 2016013199
ISBN 978-0-06-240236-3

Typography by Carla Weise
17 18 19 20 21   SCP   10 9 8 7 6 5 4 3 2 1
❖
First Edition

For Dylan & Sharon Baltazar
and my friend
Kevyn Lee Wallace

Prologue

Our world did not end the way you might expect. It wasn't caused by any of the things you hear so much about today: the wars, the unrest, the changing climate. It wasn't our arrogance, our pride, our selfishness. No, in the end, it was our creativity and brilliance. We thought we were making history by changing the future.

Turns out, we did both.

It came from beyond the stars, a cosmic event we could never have predicted, a rupturing of the space-time continuum that tore apart our entire existence. Not just our present, but our past, our future—everything that humans had been or would be. Gone. And what remained was a void, echoing with the faint whispers of a world that no longer existed.

But that was not the end.

Humankind was granted a second chance.

Out of the great silence, the earth was reborn, but like

nothing we had ever fathomed. Dinosaurs roamed the great plains beside woolly mammoths and buffalo herds a million strong. Great steamships and ancient sailboats crossed the harbors among the legs of towering robots. The past, the present, the future—all thrown together. The continents reshaped, oceans re-formed, and mountains sculpted anew. This was the world after the Time Collision.

The hundred million or so humans who survived the cataclysm came from all points in time and found themselves scattered across the planet. The people of the civilized past were called Steam Timers, the people from the in-between times were called Mid Timers, and the people from the future came to be called the Elders. As these refugees from different eras struggled to survive in a dangerous world without order, conflict was inevitable. It was not long before this savage yet beautiful new landscape became a backdrop for war.

After years of fighting, the desperate people finally saw the pointlessness of hurting one another and realized they needed to work together. They declared an end to what came to be known as the Chronos War and grudgingly united to form governments, laws, and communities.

Their fragile peace allowed the surviving cities to rebuild and countries to be remade. Children were born, and the mysteries and wonders of this new world were explored.

But the darkness had not been vanquished. Despite all of humanity's efforts, there were still those roaming the undiscovered wilds who would never submit to peace and order, and who would strike down anyone who stood between them and the power . . .

. . . to make the world their own.

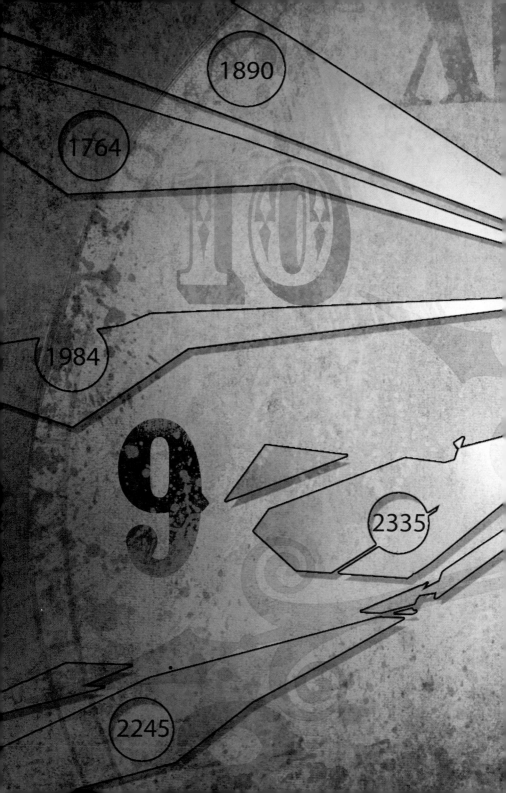

PART ONE
A World Remade

The two most important days in your life are the day you are born and the day you find out why.

CHAPTER ONE

A Dream of Flight

On the morning of his thirteenth birthday, Diego Ribera glimpsed his future in a dream. It was a dream he'd had before, one that he feared, and it always began with his father calling to him through darkness.

"Diego. We need more light."

Santiago's voice echoed through the vast workshop. He stood high on faded blue scaffolding among the enormous robots that ringed the room. He wielded a wrench the size of his arm, and was leaning dangerously far into the oily gears of a massive shoulder socket. The head, arms, and legs of the robot were spread around the floor in various stages of completion.

Diego sat on a stool, gazing at one of the robot's enormous eyes perched on the center workbench. He'd been studying the geometric kinks of its iris. It functioned like a Mid-Time camera aperture. Diego imagined the steel plates sliding open in sequence like flower petals. He pictured the tiny pistons firing one by one, how they connected to the steam processors. He seemed to *know* how these mechanics would work, sensed their purpose. He wondered if this was how it felt to be his father.

Everyone in New Chicago called Santiago a genius: the greatest mind of the new age. He was a builder, an inventor, a visionary. Some had even called him a charlatan, claiming that his creations were so ingenious that there must be some kind of trickery or fraud at work, but those people had never seen Santiago when he was engrossed in his work.

"Diego, did you hear me?"

"Yeah, sorry, Dad." Diego slid off the stool.

All at once he was standing at one of the workshop's towering windows.

Moved without moving.

I'm dreaming, Diego thought, though the awareness was fleeting. The edges of his vision swam in watery darkness.

He yanked the heavy curtains aside. Brilliant morning light spilled into the room.

"Is that enough?" Diego asked over his shoulder.

No answer.

"Dad?"

Diego turned. He found himself back in the middle of the room again. . . .

But Dad was gone. So was the robot he'd been working on. And all the others. No scaffolding, the workshop floor empty in all directions.

Except for the table where Diego had been sitting. The robot eye had also vanished, but now something far more interesting had appeared in its place, gleaming in the golden sunlight.

A gravity board.

Five feet long, made of alder wood, Kevlar, and chrome, and decorated in red and white stripes. The portable steam backpack and navigating gloves lay beside it. Of all his father's wondrous inventions, the gravity boards were Diego's favorite. He and his friend Petey had flown them around the workshop on many occasions.

And yet the sight of the board filled him with worry: he'd had this dream before.

The board always appeared right after Dad vanished.

There was danger here, something he couldn't quite grasp.

"Diego."

"Dad?" Diego peered into the shadows. But that hadn't sounded like his father. "Who's there?"

The disquiet grew in his belly. This may have been a dream, but his fear felt all too real.

He spied a silhouette in the dark space between two windows. The figure stepped into the morning light. Not his father. Shorter. A girl? It was hard to tell. She was wearing thick goggles and an aviator's cap. She looked about his age.

"Who are you?" Diego asked.

The girl stood motionless. When she spoke again, her mouth didn't move, her voice instead echoing in Diego's mind:

Fly.

Then she vanished.

A gust of air.

Diego spun to see the girl leaping out the window.

"No, don't!" Diego rushed over. He gazed down at the bustling street ten stories below, but the girl wasn't lying broken on the train tracks, nor floating faceup in the canal. Instead, she was speeding away through the air, on a gravity board of her own.

Fly!

The voice burned between Diego's temples. He had to move. Had to act.

Diego grabbed the gravity board from the bench. He slung the steam pack over his shoulders. The heaviness of the miniature brass boiler and pressure converter threw him off balance, but he got his feet under him and ran for the window. He slipped on the thick leather gloves—covered in dials and fastened to the pack by slim hoses. He attached the power gauge regulator, flicked switches, and heard the familiar hiss as the boiler cycled up—

And then he was leaping into the sky.

Wind swirled around him. Windows blurred by. Diego hurtled toward the street, but he held the board firm with both hands and slid it beneath his feet. He hit a switch on his gloves, activating the magnet locks, and his boots fastened into place. The busy sidewalks rushed toward him. He pressed hard with his feet, shifted his weight, the ground speeding closer. . . .

The steam turbine whined at full strength, the board dug into the air, and Diego shot forward into a glide, skimming above the shop awnings and the Steam-Time ladies' high hats.

Diego finally breathed, his face bathed in the breeze. Yes! He felt a shimmering excitement as he soared through the

air, a feeling he'd yearned for all his life, one he knew was in his blood.

He pressed the board against the wind, sweeping this way and that. The movements felt as natural as walking, but so much better.

He sped over New Chicago, its canals and train tracks clogged with the morning traffic of steamships and trolleys, its sidewalks crowded with topcoats, leather tunics, and fine capes, a world collided in color and sound, in the smell of horse droppings and engine grease, corn roasting on food carts, and the sea. Off in the distance, the exhaust clouds from the great steamships and harbor robots colored the sunrise gold.

He spotted the girl up ahead, knifing through the sky. He had to catch her before it was too late. Diego didn't know why, just knew he had to. Something to do with time, he thought. It was always time, running forward and backward through this world, but in this dream . . .

Running out.

Diego was the wind. He was the sky. He felt light as air and knew this was all he'd ever wanted, just like his

mom. To fly free.

He spied the girl again, arcing around the next corner. Diego cut the angle so hard that his shoulder glanced off the brick-building wall, but he also edged closer.

If he could reach her, he could pull the main hose on her steam pack and disable the board. He could guide her down to the canal, and then she would be safe.

Safe from what? Diego didn't know.

They turned sharply into a wide plaza around City Hall. The building was a grand tower, a mix of Elder and Mid-Time architecture, the plaza a series of floating walkways over water, with fountains burbling in intricate patterns. Diego was surprised to find the plaza packed with people, a huge crowd. More and more were streaming in from all sides,

every one of them gazing upward and pointing.

But the timbre of the crowd changed: their gasps shifted from awe to worry. Those who weren't pointing to the sky were jostling one another, trying to leave.

Diego glanced around for his flying partner, but there was no sign of the girl. She had disappeared.

The shouts below turned to screams of terror. Panic. People knocking one another over to get away. Diego followed the pointing fingers to the great clock at the top of City Hall, gleaming in the morning sun.

At first, he thought that the clock must be broken, because the hands seemed to be missing. There were still earthquakes now and then, due to the new fault lines where the earth's crust had re-fused, but that wasn't it. The hands were still there; they were just spinning so fast that they had become a blur.

Spinning backward.

The sight made Diego's vision swim. He had to bend down and grab the sides of the board to keep his balance.

When he did, he saw the empty plaza below. All those people. Gone.

There was no one in the nearby streets either, the tracks and canals vacant, no airships in the sky, no smoke from steamers in the harbor.

It was so quiet. Diego's breathing echoed in his head. The only other sound was the humming of the clock hands.

Diego's board began to vibrate. The buildings started to tremble. The clock hands suddenly froze, and the world seemed to halt. Even Diego, his breath caught in his throat, his board stuck in the air—

Then the world began to roar.

Diego raced away as fast as he could. Water and ash swirled behind him, coming closer. Boats and trolleys rocketed up in the air, thrown by the force of the blast. The sky went dark, clouds and dust all around, swallowing Diego. He lost sight of the sky, the buildings, and . . .

A voice drifted across an infinite wind, speaking a single word as if from a hundred miles away.

"Forward."

CHAPTER TWO

The Riberas
of New Chicago

Diego's eyes flashed open, the vision of the crumbling city still fresh in his mind.

He blinked and saw a curve of metal overhead, dotted by rivets. The inside of his bed.

Diego breathed deep. It had only been a dream . . . a nightmare. He sat up on his elbows, careful not to bump his head inside the old propane tank that his dad had converted to look like a Mid-Time–era submarine. The bed had been a present for Diego's eighth birthday. These days, his feet reached to the far end when he slept.

He looked around his room and saw that everything was as it always was.

Diego shivered. He'd pushed his blankets off during the dream. He reached for them but then noticed daylight through the windows. He glanced at the clock—would the hands be spinning backward? No, they were normal; of course they were. And it was time to get up.

Still, he lay back for a moment, crossing his arms. The image of everything exploding played across his mind. He knew it was a dream, but still. There had been that gravity board. Something he wanted more than anything else.

Diego swung his legs out of bed and stood, stretching. He threw on cargo work pants and his favorite T-shirt: orange with bright white letters that spelled ATARI.

His eyes paused on the poster above his bed. It showed the skyline of Chicago the way it used to be. A long row of elegant buildings neatly arranged along the shore of a lake. The city that his father was from. Before the Time Collision. Diego was part of the first generation of children to be born in this new world. Everyone older had arrived here from some other time. Many people still identified themselves as being *from* those other eras, but not his parents. Though Santiago was a Mid Timer and his mother, Siobhan, was a Steam Timer, they thought of themselves simply as citizens of this new world.

"You are lucky," Santiago had said once. "You are a child of the future. You will never be held back by the past."

Santiago never talked about the Time Collision, or the Dark Years that followed. Some groups were still bitter about the war, but his focus was always on making this world better.

Still, he had saved a few clippings from the newspapers right after the event. When Diego started learning about the Time Collision in school, Dad had given them to him. They were on the wall above his desk.

The biggest one was titled TIME COLLISION! The article below was interesting to read now: people had known so little in the years right after, when the Chronos War had erupted. The Steam Timers had fought the other-time cultures for control of the world,

and for a while, people had become more dangerous than the dinosaurs.

A different article detailed a group of hunters standing over a

The best of days! with Anders and Diego

spinosaurus; another, the vast woolly mammoth herds that lived north of the wild lands. And below there was one about the first explorations across the fantastically changed American landscape by the great explorer Bartholomew Roosevelt. Diego stepped onto the balcony outside his room. A cool, salty breeze greeted his face. It smelled like seaweed and diesel fuel. He gripped the railing and gazed out over the city. He wanted to make sure it still looked like it always had. One last assurance that his dream had been just that.

And sure enough, there was New Chicago, shimmering in the morning sun, looking as fixed and permanent as a city made of three different time periods could.

A ship's horn blared. In the distance beyond the building tops, Diego spied the great heads and shoulders of massive, clanking robots toiling in the morning mist of the harbor. Once the cargo ships were tended to, these robots would make their way into the canals, their engineers patrolling the city for any signs of deterioration or disrepair from the salt water. The canals were once city streets, but they all lay beneath the waters of the Vastlantic, an ancient ocean that now covered a third of North America.

A bright blue robotic crane passed by Diego's building, picking its way through the crowded canal like a spider on its eight spindly legs. Another smaller robot followed not far behind. It was yellow and sturdy, more like a bulldozer on legs but with two piston-powered arms instead of a giant shovel. It towed a barge loaded with steel beams.

The streets were clogged with people and vehicles from many eras. New Chicago was unique like that. In most parts of the world, the eras of time were uniform over vast geographic regions, and they lined up neatly against each other like slices of a pie. Here, the time regions were more like splinters in a cracked mirror. Some narrow and long, some short and trapezoidal, and they wove and crossed among one another. It made life more colorful and chaotic than in other places, and

in some ways more dangerous, but compared to that skyline in the poster on his wall, Diego thought this version of Chicago seemed way more interesting.

The smell of bacon and eggs broke Diego out of these thoughts. He heard sizzling meat from inside. Then he remembered why they were having a bigger breakfast than normal.

It was Diego's thirteenth birthday.

He hurried back inside and to the kitchen. Siobhan stood by the stove wearing her pilot's jumpsuit, her thick red curls pulled back and held up with a blue chopstick. She dropped another strip of bacon into the sizzling pan just as the pressure gauge next to the stove dropped to zero. A shrill whistle burst from the gauge, and the stove went dead.

"Blimey," Siobhan muttered. "There should be at least thirty minutes of power left on that blasted thing."

"Try this one, Mom," Diego said, unclipping the pressure gauge from his belt and handing it to her. "It should have three hours of burn on it."

"Thank you, my darling birthday boy." She hugged him tightly, kissing his forehead.

"Mom . . . ," Diego said.

"What?" She smiled as she unscrewed the depleted gauge and affixed the new one, the stove snapping back to life. "Should I say 'young man' now instead of 'boy'?"

"Just maybe not '*darling*,'" Diego said.

Siobhan sighed. Her face was ivory white and smooth, her eyes a striking gray blue. "Oh, you are getting older, aren't you? And I think you grew another inch overnight." She tapped his nose with her index finger. "Sit. You need to eat and get off to school. And don't forget," she added as Diego moved to the table, "you're meeting Dad after school today at the Arlington Geothermal plant."

"I know," Diego said.

"You're supposed to report to the ferry dock right after

school. No messing around with Petey. Dad says that installing this new steam converter will take all afternoon."

"I know," Diego said. "Man, it would've been great if Dad could've built the power plant closer. The ferry ride is too long."

"I think you could forgive him that one oversight," Siobhan said. "This city has power, security, and prosperity because of your father."

He knew how much his father had done for New Chicago: in the short years after the Time Collision, Santiago had designed and built the power plant and the perimeter wall protecting the territories, and created most of the robots that maintained and protected the city. "It's just a long afternoon on my birthday."

"Yes," Siobhan said. "We'd been hoping to take you to the Signature Room at the 95th for dinner tonight, but this job is very important. If your father could have scheduled it for any other day, believe me, he would have. So there will be no more complaining in the ranks, boyo. Is that understood?"

"Aye, aye, Captain," Diego said. He gave his mom a salute. Siobhan flew for the City Search and Rescue now, but she'd once been a decorated fighter pilot. She fought against the Aeternum, a group of marauders who frequently raided New Chicago and other coastal cities in the aftermath of the Chronos War, and her part in the decisive Battle of Dusable Harbor had made her a legend.

Heavy boots echoed down the hall.

"Good morning," Santiago said. He was dressed for work.

Though the title Chief Mechanical and Civil Engineer might sound like it required a suit, Santiago was not one to put on airs, never mind wash the engine grease from beneath his fingernails. He was happiest when he was right there among his crew, up to his elbows in machines.

He hung his heavy, weather-beaten satchel on the back of a chair and then filled a mug with coffee.

"Good morning, Santi." Siobhan handed him a plate of food, and he leaned over to kiss her.

"You always look fetching and official in your uniform," he said.

"I thank ya kindly," Siobhan said, her words seeped in a light Irish lilt that always seemed stronger when she was either embarrassed or furious. "Turns out I got all fancied up for nothing. The whole fleet's grounded. Colonel McGregor sent word that the batch of fuel they put into the squadron last night was bad."

"Bad?" Santiago asked as he sat down. "How could that be?"

"Full of impurities," Siobhan said. "So, instead of flying, we're going to spend all day draining the tanks and flushing the fuel lines. It's affected most of the navy ships, too. Nearly every vehicle at the base is out of commission."

"Sorry to hear it," Santiago said. "That's odd, though. The Calumet refinery is usually so reliable. Did they say how it happened?"

"Not in the report I got," Siobhan said.

Santiago frowned. "I'll give them a call later this morning.

If there's a problem with one of the pumps, the sooner I can send a team the better." After a bite of eggs, he glanced at Diego. "I heard you call her 'Captain.' You'll be a captain yourself this afternoon."

Diego smiled nervously. "And what will I be *captain* of?" he asked, thinking, *Say a gravity board, say a gravity board. . . .*

"Hah." Santiago chuckled and ate his bacon. "The loader, of course, driving the big blue Centauri bot. This Goliath steam converter is a big deal. I hope you're still up for it."

"Oh," Diego said. "Right. That bot is kinda tricky."

"I've seen you handle it like a pro," Santiago said.

"I'm not *that* good at it," Diego said. "I mean, I guess when we're installing pressure valves or something, but . . . maybe you should have Stan Angelino do it. He's the top robot driver at Arlington."

"Come on," Santiago said. "You are my son. How could you help but be one of the best, someday maybe even *the* best?" Santiago rubbed the top of Diego's head, messing up his hair. "This converter came to us all the way from London. The queen's top steam propulsion designer and his son are here to help us install it. Stan is very good, but I need my top man on the job."

Diego felt his cheeks burn.

"And besides," Santiago said, "you've got to see this thing. It's massive!"

Dad always sounded like a kid when he talked about work. He liked to say that it kept him young, though lately

Diego had noticed the gray hair at his father's temples and the occasional white whisker in his broad mustache.

But instead of smiling back, Diego stared down at his plate.

"What is it, Diego?"

"Well, I just don't understand why Magistrate Huston thinks that we need some old-fashioned steam technology. First, there was the engineer from France with his revolutionary gas lamp systems, then that awful crude oil expert from Texas. Now we have to put up with some stuffy British guy?" Diego flashed a glance at his father. "I mean, you're ten times the engineer that he is."

Santiago sipped his coffee. "Sharing our technology helps strengthen our alliances. It's my duty to help them, and this converter is the queen's way of doing the same." Santiago smiled. "There's more to being chief engineer than gears and pistons. There's also the workings of people. And sometimes they're more complicated. You'll have to learn that if you are ever going to take my place."

Diego wished he hadn't said anything. "I don't know, Dad. . . ." He didn't think he could ever take Santiago's place. He didn't know if he had that kind of greatness in him, and he didn't want to see the disappointment in his father's eyes if he didn't.

"Listen," Dad said. "I realize it's not as exciting as taking your pilot's test. But I need you."

"I know," Diego said.

"And someday when you finally turn thirteen and take

that test, you'll still be the youngest pilot in New Chicago."

"Dad . . . ," Diego muttered. He shoved a whole piece of bacon into his mouth.

"What is it?" Santiago asked.

"*Today* is my birthday."

"Wait . . . today? But . . ." Santiago started counting on his fingers. "It can't be. Today is Tuesday, yesterday was Monday. Before that it was Sunday, so today must be . . ."

Santiago's face cracked, and he started to laugh.

"Dad!" Diego said.

"You're horrible," Siobhan said, punching Santiago's shoulder lightly.

"Sorry," Santiago said, grinning. "But I had you going." He pulled a small package from his satchel and held it out. "Don't worry, I didn't forget. Here."

This was not the size of a gravity board, but Diego pulled off the brown paper, revealing a small box wrapped in white paper, with a blue bow. There was a card attached.

> *To our young adventurer and son, Diego*
> *Through this, may you see*
> *A world of wonders hidden from most.*
> *Love, Mom & Dad*

He unwrapped the package.

"What is it?" Diego asked, raising the tube to his eye. Through the lens, he saw tiny broken fragments. They formed a fractured pattern of beautiful colored shapes.

"Now turn the other end," his father instructed. Diego rotated the cylindrical collar at the front. The image began to move and change, forming new patterns even more beautiful than the last, the colors tumbling and rearranging.

"Wow," Diego said.

Santiago smiled. "It's a kaleidoscope. It has mirrors and bits of different-colored glass inside. That's what creates those patterns when you rotate it."

"It's amazing," Diego replied. He turned the device over in his hand.

"Don't you like it?" Siobhan asked.

"Yeah, I mean—it's awesome." He tried to sound thankful, and he was just . . . Was this it? "Thanks, guys."

"Never discount the potential in all things, no matter how humble their appearance," Santiago said.

"Okay," Diego said, doing his best to smile.

But his parents were still grinning.

"Santi," Siobhan said, nearly cracking up. "Isn't there something else?"

"Maybe." Santiago's eyes glinted mischievously.

Diego jumped. "Is it—"

"Hold your horses," Dad said. "It's still down in the workshop. I have a few last touches to do, but it will be ready by tonight." He saw Diego's face fall. "I think you can survive.

Besides, we have lots to distract us between now and then. I . . ."

Santiago paused and looked at Diego curiously.

"What?" Diego asked. It was almost like Santiago was studying him. "Dad . . ."

"Sorry." Santiago shook his head, like he was returning from a daydream. "You know what? On second thought, I tell you what: Why don't we stop by the workshop before school?" He checked his watch. "There's enough time if you eat fast. And then you can have that present now, after all."

"Okay, cool." Diego wolfed down his food.

"I'll meet you at the front door," Santiago said, gathering his belt and refilling his coffee mug.

Diego shoved in his last bites and jumped to his feet, still chewing.

"Bye, sweetie," Siobhan said, kissing Diego's head. "We'll have cake tonight when you two get home."

CHAPTER THREE

A Workshop of Wonders

D iego and Santiago rode the elevator down to the
workshop. The elevator clacked and shimmied, its
gears grinding. Like so many things, it had once
run on electricity, but the Time Collision had made the
earth's magnetic field violently unstable. As a result, virtually nothing electric worked. Some simple devices worked
with the help of Elder fuses but only in limited capacity and
only for short amounts of time. Limited use of old-fashioned
telegraph devices was the only form of long-distance communication. Anything that had used circuit boards needed
to be resurrected using steam, hydraulics, limited diesel, and

manual labor. The work that Santiago had pioneered, mixing Steam-Time and Mid-Time technologies, had been the key to rebuilding the world safely. He had replaced this elevator's smooth plastic buttons with brass ones that triggered little pistons, which in turn connected to gear works. The elevator lowered with a rhythmic pumping of steam compressors. Like most things in the city, it smelled of machine oil.

The elevator lurched and clanged to a stop, the doors grinding open.

As they did, Diego felt an odd sensation in his head. The world swam slightly, and there was a faint ringing in his ears. He put his hand against the wall to steady himself.

Santiago stepped out into the hall and glanced back at Diego.

"Diego, are you okay?"

"Yeah, I just . . . I'm fine," Diego said, following him out. He took a deep breath and felt normal again, but when he looked up, Santiago was still gazing at him oddly.

"Dad, what?"

Santiago shook his head. "You just looked green for a second. You sure you're all right? It's going to be a big job today. I'll need your best effort."

"It's just driving a loader," Diego said, walking beside Dad. "And I'm sure their steam converter is nowhere near as sophisticated as yours."

"No," Santiago agreed. "But its designer, George Emerson, is a tough nut to crack. Don't take his attitude personally. He's been here six months already, working on the retrofit, and the encounters I've had with him have been ... less than pleasant. His son Georgie has been helping too, though, and he's much nicer. Maybe you two will have something in common."

"Maybe," Diego said.

They walked down a high-ceilinged hall, their footsteps echoing on the long, warped boards.

"Hey, have you thought any more about what you want to do this summer?" Santiago asked.

"Nah," Diego said. "I'm not sure yet."

"Time's getting short," Dad said. "If you want to fly and service the planes with your mother at the air base, I'll need to find an apprentice for the shop. And that will be hard, since I already have the best young engineer in New Chicago."

Diego knew that if he looked up, he'd find Dad smiling proudly, so he kept his eyes on the floor. "I like working in the shop, Dad. It's just ..."

Santiago sighed. "I know. You love to fly. Besides, Mom should get a summer with you for once." Santiago patted Diego's shoulder. "She's jealous of all the time we get together."

"I could still come by in the evenings," Diego said. "I mean, to check in on the robots and stuff."

"I'm sure that won't be a problem. I'd be glad for it. Whoever I find will no doubt need a lot of training."

"Well, yeah, but then you'll have someone around who can really help out, long term."

Santiago shrugged. "Someone who will need things

explained three times when you barely needed once."

"That's not true," Diego said. "I wrecked that plasma torch last month, even though you showed me how to use it."

"That plasma torch would be hard for even my most experienced men to operate."

"Yeah, but . . ."

Santiago stopped and patted Diego's shoulder. "It's all right. I hear you. Flying sounds more exciting."

Diego wasn't sure that was what he was saying at all. And he hated this feeling that he was letting his father down, but also that Dad kept assuming Diego was a genius builder like he was. Actually, there was little chance he'd ever be the pilot that his mother was either. Both his parents cast tall shadows.

"You know working with Search and Rescue will be a lot more swabbing decks and windshields than flying patrols or performing rescues," Dad said.

"I know." Diego understood that what he most often pictured—spotting Aeternum scout ships, arcing through the air with his cannon rifles firing—was unrealistic for his summer.

A shrill bark echoed in the hallway.

"Hey, Daphne." Diego bent, and the little orange-and-white Shiba Inu nearly jumped on his face. "Whoa, girl." Diego wrestled the dog down and gave her a quick, furious scratch. "Nice to see you, too."

He stopped at a large metal door on runners and twisted the big dials on its lock. The door hissed and began to grind open.

"Over here," Santiago said. He stood by a large iron workbench, its faded red paint chipped and worn away. The sunlight bathed a black tarp covering something on the table.

"Now," Santiago said, grinning like a kid. "Back to your birthday . . ." He whipped off the tarp.

There it was: a gravity board, the magnet-bottom boots, steam pack, and gloves beside it.

"Awesome," Diego breathed. He gazed at the polished surface, at the fans and machinery. The design was so cool. Diego could barely keep himself from grabbing it and jumping headlong out the window.

"Oh," he said. "Hey, you weren't kidding . . . it's not finished."

"What do you mean, it's nearly there . . . isn't it?" Santiago asked, eyeing him.

Diego pointed to the board. "Well, the rear thruster and the mercury accelerator haven't been installed yet." It seemed obvious to Diego, but that was strange; he'd never really studied exactly how these boards worked. He'd been too concerned with how to fly them.

"I was going to finish it today and give it to you tonight," Santiago said, stepping over to a bench by the wall. He returned with an armful of parts. "But maybe you should try to finish it yourself." He placed the parts on the table.

"Me?" Diego said. "But I've never worked on one of these."

"I think it will be different today."

"Dad—"

"Diego. Try." Santiago's hand fell on his shoulder. "I want you to place your hands on the engine components and close your eyes."

Diego glanced at his dad.

Santiago nodded at the parts. "I'm serious. Go ahead."

Diego shrugged. "Okay . . . but this would probably go a lot faster if you did it." He placed his hands over the cool metal pieces and closed his eyes.

"Now, try to *see* how the engine should be put together in your mind."

"But I have no idea how—"

"Just try."

Diego almost pointed out that birthday presents were a lot less fun when they were tests. Also, what if he couldn't do it? He wanted to fly this thing today!

But even as he was wondering this, a strange thing began to happen in Diego's mind. He saw flashes . . . images of the parts. Not just the parts, but how they fit together. It happened in bursts of white light against darkness. He focused on two pieces and saw them connect. Two more, now three. And not only that, he sensed their relationships, how the different pieces functioned together, how each gear, each material had a purpose.

Distantly, he felt his muscles working, his hands and

arms moving, following the images in his mind. He lined up pieces, grabbed a screwdriver from the far end of the table, made a connection. . . .

It was like watching a movie about how to put the parts together, except that movie was playing *inside* his mind, almost like some part of him already knew. *But how do I know this?* he wondered.

The thought broke his concentration, and the images sank back into the darkness.

"Ow!" Diego felt a stinging sensation as he opened his eyes. He'd stabbed his thumb with the screwdriver. He hadn't drawn blood, but there was a red indentation.

"What just happened?" Diego asked, looking up at Santiago. "I saw something, but I lost it."

"Relax," Santiago said, his voice nearly a whisper. "Concentrate on the pieces and try again. Clear your mind and think only about the build, and nothing else."

Diego closed his eyes and focused harder. The flashes returned, showing him more. His hands moved faster, his brow starting to sweat. He finished the accelerator and moved to the motor, calibrated it, and finished the assembly.

I can't believe this is happening, he thought. *What is making this happen—*

Just that simple thought seemed to snuff out the images again. Diego took a deep breath and concentrated again, but the images didn't return. *Come on.* He tried to think of nothing else, to clear his mind and *focus,* but there were only distant impressions in the dark, like shapes through a fog.

Diego sighed and opened his eyes. "I lost it," he said. The board was nearly complete. He stepped away from the bench, breathing hard. His brain felt stretched, his head tingly. He eyed the board. "Dad, what was that?"

"I'll show you." Santiago shut his eyes and reached to the parts. His fingers traced over the last small pieces, then fit them together to make a compression valve, which he placed in the motor. He flipped a switch, and the mercury accelerator purred to life. The board rose in front of them, hovering a foot off the table.

"How did you do that?"

"We did it," Santiago said, "by *seeing* it and only it. There can be no other thoughts or feelings. Your total focus must be on the thing that you make."

"That doesn't make sense," Diego said, except it *had* made sense as it had been happening. "How is that possible?"

"First things first," Santiago said. "Tell me this: Did you notice anything different about that engine as you were working?"

Diego was surprised to realize that he had. "You replaced the titanium mounts with destabilized aluminum alloy."

"And why would I have done that?"

"Um . . . because it is lighter and more powerful," Diego said. "So it will stay flexible under increased pressure without becoming brittle." That made sense; Diego had heard his dad talk about things like alloy properties, but it wasn't like he'd ever studied them.

"And that means . . . ?" Santiago probed.

"It means that I can make a near ninety-degree full-throttle turn while absorbing the violent vibrations that would normally tear the motor out." Diego shook his head. "How do I . . . *know* all this? I've never even worked on a gravity board. I don't—"

"But you do," Santiago said. He put his arm around Diego. "You saw it, Diego, just like I knew you would. Because you are my son."

"Dad, that doesn't make sense."

"But it does. There's a reason why I can build the things I build, why I can see how to bring together the technologies of the different times in a way that very few can. I have a gift."

"You're really smart."

"No, it's more than that. I have a . . . power."

"What, like a superpower?"

"Not exactly. But it is, was, unique to me."

"Were you born with it?"

"No, it manifested in me after I came to this world. I was sixteen the first time I used it successfully; I was volunteering to help build a well for the Natives living in the western territories. The design I came up with, everyone claimed it was impossible. The Steam-Time engineers said it was a miracle or maybe witchcraft, but an old Algonquin shaman there called it something else . . . the Maker's Sight."

"A shaman," Diego said, trying to fit all this into the

nuts-and-bolts image he'd always had of his father. "The Maker's Sight? And you're the only one who has it?"

"Maybe not the only one. The shaman said that she'd seen this kind of thing before, but she wouldn't speak of it further, except to warn me to keep the power secret. And I have, until today."

"You knew I had it," Diego said. "Didn't you?"

"Yes, but not until today. Your mother and I always suspected that you might inherit the Sight, but we were never quite sure."

Diego peered up at his father. "Why today?"

"I can't say. But this morning at breakfast I saw these flashes of light in my mind that tingled and burned. They reminded me of how I experienced the Sight, but they weren't quite the same. In between each flash, I saw the gravity board. I suspected that the power had come alive in you, but I couldn't be sure until we came down here. When you first gazed at the unfinished gravity board, I could feel the Maker's Sight in you . . . around you, coming off you in waves."

"So are you saying that it, like, runs in our family?"

"Yes, but it begins with me. Or, more precisely, with the Time Collision. Before that, I was just a normal boy. The Sight is just another way that the world was made new."

"And it lets you build things."

"It shows me a series of images that allow me to make or fix anything. Like what you just experienced, but to use it at the level I do requires supreme concentration, and it takes years to master. I am not certain that this is what the power is for, or even the only way to use it, but this is what I have chosen to do with it. In the world after the Collision, building and fixing things seemed like the best way for me to help the world."

"So," Diego said, "what am I supposed to do with it?"

"I'm not sure. It may be the same, or it may have a different purpose that is unique to you. You will figure that out as your Sight grows."

Diego looked back at the board. If he could assemble the parts needed to construct the gravity board, what else could he make? "What's the best thing you've used the Sight for?" he asked.

"I'm not sure. I never really thought of it like that."

"Come on," Diego said. "Did you ever enhance the fighter planes, like with better engines or weapons? Or, like, what about robots that could seek out the Aeternum to defeat them once and for all?" Diego remembered the picture of his uncle Arden and his parents. "Then maybe Uncle Arden wouldn't have died in the Battle of Dusable Harbor—"

"No," Santiago said. He'd stiffened, his gaze lost in the table. "During the Dark Years, my first instinct *was* to build machines to match the violence around us, and to save lives. I saw so many terrible things in the Chronos War: Mid-Time towns gouged apart by Steam-Time cannon fire while their armies were laid waste by Mid-Time missiles, so much violence brought on by people's hatred of each other's time culture. But the thing was, there were so few humans left, a superior weapon might have ended the conflict, but it also would have caused unforgivable destruction, and I didn't think humanity could survive it.

"I realized that to survive in this world, what we really needed was each other. Mid Timers and Elders needed the Steam Timers. And as much as they hated to admit it, Steam Timers needed us, too. The Steam Timers had technology that still worked, the Elders had their advanced science and medicine, and the Mid Timers could bridge the gap.

"Now, years later, this world faces an enemy more dangerous than we ever faced during the Chronos War. We can beat the Aeternum, but not through the creation of superior weapons. It must be through our prosperity and by making a stronger world. Does that make sense?"

"Sort of," Diego said. "But just making the world more prosperous won't stop the Aeternum, will it? Not like a better fighter plane. Why not show them how powerful you are? Then they would fear you."

Santiago sighed. "In my experience, fear never leads to freedom. This was proved true all too often in the world before the Time Collision. Making the world more prosperous will rally the people to stand against those who'd take their future away from them."

"Could you build defenses then? Instead of weapons. You know, like shields, or . . ."

"Diego, that's not the point. I understand where you're coming from, son, but the power has to be used carefully,"

Santiago said. "There are those who would use it toward self-ish ends, and still others who would fear what we can do and want to destroy us because of it."

"Destroy us?" Diego repeated. "Who would want to do that? You mean like the True Believers?" The True Believers were Steam Timers who had become time supremacists. They wanted to form a society free of Mid-Time and Elder influence.

"Perhaps," Santiago said. "By combining their technology with that of the Mid Timers and Elders, I do what they are sworn to stop. And we know how ruthless they can be."

"There's more of them around town now, too," Diego said. "There are even Believer gangs at school these days."

"Yes," Santiago said. "That is why, for now, you must keep this power secret, as I have. For our safety, for our family's safety."

"But for how long?"

"Until the world evolves. We are still a civilization heal-ing from a traumatic wound. Much of the hatred comes from people's fears. They want to hold on to what little is left of what they know rather than embrace what they could learn."

"Was your old time better than this one?" Diego asked.

"No," Santiago said. "It was different: in some ways better but in other ways much worse, despite what the Believers say."

They both fell silent. The din of the outside streets bled in through the walls. Diego gazed at the gravity board, trying to comprehend everything he'd just learned.

A rolling sound reached his ears, and Daphne barked.

"Heads-up!"

Diego turned as Petey Kowalski swept through the door on an old skateboard. He swerved to avoid Daphne, who hopped excitedly on two legs.

"Good girl," Petey said. He bent down as he passed and tried to rub Daphne's head, but lost his balance and stumbled off his board. He careened into the table, catching himself against the edge as the skateboard shot across the room and smacked into the far wall.

"Whoa!" Petey said, breathing hard. "Almost lost it."

"Almost?" Diego said.

"Well, I mean, I was just—Oooh, no way!" Petey spied the gravity board.

"Birthday present," Diego said.

"And we are going to ride it to school, right? Tell me we are going to ride it right now!" Petey exclaimed.

"The board is only safe for one rider," Santiago said.

"Dad," Diego said, "could we bring Mom's board to school so that Petey and I could both ride during lunch?"

"Hmmm." Santiago scratched his chin as if deep in thought. "You do deserve some birthday fun. Okay. If you promise to be careful with it, and if you clean up these tools before you leave."

"Definitely!" Diego said.

"It's not like you haven't tried the boards out before." A smile played at the corners of Santiago's mouth.

"Um . . . ," Diego said.

Santiago laughed. "It's okay, son. You're old enough now to

pilot one yourself anyway."

"Oh hey," Petey said, "I ran into your mom on my way down. She's looking for you, Mr. Ribera."

"I wouldn't want to keep her waiting." Santiago gave Diego a meaningful glance and then patted him on the back and headed for the door. "Have a good day at school. Remember, the power plant. Don't be late."

"Right," Diego said, knowing that glance had been about the Sight. Telling no one included Petey, which would be tough. "And thanks again!"

"Whoa, D, look at this, huh? This board is berries!" Petey ran his fingers over the smooth surface.

"It's pretty great," Diego agreed, gathering the tools scattered across the workbench and sliding them into drawers. "It flies real smooth."

"I thought you just got it?"

"Oh, right," Diego said. He'd been thinking about his dream. "I mean, I'm sure it's going to." He crossed the shop and started hanging tools in their correct places on the far wall.

"What's this bot doing back here?" Petey's voice was coming from a different spot. Diego turned to find that he'd climbed up into the cockpit of an eleven-foot-tall robot that Diego had nicknamed Marty. "I haven't seen him since you built him last summer."

"Yeah, with Dad's help. Now be careful; he's back in the shop for repairs."

"Okay, sheesh, settle down." Petey put his boots up on the

controls and laced his fingers behind his head. "He's fine, but not nearly as cool as Redford."

"Yeah," Diego said. "Redford came out great."

"That still blows my mind," Petey said as Diego coiled a hose from the floor. "You saw that old red tractor and turned it into a giant robot. Someday you'll be even more talented than your old man."

"Mmmm," Diego said. "Actually, Marty could do circles around Redford, but yeah, Redford has the best origin story, for sure." They'd discovered the tractor out past the perimeter wall, searching for parts in the northern wild lands.

"Yeah!" Petey agreed. "Hiking along, keeping our eyes peeled for Algonquin warriors. And then running into that dimetrodon. I'm still pinching myself to make sure we survived that! It was like being Bartholomew Roosevelt, or a mercenary explorer or something."

"I know," Diego said. Actually, it had been terrifying, but if Petey hadn't walked across that angry giant reptile's nest, they would've never run and hid in the pile of abandoned tractors where Diego had found Redford.

A horn sounded from out on the canal.

"Ah, shoot," Petey said. "School bus boat!"

"We should go." Diego yanked up the last of the hose and tossed it over on the bench.

"My mom's going to kill me if I get another tardy." Petey

scrambled to sit up.

There was a shrill whine and a grinding of gears, and Marty lurched forward from his spot.

"Ahh! Sorry!" Petey cried. "I kicked something!"

"Petey! He hasn't been properly oiled. . . ." Diego had barely moved when Marty took another lumbering step and then froze up in midstride.

"What did I do?" Petey said, throwing up his hands.

The robot lurched sideways and crashed over onto his back, shaking the whole building.

"I'm stuck!" Petey shouted.

Diego rounded the side of the bot. He reached the cockpit and tried to pull open the hatch, but it was jammed. Smoke poured from the seized-up gears.

"Petey, shut it down!" Diego shouted over the earsplitting hiss.

"What?" Petey shouted back.

Diego prodded at the cockpit, trying to point at the controls inside. "Shut it down! Right there! If those gears stay seized up much longer, they'll be warped and ruined." Not to mention cause a dangerous fire.

Petey inspected the controls. He placed his hand over a large yellow button. "This?"

"No, Petey! Not that—"

But Petey slammed his hand down.

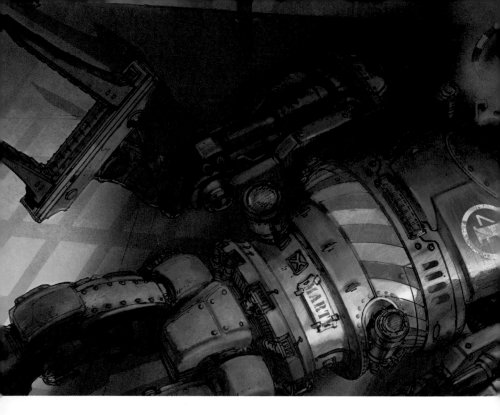

"Jeez, Petey," Diego said, rubbing his shoulder.

"Sorry," Petey said, shaking his head.

Daphne barked, hopping away and nursing one leg.

Diego scrambled to his feet and hurried back to the robot. He leaned into the cockpit and hit the shut-down button. The leg stopped hissing.

Outside, the bus horn blared again.

"Aw, man," Petey said. He rushed over to the window and peered out. "There it goes. What are we going to do? Boy, am I gonna get it!"

"Hold on," Diego said. He glanced to the corner of the

shop, where a small vehicle was covered by a tarp, and hurried to it. "How about this?"

He threw the cloth aside, revealing one of Diego's favorite father-son creations: an orange-and-white 1960 BMW Isetta that had been converted into a submarine. Petey had even managed to build the periscope for it.

"The *Goldfish!*" Petey shouted. "Your dad won't mind?"

"Nah," Diego said. "It's my birthday. And he definitely wouldn't want me getting a detention for being late. I need to work with him this afternoon."

"Great. But we still need to hurry," Petey said.

"Yup." Diego darted over to his father's desk for the keys. "Ah, shoot." Dad's stuff was scattered everywhere. He was going to be so annoyed, but Diego did not have time to clean this up, too. He scoured the mess for the keys but couldn't find them. Dropping to his knees, Diego looked under the desk, then finally spotted them under the propane tank.

Daphne hopped over beside him and started yipping excitedly.

"Not now, girl," Diego said, "I'm busy." He strained to reach the keys, but they were beyond his fingers. *Crud*, he thought, glancing around. *I've got to get those keys!* He grabbed a pencil off the desk and tried with that, each time to no avail. *Have to get them—I just have to.*

Daphne's rapid panting became slow, even breaths, and then she darted forward, flattening herself and scooting under the tank. She slipped back out with the keys in her jaws.

"Whoa, good girl!" Diego said. He bent down and held out his hand. As Daphne dropped the keys onto his palm, Diego saw a strange, silvery glint in her eyes . . . but then Daphne trotted off, tail wagging, like nothing had happened.

"All right, Daphne!" Petey said, standing behind him.

Diego stood. He watched Daphne go, his head tingling, similar to the way it had after building the gravity board.

"What's up, D?"

Diego shook his head. He figured he was still a little woozy from his experience with the Sight earlier. A ghost of a headache knocked at the back of his skull, and Marty throwing them across the room hadn't helped. "Nothing," he said.

"Come on, man," Petey said. "We need to scramble."

"Right."

"Should I get your mom's gravity board?" Petey asked.

"Nah, I'll get it," Diego said. "You've caused enough trouble." He smiled and punched Petey in the arm, then hurried around the shop, putting a few more things away and grabbing the two boards.

Petey and Diego pushed the *Goldfish* into the freight elevator and rode to the ground floor. Petey sat in the passenger's seat as Diego ignited the main boiler. The little car chugged to life. Diego hopped inside and jammed the control levers. The car rolled down the street-level dock and into the green water.

Horns sounded in the traffic-clogged canal as Diego veered among the slower paddle wheelers and faster boiler

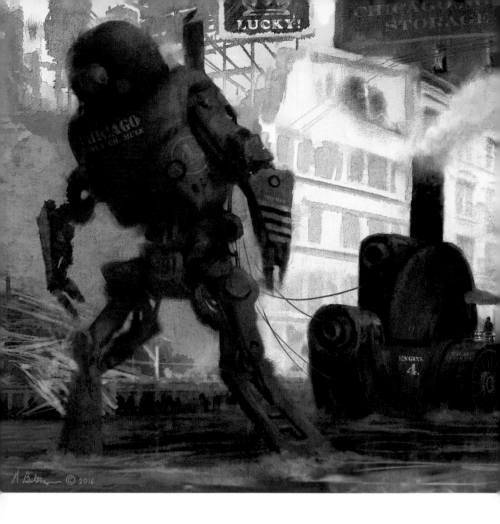

taxis while watching out for the tromping legs of robots. The little craft was barely visible to the larger ships, sitting just above the water as it did.

As the world bustled around them, Petey pulled an old Sony Walkman cassette player from the glove box and plugged in the cable from a simple set of speakers in the back.

"Which one of these do you like?" he said, flipping through a stack of plastic cassette cases. Petey handled these

gingerly; in his house, he was used to music being played from delicate wax cylinders.

"That one," Diego said, glancing over.

"The Replacements," Petey said. "Which song?"

"'Can't Hardly Wait,'" Diego said. "It should be cued up."

Petey slid in the tape, and the speakers burst to life.

"Your dad's music is loud!" Petey shouted.

"That's the best part about it!"

CHAPTER FOUR

Where Giants and Monsters Be

Diego surfaced beyond the public docks in front of their school. The Field Museum of Natural History loomed over its surrounding streets, a great stone building built back in 1893, sturdy enough to survive the Time Collision with only a few busted windows. With so many other structures destroyed, and with unknown seismic activity still lurking, the museum had been chosen to be the first primary and secondary school in the city. It still held most of its vast collection of artifacts and specimens, including skeletons of many giant creatures that had returned in the new world.

"Just in time!" Petey called, leaping out and tying off the

ropes. "We should charge fares for getting kids to school in style. Diego and Petey's Underwater Cab Service!"

Diego smiled. "Too bad there's no room for more passengers."

"The girls can sit on our laps!" Petey said. "Speaking of which . . ." He pointed toward a crowd gathered in front of school. "Get a load of this."

Diego joined Petey at the edge of the crowd. Everyone watched as two girls skated on the stairs, grinding the rails. The crowd was a mix of times and culture, Steam Timers and Mids, even a few Elders here and there. A teen couple passed in front of them, an Elder boy and a Steam-Time girl, holding hands.

"Dating a Steam Timer would be swell," Petey said, watching the couple wistfully.

"You'd never be able to handle all the proper manners," Diego said.

"How do you know? Maybe I've been practicing on my own. Good day, m'lady," he said, bowing like a gentleman.

"Hey." Diego nudged him. "Not now."

He nodded to the side of the crowd, where a group of older kids were catcalling at the Elder-Steam couple. The two hurried in the other direction, but not before enduring a barrage of insults. Diego recognized the boy at the center of the group, his fire-red hair springing from beneath a derby cap.

Petey slapped Diego on the shoulder. "Don't pay him a nickel, D," he said. "Come on, let's get a closer look at this rumpus."

A. Betts © 2015

"I should have guessed it was Paige Jordan," Petey said as they watched. "She's something, huh?" he said, leaning into Diego's shoulder.

"She sure is," Diego said, not talking about Paige.

"Uh-oh," Petey said, noticing Diego's stare. "Somebody's got a doe in his headlights!"

The girl met his gaze, just as she was about to jump her board up onto the rail—

But the board hit wrong, and she crashed to the steps.

The crowd gasped. Paige hurried over to her.

"Girl, you know you're gonna eat that rail if you pop your board up too soon," Paige said, hands on her hips. But then she knelt down. "You all right?"

"Fine," the girl muttered. Her eyes flashed to Diego again.

This time, Paige noticed, and when she saw that Diego was on the other end of that gaze, she rolled her eyes. "Oh, no way. You're face-planting because of *that* boy? Get your head in the game, Lucy! He's just some seventh-grade runt."

A few in the crowd heard this and laughed in Diego's direction. His cheeks burned.

"Hey . . . ," Diego started, but Petey tugged on his arm.

"Settle down, D. You do *not* want to pick a fight with Paige Jordan."

The school bell rang, and the crowd dispersed.

"Come on," Petey said, pulling Diego along. He kept craning his neck, but he'd lost track of where the girl had gone. *Lucy,* Paige had said.

Petey and Diego were swept up by a group of their classmates. Everyone was chatting about the gossip of the day, but Diego barely paid attention.

"Hey, this way," Petey said when Diego started toward their class. He saw that his classmates were heading the other way. "We're touring the Ice Age exhibit today, remember? For science? Two hours less of class time."

"Oh," Diego said, catching up. "Right."

"Uh-huh," Petey said, grinning. "I know what's got you distracted."

They fought through crowds of lower-grade and high school students and visitors to the museum, finally catching up to the rest of the class as their teacher, Mr. Nelson, was taking attendance. "All right," he said, "we'll be joining the other upper-grade classes in the exhibit hall. Right this way."

"Wait, hold on," Petey said. He grabbed Diego by the shoulder and turned him toward Sue, the famous T. *rex* skeleton, a relic from before the Time Collision. "Is that the blond skater that was outside with Paige?"

"No way." Diego saw that Lucy had traded in her skater clothes for a prim dress with a white collar and high boots, her hair tied back.

"Looks like your crush is actually a Steam Timer." He punched Diego's shoulder.

"Maybe," Diego said. He couldn't get over how different she looked.

"Come on, you've gotta say hi," Petey said, elbowing him in the ribs.

"Nah," Diego said. "She probably won't even talk to me."

"Come on, D. Besides, she's gorgeous. If you won't, I will."

Diego took a deep breath.

"Okay, fine, but you're coming with me." He dragged Petey along by the arm and made his way around the back of their class, keeping out of Mr. Nelson's sight.

Paige spotted them approaching and whispered to Lucy. They shared a laugh, and Diego wanted to die. Still, he wasn't going to turn back now. He willed one foot in front of the next until they were right beside the girls, who were now acting more interested in Sue, as if Diego and Petey didn't exist.

"Hey," Diego said, shoving his hands in his pockets.

"What you want, North-sider?" Paige snapped.

Diego looked at Lucy. She eyed him curiously. "I'm Diego," he said. "This is Petey. We just want to, um, welcome you to our school, and . . ."

Lucy smirked. "Are you the official Mid-Time welcoming committee?"

She had a thick accent, and it took Diego a second to decipher what she had said. "Oh, you're from . . ." He was trying to place it. "Over there . . ."

"Over *there*?" Lucy said. "Indeed . . . if by 'over there' you mean across the Vastlantic. And how uninformed of you to think that you're from *here* and we're from *there*, as if one is superior to the other. If that were true, it would *certainly* be that there was here and here was *there*."

"Wait," Diego said. "I wasn't, um, saying that. I just . . . your accent . . . it's . . . Irish?"

The second he said it, Lucy's mouth dropped open.

"Oh, sorry, I mean Australian." There was a more obvious spot he could have named, but it was like his brain was a steam compressor on the fritz.

"My manner of speech is neither from an island of peasant farmers nor one of criminals," Lucy said.

"Hey," Diego said. "Watch it. My mom's from Ireland."

Lucy made a face Diego couldn't decipher. "Be that as it may," she said, "for your information, Mid-Time *American*, I am a loyal subject of the true sovereign of the United Kingdom, Her Majesty Queen Victoria—"

That was it! England!

"And I'm not new to your school," Lucy continued. "I was homeschooled when we first got here, but I've been here in your eighth grade for a few weeks now. And I will be for the rest of the semester while my father is in town on important business. Now why don't you little boys go find some other tikes to play with."

"We're not little boys," Diego said. "We're both thirteen."

"You sure act like little boys," Paige said. "Now step off and go back to your playdate." She and Lucy turned toward Sue.

"Come on," Petey said. "Let's go find some real girls to talk to." He started to turn away.

But Diego stood his ground. There was something about this girl.

"Why are they still hanging around?" Paige said, her back to the boys.

"I haven't the foggiest idea," Lucy said.

"Hey," Diego heard himself blurt out. "You think that T. *rex* is so cool, maybe you'd like to see a real one."

This made Lucy glance over her shoulder. "How's that?"

"Well, my dad loaned the museum some equipment to help install their new T. *rex* exhibit, and when I helped deliver the loaders, I memorized the combination to the service entrance door. It's here in the Ice Age hall. That new dinosaur's got skin and everything. It looks alive."

"D," Petey said quietly by his shoulder. "We're not supposed to leave our class. We'll get in huge trouble if we're caught, and our parents will kill us."

"Well, then, we won't get caught," Diego said, shrugging. "Come on, Petey, where's your sense of adventure?" He grinned at the girls.

Lucy and Paige shared a glance.

"We're not going to let these North-side runts show us up, are we?" Paige said.

Diego was surprised to see uncertainty on Lucy's face.

Paige leaned toward Lucy. "It's not gonna bite."

"It's really cool," Diego added. "Besides, you've got me and Petey to protect you."

"Please," Lucy said. "I don't need a *boy* to take care of me." She nodded and glanced at Paige. "Let's humor them." She took a deep breath as she said it.

Diego glanced back at their classes. "We should stay with our groups until we're down the hall a little farther. Then watch for my signal."

After what seemed like a never-ending lecture by Mr. Nelson, the classes split into four-person groups and were allowed to take in the rest of the exhibit on their own. Each student was given a small chalkboard to gather at least three interesting facts from the displays. The boys scribbled down as much as they could at the first exhibit about mammoths and then announced that they were headed for the restrooms, and set off to find Lucy and Paige.

They spotted Lucy with her school group over by an exhibit about glaciers. Paige was with hers by the mastodons. Diego nodded to each of them, then waited over by a diorama featuring Neanderthal hunters confronting a saber-toothed tiger.

"Those would be good friends for you two," Paige said as she and Lucy arrived.

"Actually," Petey said, waving his hand dismissively at the exhibit, "that's not even close to what a real Neanderthal looks like."

"Like you would know that, North-sider," Paige said, one eyebrow raised.

"Actually, Petey and I have been out to the wild lands," Diego said. "We've seen the Neanderthals firsthand."

"Oh, really?" Lucy asked.

"Yeah," Diego said. He didn't add that technically they only *thought* they'd seen a Neanderthal tribe, from a far distance. At the time, they'd been running from that dimetrodon.

"You've actually been out to the wild lands?" Lucy asked.

"Yeah, right," Paige said. "These two couldn't even survive a walk in Cicero. There's no way they've been out in the wild lands."

"We've been there a few times," Diego said. "And I'm not sure *you* could handle it."

"Oh, I'm about to show you what I can handle," Paige said, putting her hands on her hips.

"Hold on," Lucy said, grabbing Paige's arm. Diego noticed

that her eyes had widened. "But aren't there . . . dinosaurs out there? Like, real ones?"

"Oh yeah," Petey said, "lots of different kinds. Man-eaters, giant herbivores that could squash you with a single step."

"It's not that bad," Diego said, watching Lucy's face as Petey went on. "They usually keep to themselves. It's actually more dangerous if you cross into Algonquin lands without permission, or run into one of those Neanderthal hunting parties."

"Yeah, right," Paige said. "You two talk big. I bet you've never really been out there."

"We have, too," Diego said. "My dad leads salvage expeditions, and he takes us along to help."

Paige opened her mouth to add more when snickering distracted them.

A group of boys lurked across the hall, with Joe Fish standing in the middle.

"Ugh, I thought I smelled Believers," Petey said, but he kept his voice quiet enough that the gang wouldn't hear.

"True Believers?" Lucy asked.

Just then, Fish blew her a kiss. His gang cracked up.

"They're a lot of filthy hooligans," Lucy said. "Let's get out of here."

"Come on, y'all, we don't need to waste time with them," Paige said.

"You heard the ladies," Petey said, catching up.

Diego started after them but paused and turned back to Fish.

Fish's buddies laughed at this, too. Fish scowled at Diego and made a circular motion, with his finger pointing at the ground. *Turn around and walk away.* He then raised his thumb to his throat and made a long, slow, cutting motion.

It was all Diego could do to keep his cool. Not even two years ago, they'd been friends, and Fish had even come by the workshop sometimes. Now he was well on his way to being a Time-separatist thug.

"D," Petey said from a few steps behind him. "Come on."

Diego tried to swallow his anger. But before he turned away, he held up a hand to his ear, then with the other hand pretended to be turning up the volume dial on a radio. He moved his hand away from his ear and slowly raised his middle finger in time to the dial spinning.

Fish shoved his hands in his pockets, his face so red it looked like he might boil over.

"Why would you do that?" Petey asked as they hurried to catch the girls. "I really don't want a busted jaw, or worse. You know those guys have roughed kids up, bad."

"He needs to know that not everyone is afraid of him," Diego said.

"But I *am* afraid of him," Petey said. "I'm sore at him for turning on us as much as you are, but we can't do anything about it."

"They shouldn't act like that toward a girl," Diego said.

"You two speak for yourselves," Paige said as they caught up. "Them hoods wouldn't dare mess with me, or they know what they'd get."

"Yes," Lucy said, "we don't need seventh-grade bodyguards, if you please. We can handle ourselves."

"Fine," Diego said.

Petey said, "There's the service entrance." He pointed to a door with a keypad lock. "Right, D?"

"Yeah." Diego led them to the door. He punched in the code. The door didn't move.

"I thought you said you had this?" Paige asked. "Or is this just more of your bull?"

"No." Diego typed in the code again. He'd gone over it in his head. This was definitely it.

Still nothing.

Lucy huffed. "What a bore."

"Try it slower," Petey said, "in case the buttons are sticking, or a number isn't registering." He gazed back over his shoulder. "But, you know, hurry. Mr. Nelson could come by any second."

Diego typed the numbers again, and when the door still didn't budge, he slammed it with his palm.

"Knew you were all talk," Paige said.

"We should just head back," Petey added.

"No, wait," Diego said. "Just . . . hold on." He closed his eyes and tried to block everything else out. He placed his hand on the keypad. Imagined only the door, the inner workings of the lock. How the keypad mechanism might work . . .

Images flashed in his mind: the pins of the lock, the gears

that would twist them into the right shape, the connections to the keypad—

Diego's fingers found the numbers flashing in his mind. He tapped them in.

A click. He opened his eyes and pushed the door. It yawned into the stairwell.

"Okay, let's hurry."

Diego stepped through the doorway, then looked back to find Petey, Lucy, and Paige staring at him.

"That was weird," Lucy said. "What did you just do?"

"Nothing, I just had the numbers reversed in my head."

"You did it with your eyes closed," Paige said.

"I had to remember them from the other day. So are you coming or what?" He held the door and motioned for them to go by.

They filed through, and Diego pushed the door shut but paused. "Ah," he said, studying the door controls.

"What is it?" Petey asked.

"There's no lock on this side. We have to leave it open if we want to get back up this way."

"But if someone notices the door open . . . ," Lucy said.

"It will be fine," Petey said. "Won't it, D?"

"It's no problem," Diego said. He closed his eyes again, tried to clear everything and see the door. There had to be a way to make this work—

"This is what you call a plan?" Paige said.

The comment distracted him. Diego breathed deep, trying to shut out the world again.

"I knew this was rubbish," Lucy said.

Diego lost it again. He spun around. "What are you all afraid of? No one comes down here during the day, and the door will look like it's closed. I'm going anyway." He brushed past them and started down the stairs, stopping after a few steps. He turned back to see the three looking from one to the other.

"I'm not letting *him* call me a coward," Paige said. She took Lucy by the arm and started down the stairs.

Petey glanced at Diego, then shoved his hands in his pockets and followed.

"I feel like they're watching us," Lucy said, glancing from side to side.

Diego felt like there were eyes in the dark too, but Lucy sounded terrified. As if she thought one of these creatures would come alive and devour them all on the spot.

"Hang tough, girl," Paige said, squeezing Lucy's arm. "You got this. Remember, these things are dead and stuffed."

Lucy nodded. "Of course they are."

They passed through the hall and out into a wide rotunda. It was brighter in here, the morning sunlight casting angular beams through round windows in the domed ceiling. In the center of the room stood the giant T. *rex*.

"Say hello to Wendell," Diego said.

"Whoa," Paige said. "Now that's a carnivore."

"Largest tyrannosaurus ever recorded in the wild lands," Petey said.

"He's majestic," Lucy said, but she stopped a few feet from the felt ropes that ringed the specimen.

Paige jumped right over them and stepped around one of the dinosaur's thick legs. She moved under the creature's chest, running her hand along its skin. "Wait, what," she said, "this thing has feathers?" She brushed her fingers over soft, scalelike feathers around the creature's leg. The pattern extended up around the underside of its neck.

"That's going to be Wendell's big surprise to the world," Diego said. "She's a species of T. *rex* never before seen."

"She?" Lucy said. "But . . . her name's Wendell."

"She's actually named after Wendy Dykstra," Petey said, "the game warden who found the body out beyond the perimeter wall. She knew how important a specimen this was, so she hot-wired a class-four loader robot to get her over the wall before scavengers could."

"But Wendell is a boy's name," Paige said.

"The museum wanted the dinosaur to have a boy name since the skeleton upstairs is Sue, so they changed Wendy to Wendell."

"That's how they reward her for her heroics?" Lucy said.

"There's going to be a plaque by her that explains it," Diego said. "Everyone will still know about her and what she did."

"A plaque?" Lucy said. "Well, I guess the Time Collision didn't change everything. It's still a man's world."

"You got that right," Paige said.

"Actually, Diego's mom was part of it, too," Petey said.

"Yeah," Diego said, "she caught a glimpse of her on a training flight. She didn't quite know what she'd seen, but she gave the coordinates to Wendy."

"Your mom's a pilot?" Lucy asked, turning away from Wendell. "Is she an explorer, or a bush pilot, or what?"

"She flies search and rescue for the air corps, but she used to be a fighter pilot. She fought against the Aeternum in their raids against New Chicago."

"A *famous* fighter pilot," Petey added.

"You—" Lucy's mouth fell open. "You're not talking about Siobhan Quinlan, are you? Not *the* famous fighter pilot, the hero of Dusable Harbor?"

Diego couldn't help a wide grin. "Quinlan-Ribera now, but yeah. One and the same."

"That's—" Lucy shook her head. "Your mother is my hero. A woman who went well beyond her station in the Victorian world. But hold on . . . did you say Ribera? Like *Santiago Ribera*?" Suddenly her eyes narrowed. "You're messing with me, aren't you?"

"No," Diego said. "Those are my parents. What's it to you?"

Lucy kept peering at him. "So . . . you're saying that the fact that your mother is Siobhan Quinlan, my hero, and your *father* is Santiago Ribera . . . the purported genius engineer whose own steam converter was found wanting and had to be replaced by my father's superior Goliath steam converter . . . you're saying those two things are just coincidence?"

"What do you know about my father?" Diego said.

"Your father is the entire reason we're here," Lucy said. "It's his inadequate steam converter that's the reason I'm stuck in New Chicago for half a year. So that my father can save your city."

"Wait," Diego said. "You're saying that your father is that Emerson guy my dad was talking about?"

"He's not some guy; he's George Emerson, the world's preeminent steam engineer, who will be knighted by the queen herself, I'll have you know."

"Right, him," Diego said. "We're only using *his* old-fashioned steam tech out of pity."

"Pity?" Lucy nearly shouted. "How dare you? My father is a genius. His converter design is superior to your city's. Everyone says so."

"Who's everyone?" Diego said. "Everybody still living with gas lamps and locomotives? Maybe that's nice by *your* standards, but you should open your eyes around town. My dad is a visionary."

"How much of a visionary could he be if his son is such an arrogant fool?"

"You tell that wannabe," Paige said.

"Okay, okay," Petey said. "How about if we rejoin our classes before someone gets hurt?"

"Oh, I'd hate to miss that opportunity!"

The voice echoed out of the darkness. The four whirled toward the hallway they'd come from.

A match was struck, lighting four figures.

Fish sucked on his cigarette, the end glowing, as he and his gang stepped out of the shadows.

"Get out of here, Fish," Diego said. He tried to sound tough, but his heart was racing. This wasn't a public place like the exhibit hall.

"Can't do that," Fish said. He plucked his cigarette between two fingers and waved it in their direction. "Have to rescue the damsel."

"What are you talking about?" Petey asked.

"It's a classic tale, really. Damsel in distress and then along comes a hero and his mates."

"That punk better not think he's talking about me," Paige muttered.

Fish scowled. "Not you, love. That one." He pointed at Lucy.

"Oh, I'm in no need of a rescue, thank you very much," Lucy said.

"Sure you are. Look at ya: led into associations with a Mid-Time colored girl and a half-breed clock mongrel."

"Shut up, Fish!" Diego shouted. "What happened to you anyway?"

"I wised up."

"Sounds like the opposite," Petey said.

"You need to step off before you step *in* it," Paige said.

Fish shook his head. "It's like there's this barking and yapping, but I can't quite understand what it's saying. Come on, damsel. Before things get ugly."

"I think the ugly's already here." Paige slapped a fist into her palm and glared at Fish.

"Ooh," Fish said. "I normally wouldn't hit a lady, but you don't count."

"You'd do well to pay her mind," Lucy said. "And just because I'm a Steam Timer doesn't mean I'd want anything to do with you hooligans."

"I see how it is." Fish flicked his cigarette aside. "Tommy, Seamus: get Ribera and hold him down for me. Billy, grab the skater girl. She'll be next. And make sure that Petey-boy sees stars!"

"Run!" Diego shouted. He curled his fingers into a fist as the boys advanced.

"Yeah, right!" Paige replied. She'd already dropped her backpack and skateboard. Billy was just reaching for her arm when she darted toward him, grabbed him by the forearm, and judo flipped him to the floor.

"Whoa!" Petey said.

The move made Fish and the others freeze for a second. Diego saw his chance. He lunged for Paige's skateboard, grabbed it with tingling fingers, and slammed Fish across the face with it.

Fish crumpled to the floor, rolling back and forth, holding his nose and cursing. Tommy and Seamus rushed over to him.

"Okay, *now* we might want to run!" Lucy said.

"Let's go!" Diego darted for the hallway, Petey, Lucy, and Paige right behind him.

When they reached the dark corridor, Diego glanced back and saw Billy staggering to his feet, the other two crouched beside Fish.

"Let's keep moving," Petey said. They hurried back to the stairs and up to the service door.

Diego shut it and then punched in the key code, but the lock didn't engage.

"Are you sure it's the same code to lock it?" Petey asked.

"Please tell me you thought to check that beforehand," Lucy said.

"Nah, it's the same," Diego said. He had no idea. "Just gotta get it right."

Footsteps thundered up the stairs from below.

"Hurry up!" Lucy said.

"I'm trying." Diego glanced through the window and saw Tommy and Seamus coming. "Grab the door and hold it shut!" Diego shouted.

As they crowded around him and grabbed the handle, Diego closed his eyes again. Had to push everything out, had to focus. Just the door. Just the intricacies of that lock . . .

Fists pounded on the door, breaking his concentration.

"We . . . can't . . . hold them!" Petey shouted.

Diego took a deep breath and held it. Sank into his head. Nothing but the lock. Flashes exploded in his mind. He let the visions reach his fingers, tapped at the keypad, and the lock slid shut.

"Mongrel!" Fish shouted, his face pressed against the window, steaming up the glass. Diego could see the blood dripping down his nose. "You're gonna pay!"

Diego stepped back, panting, and offered Fish a wordless smile and shrug. Angry muffled shouts and thuds continued behind them as they stepped away.

Once they rounded the corner, they stopped to catch their breath.

"Where did you learn to do that?" Petey asked, gazing at Paige.

"One of our neighbors is a jujitsu master," she said. "My brother . . . and I used to practice with him."

"Thank you," Lucy said, her breath still short. "For getting us out of trouble."

"No problem," Diego said.

"She meant me, fool," Paige said. "You're the one who got us *in* trouble." She took her skateboard back from Diego. "You're just lucky you're so . . . lucky. And that I was there to bail you out."

She and Lucy started across the hall.

"But . . . ," Diego said, "you have to admit: not bad, right? For a couple of *kids*?"

"Whatever," Paige said, not looking back.

Lucy glanced over her shoulder but didn't say a word.

Diego and Petey wound their way through the Ice Age hall looking for their class.

"So?" Petey asked.

"So what?" Diego replied. "I wish I could've hit Fish again for what he said."

"Ah, don't listen to him," Petey said. "Fish doesn't know nothin', and his people are ignorant. You just gotta ignore it."

"It's not that easy," Diego said. "Clock mongrel." The words made him clench his fists. The name was vicious and hateful. He wanted to believe that Joe didn't really mean it deep down, that he was only imitating his father and his brothers. But Fish had changed.

"Well, you showed him. And you'll show him again. But hey . . ." Petey draped an arm around his shoulders. "Besides, that's not even what I meant."

"Huh?"

"I meant, what do you think *about Lucy*?"

"Oh," Diego said. "I'm trying not to."

The school day passed in a blur. Diego and Petey decided not to fly the gravity boards at lunch, worried that Fish and his gang might be waiting for a chance at payback, and instead stayed in the cafeteria. Diego kept an eye out for them in the halls after lunch too, and also for Lucy.

After school, Petey drove the *Goldfish*, delivering Diego to the ferry station.

"What's up?" Diego asked over a new cassette, this one by another of his dad's favorite bands, U2. Petey had been quiet all day since the fight with Fish.

"Nothing," he said.

"Come on," Diego said. "Something's bugging you."

Petey grimaced. "I don't know, D. You were kinda reckless this morning, that's all."

"What do you mean? Hitting Fish? Come on, he was going to pound us."

"I know, but, like, before that. The way you taunted him? It's like you were trying to pick a fight."

"I wasn't *trying* to. They were being jerks. They got what they deserved."

Petey shrugged. "I don't know if it's your birthday, or if it was just having a couple of pretty girls around."

"My birthday doesn't have anything to do with it," Diego said. "Come on, what's so wrong with giving punks like Fish a bit of their own medicine?"

"You sound like Paige," Petey said.

"Well, she knows how to stick up for herself."

"Yeah, well, I just don't want to spend the rest of the year having to watch my back. You know Fish won't let it go."

"Let him try," Diego said.

"Great," Petey muttered.

They were silent for the rest of the ride.

• • •

Diego hopped up onto the dock. A steady breeze whipped at his hair. Gulls circled overhead, making shrill calls. Diego looked out over the harbor and saw dark clouds on the horizon.

"Get her home safe, okay?" Diego said, slapping the side of the *Goldfish*. "Stay ahead of that storm." He was second-guessing the idea of leaving such a prized invention, not to mention the pair of gravity boards in the trunk, in Petey's not-always-sure hands, but he didn't have time to get the *Goldfish* home and still make the ferry.

"Sure thing," Petey said. "I got it. See ya tomorrow."

As the *Goldfish* puttered off, Diego made his way through the crowds of people and cargo. Different languages tumbled over one another, and Diego caught a hundred smells: the sour sweat of livestock, the sweet burn of frying food, a burst of exotic spice, a flash of citrus.

He made his way between piles of crates and around break-dancers and a brigade of Napoleonic soldiers playing cards, carts heaped with furs. A band of Algonquin warriors inspected a caged beast: something like a rhinoceros but with three horns.

He boarded the hulking ferry as its horn sounded across the harbor.

CHAPTER FIVE

Serpents and Soldiers

"**D**iego!"

Diego was surprised to see a young man standing on the dock, waving in his direction. As he stepped down, he tentatively waved back.

The man smiled and put out his hand. "I'm George Emerson Jr., but you can call me Georgie. It's great to finally meet you!"

Diego shook his hand, wondering if Georgie was going to be anything like his sister. "Nice to meet you, too."

"Splendid that our fathers get to join forces, wouldn't you agree?" Georgie said as they crossed the busy platform.

"Pretty cool," Diego said.

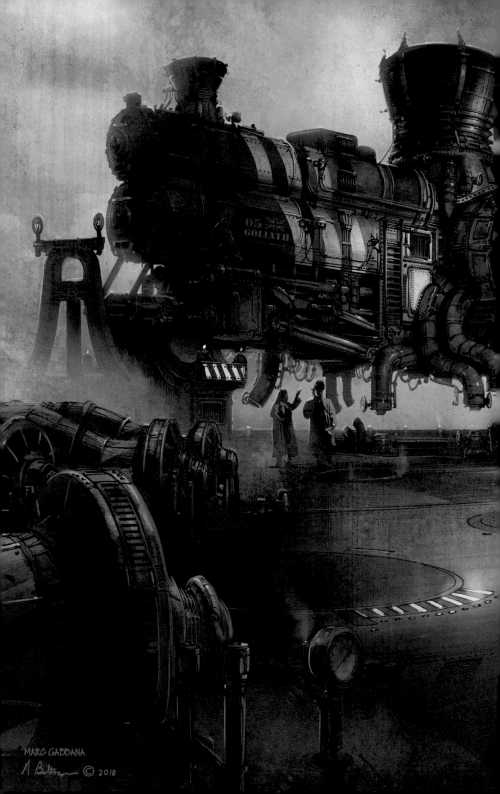

MARC GABBANA
A Belt... © 2016

"I'm looking forward to seeing this retrofit completed," Georgie said. "It's been painstaking work out here, that's for sure. But more interesting than hitting the books back in London. I hear they brought you in to drive the bot. You must be an ace operator."

"I'm okay," Diego said. *This Georgie wasn't half bad.*

"I appreciate your modesty," Georgie said. He lowered his voice. "But if you want my advice, don't sell yourself short to my father. He can be tough to take, especially when he smells uncertainty."

"Thanks," Diego said. "Actually, I'm really good."

Georgie patted him on the back. "That's the spirit."

They reached the center of the open area, where George Emerson Sr. stood beside Santiago near a neat stack of eight large mechanical steam converters. Diego recognized his father's work, now being replaced with the single Goliath converter that Emerson had designed.

"Careful with those pressure regulators," George said curtly to two of Santiago's workers. "And you there," he barked, pointing at another man who was preparing the housing. "Do you even speak English? I said to *scour* that piping, not give it a massage."

Diego was surprised to hear Emerson speaking to his father's men that way. He watched Dad for a reaction, but Santiago only glanced up, then back at his clipboard.

"Hi, Dad," Diego said.

"Oh hey, son." Santiago rubbed his head. "George, this is

Diego, our driver for today."

George glanced over. "The prodigy, huh?" He gave Diego only a passing glance before returning to the clipboard. "You sure he's up to this? It's not a toy we're installing." His eyes flashed to the massive orange steam locomotive retrofitted with pistons and gears. "I would have preferred someone a bit more . . . qualified."

Diego was about to stick up for himself when Santiago's hand fell on his shoulder.

"Diego can handle it."

Emerson lowered the clipboard, still frowning. "Only my top drivers in the Royal Engineering Corps are rated for a class-three loader. Has your boy completed any formal training?"

Diego glanced at his dad. Santiago's lips pursed, but he breathed deep and spoke diplomatically. "I can assure you that your steam converter is in the best of hands."

Come on, Dad, Diego thought. He wished Santiago would give this arrogant man a piece of his mind.

"Well . . . ," George scoffed. "I'll be the judge of that."

"Your drivers wouldn't have the first clue how to pilot that Centauri loader bot," Diego blurted. "My father designed it specifically for this station. You have to know what you're doing, handle it right. Tear the wrong thing out and you could blast us all to pieces."

"How dare you speak to me like that, you insolent whelp!" George bellowed. "Mr. Ribera, if you can't control your *crew*, I can pull my team and take my converter back home with me."

Santiago's hand closed around Diego's arm. "My apologies, Mr. Emerson." Santiago yanked Diego away, guiding him across the platform toward the foreman's office.

Once the door had closed, Santiago threw up his hands. "Diego! What has gotten into you? Do you realize who you were talking to?"

"Yeah," Diego said, "a real blowhard."

"George Emerson is the chief technical officer of the—"

"I know who he is, Dad! But that doesn't mean he can talk to you like he did! Why are you defending him? You've done more for New Chicago than he's ever done for his home. Why do you let someone like him push you around? Why do we even have to use someone else's stupid converter when yours are twice as good?"

"That may or may not be true," Santiago said. "There is always something to be learned from cooperation and sharing ideas."

"Not with him!" Diego said. "If I were chief engineer, there is no way I would accept being treated like that."

"What else would you do if you were chief engineer?"

"After I sent Emerson home? I'd make machines that would prove how strong we are, a city to be respected."

"You sound like you mean *feared*."

"Well, what would be wrong with fearing us? If you showed Emerson what you could really do, he wouldn't come in here acting like he does."

"You would have us be mighty and strong," Santiago

said, shaking his head, "but the mightiest are also often the loneliest. We need each other to survive in this world, even the more . . . difficult people. I can't believe that is all you have learned from me. You have a lot of growing up to do before you'll be ready to be chief engineer. Maybe you're not ready for the Maker's Sight."

"Maybe I'll never be good enough to be chief engineer. I mean, have you ever asked me what I wanted?" Diego shouted. "And the Maker's Sight—I didn't ask for that either! Why would anyone want to have an ability that they'd have to hide from the world? I'm not you, and I don't want to be!"

A silence passed between them.

Suddenly, the floor shook violently.

"What was that?" Diego asked as he regained his balance.

"Trouble," Santiago said, peering out the window. He pushed Diego toward the door. "Back outside. Hurry!"

The two emerged from the foreman's shack into the deafening wail of warning sirens.

Workers darted in all directions. The wind had kicked up, the sky to the west darkening with the approaching storm.

"What's wrong with your plant now?" George thundered over the din.

"There's nothing wrong with the plant!" Santiago replied.

Another explosion tore through the station from below, shaking the floors. Diego stumbled and fell to his knees.

Something shrieked above them.

"Look out!" Santiago called.

George threw himself backward as part of a venting tower crashed to the deck. "Ahh!"

Diego scrambled to his feet to see Georgie pinned beneath the wreckage, screaming in pain.

"Diego!" Santiago shouted as he raced to Georgie. "Get the Centauri bot!"

Diego sprinted across the deck, dodging fiery debris as it crashed around him. A giant piece of the cooling tank knifed into the deck just feet in front of him, forcing Diego to dive out of the way. He stumbled to get up, regaining his balance as another steel girder slammed into the deck.

Diego reached the Centauri bot, clambered up the side, and slung himself into the cockpit. He powered it on, and the diesel motor revved to life. Diego jammed the throttle, and the Centauri lurched forward. The robot took one huge step but stalled as Diego fumbled with the controls. He could operate this robot with his eyes closed usually, but nothing about this moment was usual. Diego watched Georgie struggling. *No time to think.* He eased the robot forward and moved quickly.

The Centauri reached Georgie after several thundering strides. George waved his hands in the air, pleading with Diego to hurry. But the robot's pneumatic claws could crush Georgie like a gnat if Diego wasn't precise. He maneuvered the claws like they were an extension of his own hands and clamped down on the beam, lifting it free and flinging the beam out of the way. As he spun the robot back around, Diego looked to the horizon.

"Dad!" Diego shouted. "Three warships! Headed this way!"

He pointed toward the horizon, and Santiago raced to a maintenance ladder, scrambling up until he could see.

Blinding flashes of light . . . whistling. Three more explosions shook the platform to its core.

A section of the scaffolding exploded. Diego heard a terrified scream and saw a worker throw himself off the side into the sea to escape the flames.

"It's the Aeternum!" Santiago shouted, dropping back to the deck. He waved to Diego. "Get to the command center!"

Santiago and George bent to help raise Georgie to his feet. Getting his arms around their shoulders, they lurched across the damaged deck, making their way around flaming piles of debris.

Diego powered off the robot and risked a glimpse back to the sea before climbing down. The ships were closing fast, but their cannons had stopped. The water all around them roiled. Shining backs broke the surface, surging ahead of the ships. Flicking tails, whitecaps and wakes forming as if behind invisible vessels. Diego wondered if they were machines, but as they neared the platform he saw something much worse. Pointed snouts, the glint of massive jaws. Mosasaurs, the most fearsome predators of the Vastlantic.

The station shuddered, swaying to one side, then back in the other direction with the next hit. Violent plumes of ocean spray exploded into the sky. Diego struggled to hang on to the railing and Georgie as they stumbled to the command center.

"In here! Hurry!" A marine sergeant waved to them from the doorway.

Diego lunged through as a terrible shriek sounded. The walkway they'd just been standing on twisted and collapsed out of sight. The command center teetered, and, for a moment, it seemed like the whole thing would fall into the sea. But the support towers groaned and the room stopped, frozen at a steep angle.

Diego fell against the wall, catching his breath. A medic grabbed Georgie and laid him on the floor to assess his condition.

"What's the situation, Captain?" Santiago called.

Captain Halsey stood over the control banks, gazing through binoculars at the attacking ships. "Not good, Ribera. We've lost most of the stabilizers. If the station takes much more of a beating, we'll be swimming with those monsters!"

"What about our defenses?"

"Their initial cannon attack effectively crippled us. Security bots were knocked out, and we've lost our submersibles. Even the ferry's been taken out. I sent a distress call to the air corps—"

"No one's coming," Santiago said. "They're all grounded, so we're on our own." He gazed at the looming ships.

"There must be something you can do!" George shouted over the deafening sound of vibrating, twisting metal.

Then all at once, the battering ended. The platform stopped swaying.

The cannon fire ceased . . . replaced by the much closer sound of rifle fire.

Captain Halsey looked through the security scopes. "They're boarding us."

"How many men?" Santiago asked.

"At least fifty," Captain Halsey said. "And an assault robot."

Diego could barely breathe. Outside he heard shouting, frantic footsteps, the crackle of gunfire.

"Seal the door," Santiago said.

"You heard him," Captain Halsey said to the two marines by the door.

"We're just going to hide in here?" George said.

Santiago whirled, and, though his voice remained low, he sounded as angry as Diego had ever heard him. "It's not hiding when the enemy knows where you are. We're buying time."

"Buying time for what?" George said.

Santiago didn't answer.

A blowtorch burst to life. The marines began to melt the edge of the door to the frame.

"Sir!" one of the workers shouted from the back of the room. "This air vent could lead down to the lifeboats."

"What good are lifeboats against those Aeternum ships?" George said.

"They might be small enough to escape unnoticed," Santiago said. "And since they're sail powered, they shouldn't attract those mosasaurs." He motioned to the workers. "Go!"

They dropped to their knees and began unscrewing the air vent grate in the wall.

A burly hand fell on Diego's shoulder. "Come on, kid," Stan Angelino, Dad's foreman, said. He pulled Diego toward the vent.

"Wait, no!" Diego shouted.

"We've got it!" one of the workers shouted, tearing away the grating while the other began to slide his feet down into the airshaft.

"Let go!" Diego said.

"Can't do it," Stan said. "Your father ordered me to get you to safety."

"I want to stay here!" Diego said. He turned and found Santiago across the room. Dad nodded at him, his face stern.

"Go. That's an order."

"I—"

Small-caliber bullets smashed against the armor of the command center door. The door shuddered under the pounding. The gunfire ceased, and there was a moment of silence, and then the sound of groaning metal as the assault robot tore the bulkhead door out.

"Come on," Stan whispered. Diego didn't protest.

He dropped to his knees beside Stan, grabbed the edge of the vent, and pushed himself in, feetfirst.

"Here." Stan handed him the grate for the vent. "I'm going to help hold them off," he whispered, and darted away into the smoke.

Diego slid until his shoulders were through, then twisted back around and replaced the grate. He couldn't screw it into place, but he leaned it as flush with the wall as he could just before—

Gunfire cracked. Shouts echoed. Cries of pain. The smoke began to dissipate, and Diego saw shadows darting back and forth.

He spied his father standing beside Captain Halsey, a handgun raised. They were flanked by two marines, with the other engineers and George behind them, all using the station's control console as cover.

Diego began to shimmy backward. His feet left metal over the vertical shaft that he would need to climb down.

And yet he didn't move. He couldn't.

He kept peering out the grate. A marine lay on the floor nearby, unmoving. There was a flash: the gleam of the Aeternum warrior's sword. He wanted to call out to his dad, but he couldn't risk it.

Shouts. More gunshots. Fists colliding, the thumps of bodies hitting the floor. The smoke was almost gone now, and Diego saw another man step through the doorway, making no effort to defend himself.

"Santi, my boy," the man called, "we can kill everyone in here, or you can show yourself. One of those two options sounds much easier."

Don't do it, Dad, Diego thought, but he heard footsteps, and his father stepped out from behind the control consoles.

"Hello, Balthus," Santiago said. "I wish this were a surprise."

Balthus Tintoretto smiled at Santiago and raised a gun toward him. "Oh come on. No hug for an old friend?"

Santiago lowered his gun. "If it's me you want, then take me. But leave the rest of these innocents alone."

Diego glimpsed a shadow, a figure slipping up behind Santiago. He wanted to call out—but the man had a sword against Santiago's throat in less than a second.

"No one is innocent," the man said.

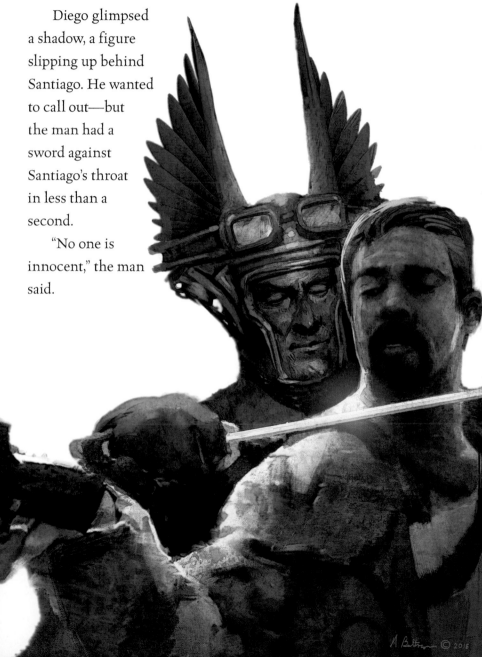

Diego recognized the Roman battle armor from the news reports, and he saw the Aeternum symbol etched in gold on the man's uniform: a Roman sword facing up, with a bow facing down.

"Hello, Magnus," Santiago said tightly against the blade.

"Still the compassionate fool," Magnus said. "Some things never change."

"No, Magnus," Santiago grunted. "I can see that they don't."

It was all Diego could do not to scream. Why was his father speaking to the leaders of the Aeternum, the vilest enemies known to this world, like they knew each other?

"The time has finally come," Magnus said, lowering the blade but only to place the point against the small of Santiago's back, "to complete the great work that we started together so long ago, back when you had purpose!"

More Aeternum soldiers swept into the room.

"It's me you want," Santiago said. "Leave my people be."

"I'm afraid we can't do that," Balthus said. "We'll be needing all your engineers for our cause."

The soldiers rounded up George Sr., Georgie, and about a dozen of Santiago's engineers, and marched them toward the door.

A soldier appeared before Santiago, holding a set of chained cuffs.

"Hold out your hands, brother," Magnus said. "Just need to be sure you don't have any heroics left in you."

Diego watched his father raise his arms, heard the cuffs click around his wrists. He held his breath, fighting the urge to leap out, but it would be pointless. He'd only be captured as well.

And suddenly he realized: *Dad knew they were coming for him.*

Balthus turned to leave. Magnus gave Santiago a shove, and he moved to the door.

The room shuddered, and Diego heard a distant whine of metal. This place was still in danger of collapsing into the sea.

The shaking loosened dust in the vent. Diego tried to hold his nose, but a cough slipped out of him.

Magnus froze. He turned and peered around the room. His cold, ruthless stare fell on the grating, studying it. . . .

He stepped toward the vent, tapping his sword against the floor.

Diego couldn't move, couldn't think—

"Magnus." Balthus was back at the door. "We need to depart."

Magnus nodded. "Of course." He glanced again at the grating and then strode out of the room.

It was some time before Diego could bring himself to move. When he finally did, he carefully lifted the grate aside, crawled out of the vent, and then collapsed against the wall and began to cry. His body shivered, all his fear pouring out of him, his face in his hands.

A horn sounded from out on the water. Diego dragged

himself to his feet and hurried onto the deck. The three Aeternum ships were sweeping back out to sea.

He pictured his father on board, maybe in a cell, in chains.

He had to find a way to help him. But first he had to get out of here and tell the world what had happened.

And I have to tell Mom.

Diego stepped back into the control center. He found the radio. It had been blasted to pieces. *Dad would have known how to fix it.*

But maybe Diego did, too. He placed his hands over the broken pieces and tried to calm his thoughts. It wasn't easy, with images of the firefight, of the mosasaurs, of Magnus with his sword to Santiago's throat . . . but finally he pushed the thoughts away and felt the tingling sensation of the Maker's Sight. It ignited like a match in his mind, illuminating the connections between the radio parts, only to be snuffed out as flashes of the battle and his father bulled their way into his mind.

He started over, and then again, searching for his focus. Finally, his hands started to move, to reach for tools, and slowly, he reassembled the radio.

CHAPTER SIX

Streets of Fire

Diego sat at the kitchen table, unmoving. Numb. He pushed the glass of warm milk a few inches away from him. Picked it up, put it down. He ran his spoon through the Irish stew his mother had made, stirring dark broth and chunks of potato and carrot back and forth, but he didn't take a bite.

"It's not your fault," Siobhan said gently from across the table.

Diego glanced up. He'd barely been able to look at her since he'd been brought home. She offered him a supportive smile, but her eyes were red, her face tight with worry.

Tears sprang from his eyes again. He couldn't hold them

back. "I wanted to stop them, but I didn't know what to do."

"There was nothing you could have done," Siobhan said. She reached out and rubbed his hand. "You'd be no match for Magnus and his warriors. Few people are. And you were doing what Dad wanted. He would never have forgiven himself if you were captured, too."

Diego nodded. He knew this. But it didn't make him feel any better. "I just . . . I wish there had been something . . . some way I could have used the Maker's Sight. Anything."

"So . . . Santiago was right after all," Siobhan said. "You have the Maker's Sight."

"Yeah." Diego shifted in his chair. "And I know it needs to be kept secret. I just . . ."

"What is it, honey?"

"Nothing."

Siobhan rubbed his hand again. "All that matters is that you're safe. Now eat up and then get some rest."

She stood and took her sidearm holster from the counter and slung it over her shoulder. He'd seen her wear it to military functions, but she'd never had it out around the house. "I'm going to check with the guards." She headed for the front door. Two marines were stationed outside.

Diego shuffled through his nighttime routines, then lay in bed, staring at the curved inside wall and wondering how he would ever sleep. His mind replayed the attack. He could hear the explosions, feel the station rattling, smell the smoke.

Siobhan came in a few minutes later and sat on the edge of his bed.

"Any news?" Diego asked.

"No," Siobhan said. "There won't be until morning. Magistrate Huston has called a meeting first thing tomorrow at Union Station. We'll know more then. Now, try to sleep." She kissed his forehead.

"Mom . . . ," Diego said cautiously. There was a question he'd been yearning to ask. "Those Aeternum . . . Magnus, Balthus— Dad knew them. They talked to him like they were old friends."

Mom's lips pursed. "Not friends, exactly. But yes, your father worked with them in the past, before they were the Aeternum. It was during the Dark Years. He doesn't like to talk about it, and he's never told me very much, but I do know this: when your father met Magnus, he was a great warrior, and he helped the allies turn the tide and end the fighting in the Chronos War. But after that . . . he changed."

"What made him evil?"

Siobhan looked away. "Your father never told me exactly."

Diego wanted to ask more, but Siobhan stood up. "I love you, honey. Go to sleep."

"Mom?" Diego asked anyway. "Are you okay?"

Siobhan paused halfway to the door. "Not at all."

Diego thought he might be awake all night. He'd woken up this morning with his thoughts only on his birthday—no, that wasn't true. There had been the dream. His world falling apart . . . and now it had.

. . .

The great hall at Union Station was packed to capacity. All schools and nonessential services had been shut down in the wake of the attack. People crowded the doorways, perched on the bases of the columns, and sat on the sills of the tall windows to get a better view. The room was dimly lit with gas lamps, and everyone buzzed with frantic, nervous conversation.

Diego sat among the Mid Timers on the benches along the center floor of the hall. Siobhan sat on one side of him, Petey on the other.

Across the aisle, Diego spotted Lucy among the Steam Timers. She wore an austere black dress with a white collar, a black choker, and high-laced black boots. Her hair was pulled back into a tight braid, her face shaded by a short-brimmed hat. Despite its shadow, Diego could see the dark circles around her eyes. Lucy's mother, Margaret Emerson, sat next to her in similar dress, her stony expression betraying nothing.

"Ladies and gentlemen, let's begin." Conversation hushed, and all eyes found Magistrate Huston. He loomed over the crowd, with powerful shoulders and a stern gaze, wearing the customary Elders clothing. When he spoke, no one dared turn away.

"Here are the facts," he said. "By now you've all heard about yesterday's attack on the Arlington plant. We can confirm that an Aeternum assault force carried out this assault, but unlike prior aggressions, this time we believe that attacking the city was *not* their objective. Their goal was to capture a dozen of our best engineers, for reasons we have yet to determine. Hundreds of lives were lost in the raid, and hundreds more were wounded.

"While emergency crews and mechanized construction bots work around the clock to restore Arlington, the assault has left the city nearly without power. In the meantime, all pressurized propulsion and natural gas systems are now running from emergency boiler hubs around the city. We will have water running again later this evening and hope to have lights, heat, and limited steam power sometime tomorrow. But more importantly, we are fortifying our defenses against future attacks. For these reasons, the council has decided that we will not be launching a rescue operation at this time."

"What?" Diego exclaimed. The crowd exploded into accusatory shouts.

"That's gotta be wrong," Petey said.

Diego clenched his jaw and gripped the bench on either side of him, his fingernails nearly gouging the wood. He glanced over and saw that Lucy had her face in her hands, her shoulders hitching like she was sobbing. Meanwhile, a boy who looked like a cross between her and Georgie had leaped to his feet beside her and was shaking an angry fist at the magistrate.

"Believe me, people, as a former military commander of our armed forces, it would not have been my decision," Huston said against the uproar. "But there is wisdom in remaining calm and choosing patience before military action. We need to protect the city first."

Some in the crowd still jeered, but a new chorus of support emerged.

"We must rebuild and work toward bringing the city back to normal. Again, all city and civilian resources will work with your districts—Old Chicago, Mid-city, and Elders' town—to get power, water, and supply lines up and running. Until further notice, only essential services and businesses will operate, and we ask that any nonessential canal travel at night be avoided until lights and traffic systems can be restored. Please, work with us toward this end, not against us. Thank you. This meeting is adjourned, but I would like all families of the captives to join me for a private briefing."

Huston left the stage to some shouts of support, yet anger and confusion still stalked the fringes of the crowd in anxious whispers.

Siobhan stood, sighing and shaking her head.

"It's wrong, Mom," Diego said.

"Let's go talk to the magistrate," Siobhan said.

The crowd filed out, murmuring and grumbling to one another. Diego, Petey, and Siobhan made their way up to the front of the hall, where they gathered with the other families around the magistrate. There were forty or so standing silent as the hall emptied.

When the last footsteps had echoed away, Huston spoke. "Thank you for staying—"

"Magistrate," Siobhan interrupted.

"Yes, Captain Ribera?"

"Sir," she said, her voice firm, "I understand the need to keep our defenses close, but we must meet their aggression with force and take back our people!"

"What do you propose, Captain?"

"Let me lead a rescue team," she said. Others murmured their approval. "Give me *Skywolf*, and one fast-attack boat of commandos and sharpshooters, and I'll get them back."

"Siobhan," Huston said, "I'm afraid that's not feasible. You and our best soldiers are needed here. The council has reappointed me as commander of all New Chicago city and territorial defense forces. All military personnel are being reinstated to active duty as of this moment, to defend the city. The decision has been made not to engage the Aeternum until we are back at full strength. It's simply too risky."

"But—"

"The answer's no, Captain," Huston said. "And that's an order. Are we clear?"

Siobhan stood at attention. "Yes, sir."

"What have you learned about the hostages?" Lucy's mother asked, her voice thick with worry.

"I'm afraid we have no new information about them," Huston said.

"How can you do this?" an older woman asked. "Just leaving our loved ones in the hands of the enemy?"

"It's more complicated than that," Huston said. "Listen,

everyone: we've gathered credible intelligence that Aeternum agents have infiltrated the city, with orders to kidnap the family members of the engineers they're holding prisoner."

"But why us?" Lucy said.

"To use you as leverage," Huston said, "in case the captive engineers refuse to follow Magnus's commands. We're placing you all in protective custody immediately. You will be escorted home to gather essential belongings and then brought to the air corps base at Meigs Field, where we can keep you safe. Police boats are waiting outside. You'll need to go immediately."

The crowd started toward the door. Siobhan didn't move at first, and Diego held back when he saw Huston coming over.

Huston put a hand on Siobhan's shoulder. "If it had been up to me," he said, "I would have let you go."

"I know," Siobhan said.

The families filed out, no one speaking other than in a stray whisper. Diego saw the scowl on his mom's face, and he felt the same.

Petey was waiting for him outside the doors. "How you holding up?" he asked.

"Bad. They're putting us in protective custody. So I guess you'd better not hang around me."

Petey smiled. "But hanging around you is where all the action is."

They stepped out into the fading glow of sunset on the front steps of Union Station.

"It'll be okay," Petey said, patting Diego's shoulder.

"No, it won't," Lucy said, appearing beside them. "Nothing's going to be okay. We'll never see our fathers again."

"You don't know that!" Diego snapped.

Lucy bit her lip. "Sure feels like it."

"Lucy," her mother said. "What's going on? Do you know these boys?"

Lucy's eyes dropped to the ground. "No, Mother, of course not."

"You—" Diego began, but he understood when Mrs. Emerson's disapproving gaze traced over him. Lucy had said that her parents weren't True Believers, but clearly they ascribed to some of the discrimination that was common among people from the Steam era.

"Siobhan!" Diego saw Officer Leahy waving to them from one of the boats tied at the base of the stairs. "You and the Emersons can come with me."

Siobhan glanced at Margaret. "I'm Siobhan Quinlan-Ribera," she said, extending her hand.

"I am aware of who you are," Margaret said, her hands remaining clasped in front of her. "It was . . . noble of you to suggest a rescue mission, if a bit improper."

Siobhan lowered her hand. "Not to me it isn't."

Margaret nodded. "These are my other children: Lucy and Archie."

"How do you do, ma'am," Archie said flatly, but still doffing his cap.

"It's an honor to make your acquaintance, Captain Quin-lan," Lucy said. "I mean, Quinlan-Ribera, I—" Her face reddened.

"You can call me Siobhan."

"Lucy, compose yourself," Margaret said. "And you'll address her properly, as your manners dictate."

"Yes, Mother," Lucy said.

"So, will it be all right for the Emersons and Riberas to ride together?" Siobhan asked. "We do have much in common at this moment."

Margaret's lips pursed, but she nodded. "That will be fine."

Diego saw that Lucy was still gazing at Siobhan like she might say more, but then Margaret nudged her in the back.

"Let's move along then," she said, and they all started down the steps.

"Lucy!" a voice called as they reached the dock. Diego saw Paige rushing over, skateboard under her arm.

"Hey," Lucy said, a relieved smile lighting her face as Paige hugged her with her free arm. "I'm so glad to see you." Tears sprang from her eyes.

"Lucy," Margaret scolded. "Hello, Miss Jordan."

"Ma'am, I'm sorry to hear about Mr. Emerson and your son," Paige said.

"Thank you, my dear." Margaret gave a faint smile.

"Mother," Lucy said, "would it be all right if Paige came with us? She was going to ride back with her cousin, but we could drop her off on the way. Please? With everything that's happened, it would mean the world to me to have her company right now."

"That's all right with me. Is it all right with you, Officer?" Margaret asked. Diego wondered why Margaret's cold vibe didn't extend to Paige.

"It's fine," Officer Leahy said. "Kowalski, you're riding with us, too. Diego could use a friend along, and I already cleared it with your folks."

Engines roared, and the armed escort boats that would lead the convoy began to pull away from the moorings.

"Let's go, everyone," Officer Leahy said, motioning them into the boats. "We need to keep these formations tight."

Diego climbed into the back of the boat, sitting between Siobhan and Petey. Lucy ended up across from him. She and Paige spoke quietly to each other.

The boat churned up the canal.

"People were saying the Aeternum kidnapped those engineers to help run their conquered cities," Petey said over the roar of the boat engine. "But then I heard a guy earlier today saying that it was to build their own geothermal station at some secret location."

"Huh," Diego said. He stared into the shimmering spray of water arcing off the back of the boat.

"Hello?" Petey said. "Earth to Diego."

"Sorry," Diego said. "Just thinking about Dad. And these undercover agents." He glanced at the sides of the canal. "They could be anywhere."

Someone tapped his shoulder. Diego turned to see Siobhan standing up. "Leahy wants me up at the wheelhouse," she said. She leaned into the stiff wind and made her way around to the cockpit of the boat.

"Okay." Diego kept a wary eye on the walkways around them. The boat passed in and out of the crisscrossing shadow of an Elder maglev train overhead. They wove around a Chinese dumpling house resting on pontoons and barrels, veering close to the floating sidewalks. Their police escort was causing bystanders to turn their heads.

"We're not exactly sneaking through town like this," Petey said.

Raised voices caught Diego's attention over the wind. He turned toward the bow. Siobhan and Leahy seemed to be arguing. Diego craned over the seat, trying to hear better—

Something tore through the air with a searing crack. Diego glimpsed a flash in the corner of his eye before being knocked down by the blast.

"Get down!" Siobhan yelled.

The boat was tossed violently, everyone falling into one another. Leahy spun the boat, throwing them again.

More pops. Splintering cracks. Diego scrambled up from the floor of the boat, trying to get his bearings and afraid to lift his head. The gunfire seemed to be coming from everywhere.

Leahy shouted over the barrage. "I think there's just one—"

Crack! Snip snip! More bullets strafed the side of the boat. They pitched right, nearly capsized, and slammed off a parked barge. Metal whined, wood splintered, the hulls momentarily fusing together . . . then their boat lurched free.

"Diego!" He popped up to see Siobhan shouting to him. She held Officer Leahy in her arms. He was slumped over, blood spreading across the back of his coat. "Get up here!"

Diego dropped to his elbows and knees and made his way to the cockpit, his heart pounding.

"Take the wheel!" Siobhan said. She dropped to her knee and peered back at the pursuing skiff. "Keep our speed up!"

"Got it." Diego jammed down the throttle.

"Do you have any weapons?" Siobhan asked Leahy.

He only moaned but managed to point toward a locker in the floor.

Siobhan grabbed the keys from his belt, fumbling with them before finding the right one and opening the locker. Diego saw a flare gun, a loaded service pistol like Siobhan's, and two World War II–era hand grenades. She slipped the extra gun and one of the grenades into her jacket, cocked her pistol, and grabbed a grenade with her free hand.

"Can I help up there?" Archie raised his head above the rail, but bullets zipped around him and he ducked quickly.

"Stay down back there!" Siobhan shouted. "Diego, I need your help." Diego nodded.

Siobhan checked the position of the enemy boat, then ducked back down. "I want you to slow down, let them get close."

"But, Mom—"

"Diego! Trust me. We can't outrun that skiff. We have to take them out."

"Okay." Diego eased off the throttle.

"Hey, what are you doing?" Paige shouted from the back. "Don't slow down! They're going to waste us!"

Siobhan watched over the side. "Now, when I say . . . turn hard right."

Diego gripped the wheel. The skiff was gaining fast. Almost beside them. Bullets zinged past Diego's head.

Siobhan held the gun close to her nose. "Blood to bones be true," she said quietly.

"What?" Diego shouted.

Siobhan didn't answer. She checked behind them. "Wait."

The skiff churned closer. Diego heard their pursuers calling to one another, laughing at their victory.

"Wait . . ."

Diego heard Lucy scream as the faces of their attackers appeared over the side of the boat.

"Now!"

"Full throttle!" Siobhan shouted as she dropped back down.

As they roared away from the explosion, the shock wave pitched the police boat forward, its nose plunging beneath the surface. Diego struggled to keep control. He jammed back on the throttle, and the nose popped free, but then they swerved wildly, nearly broadsiding a paddle wheeler. Diego yanked the wheel the other way, then back again, and finally they steadied. He slammed the throttle to full speed, and they shot down the canal.

"You okay?" Siobhan said, standing beside him, breathing hard.

Diego nodded, catching his breath. For all the stories Diego had heard, he'd never seen his mother like he did right now: as a warrior and a hero.

"I'm going to check on the others," she said. "You know the way to the base?"

"Yeah."

Diego leaned forward and gripped the wheel, focusing on keeping their speed up and avoiding the traffic in the canal. He tried to stay calm, to see in all directions at once, to spot anything out of the ordinary. More attackers could be anywhere.

By the time Siobhan returned a couple minutes later, Diego had discovered a problem with their plan. "We're not going to make it to the base." He tapped the fuel gauge. It was falling fast, past a quarter full and on its way to empty.

Siobhan peered over the side of the boat. "A bullet must have hit the tank."

"We're not far from home," Diego said. "What about those extra boats Dad has at the dock there?"

"Good idea."

It only took two minutes to get to Marina Towers, but they coasted in on the very last of the fuel, the engine sputtering out as they reached the dock.

They filed silently off the police boat. Archie helped Diego and Siobhan carry Officer Leahy. They laid him carefully on the back bench of one of Santiago's service boats.

"This boat isn't big enough for us all," Archie said, looking at the small cabin.

"There's another boat at the dock closer to the tower," Siobhan said. "I'll bring it around."

She started off. Diego watched her go but then jogged after her. "Mom, wait up."

He thought she might protest, but instead she paused and then put an arm around him as they walked. "How are you holding up?" she asked.

"I'm dealing," he said. "I saw you arguing with Leahy before the attack. What was that about?"

"Oh." Siobhan glanced at him but then looked away. "It . . ."

"Don't say it was nothing," Diego said. "Not after everything that's happened."

Siobhan smiled. "You're right. Sorry. Leahy was giving me a message from Magistrate Huston. He wanted me to know that he *does* plan to launch a rescue mission, but he fears that the sabotage of the air corps fuel was an inside job and that the city council has been compromised. It's got to be a secret operation. So he's decided to enlist the help of mercenary pirates to find your father."

"Wait . . . what pirates?" Diego coiled up. "It should be you going, Mom! Or at least the city's air corps or navy. Hell, I should be allowed to go before some hired guns!"

Siobhan waited for him to take a breath. "They're sworn enemies of the Aeternum," she said, "but my reaction was like yours. I don't know how we can trust them. Then again, if we can't trust our own people, then we don't have many options. Huston trusts them, and while he and I don't always agree, I do trust him. I just don't agree with how we're paying them."

"What do you mean? What are we paying them?"

"Cash mostly, but also supplies, and . . . they asked for two of your father's robots."

"Our robots? We're giving them to pirates?"

"I don't like it either, but they were very specific. They want a marine salvage bot and a construction bot. Magistrate Huston is offering them Seahorse and Redford."

"No way!" Diego exclaimed. "Mom, Redford? That makes no sense. That old robot doesn't even work that well, and besides, he's mine!"

Siobhan shook her head. "I know, but they have it all worked out. Huston's arranged a secret deal to pay the mercenaries without the council knowing. After tonight there will be nothing anyone can do about it. I know you're upset, but if Redford and Seahorse are what it takes to get your father back, it has to be worth it.

"I understand how you feel, but I swore an oath. To this city, to its people. Believe me, I want to do exactly what you're saying, but I'd be betraying my honor. And your father would never want that."

Diego bit his lip, but inside, his blood boiled.

"Damn," Siobhan said. They'd reached the second boat, and Diego saw that it wasn't going to be of any help. "What are we going to do now?"

Santiago had removed the boat's engine for one of his works in progress. Diego could picture it now, hanging from giant chains in the workshop.

"How about the *Goldfish*?" Diego pointed to the end of the dock, where Petey had parked the little craft yesterday. "We can probably fit Petey and me and the girls in there. The rest of you can take the service boat."

"Only if you stay close behind us. I mean *close*."

"Got it," Diego said.

"Okay, bring it around," Siobhan said. "And listen . . ." She looked at him strangely, her brow furrowing almost like she was mad, then she reached behind her and removed the service pistol and a spare clip that she'd taken from the police boat.

Diego didn't move for a second.

"Take it," Siobhan said. "You remember what I taught you about shooting?"

"Yeah." She'd taken him to the firing range several times. *Line up the sights. Keep the gun still. Never lock your arm.* You had to be a good shot if you were going to be a fighter pilot.

Diego took the gun. Felt the cold weight of the metal in his hand.

"If anything happens when we're on the way to the base," Siobhan said, "you submerge and get out of there. You do not stick around. Understand?"

"Yes," Diego said, though the thought of leaving his mom after he'd already lost his dad made his gut clench tight. He checked the safety and slipped the gun into the back of his pants. Once it was in his belt, he made sure his shirt covered it.

"That's only to be used as a last resort," Siobhan said. "If you and your friends have no other way out."

"I got it."

Siobhan nodded. She turned away, then spun back around and wrapped Diego in a tight hug. "I love you," she said, and kissed his forehead.

"I love you, too, Mom."

"Guys!"

Diego spied Petey over Siobhan's shoulder.

"Officer Leahy's coughing up blood!" he called. "We need to hurry."

Siobhan pulled away. "You ready?"

Diego nodded. "Petey!" he called. "Get the girls and get down here! We're taking the *Goldfish*."

• • •

"Your elbow's busting my ribs!" Paige groaned.

"Sorry!" Petey said. "There's nowhere else to put it."

"I'm gonna put you out the roof of this thing unless you get out of my business."

"Working on it," Petey said, worming around.

"Ow, watch it!" Lucy snapped.

"Guys!" Diego said. "Knock it off. You're shaking the whole car." He was crammed far against the side, his head pressed into the curving glass. It was a struggle even to move the wheel. "Lucy, shift to third gear," he said.

Lucy reached down by her knees. "You and your father built this contraption?" she asked as she moved the shift and the *Goldfish* lurched into a faster gear. She'd been appraising the controls and construction with a skeptical look since they'd taken off.

"Don't forget I helped," Petey said.

"I hope you weren't in charge of the waterproofing," Lucy said to him. She sat back, adding, "That said, it is quite a nifty device."

Diego smiled to himself.

Suddenly there was a shrill growling sound.

"Ow!" Petey shouted. "What in the—"

"Petey, settle down!" Diego said as the *Goldfish* rocked back and forth. Diego swerved, barely avoiding the lumbering leg of a robot beside them.

"Ah, what is that?" Lucy shouted. She started grabbing at

her head and then threw something forward in a blur of fur. Paige screamed.

"Hold on, you guys!" Diego shouted. He lunged toward the floor of the *Goldfish* and scooped up the writhing thing in his arms.

"It's Daphne!" he said, holding up the panting, terrified dog. "How'd you get in here, girl?"

Daphne yipped.

"Must have been when we loaded the gravity boards yesterday," Petey said.

"You didn't take them out?" Diego asked.

"No, totally forgot." Petey glanced down behind him. "They're still right here."

"You poor girl," Diego said, nuzzling Daphne. She was breathing faster than an engine, her little chest heaving. "You must be starving."

"It kinda smells back there," Petey said.

"Aw, gross!" Paige said. "Did the dog . . ."

"What was she supposed to do if she's been trapped in here for a day?" Diego said. He passed her to Lucy.

"I don't really. I . . ." She grimaced and held Daphne at arm's length.

"Lucy, move her. She's blocking my view."

Lucy bit her lip and cradled the animal. "I hope you don't have any more *business* to do."

Daphne nuzzled into her arm and panted.

Diego focused on keeping up with the service boat.

Siobhan wasn't too far ahead of them, but a maintenance bot was tromping along right in stride with them, making frothy waves and spraying the windshield with each lumbering step.

"Can't you go around that thing?" Paige said. "Any more of these waves and I'm gonna barf."

"Relax, you landlubber," Petey grumbled.

"When I can move my legs, you are so going to get the beat down of your life," Paige said.

Diego glanced at Siobhan. She motioned for him to submerge and pointed off in the direction of the base. She was already turning her craft in the other direction, toward a side street.

Diego hated to see her go but swallowed that fear and nodded back to her.

"We're separating?" Lucy asked, craning her neck to glimpse her mother and brother.

"Those are enemy agents blocking the canal ahead, and they stopped a boat that looks like the one we were just on. We're splitting up so we don't attract attention," Diego said. He took one last look at the other boat, then put the *Goldfish* into a dive. As they submerged, Diego surveyed the surface view of the canals around them one last time. "We can get to Meigs Field a lot faster if we cross Dusable Harbor."

"You sure that's a good idea?" Petey asked. "Being out in the open like that?"

"Better than being penned in on these canals," Diego said. "Besides, they won't expect it."

Diego flicked switches, activating the exhaust covers and seals, then plunged them into a steep dive. The surface world slid from sight, replaced by murky shadows and shimmering light.

"How deep are we going?" Petey asked.

"We'll skim along the bottom," Diego said. "Shouldn't be too much—"

CLANG!

The *Goldfish* shuddered and rattled, and all of them were thrown into each other. Silt and mud rose up from the sea-floor where they struck.

"What was that?" Lucy said.

"Guess I dove a little faster than I thought," Diego said.

"Watch where you're going!" Paige shouted.

"Crud!" Petey squirmed again. "We've got a leak in the floor."

Diego heard the hiss of spraying water.

Lucy screamed. "We have to get to the surface!"

Daphne started barking.

"Hang on," Diego said, peering out the top of the *Goldfish*. "This is all for nothing if we go up now."

"It's all for nothing if we drown," Paige said.

"Water's coming in fast," Petey said.

"Just a little longer," Diego said. He felt the frigid water clutching at his ankles.

"Take us up this instant!" Lucy shouted. "I insist—"

"Ssh!" Diego pointed toward the surface and lowered his voice to a whisper. "We're passing beneath them right now. If they hear us, we're done for."

Everyone gazed up at the underside of the boat, directly above them.

Diego held his breath. *Almost there . . .*

His gaze flashed back and forth from the hulls above to the murk before them . . . then they were through. Diego dared to turn on the headlights. He picked up speed, weaving around dock supports and the legs of parked robots, making for the harbor.

"My dress is soaked, and my feet are going numb," Lucy said. "We *have* to surface."

"Just pick your feet up," Diego said. "A little water never hurt anyone."

No one responded.

Outside the *Goldfish*, the water deepened, the colors muting, and the currents settled. They blurred through a world of slow-moving fish, silt, and trash.

"What's that smell?" Petey asked.

Diego hadn't noticed, but now he sensed the acrid tinge of burning pistons. He checked the temperature gauge. If he kept it at full throttle much longer, they would overheat. He backed off the speed.

"Petey, is there any water getting to the engines?"

"No . . ." Petey checked the dials in front of him. "We're okay right now but not for much longer."

"The water's almost up to my knees," Lucy said.

"You better do something fast, Ribera!" Paige shouted. "I'm gonna kill you if we drown!"

"Thanks for the update," Diego said.

"Let's check to see if they're still following us," Petey suggested.

"Good idea." Diego rose to periscope depth.

"'Scuse me, m'lady," Petey said as he wormed his way out of his seat and wriggled back to the periscope, nearly crawling over Paige in the process.

"Man, I did not sign up for this," Paige said.

"Okay," Petey said, "putting up the periscope." He wound the crank and watched through the lens.

"See anything?" Diego asked.

"Nope," Petey said. "I don't think anyone's following."

Diego exhaled hard. "Okay, we're going up."

He hit the tank switches and turned the pump crank. The *Goldfish* popped to the surface. Paige threw back the bubble hatch, and cool night air flooded in, along with the sounds of the harbor.

"I'll get the pump going," Petey said, returning to his cramped spot.

They rode in silence, except for the chugging of the engine and the rhythmic cycle of the pump.

Diego wondered how Siobhan and the others had fared. Lucy's worried expression suggested she was thinking the same thing. Paige and Petey stared out at the water, no doubt wondering what they'd gotten themselves into.

Halfway across the harbor, Diego spied the lighthouse near Meigs Field, where the air corps base was located. Closer, they would soon be passing Navy Pier.

"We shouldn't even be here," Lucy said, breaking the silence. "I should be back in London, in school with my friends. If it wasn't for those stupid steam converters, we'd be home, and Dad and Georgie would be safe."

Diego thought of his dad. Of their fight. "It sucks," he said, for once agreeing with her.

"How dare Magistrate Huston be such a bloody coward!"

"He's not a coward," Diego said. "It's the senate and the city council."

"Oh, come on, how can you even say that?"

"Because," Diego replied. "Look . . ." He knew he wasn't supposed to say anything, but didn't Lucy deserve to know, too? "There is a plan, actually. . . ." Diego explained about the secret mission.

"Pirates . . . bloody hell!" Lucy said. "Why on earth would we trust *them*?"

"I don't know," Diego said, "but Huston trusts them, and my mother trusts him."

"And that's supposed to be enough for the rest of us?"

"I guess."

Lucy slammed the dashboard. "I hate this! What are we supposed to do? Just sit around and wait for word from a bunch of mercenaries?"

Diego gripped the wheel. He agreed with her, in so many ways. All this made him feel so helpless. He felt something snap inside.

"No," Diego said. He veered the *Goldfish* sharply toward Navy Pier.

• • •

"Why'd you bring us here, Ribera?" Paige demanded.

"Yeah, D, what gives?" Petey asked.

"Petey, get the girls back in the *Goldfish* and safely to the air base."

"Um, and what exactly are you scheming to do?"

"No more running for me," Diego said. "No more hiding."

"Which means what, exactly?" Lucy asked.

"Huston is sending pirates to rescue our parents." He hoisted his backpack over his shoulder. "My mom said that they were getting two of our robots as part of their payment tonight. Those robots are stored here, which means those pirates have to come here to get them. And when they do . . . I'm going with them."

"Slow down," Petey said. "You gotta think this through."

"No, I don't."

"Yeah, you do! Because you sound like a fool!" Paige shouted. "If you think it's a good idea to run off with a bunch of pirates, you're a bigger idiot than I thought."

"What else am I going to do?"

"How about not get yourself killed?" Petey said. "Magistrate Huston has a plan. You don't see your mom running off and disobeying orders. Why should it be any different for you?"

"Yeah," Paige said. "You think you can go and play the hero just because your momma's one in real life?"

"That's not it," Diego said. "You guys don't understand."

"We—" Petey sighed and turned to Lucy. She stared out at the distant city. "You haven't made a peep; what do you think?"

Diego watched her. Lucy would understand; it was her dad, too.

But the gaze she turned on him was frigid. "I think you're bloody bonkers," she said. "You'll probably make it worse!"

Diego shrugged. "Fine. Think what you want. I guess this is good-bye, then." He started up the pier.

"Hold on," Lucy snapped. "I wasn't finished."

Diego paused. "What?"

"You *are* acting like a lunatic, but there is no way I'm letting my father and brother be rescued by a Ribera alone. . . ." Lucy glanced up at the sky. Her eyes looked glassy. "I'm coming with you."

"What?" Diego said. "You? There is no way I'm letting some prim-and-proper girl come along on this mission."

Suddenly everyone was shouting at once.

"How dare you!" Lucy shouted. "Of all the arrogant—"

"I told you!" Paige said to Lucy. "Let him go! Stupid fool's gonna get himself killed."

"You guys can't just go!" Petey said. "Pirates are one thing. You're forgetting that we're talking about the Aeternum!"

"Well, I'm going," Diego said. "And you can't stop—"

"Watch out!" Paige lunged at Diego before he could even flinch, tackling him to the dock. Something singed the air overhead, and Diego heard splintering pops. He looked up to see bullet holes dug into the hangar wall behind them.

Now the sound of an approaching motor, and shouting: "Careful! We need that clock mongrel alive!"

Diego scrambled to his feet. "Run!"

He grabbed his pack and board. Petey grabbed the other board, and they all sprinted down the dock, Daphne right at their heels. Diego heard the engine revving behind them. He risked a glance over his shoulder. There was the enemy skiff emerging from the dark.

"So much for our clean getaway!" Petey said.

"Where do we go?" Lucy said over the pounding of their feet.

"This way!" Diego veered to the right. He'd been here many times with Santiago. The actual hangar he wanted to get to was in the other direction, but maybe they could throw their pursuers off their scent. As they ran, Diego noticed that the pier around them was oddly silent and still.

He led them into a cavernous, empty hangar but didn't stop, sprinting straight through.

"What are we doing?" Paige shouted after him.

"Just keep going!" Diego said.

He turned hard out the back of the hangar, doubling back and running past several more, and then stopped at Hangar 9. He pushed open the door. "This way." As the others filed through, he peered into the dark the way they'd come, watching for movement in the shadows . . . but the night was still.

Diego ducked in behind his friends and saw a familiar sight: Redford and Seahorse, standing in the dark, a stack of cargo containers now placed between them.

"I built the red one," Diego said, pointing out the robots to Lucy.

Lucy shot him an impressed look. "Really?"

"Yeah, I—"

Gunfire cut him off, echoing from several hangars down. Diego scanned their surroundings. There were few places to hide.

Voices echoed from behind them.

"They're getting closer," Petey said.

"Follow me," Diego said. He could only think of one place to hide. He ran to the scaffolding beside Redford, scooped Daphne up in his arm, and led the climb. Diego stopped at Redford's equipment locker and threw open the door. "We can hide in here," he said, pushing them all in.

"This is disgusting," Lucy said, gathering her skirt as she surveyed the cramped, grimy interior.

Diego heard footsteps below. "Just deal," he whispered. "They're here." He pushed Petey and the others inside and stepped half inside, still leaning out so he could hear.

The heavy boot steps thudded closer. Diego craned his neck and spied a team of eight thugs.

"Outside is clear, Mr. Thompson," one of the guys reported to the skinny man in the lead.

Thompson nodded. "Mr. Barnaby," he said to the man beside him, the largest of the group, "search every inch of this place."

The men spread out. Diego watched for an opening, a chance for him to lead his friends back to the door, but the men had every angle covered.

They searched in the gloom, rifles tapping against crates, container doors creaking open.

Something clanged against the base of the scaffolding, and Lucy stifled a squeal.

"Anything?" Thompson called to his team. "That Ribera boy's got to be here somewhere."

"What about the rest of them?" Barnaby asked.

"Take the English girl if you can," Thompson said. "Kill the rest."

Diego's insides froze. Paige made fists and held her breath. Petey stared at the ceiling like he was praying.

Diego breathed deep and slid the gun from his belt. He flipped the safety off. He found his friends gaping at him, and he dismissed them with a nod.

He placed the gun on one of the storage shelves and felt around the compartment, looking for something to brace the door shut. He tried to see if the boards or maybe something on the steam packs might work, but they were no use.

His foot landed on Daphne's tail and she yipped.

"What was that?" The voice was right below them.

Diego watched as Thompson approached Redford and began to climb the scaffolding.

Diego slid back into the locker. He heard grunts as Thompson climbed and then the clangs of his footsteps on their level. Diego leaned back, squishing himself in. Petey grunted and tried to move out of the way, but he fell over.

His knee bumped Diego's gun, and it clattered off the shelf.

"No—" Diego lunged for it, but the gun slipped just past his fingers, down through one of the wide ventilation gaps in the locker floor. A moment of silence . . . then the gun clanged against the next floor down, a bright explosion of sound that reverberated throughout the entire hangar.

"Over here!" Footsteps pounded toward the locker.

"Hold the door!" Diego shouted.

They all grabbed it and had just started to pull when Thompson slammed into it. The girls screamed.

"Come on, you brats!" Thompson shouted, yanking on the door. "Barnaby! Get up here."

Diego heard the heavy thumping, the scaffolding swaying, as Barnaby came closer. They held the door with all their strength, but it wasn't going to be enough. Diego looked around the dark container uselessly.

The door wrenched partially open for a moment. Through the crack, Diego saw Barnaby joining Thompson, his thick arms flexing.

"We'll never hold it!" Petey shouted through gritted teeth.

"Wait!" Diego let go of the door. "Keep holding it!"

"What are you doing, you idiot?" Paige said as the door swung outward again.

"Just give me one second. . . ." Diego put his hand against

the wall of the locker and closed his eyes. He shut out the yelling, the clanging, the panicky breaths of his friends and concentrated only on the container, on the metal and where it welded to Redford, on the spaces between the walls . . . focused. Images flashed in his mind, and the Maker's Sight revealed a panel behind him, in the corner of the locker, and the mechanism inside. Diego spun and tore it open, revealing a power junction coupler.

"Whatever you're doing, hurry!" Petey shouted.

The door flew open wider this time and slammed closed again.

"There's no use fighting it!" Barnaby growled.

Diego's fingers flicked through the circuitry, finally set-tling on two wires. He tapped them together, and an enormous surge of electricity coursed through the walls and his body all at once. It tossed Diego across the locker. He slammed against the wall, his head smacking the metal, and he crumpled to the floor.

His vision filled with pinpricks of light. He heard voices around him:

"What's happening?"

"We're moving!"

And also the grinding hum of pistons firing and boilers coming to life . . .

But it all grew distant, like he was sinking into darkness.

And then silence.

PART TWO
The Rangers of the Vastlantic

We can easily
forgive a child who is
afraid of the dark; the
real tragedy of life is
when men are afraid
of the light.

CHAPTER SEVEN

Pirates and Stowaways

Diego's eyes fluttered open. For a moment, he thought he recognized his bed at home. Maybe the fight in the hangar had been a dream, the chase, even his dad....

"Oi, Ribera's awake."

Diego blinked. Above him was another bed. He was lying on a bottom bunk. He rolled over and found Lucy sitting on the floor next to him, and Paige eyeing him from the doorway.

Daphne jumped up and licked his face.

"Where are we?" Diego asked groggily. His first thought was that they were in the air corps infirmary, but then he felt a rhythmic rocking, back and forth.

"I'm not sure," Lucy said, glancing toward a porthole window. "But I'd imagine we're far from New Chicago by now."

"The pirates?" Diego asked.

"Right. Not a friendly bunch." Petey leaned over from the bunk above. "Course, you slept through the part where they found us in the robot's storage and threw us in these cabins and haven't come back for hours, no food or water or nothing."

Diego rubbed his head. "Yeah, I wasn't exactly sleeping."

"Someone's coming!" Paige said. She was sitting on the floor, leaning against the door.

Heavy footsteps thudded up to the door. A key rattled. Paige jumped as the door swung open. She recoiled as a huge grizzled man squeezed through the narrow doorway.

The man stood silent at first, but his glare felt like molten steel. He filled the door, his breaths short and hard, more like a bull than a man. When he spoke, the words shot out like nails.

"Before I feed you to the beasts of the Vastlantic," he said, his thick Russian accent like a wool blanket over his words, "I will have your names. Now."

He stank of smoke and gasoline. Diego felt certain that this was a man who meant what he said, and only said it once, including the part about making them a sea reptile's lunch. Still, he summoned all the courage he could find. "Tell us who you are first. How do we know you're not an Aeternum soldier?"

"Bah!" The man scowled and spit on the floor. "How dare you! I am Captain Aleksandr Anatoli Boleslavich. Leader of the Vanguard. Sworn enemy of the Aeternum. Now, tovarich." He stepped closer, and his voice lowered to an engine-like growl. "Your names."

"I—I'm Diego, Diego Ribera." He tried to keep his nerves out of his voice. "This is Lucy, Paige, and Petey. My father, Santiago, and Lucy's father and brother are among the kidnapped men you're searching for. We want to help rescue them."

The captain narrowed his eyes at Diego. "I see." He spun on his heels and stalked out of the cabin without another word, slamming the door behind him. There was a clicking sound as the door locked from the outside.

"Is it just me," Petey said, "or did that not go so well?"

"At least it was him instead of that big cyborg who dragged us out of the storage locker," Paige said.

"There was a cyborg?" Diego said.

"Yeah," Petey said, "big fella, bigger than that Russian captain. Part of his crew, I figure."

Diego rubbed his head. "What happened back at the hangar?"

"After you were out cold?" Petey said. "Whatever you did got Redford moving, and he knocked down the scaffolding, but he only went a few steps before he shut down again and fell over. We all got walloped from that, though not as bad as you. They found us after Redford was already loaded on their barge and they'd set sail."

"Those Aeternum bastards almost had us," Paige said. "Whatever you pulled back at the pier actually worked, except for electrocuting yourself."

"I'm just glad it worked," Diego said.

"Yeah, in one way," Paige said. "But, shoot, look where we are now! You went and dragged Petey and me onto this god-forsaken pirate ship in the middle of the ocean!"

"Which is better than being dead," Petey said. "I guess."

"You mean not dead *yet*," Paige said.

Diego didn't bother to respond. He dragged himself out of bed and made his way to the bathroom. He was woozy on his feet, and the swaying of the ship didn't help. He splashed water on his face, then glanced out the window at the open sea. He hoped this had been the right move, because there was no turning back now.

He stepped out of the bathroom to see Paige rubbing Lucy's back.

"What is it?" Diego said.

"My mother has no idea what's become of me," Lucy said, sniffling. "We don't even know if they escaped."

Diego thought of Siobhan and felt a cold stab of worry. "If they were captured," he said, "then that's all the more reason why we should be here."

There was another rattle of keys at the door, and a new pirate appeared, this one maybe just a year older than Paige. He removed his strange-shaped hat as he stepped in.

"Here they are, the young rapscallions." He moved to

Lucy and took her hand. "Forgive our treatment, mademoiselles; we are not used to guests." He kissed Lucy's hand, then took Paige's and did the same.

"Oh please," Paige said, yanking her hand away.

The pirate stepped back. "Ah, my apologies, mademoiselle. It is a custom where I—"

"It's a custom you can drop or next time I'll drop you," Paige said, raising her arms into a fighting stance.

"Oh, very feisty, I see." He smiled. "It makes meeting you even more of a pleasure."

"Who are you?" Diego asked.

The man stood straight and put his hat back on. "I am Gaston Le Baptiste, second pilot, navigator's apprentice, and deck officer, at your service," he said, still focused on Paige and Lucy.

"*N'êtes-vous pas un peu jeune pour un pirate?*" Lucy asked.

"Ha, young for a pirate." Gaston laughed. "*Je compte mon âge en milles parcourus. Ma belle, vous me semblez être quelqu'un qui a voyagé loin.*"

"What the heck are you two saying?" Petey asked.

Lucy giggled. "*Peut-être.*"

Gaston took Lucy's hand. "*Quelle dommage pour tous les hommes que vous ayez voyagé si loin toute seule.*"

"Okay, okay, break it up," Paige said, knocking Gaston's hand off of Lucy's. "You served up enough of that bull for now."

Gaston laughed heartily. "By all means, mademoiselle."

"Don't push me, kid," Paige said. "You don't know who you're talking to."

"Can we *help* you?" Diego said.

Gaston turned, and his smile faded. "Ah, so you are the young Ribera boy, I take it."

"What of it?"

Gaston glanced at Lucy. "*Très courageux pour un de onze ans.*"

Lucy smiled.

"What did you say?" Diego asked.

"He said you were very brave for an eleven-year-old," Lucy said.

Paige cracked up at this. Petey just shook his head.

"I'm thirteen," Diego said, standing up straighter.

"My apologies," Gaston said. "I meant no disrespect. . . . You are short for your age, are you not? But who's to say that you will not grow up to do great things someday. A future-world Napoléon, perhaps!"

Lucy laughed again.

"All right," Diego said.

"Steady on," Lucy said, still smiling. "He's just giving you a go is all."

"Yes," Gaston said. "I didn't come here to start a fight."

"Then why exactly are you here?" Petey asked.

"I am to bring you to the galley to meet with the captain. So, if you'd please follow me." Gaston walked out without waiting for a reply.

"This kitchen is amazing," Paige said, gazing around like she was making an inventory of the supplies and devices. "I could do my momma proud in this place."

"Good," a voice boomed from the doorway. Captain Boleslavich trudged in. "At least *one* of you may get to live."

"What's that supposed to mean?" Lucy said.

The captain stopped before them and crossed his arms. He studied them, the engine-like sounds of his breath filling the room.

"We have a right to be here," Diego said. "It's our parents who are in danger out there and—"

"You have no rights here—*half*-Ribera!" the captain said as he took a seat on a bench behind a long galley table. "And . . . danger? What of the danger you've already put my crew in? I lost several men back at the pier, all because *you* led Aeternum agents there. We arrived to find our payment buried beneath ruined scaffolding and surrounded by armed killers. We dispatched those wretched dogs, but not before taking losses of our own."

"I'm sorry," Diego said. "I didn't—"

"My men have value and purpose on this ship, boy. And so far you do not."

"We can have a purpose," Diego said. "You just give us a try. Paige can cook. Petey is smart, especially with history and numbers, and—"

"And I can master any duty on this ship," Lucy said, cutting him off. "Just tell me what's needing done, and in a week I'll do it better than your crewmen."

"And Lucy's good at being superior," Diego said.

The captain spoke before she could respond.

"And you, half-Ribera," the captain said. "What worth do you possess besides wearing your father's good name?"

"I can . . ." Diego hesitated for a second. "I can fix anything," he said. "I can make anything like new, and sometimes even better."

The captain was silent again, arms still folded. Finally, he said, "My deal with Arthur Huston is to return the men and women taken from New Chicago. This does not include taking care of their worthless, undisciplined runaways. I would've taken you back and thrown you out in the harbor if there had been time, but every moment counts on our mission. So, show me you are worth keeping, and live. Fail me . . . and you can test your mettle against the sea."

Kurt Kaufman

CHAPTER EIGHT

Trials at Sea

C aptain Boleslavich led Diego and his friends out to
the top deck. Diego wasn't prepared for how big the
ship was.

"We must be at least four stories up," Petey said, leaning
against the railing.

"Check it out," Diego said, pointing out on the water.

"Liopleurodons!" Gaston called from above. "A pod of ten
at least!"

"Are they a danger to the ship?" Lucy asked.

"Not to this ship," the captain said. "Now, you'll each
have a task, and a week to learn it. Prove you can handle it,
and you stay. Show yourselves to be unfit for ship duty . . ."

He nodded to the great beasts in the sea.

"And just to be clear," the captain said, "until you prove otherwise, you're barnacles, you understand me? No one should hear you except when you're doing what you're assigned to do. You will follow the officers' orders at all times. You may go anywhere you need to go on the ship, but under no circumstances will you be allowed in the captain's and officers' personal quarters. Also, you are restricted from the weapons and munitions storage. Break any of these rules and . . ." He glanced out to sea again. "Understood?"

"Yes, Captain," they all murmured.

"The bridge is this way." The captain stalked off.

Diego and his friends fell into line. They entered the bridge, empty except for Gaston. Diego wondered where the rest of the crew might be. It seemed like there must be more people, given the size of the ship.

"We sail on the USS *John Curtis*, a one-of-a-kind vessel," the captain said. "Powered by both steam and diesel. The man who built it was John Curtis himself, and he had a talent like few others to build impossible machines."

"Is Mr. Curtis aboard the ship somewhere?" Diego asked.

The captain patted the wall. "No. John is with us in spirit only. He was an amazing builder. He combined ships and parts from a mysterious ship graveyard surrounding the island we found him on. The place that is the base of our operations now. And our home—"

"Why do you have a steam and diesel engine, and also

paddle wheels?" Paige wondered.

"Do not interrupt when the captain speaks!" the captain roared.

Paige looked to the floor.

The captain breathed in deep, a sound like inflating bellows, before he continued. "Out here in the deep, the vibration of the propeller attracts the larger predators. They are drawn to it and have been known to swarm and attack ships. Mostly we travel by paddle wheel, but the propellers are necessary for combat and operations in secured harbors. The steam and diesel engines give us flexibility. People cannot always be persuaded to sell their fuel to pirates."

"That's why all the ships in Dusable Harbor are sail, paddle, or hybrid propulsion," Petey said. "The early Vastlantic sailors learned the danger of propellers the hard way."

The captain fumed, his gaze boring into Petey.

"Sorry, interrupting. My bad."

"These levers control the ship's speed and fuel source," the captain continued, pointing to the controls surrounding the large ship's wheel.

"Is it hard to pilot the ship?" Lucy asked.

"I hope not, for your sake," the captain said. "You say you're good at anything we put you to. Well, you'll be replacing Calvin Roberts, the pilot that I lost at Navy Pier. We will see if you are everything that you claim to be."

Lucy didn't miss a beat. "I claim to be nothing more than an Emerson. By this time next week, you'll wonder how you ever sailed the Vastlantic without me."

Paige exhaled slowly. Even she was shocked by Lucy's boldness. Diego tensed, waiting for the captain to explode at her insolence.

The captain crossed his arms, his eyes narrowing, but then he kicked a small wooden box over to the wheel for Lucy to step on so she could see over it.

"Thank you," Lucy said. She bent to position the box, saw the deep layer of grime on it, and removed a lacy handkerchief from her small black purse, which she used to maneuver it. Then she took her perch atop it and grabbed the wheel.

Petey leaned over to Diego. "It's small wonder Her Majesty hasn't gotten us all killed already."

Paige sucked her teeth and glared at the boys. "Looks like she's doing better than either of you two."

"Yeah, well—" Petey began, but then darted over to a large table. "Whoa, now we're talking. Get a look at these!"

"Is this our country?" Petey asked, studying the maps. "What the United Territories—I mean, States—looks like now?" He ran his finger over the faded map. Diego and Paige gathered around him. "Check it out," Petey said. "Here's the route Bartholomew Roosevelt took through the California Territories, across the Native American territory."

"Please," Lucy said from over at the wheel. "If you want to talk about *real* explorers, Roosevelt has nothing on Sir Francis Drake. Not only did he discover your California and claim it for the queen, but he established the northern route from Britain to New Chicago. Far more impressive, I'd say."

Petey rolled his eyes. "You would." He lowered his voice and said to Diego, "Drake may have found the way to New Chicago, but the Portuguese got to California before Drake ever did in the old world anyway."

"You know your history," the captain said to Petey. "Perhaps you will live up to half-Ribera's claims."

"Thank you, sir."

The captain snatched up the map that they'd been studying. "You will show me." He laid a fresh piece of blank paper on the map table. "Draw me exactly the map you were just looking at, as best you can remember. Do it now. I have need of a new cartographer and assistant navigator. By the end of this week, you will need to be able to plot our way through treacherous waters. Any mistakes in your calculations could kill us all."

Petey nodded, his face pale.

"Gaston," the captain said, "take this one to the kitchen to learn her trade. Her first test will be to make the crew dinner. Tonight."

"It would be my honor." Gaston stepped beside Paige and held out his elbow. "Right this way, mademoiselle."

Paige grabbed Gaston just below the elbow, twisted his arm right around his back, and pushed, doubling him over. "How about we walk like this instead?"

"Ow, okay, okay."

Paige released him, and he stumbled away. "That's what I thought," Paige said. "I'm not some decoration you get to wear on your arm." She turned to the captain and saluted. "Thank you for the orders, sir!"

To everyone's surprise, the captain saluted back.

"These will be the tools of your trade," the captain said to Petey, holding out a sextant and an astrolabe. "Compasses can no longer be relied on in this world. These and the other things you'll need are kept here." He opened a cabinet on the wall and showed Petey the array of rulers, protractors, and other tools. Then he stepped to the door. "When Gaston returns," he said to Lucy, "he will begin your pilot training. Half-Ribera, you come with me to the engine room."

They stepped outside, Diego a few feet behind the captain's giant form. Daphne followed close at his heels.

"At least your dog has worth. She is loyal," the captain said.

Diego was happy to hear Daphne wouldn't become shark food, just as he spotted the large barge being towed behind the ship. It looked at first like piles of scrap metal, but something about the shapes made Diego look closer, and he began to make out the outlines of Redford and Seahorse. The scrap metal had been carefully arranged to camouflage them. Beside them were the three cargo containers from the hangar as well.

"Why all the scrap?" Diego asked.

"We trade it for supplies and like to give the impression that we are simple merchants rather than pirates."

Diego was barely listening, though, as they'd reached the rear third of the ship and he saw what at first seemed an impossible sight.

"You're like a group of Steam Pirates," Diego said.

"Bah," the captain said.

As they passed the great locomotive, awash in the whirring and chugging of its workings, Diego was struck by how few people he saw around. "What happened to your crew?"

The captain exhaled heavily. "Magnus Vorenus happened." He motioned to the locomotive.

Diego noticed a strafing line of bullet holes.

"After Navy Pier," the captain continued, "we can't afford any more losses."

They passed massive antiaircraft guns at the back of the ship and then descended a metal staircase into the dark, greasy bowels of the ship. Pipe work crowded around them. Joints steamed, gears ground and creaked, and beneath everything, a persistent rhythmic sound—*ka-chung, ka-chung*—vibrated up Diego's legs and into his chest. It reminded him of the workshop and gave him a sense of comfort, even so far from home.

They wove their way through the maze of pipes. The smell of gas and grease grew stronger. There was a brown sheen of oil on every surface, and Diego's feet skidded with each step.

They emerged in the labyrinthine engine room. The twisting pipes and gear works all knotted around two massive diesel engines. The pipes steamed, and condensation dripped in the red light.

A form moved up on a catwalk, and at first Diego found himself trying to identify a . . . another robot? No, instead this was a goliath of a man fused to a machine.

"Ajax!" the captain called. The dark-skinned man turned and slid down a staircase by the railings. When he landed, he only seemed bigger, more than seven feet tall. His one arm was like a tree trunk, while the other resembled a small locomotive grafted to a man's shoulder.

"This is my engineer . . . Abraham Jackson, but he is known simply as Ajax. This is Diego, son of Santiago Ribera . . . a half-Ribera," the captain said, gripping Diego's arm in a way that didn't feel friendly. "He will build a backup generator for the diesel and steam engines. He has one week to do this, and you will oversee him, but do not help him in any way. Understood?"

"Yes," Ajax said, his voice like a deep foghorn. "But what is the point of asking the boy to do the impossible?"

"To find out if he is merely a braggart or a liar," the captain said, turning his back on the boy. "I do not suffer liars aboard my ship. And braggarts will be made to suffer."

The captain gave Diego a light but unfriendly push forward, then turned and stalked up the stairs.

Diego's gaze fell. His head still ached from the night before, and the din around him wasn't helping.

"He does not like you," Ajax said.

Diego looked up at him. "Guess not. And I don't like being called half-Ribera."

"But he did not throw you overboard." Ajax clapped him on the shoulder. "That is something."

"Does Captain Bowlsa . . . Baleslamich . . . Balsamic like anyone?"

Ajax exploded in a single burst of heavy laughter. The sound was shocking: loud and curt. Diego didn't realize what he'd said.

"Balsamic, like vinegar. That's pretty brave, kid."

"Oh," Diego said, allowing a smile, "I was just trying to pronounce his name right. I . . ."

"I think that is much better," Ajax said. "Come on, let me show you the workings of the engines."

When Diego finally emerged from the engine room many hours later, he felt like his brain had been run through the steam boiler. Ajax had explained every facet of the diesel and steam engines, and while Diego managed to grasp most of it, he had no idea how he was going to build this backup generator the captain was talking about. He felt ready for a long nap.

Petey and Lucy were in similar states of exhaustion and frustration. Diego sat down beside them in the galley for dinner. They glanced up at him but didn't say a word.

The galley door slapped open, and Paige and Gaston carried out two trays each of food.

"Man, I'm so hungry, I'd eat anything," Petey said. Then the trays landed on the table. "Well, except maybe that."

Diego sniffed apprehensively at the food before them. There was a tray of meat, charred black beyond recognition and lying on a bed of wilted leaves that could no longer be called greens. Another tray held two bowls of something mashed— they seemed too brown and gray to be potatoes—covered in what appeared to be purple gravy. The next tray was a mystery. There were things like vegetables in shape but covered in some mealy coating, and then what seemed to be fried fish heads.

"One week to live and this is what we're going to spend it eating?" Diego said quietly to Petey.

"Speak for yourself," Petey said. "I'd rather starve."

"Petey!" Lucy scolded.

"You try to do better with what's in that fridge." Paige's voice wavered beneath the anger.

"Sorry," Diego said.

The captain cleared his throat. He spooned some of each dish onto his plate, then stabbed one of the fish heads and paused with it dripping over his plate. "*Everyone* will eat

what your cook has prepared. That is an order."

He waited, the fish head dangling there, as the rest of them slowly spooned out their own portions. Then he slid the entire head into his mouth and bit down on it with a sickening crunch. Diego chose a scoop of the maybe-potatoes. The purple gravy might taste sweet.

Wrong. It somehow managed to taste both sour and too salty at the same time. The potatoes had the consistency of starch and paste. He puckered, barely able to get a bite down. He chugged his water.

The captain was still chewing. Then he pulled the hat off Ajax's head and held it before him as if he were going to be sick. His face seemed to turn three distinct shades of green. Finally he picked up his water glass and forced the mouthful

down with a gigantic gulp. Then he stood and gazed at Paige, who sat with her head down.

"Let's hope your skills improve over the next few days," the captain said. "I'll be on the bridge." On his way, he grabbed an apple from the counter.

Everyone else finished a bite or two and then put down their forks.

"It is not that bad, mademoiselle," Gaston said, "especially for a first try."

"Thanks," Paige muttered.

Gaston left with Ajax, who offered her a strained smile before leaving.

"It was a good try," Lucy said once the four of them were alone.

Paige bit her lip. For a second, Diego thought that she might cry, but then she looked up and exploded. "What else was I supposed to do? I know a thing or two, but all that cranky Russian bear had in the kitchen was fish heads and those gray turnips, beets, and some weird meat! How am I supposed to make anything good with *this*?"

"It's okay," Lucy said, putting her arm around Paige. "I had a tough day, too. I could barely figure out where we were going the whole time."

Paige nodded. She tried a bite of her turnips and threw down her fork in frustration.

Diego and Petey each suffered another bite or two in silence and then began clearing the dishes.

Diego ended up beside Paige in the kitchen. "I'm sorry Captain Balsamic had such bad ingredients for you to work with," he said.

A grin slipped across her face. "Balsamic," she said.

"That's a good one, Diego," Petey said, passing by.

"We'll figure this out," Diego said. "And no one's going to get fed to sea monsters. I promise."

"You better," Paige said. "It's your fault I'm here."

"It was a pretty tough day," Petey said when they were back in the dining room getting more plates. "How'd it go down in the engine room?"

"Good . . . actually," Diego said. "I should have no problem."

Petey just shrugged. "Well, I guess one of us will survive, then."

"Come on, Petey," Diego said. "Pep up. We've got time."

But the truth was, things hadn't gone great at all in the engine room. Sure, he'd liked Ajax, but when it had come time to get to work on the generator . . .

Nothing had happened. Diego hadn't been able to find the Sight, no matter how hard he focused. There was darkness, but no flashes. He tried for hours, but it never came, and he was starting to worry that the power had left him forever.

CHAPTER NINE

Those Who Help Themselves

That night, Diego lay awake long after lights-out. His stomach burbled, whether from the rolling seas, the strange food, or his worried thoughts, he didn't know.

"You awake?" he said when he heard Petey roll over on the bunk above his.

"Yup."

"I'm sorry for bringing you out here," Diego said. "For getting us in this mess."

Diego heard Petey sigh. "I know you didn't mean to, D . . . but you were crazy for wanting to run off with these pirates. And now we're all in deep."

Diego laced his fingers behind his head. "I couldn't just

wait around doing nothing. It was like, every day we waited, the Aeternum and my dad were getting farther and farther away. I . . . I couldn't live with what I did."

"What are you talking about?" Petey asked.

Diego almost told Petey about the fight with his dad back at the power station. "That I didn't do enough when it mattered, and I had to fix it."

"Yeah, well, we all have to fix it now," Petey said under his breath.

"What?" Diego asked.

"Nothing." Petey rolled over. "Get some sleep."

Diego shut his eyes and ran his hand gently over Daphne, curled up beside him . . . but sleep was a long way off.

On the third morning at sea, Diego woke before his friends and skipped breakfast, heading straight to the engine room. He gathered the supplies that Ajax had set aside for him as well as every other component that he thought might be useful for building the generator. When everything was laid out, he placed his hands over the pieces and closed his eyes. . . .

Nothing.

Again . . .

Nothing.

Diego pushed back from the table and kicked a nearby metal bucket. It clattered across the floor and clanged off a series of pipes. What had happened to the Maker's Sight? And, he couldn't help wondering, did losing the Sight mean that something had happened to his dad? He had no idea why that would be true, except that he feared it deep in his bones.

"There's no need to kick things," Ajax's voice called from somewhere behind the turbines.

Diego jumped. He'd assumed he was alone.

Ajax appeared at the top of a catwalk, pausing to lace his boots.

"You sleep down here?" Diego asked.

"I find the sound peaceful. Can't stand all that silence topside." Ajax slid down the staircase railing. "Go clear your head. And by that, I mean go get my tool kit from the barge. It's by that odd red robot. I was trying to decipher how it was constructed. Whoever built that sure had a unique style."

"Huh, I'll have to check it out," Diego said.

Diego headed topside and made his way aft. A rope bridge connected the ship to the barge. It wobbled and bounced as he crossed. He was halfway there when he spotted Lucy and Gaston picking through a pile of scrap metal not too far from Redford, chatting and laughing. Diego jumped down to the barge and gave them a wide berth. He circled around behind Seahorse, reaching Redford without them seeing.

Diego patted Redford's shoulder affectionately. "How you doing, big guy?" he asked. "You didn't happen to see a yellow toolbox, did you?"

Diego searched through the disorganized piles of scrap. He could hear Lucy and Gaston rummaging around on the other side. They were looking for parts to fix something on the bridge, but Diego couldn't care less. He didn't know what bothered him more, hearing Gaston's lame jokes or Lucy's fake laughs.

Finally, he spotted the toolbox in the shadow beside Redford. He bent to pick it up and froze. A few feet behind the toolbox was a boxy device. Diego recognized it in an instant: a generator. Just like what the captain had tasked him with building. This must've been the one he was making the replacement for. Maybe he'd intended Diego to find it. *Who knows why it doesn't work? At least if I copied this, I'd have a chance,* Diego thought.

He wondered if the Maker's Sight would work now. He placed his hands on the generator housing and closed his eyes, trying to clear his thoughts, trying to see the way the parts linked together.

Darkness . . . then a flash, but not of the generator. Instead, Diego saw something he didn't recognize. A metallic device shaped like an octopus. Possibly Elder technology, yet it was . . . strange. He felt like it was something he needed—

But then it was gone, and his eyes popped open.

Diego gasped. Somehow, he was now standing next to Redford, and clenched in his hand was an early-twenty-first-century computer tablet. It was filthy and broken. What had happened? He had no memory of moving, or picking it up!

The vision of that strange octopus-shaped device was

already fading. Diego considered the tablet. Something in the back of his mind whispered that it was important. He tucked the device under his arm, grabbed the toolbox, and headed back.

Diego spent all day in the engine room. He had no luck with the Maker's Sight, so instead he labored for hours trying out various possibilities for the generator construction, his thoughts drifting back every now and then to that weird moment on the barge. When he got frustrated, he helped Ajax, who was calibrating the bearings on one of the engines. That work was more satisfying, as Ajax was a good teacher, and it took Diego's mind off his roadblock with the generator.

By the time he returned to his and Petey's room that evening, he was covered in smudges of grease from his head to his feet. He brought the tablet with him, and despite spending a few moments fiddling with it, he'd had no luck making it work either.

Petey was sitting on the floor surrounded by maps, measuring distances with the sextant. He found Paige lounging on his bunk, flipping through a cookbook.

"Had to get some time away from Her Highness?" Diego asked, leaning on his desk.

"Looks like I'm off the hook, suckas," Paige said. "Look what I found stuffed inside one of the pots in the back of the kitchen." She held up a book with illustrations. "This tells you how to actually prepare some of that nasty crap in the food stores into something that even you North-side dorks might like."

"That's great," Diego said.

"I'm making progress on these charts," Petey said. "Gaston was a big help with the basics."

"I'm sure he was," Diego said.

"What, you don't like him?" Petey asked.

"Sometimes he's kind of . . . too much."

"He seemed cool to me," Petey said. "He has all these amazing stories about traveling the world, strange ports, and huge battles."

Diego shrugged and sat on the floor. He ran his fingers over the tablet.

"What's that you're fiddling with?" Petey asked.

"Just something I found," Diego said, running his finger over the dark glass surface.

"You know it's not going to work, right?" Paige said.

"How do you know?" Diego said.

"I *know* that magnetic-field spikes act like intermittent electromagnetic pulses and render tech like that useless," Paige said.

"True," Petey said.

"Thought so," Paige said. "Well, you boys can sit around and play with that janky old tablet. The captain wants to show me something that he thinks might make things run smoother in the kitchen, then I'm off to meet Lucy in the galley. Later, fools."

"Man," Petey said as the door closed behind her, "why do they have to make everything so hard?"

Diego didn't answer. He fiddled with the tablet again.

"Hey," Petey said after a minute. "You all right?"

Diego thought about explaining that weird moment by Redford. The more these strange things started to add up, the more overwhelming it felt to keep it to himself. And yet Santiago's words echoed in his head: *You must keep this power secret.* "Petey," he said instead, "I don't know if I can live up to what I said. Balsamic wants me to build this generator, and I spent all day staring at it and got nowhere."

"Come on," Petey said. "You're Diego Ribera. You've built entire robots. You just need a little more time. It's a lot of pressure. You'll figure it out. You always do."

Diego laughed. "Maybe not this time."

"Here," Petey said. He stood up and tossed Diego a stack of folded clothes.

"What are these?" Diego asked, sitting up.

"The captain brought them. Spare clothes. I'm pretty sure they're World War I uniforms."

"Ugh, they reek," Diego said, holding up the bristly material.

"Yeah, but our own clothes stink worse," Petey said, slipping on one of the shirts.

They had to roll up the pants and sleeves to get them

to fit, and once they were dressed, they had a laugh at their appearance. Soon after, Diego settled back into silence, lying on his bunk, listening to the slow rhythm of the sea, worrying about the strange silence in his head.

Diego and Petey headed to the galley a few hours later. They were about to enter when they heard voices from around the corner.

Is that the girls? Diego wondered. He moved quietly down the passageway and peered around the corner. Paige and Lucy were standing at the rail outside the galley, speaking in hushed voices.

"I'm holding up the best way that I can," Lucy said. Diego was surprised to see her wipe at her eyes. "But I . . ." She held up her hands. "I've got blisters everywhere; my back feels like a broken spring. I can't even make my bed up to the captain's standards, or lace these silly boots. I'm useless."

"Come on, girl. That ain't true, and you know it. You'll get the hang of it."

Lucy shrugged. "I *should* be able to, but I've never had to do any of these things before, being raised the way I was. And I would have gotten in trouble if I'd been seen doing such things. Now, trying to learn them all at once, while also learning to be a ship's pilot. It's . . ."

Paige rubbed Lucy's shoulder.

Lucy sniffed, wiped her nose, and then looked at her hand

in disgust. "If my mother saw me leaking like this, she'd box my ears and ground me for a week. Must maintain proper form and all."

"Who gives an Elder rat about proper form?" Paige said.

Lucy laughed. "You're lucky. *Everything* is about proper form where I'm from. She'll disown me for running off in the first place."

"Not if you save your father and brother she won't."

Lucy sighed. "Well, that's only if my father doesn't cast me off the second he sees me out here."

"They sound mad harsh."

Lucy nodded. "You don't do what's not done. That's the Emerson way."

"But I don't get that," Paige said. "I thought your mother was a suffragette back in London. Wasn't she doing 'what's not done'? Those women went against the times fighting for the right to vote, trying to make it better for our kind."

Lucy half smiled. "Mother believed that a woman should have the right to be a whole person in the eyes of the world. But you should have seen Father's reaction when he found out about *that*. He snuffed it right out."

"And your mom let him do that?"

"Ours is a different time," Lucy said. "That's what she says."

"Yeah," Paige said. "But now is a different time, too. Listen, what happened to your mom really sucked, but you don't have to repeat your parents' mistakes. You're allowed to be *you*. You can try to change the world. You can even have a black Mid-Time friend. Go for broke."

This made Lucy smile. "Why isn't all this as hard for you?"

"It is," Paige said. "But where my parents came from, speaking up and being yourself was all they had. It's one way that I don't mind being like them. They had it real hard, but they took care of their own."

"I wish I had your parents," Lucy said.

Paige wrapped her arms around Lucy. "You got me, girl," she said. "That's even better."

Lucy laughed but then slumped and started crying again.

Diego pulled back and tapped Petey on the shoulder to say they should leave.

"What was that all about?" Petey wondered quietly as they headed for the dining hall.

"Let's leave them be," Diego said. He found himself feeling bad for Lucy and also guilty for how frustrated he'd been with her. She was fighting her own battles in her head, like he was.

Petey and Diego joined the crew as they gathered in the dining hall, no one saying it but everyone worried about what Paige would produce next. To their surprise, the trays that emerged from the kitchen contained a delicious beef burgundy, fluffy wild rice with roasted carrots and shallots, and even a sweet and satisfying bread pudding.

"Mmm." The captain grunted once, and then again, and then a third time, polishing off two helpings as the others were finishing their first.

"That's a good sign," Gaston said to Paige, who was seated on one side of him, with Lucy on the other.

"Ms. Jordan." The captain stood up from the table. "That was less terrible than your other meals. Continue to cook in this manner." He grunted to Ajax, and the two departed.

Paige looked down at her lap, but a satisfied smile pulled at the corners of her mouth.

"Great job, Paige," Petey agreed around a mouthful of stew. "How'd you pull it off?"

"Because I got mad skills," Paige said. "But also, it turns out one of those storage containers they had back at Navy Pier was full of fresh food supplies. Captain took me over and showed me tonight. Would've been nice if that old bear showed me that sooner." Paige shook her finger at them. "But *nooo*, that'd be too easy. He said he wanted to see how resourceful I could be those first nights with nothing but that old garbage!"

"Mademoiselle," Gaston said, "for you." He'd been fiddling in his lap and now handed over his napkin, re-formed in the shape of a swan. "From an ugly duckling on the plate to grace and beauty."

Paige eyed him like she was readying a comeback, but then she smiled and took the swan. "Thanks."

"What's with Ribera?" Lucy asked a few minutes later. Diego hadn't said a word and had barely touched his food.

"Ah, give him a break," Petey said.

Diego looked up. "No, it's fine. I'm having trouble building that generator."

"I thought because of your father, you were some kind of building prodigy," Lucy said.

"Well . . ." Diego looked from one face to the next. "It's fine. Just going to take a lot of work these next couple of days."

Gaston got up to refill their water pitcher.

Once he was out of earshot, Diego lowered his head and whispered to his friends: "Listen, you guys meet me in the engine room later, and I'll tell you what's up."

"Is this more of your shenanigans?" Lucy said.

"No, I swear."

Lucy studied him. "Very well."

Diego felt a rush of nerves. They were halfway through their trials, and everyone was forging ahead . . . except him. The power had deserted him, no matter how hard he tried. He'd counted on the Sight, but without it, what did he have left? His wits, and his friends.

That would have to be enough.

His life depended on it.

CHAPTER TEN

Maker's Sight

"What's down here?" Petey asked. "There's a bucket of minnows."

"I would not get too close," Ajax warned. He sat on a nearby catwalk, working on a small engine component in his lap.

"Why not?" Petey said when the water splashed and something rocketed upward. "What the—" Petey toppled backward. A turtle the size of a bowling ball landed in his lap. It clamped down with a vicious bite on Petey's belt buckle. "Get it off me!" he shouted, slapping at the thick, weathered shell.

"Beauregard likes you!" Ajax called down, his deep laugh booming throughout the engine room.

"Don't hurt him," Diego said.

"Hurt him?" Petey gasped. "That's an alligator snapping turtle. He's about an inch away from changing my life forever! Get him off!"

"I'm trying . . ." Diego tugged on the turtle, but Beauregard's fierce bite wouldn't relent.

"He's not going to let go until he feels like it, or finds something more interesting to bite," Ajax said.

"More interesting?" Petey shouted.

"It's no use," Diego said. "You've got to give him your pants."

"What? The girls are coming!"

"We'll get him away from you and then put out some minnows to draw him off," Diego said. "But we can't do that while he's right on your—"

"All right, I get it!" Petey shimmied out of his pants.

Diego grabbed the pants by the legs and dragged them until Beauregard was a few feet away. Then he plucked a handful of minnows and made a trail from Petey's pants back to the tank, but the turtle didn't move.

Diego looked up to see Petey standing in his boxers, arms crossed, scowling. "What am I supposed to do now?"

Diego grabbed a roll of duct tape from the nearby boiler and a length of tarp off the ground. "Maybe you could improvise?"

"This is not funny. And who keeps a snapping turtle as a pet anyway?"

"Beauregard is quite a guy," Ajax said. "He is both ancient and modern at once. Timeless. The world will keep changing, but he will still be him."

Diego grinned. Ajax smiled too as a puff of steam escaped from a piston on his mighty arm.

"By all that is holy!" Lucy threw her hand over her eyes.

Paige covered her mouth like she was going to barf. "I did not climb all the way down here to see Kowalski in a skirt!"

"It's his fault!" Petey cried, pointing to the turtle, who had finally disengaged from Petey's pants and started gulping down the minnows.

Petey edged over, grabbed his pants, and darted to the far side of the space. "Now, nobody look!" he shouted, dropping the tarp and slipping his pants back on.

"Are you decent yet?" Lucy asked, her eyes still mostly covered.

"Yes," Petey huffed, cinching his belt and then gazing at his damp fingers. "Gross, turtle spit."

There was a plunk as Beauregard dropped back into the tank. Diego slapped the floor panel closed.

"I'll be going topside now," Ajax said, eyeing the girls.

"Thanks, Ajax," Diego said. Before Petey had come down, Diego had asked Ajax for privacy once everyone had arrived.

Diego listened as Ajax's boots clomped away along the catwalk, then up the stairs, fading into the din of the machinery.

"So, why'd you bring us here?" Lucy asked. She scanned the room, then used a handkerchief to wipe off a railing before leaning against it. "Other than for Kowalski's striptease."

"Shut up," Petey said.

Diego sat on the floor, the others joining him. "Seems like forever ago, but the other day was my birthday. And that morning, before we met you in the museum, my dad told me a secret about my family that I'd never known."

"What secret?" Petey said.

"Well, there's this . . . talent that runs in my family. It's the ability to visualize how things connect, or how they're meant to be. So I can see how technology can be put together and made to work."

"You mean like drawing up schematics?" Lucy wondered. "Like Leonardo da Vinci?"

"No, not really like that. More like I can *see* an image of how things could be, or should look when they're built. Once I learned that I could do this, I tried it on the gravity board my dad gave me, then on that lock at school, and then in Redford's locker that night."

"That's how Redford came to life," Petey said. "I figured you knew where the right thingamabobs were to start him up."

"I had no idea, until I saw it," Diego said.

"You're seeing images in your mind . . . ," Lucy said. "You sound like one of those spiritual mediums we have back in London, communicating with the dead through their crystal balls."

"I don't have a crystal ball," Diego said. He tapped his head. "It's in here."

"That sounds like a lot of bull to me," Paige said.

"Thanks," Diego said.

"Do your parents know about this?" Petey asked.

"Yeah . . . they do."

"So that's what had you acting like you was *all that* to Balsamic, like you can fix anything?" Paige said.

"Except now it's stopped working."

"So, what, you want us to feel sorry for you 'cause your high-and-mighty imagination disappeared?"

"Maybe you should just explain this to the captain," Petey said.

"I don't think so," Diego said. "I don't trust the captain. Plus, Dad said I should never tell anyone."

"So you're saying we're less than *anyone*," Lucy said.

"I didn't—"

"Settle down, Diego. I'm giving you a go is all."

"Sorry," Diego said. He noticed that she'd called him by his first name for once.

"So why *are* you telling us this?" Petey asked. "How can we help?"

"If I'm going to hold up my end of this and not get us all thrown overboard, I need your help carrying that generator back over from the barge so I can study it in my room."

"Who says we'd all get thrown over?" Lucy said. "We've all excelled at our tasks. I'm fairly certain it would just be you."

"Jeez Louise, Lucy!" Petey groaned.

Lucy smiled. "In all seriousness, we wouldn't be here if it

weren't for you, Ribera. I'm glad to help." Lucy elbowed Paige gently.

"Yeah, I'll help. But don't try and sell me on all that voodoo magic images crap. Be straight up. If you need help, ask for it."

"Okay," Diego said. "Let's go now so I can get to work. Thanks, you guys. And please . . . it has to stay a secret, okay?"

"Definitely," Petey said.

Lucy made a face like she was thinking it over. Then she cracked up. "Oh, you are too easy to torment."

Three days later, Diego felt more alone than he ever had. He'd barely seen his friends at all. They'd been working hard in their corners of the ship. Other than the occasional gruff check-in from Boleslavich, Diego was alone with his generator parts and Ajax. Occasionally, Beauregard joined them, trudging around the engine room, biting various shiny levers and valves in the hopes that they were fish.

Diego had studied the generator they'd smuggled back to his room, but it hadn't helped nearly as much as he'd hoped. And so he'd worked down in the boiler room, forgetting to break for lunch or even for a breath of fresh air. His hands were grimy and blistered, greasy black under his fingernails, smears across his face. He often returned to the bunk room after the others were asleep and then couldn't sleep himself.

In the midafternoon of the sixth day, the loudspeaker crackled to life. "*Fortuna lyubit gotov,*" the captain announced in Russian. "The stowaways Peter and Lucy have passed their tests. You have all tasted Paige's success. These three will be henceforth considered part of the crew."

Diego's hand slipped on his generator parts. "Ow," he yelped, finding a slice along his index finger welling with blood.

"You okay?" Ajax asked, half hidden inside a nearby gear works.

"Fine," Diego said, wrapping his finger in his filthy shirt. "What did that Russian mean?"

Ajax stood, putting a large wrench under his arm and wiping both hands on a rag. "'Fortune favors the prepared,' I believe."

"Oh." Well, of *course* Petey and Lucy had been prepared. It seemed to Diego like Gaston had been helping them every step of the way, especially Lucy. They'd find books left at their stations about reading charts and wave patterns, or notes about the winds of the day.

Of course, they'd both worked hard, too. The captain had announced last night that they would be tested today: Petey would have to chart the course to some secret location where Boleslavich was meeting with another ship to get vital information, and Lucy would have to pilot the ship through the treacherous waters, full of submerged reefs and all manner of armored fish and giant orthocones.

"Good luck, you guys," Diego had said to them both as they'd left early this morning.

"Thanks," Petey had replied quietly, looking greener than

the seaweed floating near the ship.

"I don't believe in luck," Lucy had said.

And now they'd passed.

"How come you're not happy for your friends?" Ajax asked.

"No, I am. I . . ." *I'm going to be shark food.* "I've only got a day and a half more, and I'm only halfway there with this generator."

"It sounds to me like you need to show some grit," Ajax said. "You don't fool this old cyborg. Think of your father, boy, and get it done. You are better company than Beauregard and easier to clean up after."

Diego smiled for the first time in what felt like a week. "Thanks, Ajax."

He mustered his courage, his focus. He tuned out the burning from the blisters and cuts on his hands to think of Dad, of his smile, of his strong arms wrapping Diego in a tight hug.

But it was slow, painstaking work, and every hour or so he would try to use the Maker's Sight again . . . only to find a blurry blankness in his head. Diego took off his watch and shoved it into his pocket. Time was not his friend.

And so he kept working, on and on.

Ajax disappeared for a while. Later he walked by, and shortly after that, he appeared beside Diego and handed him a muffin. "You should eat," he said.

"Thanks. I forgot I was hungry." Diego took a huge bite of the muffin. "This is a strange thing for Paige to make for dinner, isn't it?"

"Ha!" Ajax's laugh caught Diego off guard again.

"What?" Diego asked.

"It's breakfast. You've been at it all night."

Diego rubbed his head. "I lost track of time." His body did feel tingly and loose. And once he took a single bite, he convulsed with hunger. The muffin was gone in seconds.

Diego yawned and looked back at the generator. Nearly finished. For the third time. He'd completed it twice during the night, only to find that it hadn't worked.

"The captain told me to inform you that he wants to inspect your work at noon."

"Noon?" Diego glanced at the clock on the wall. 6:15 a.m. He'd never make it.

"Still having trouble?" Ajax asked as he climbed up to work on some piping.

"I don't know what it is," Diego said. "Maybe a pressure regulator, maybe one of the steam valves. I'm never going to get it to work!"

Diego lurched to his feet and picked up the softball-sized valve regulator. This stupid thing! He raised it up over his head. Smash it—that was all he could do at this point. His arms trembled with exhaustion. The regulator begged him to hurl it against the steel side of the diesel works.

"Oi, what on earth are you doing?"

Diego spun, but he slipped on a patch of grease. He stumbled, slammed into a pipe, and went down in a heap. The valve clanged to the floor, one of the gauges popping off. Diego rolled over on his back, his ribs and butt aching. He leaned back on his elbows—

And then started to laugh. Hysterically.

It was probably the lack of sleep, maybe she was even a hallucination, but Lucy was standing there dressed in the most ridiculous getup he'd ever seen. She wore a fuzzy lime-green bathrobe, navy-and-red plaid pajama pants, and pink duck slippers with bright yellow beaks.

"What's your problem?" Lucy said, but then she looked down at herself and laughed, too. "Oh, this. I was so tired from yesterday's test that I forgot to get dressed before I came down." She rolled her eyes and ran a hand through her bed head. Then she frowned. "You should know, a gentleman would stop laughing now."

Diego did his best, but he felt delirious, the laughter like a spell.

"I mean it, Ribera. Ugh, now I wish I hadn't even come down here."

Diego managed to swallow his laughter. "Sorry, you just look . . ." The word *cute* nearly popped out of his mouth, along with another bout of giggles, but he held it back in time. "Funny."

"This is all I had to work with," Lucy said. "The captain

had crewman clothes for us, but he said the sleeping attire was not fit for a proper girl. Now, be decent."

"It's just that usually you're so put together and—" Diego nearly slapped a hand over his mouth.

Lucy rolled her eyes, but she also smiled, and for a moment, she let that smile fall right over Diego, like it was meant for him. Their eyes met . . . but then she glanced away. "Anyway, I came down to see how it was going with the generator. And"—she smiled confidently—"to give you a chance to congratulate me on yesterday."

Diego shook his head. "Right. I meant to come up and say how excited I was for you guys, but I lost track of time."

"For the whole night?"

Diego shrugged. "Congratulations."

"Why, thank you, kind sir." Lucy curtsied, holding her plaid pants as if they were skirts.

They shared a second smile. Diego felt sweaty and light-headed at once.

"So, is it finished?" Lucy asked.

"Nope. There's something wrong with it, and I can't figure it out."

Lucy checked to see where Ajax was and then lowered her voice. "No imaginary pictures?"

Diego shook his head. He knew she meant well, but she made it sound silly.

Lucy sighed. "I wish my father were here. He'd know how to fix it. Or Georgie."

"Georgie seemed nice," Diego offered.

"My sweet Georgie," Lucy said, and her eyes welled with tears.

"I wish my dad were here about fifty times a day," Diego said. "Then again, if our dads were here, I guess we wouldn't be."

Lucy nodded. "I'm sorry about what I said, before all this, about my father being better than yours. I was not raised to concede excellence to anyone, and I'm realizing that's not the best trait to have when life gets difficult. You should know, I actually once heard my father tell Georgie that he thought your father's work was awe inspiring. I'm not sure why he behaves like he does."

"It's okay," Diego said. "We both look up to them, but no one is perfect, I guess."

"I guess."

"I always thought of my dad as a hero, that he could do anything. I mean, I still do. . . ." Diego bit his lip, unable to finish.

"What is it?" Lucy asked.

"Before my dad was taken, we had a big fight. I yelled at him and told him I didn't want to be like him. I thought I meant it. Well, I mean, I'm still not sure I want to be an engineer, but I felt like, I'm only thirteen, why should I figure this all out now? But now I get that he wasn't asking me to decide my entire life. He was trying to guide me. I could have listened to him more. I wish I could take that back."

"You can," Lucy said, "when we find him. You'll tell him." She pulled up a stool in front of the generator. "Now, let's get to work. I'm going to be an Emerson and declare that we have this generator working by noon. No excuses!"

"Aye, aye."

By 11:55, Diego could barely feel his fingers or keep his head up straight.

"Do you think that's it?" Lucy asked with a yawn.

"I don't know," Diego said.

"Well, time to be sure," Paige said. She and Petey had come down a couple hours earlier, bringing Diego and Lucy much-needed cups of coffee.

Diego sipped the last bit of his now, but it had gotten cold and bitter. His hands were shaking, his head was pounding, and his butt had fallen asleep. His armpits were clammy with sweat. He held three timing pins in his hand, shaking them like a handful of dice. One of the valves was still on the fritz, but he didn't know which.

There was a clanging from above. The bulkhead door. And now footsteps and low voices. The captain and Ajax. On their way down.

"Come on, D," Petey said. "You got this."

"I don't know which one it is."

"You have to," Lucy said. "We are here to rescue our families, so you need to get this right. Do it for them."

Diego shut his eyes tight and tried to think. He pictured

his dad, in the workshop, his mom, defending the boat. He tried to see their faces, to see them like they were right there. Like he'd found Dad, and they were back home and finally together again.

All at once, his hand shook. He felt a surge of electricity in his mind. . . .

There.

It was only for a second. But when Diego opened his palm, one of the pins seemed like the obvious one.

The footsteps reached the engine room floor. "Time to show us your worth, half-Ribera," the captain said, looming over them.

Diego's hands flew. He replaced the timing pin from the valve with the new one, then sat back. This was it. It would work or it wouldn't. He'd be part of the crew or . . . food for the sea reptiles.

"Is it ready?" the captain asked.

"Ready."

The captain nodded to Ajax. "Throw the switch."

Ajax moved to the wall and pushed the power lever. There was a click.

The generator hummed to life.

Lucy gasped with relief. "You did it!"

Diego realized he wasn't breathing and exhaled so hard he felt like he might deflate down to nothing.

"Report?" the captain said to Ajax, his face still stoic.

Ajax tapped the dials on the diesel turbine and nodded. "Full power."

"Now the steam engine."

Ajax cut the diesel line and threw a different series of switches. The steam chamber hissed to life. The giant piston arms dropped from the ceiling and began to swing like wrought iron pendulums. The generator didn't respond.

But then it roared to life again.

"Yes!" Petey called.

The captain grunted, consulting his pocket watch.

"Half-Ribera did not succeed in this test today," the captain said coldly.

Diego's heart nearly stopped.

"But Diego Ribera, son of Santiago . . . *he* did. *Pozdravleniya,* Diego," the captain said. "Continue to work . . . and you may remain on my ship."

Diego fell back on his elbows. Relief washed over him.

Lucy and Paige yanked him up off the ground and gave him a hug.

"How do you feel?" Petey said, slapping him on the back.

"Like I need to sleep the rest of the day."

CHAPTER ELEVEN

There Be Dragons

Diego's eyes flashed open to a shrill, ringing sound. The ship's alarm.

He flicked on the lamp by his bed and found the clock: three a.m.

"What's going on?" Petey asked, sitting up. "Did we hit an iceberg? There was this movie I saw, and that would be bad, trust me."

"We'd better go find out," Diego said, sliding out of bed and grabbing his boots.

"The captain ordered us in for the rest of the night," Petey said.

"Technically, it's morning," Diego said. "Come on."

"The floor's strange," Petey said as they made their way out the door.

Diego felt it, too. "We're listing," he said. "Something's wrong with the ship."

They hurried to the bridge. Gaston struggled with the wheel, while Paige stood next to Lucy, who seemed clearly shaken. "Come on, you *dame têtue*!" Gaston called, slamming his hands against the wheel before struggling to turn it again.

The ship was lurching about, but when Diego looked out the window into the lights off the bow, he saw that the sea was calm.

"We struck something, and now we're taking on water," Gaston said when he saw them.

"I didn't see a thing, I swear!" Lucy said.

Petey grabbed his charts from a pile on the floor. "There was nothing on the charts. I checked them three times!"

"You can never be completely sure in these waters," Gaston said. "Even the best charts can't account for all the shallow reefs."

"Then why did we even come to this spot?" Petey said. "I heard you worrying about this, Gaston, when we were plotting the course yesterday. You should have said something!"

"Worry? Yes," Gaston said. "Speak up against the captain's orders? Not on your life." He flung the wheel in the other direction and cursed when it made no difference. "We needed a place that was remote enough to ensure a safe meeting with our contacts."

"I think you gone and found it," Paige said.

"Where's the captain?" Diego asked.

"He and Ajax are down in the foredeck trying to patch the leak."

"Should we go help?" Paige said.

"Get on the charts," Gaston said to Petey. "I plotted our location a couple hours ago. See if you can find us a port to make repairs. The currents will need to be favorable. We won't have the power otherwise."

"What about the rest of us?" Lucy asked.

Just then the captain staggered through the doorway, soaked and grease stained. "Get belowdecks and man the pumps. Now!"

Diego, Paige, and Lucy rushed down to the engine room and wove their way forward on a narrow catwalk between pipes and gear works. They found Ajax standing in the triangular front of the ship, nearly waist deep in water.

"You three go to the machine room and bring more manual pumps!" he shouted. He manned a large pump attached to a thick hose that led up and out of a porthole.

The three hurried back and gathered the gear, then returned to the bow, ran the hose lines out the portholes, and slipped down into the water.

"It's frigid!" Lucy said.

"It will feel much colder if we sink," Ajax said. He threw his pump aside and pulled a blowtorch from his shoulder. His cyborg arm puffed as he raised a giant sheet of metal to the leaking area. The blowtorch fired, streaming sparks.

They worked until their arms were sore and their fingers numb and waterlogged, and then long past that. Slowly, the water lowered. By the time it had receded to their numb ankles, gray dawn light shone through the portholes.

"That should do," Ajax said, banging the patch.

Diego's shoulders ached, and his back felt like links of iron chain.

"Ship's nearly back to even keel," Lucy observed. "That's something."

"It is good," Ajax said, "but that patch won't last if we hit any rough seas."

Footsteps thundered on the catwalk, and the captain ducked into the space. He surveyed their work with a grim nod. "Seawater got in the food stores," he announced. "We've found a place to weigh anchor and make repairs. Get yourselves cleaned up and fed, and then rest. I'll need you all alert and ready to work when we arrive."

They staggered, sore and soaked, up to the galley. Gaston had a fire going and had made them hot tea. Petey had spread the navigation charts out on the table.

"This is where we were," he said to Lucy, pointing to one of the pages. "The chart's clear."

"You both did your jobs," Gaston said, "but the waters of the Vastlantic still hold secrets."

"I should have seen it coming," Lucy said.

"Nonsense, mademoiselle," Gaston said.

"Yeah, Lucy, don't sweat it," Paige said, patting her on the back.

"Is this where we're headed?" Petey asked, running his finger to a small cluster of islands.

"Unfortunately, yes," Gaston said.

Petey squinted at the chart. "It's called Las Islas del Diente y Terror. Why do I have a bad feeling that's somewhere we don't want to be?"

"Because its name means 'The Islands of Tooth and Terror,'" Diego said. "Is there a reason for that name, Gaston?"

Diego saw Gaston lean over and whisper something in Lucy's ear. Her eyes widened.

"What?" Petey asked.

"Apparently, those islands are infested with dragons," she said.

"*Oui,* our destination is certainly a last resort," Gaston said. "Many of the Islands of the Great Eastern Wall remain uncharted and unexplored. A seventeenth-century Spanish merchant ship discovered this section years ago when it stopped to replenish water supplies. The sailors told stories of being attacked by dragons. Over half of their crew were eaten. Since then . . . no one goes there."

Gaston winked at the girls. "But have no worries, I picked the smallest island in the cluster, the one named Diablo Pequeño: Little Devil."

"Oh great," Petey said, "as if we weren't in enough danger. Why not add some dragons, too?"

"Are you sure it will be okay?" Lucy asked.

"Of course not," Gaston said. "Out here, it is best to be prepared for the worst. That way you can be pleasantly surprised when things go better."

"How often do they go better?" Paige asked.

"Not very often," Gaston said. "But remember, you girls will have Gaston Le Baptiste to protect you."

"Great," Diego said.

When the ship's horn shook him awake, Diego felt like he'd barely slept at all.

"Maybe they found a different island," Petey said, dragging himself out of bed. "Maybe instead of dragons it's an island full of roller coasters and midway games. Why couldn't the Time Collision make that? Just once I'd like to find the archipelago of Coney Island."

"We'll be all right," Diego said, yet his belly rumbled with nervous energy.

They found Lucy already on the bridge, at the ship's wheel.

"Five degrees left!" Gaston called to her from out on the bow, watching over the railing for rocks and reefs.

Ahead, Diego saw a hilly green island and a cove lined with white sand and lush jungle. It didn't look like a sinister haven for dragons, more like a paradise, the kind that Diego had only ever seen in books. The sticky air was fragrant with the smell of flowers and hot sand. Exotic birdcalls somersaulted over one another, and a waterfall whispered along with the gentle crashing of the surf.

"All stop!" Gaston called.

Lucy brought the throttle back to neutral.

"Dropping anchor!" Gaston craned to see the stern of the ship. "Okay, Ajax!"

They went out on deck and saw Ajax pushing himself away from the stern on one of the longboats. His massive

HUNTSMAN

mechanized arm puffed out clouds of steam as he unfurled loops of thick steel cable. The cable splashed into the water, and thick netting settled down beneath it, creating a temporary security wall between the ship and the beach.

"There's something out there," Diego said, spying a midnight shadow in the teal water, something massive, moving alongside the net.

"Dunkleosteus!" Ajax called out from the longboat. "Just a juvenile. The adults can get over thirty feet long. That's why, in the Vastlantic, you never jump into the beautiful waters of an island paradise." Ajax turned the boat and paddled back toward the ship.

"Gaston," the captain barked. "Get our weapons from the armory. Diego, you know how to drive the robots."

"Yeah," Diego said, "and so does Petey."

"I—" Petey began.

"Good. Go to the barge with Ajax. We'll use the robots to haul the *John Curtis* onto shore."

Diego and Petey crossed the catwalk bridge, keeping a wary eye on the dunkleosteus as it patrolled the edge of the netting.

"Why did you lie to him?" Petey asked. "You know I can't drive those bots. I nearly tore apart your dad's workshop just sitting in one!"

"But now's your chance to learn," Diego said. "Stay calm and remember, it's like the *Goldfish*, only, you know, much bigger."

"Diego . . . ," Petey said with a sigh, but he left it there as they met up with Ajax on the barge.

Diego climbed up to Redford's cockpit, with Daphne riding shotgun in his backpack. The higher they rose, the more she barked excitedly and squirmed. She loved riding robots. Once at Redford's shoulder, Diego put her down and showed Petey how to start up his boiler.

"Now get in the driver's seat," Diego said.

"I'm not sure, D," Petey said.

"Come on, you got it," Diego said. He climbed over to Redford's head and manually started his diesel motor. Soon they heard the steam build as the pistons on the robot's back began to groan and push against the gears.

"Make sure your belt is fastened, and put Daphne in the toolbox pouch next to the seat," Diego said. "Then let out the clutch by your left foot, but only *after* you push the gear lever to *ST,* for 'sit.'"

Petey nodded and did as he was told. Diego held on tight to the handholds, grinning as he felt himself lifted up into the sky. With the sound of expelling steam tanks and groaning metal, the eight-ton monolithic robot sat up.

The feel of the metal, the view from up here, all of it felt familiar, and, after everything this last week, it was a relief to do something he was great at. Although Redford wasn't a state-of-the-art robot, he was Diego's creation, and operating him made Diego feel like a real engineer. It reminded him of when his dad had first taught him how to drive these gigantic machines.

Seahorse rumbled to life, smoke coughing from its stacks. The barge tilted beneath them as Ajax brought the gargantuan robot up to a sitting position next to them. He pointed to a spot on the beach. Diego waved.

"Okay, Petey, you got this, and I'll be right here at your side copiloting. Ready?"

"Here goes nothing," Petey said, forcing a smile, his fingers flexing on the controls, his feet on the pedals.

Redford lurched forward, throwing Diego. "Whoa!" he shouted, clawing to keep from falling off.

"Sorry!" Petey said. "One sec." Redford took another giant step, then all at once reversed, spinning on one foot like he was dancing.

"Petey!" Diego said, dangling by one hand. "Settle down!"

Redford's other leg splashed back into the water, and he stood still.

"I can't do it!" Petey said, throwing up his hands.

Diego clambered back to the cockpit. "Okay," he said, catching his breath. "Here's the thing, Redford might be huge, but the movements you make to operate him can be small. Try a lighter touch, okay?"

"Lighter touch," Petey said, flexing his fingers. "Okay . . ."

"But wait until I've got a tight grip," Diego said, "just in case."

The next step lurched again, Daphne squealing with worry, but after that, Petey calmed down, and they made their way to shore.

• • •

Two hours later, the *John Curtis* was beached halfway on shore, and Diego, Petey, Lucy, and Gaston were returning from the jungle with baskets full of fresh fruit, jugs of freshwater filled from a cascading stream, and a bunch of strange roots and shoots that Gaston had known to pick. He also carried a small wild pig over his shoulders. They emerged onto the beach in the brilliant sun and took refuge from the heat beneath the shade of a cluster of palm trees. The robots' engines were idling. They'd been left on to scare off any unwanted jungle predators while the group was foraging. The tropical plants gave off a sweet, fruity fragrance.

"So, you pull back this bolt here?" Paige asked. Gaston had been giving her lessons on how to shoot his rifle for almost the entire hike. Diego caught Lucy studying Paige. He wiped the sweat off his brow and made his way over to her.

"Gaston is doing his best, I'll say that," Diego said.

Lucy pushed matted hair out of her eyes. "All I know is that I'm fed up with this servants' work. It's hot and I'm famished and . . ." She looked at him blankly. "I'm sorry. Was there something you needed?"

"Never mind." Diego sat down in the sand next to Petey instead.

"Diego, when you have a chance, ask Gaston to put me out of my misery," Petey said. "If I have to climb one more tree to pick another coconut or bushel of bananas . . ."

"Yeah, I know," Diego said, lying on his back on the cool

sand. He gazed up through the leaves into the clear blue sky. "Hey, I have an idea," he said, sitting up. "You guys want to have some *real* fun?"

"Always," Paige said.

He elbowed Petey. "Remember what we have in Redford's storage compartment?"

"You mean these?" The captain's voice boomed as he approached them.

Diego turned and saw the captain pointing at Ajax, who was pulling the gravity boards from the longboat and laying them out on the beach.

"Oh, crud," Diego said.

"What manner of weapons are these?" the captain demanded as they walked over.

Diego gazed at his birthday board, still pristine, lying there in the sand. "They're not weapons. They're gravity boards."

"And you smuggled them onto my ship in your robot."

"No. I mean, yes. We brought them, but we never meant to hide them."

The captain tapped Diego's board with his toe. "What is their purpose?"

"My father invented it. You use them to fly around and—"

"Show me how they work."

"Sure."

Diego slipped on the steam pack and gloves and stepped onto the board. He adjusted the dials, readied his feet, and shot off at a steep angle, climbing over the trees. What a relief! The wind in his face, the world far below. He banked a series of tight turns, swooped over the group below so close that Gaston's hat blew off, then shot nearly vertical. When the whole island came into view, he killed the engine and enjoyed a weightless moment before gravity pulled him down. Then he kicked the board back to life and returned to the beach in a tight spiral, coming to a kick stop that sprayed sand on everyone.

"Aw, man, I could do some damage on one of those!" Paige said.

"Not bad, Ribera," Lucy said with a smile.

"Antigravity fields, thrust-vectoring inductive fans . . . ," the captain said. "How can this be, without the aid of complex electronics?"

"My dad could explain better," Diego said, "but basically, it uses a mercury accelerator to create a limited field of antigravity, and then this pack generates highly pressurized steam to power the thrust-vectoring fans. Those are what you use to control pitch, yaw, roll, and thrust. Everything's mechanically controlled by cable pulls that connect to the navigating gloves. Actually making the board turn is a matter of coordination and balance."

The captain picked up the second steam pack and studied it. "Your father uses technology like this in service of toys and rebuilding. This technology could be so much more." The captain eyed Diego. "These novelties are a distraction. Back to work, all of you."

"Sir," Gaston said, "we are hours ahead of schedule. With the heat of the day increasing, perhaps a few hours of pleasant distraction would make us all more productive later?"

Ajax picked up the second board and examined it. "Captain, clearly these were created by the boy's father to have fun. That's why I brought them out. The crew's been working hard, and Gaston's right. Maybe some time with Diego's boards would make an excellent reward for everyone, sir?"

"I could use the wind in my face," Paige said. "I'm about to die in this heat."

"Soldiers are no use when they're weary of spirit," Ajax said.

The captain exhaled slowly. "Yes, Abraham," the captain said. "Perhaps this is true." He patted his first mate on the shoulder. "Ribera, you and your friends have my permission to . . . fly your toys."

"Seriously?" Petey said.

"When is he not serious?" Gaston said.

The captain nodded. "Gaston may join you, once the repairs are done."

"Yes, sir!" Diego said, slinging the steam pack over his shoulders again.

"But let me be clear: stay to the beach; this jungle is full of dangers," the captain said. "You must stay within sight of the ship at all times, understood?"

"Got it." Diego turned to his friends. "I should probably take you up one at a time since we only have two boards, until you get the hang of it."

"I'll go first," Lucy volunteered. "My father designed something similar." She pulled on a flying cap and goggles. "But he deemed it a frivolous novelty. He's missing the point."

"Yeah." Diego knelt in front of Lucy and adjusted her boots. She slung Siobhan's steam pack over her shoulders. He connected the hoses and cables and checked the pressure readings. They were all safely in the black. He stepped close to her and slipped the gloves over her hands. He felt her eyes watching, and he met her gaze. He noticed a touch of emerald threads woven into the blue of her eyes like the waters in the cove.

Lucy drew a breath. "The metal actuators in the gloves tingle," she said.

"You're a little nervous."

"Emersons don't get—"

"Nervous. I got that—"

"Don't get nervous often was what I was going to say." Lucy smiled. "But I am. A little."

"I won't let anything happen to you, Lucy." He tapped a gauge on the glove. "You start by adjusting this and then use your feet to—"

"You mean like this?" Lucy shot off into the sky, skimming over the treetops.

"Don't stand there, fool," Paige said. "Get after her before she gets herself killed!"

Diego jumped onto his board and soared off in pursuit.

"This is brilliant!" Lucy said over the wind, her face red.

"Pretty sick move you made, Emerson."

"Well then, you'd better keep up! I've got a few more tricks up my sleeve!"

"Let's see 'em!"

Lucy arced skyward and pulled a tight turn, plummeting and skimming the water.

Diego dropped down beside her, the spray of her wake misting his face. He loved the feel of the breeze, the bounce of the board, the pure speed. He ducked, dug hard, and shot past her, taking the lead.

They raced away from the ship, reaching the edge of the cove in moments. Just around the next bend, Diego spied a stream's mouth, water cascading over enormous rocks. Perfect for air bounces. Diego checked over his shoulder. Heading for that stream would mean losing sight of the ship. The captain would be furious. But hey, they'd only be out of sight for maybe a minute or two at the most. He pointed to the spot and waved Lucy on.

Diego sped toward it, increasing his altitude. He focused on a large rounded rock at the river's end and aimed for it, planning to air bounce it into a three-hundred-sixty-degree flip. Emerson wasn't the only one with skills.

He raced closer, getting his balance right. . . .

When suddenly the rock began to move.

"Diego, look out!" Lucy shouted.

It wasn't a rock at all. A long snout rose from the sand,

turning to face him. Giant eyes, rows of yellow teeth. A deino-suchus! The prehistoric crocodile's tail thrashed and it lunged right at Diego. He banked hard, spraying sand in the croc's face, then arced around behind it, narrowly avoiding its snap-ping jaws.

"Lucy!"

He only got a high-pitched scream in response. Lucy's knees buckled on her board as she shot past him up the stream and into the cool, dark jungle. She glanced back, her eyes wide. It looked like she wanted to scream again but couldn't, and she plunged ahead even faster.

The croc sprang after Diego. He ducked into the wind and cranked the dials, shooting forward. He banked back and forth above the stream, shooting into the dark jungle. He turned and saw that the croc had given up the chase, returning instead to the warmth of its sunning place. Diego followed Lucy's dissi-pating steam trail. She must have really put on the jets.

"Lucy!" Diego looked in all directions. She'd been right in front of him. He glanced back again, making sure the deino-suchus was gone.

A scream echoed through the jungle.

Diego spun around and charged up the stream. The trees flickered past, the jungle growing denser, darker, reaching for him from all sides. He twisted and turned with the curving water, then broke out into a wide, grassy clearing. There was Lucy and . . .

Oh no!

Diego raced to Lucy, swooping down, his board moving at top speed. One allosaurus leaped at her, nearly knocking Lucy off her board. She shrieked. Diego dodged and dove, arriving in front of Lucy. Tears streaked her face. Screams seemed caught inside her throat.

Without thinking, Diego lunged for Lucy, grabbing her hand. He wrapped his arms around her waist and shot forward, pushing his board to full power to guide them both away. Fast.

"You okay?" Diego called over his shoulder, breathing hard.

"Oh my God, I thought I was done for!" Lucy shouted. She gripped him tightly around the waist.

Diego felt the tears streaming down her face against his neck. "Hold on."

The board wobbled beneath Diego's feet. Lucy felt heavier than she should have, too. Her board's antigravity accelerator must have been damaged.

He leveled off above the treetops, throttled forward, and then found a place to land.

Diego hopped off his board and inspected Lucy's. The damage was worse than he'd guessed. It was a wonder she could still fly. The two front fans were bent. Diego blamed himself. When that crocodile had turned on him, he'd lost sight of Lucy. She'd panicked and bolted deep into the jungle along the stream. She hadn't even seen those allosauruses until it was too late. But striking the juvenile was bad luck. The nose of the board was dented and smeared with its blood.

"I hear something hissing," Lucy said.

"Me too." Diego spun around and inspected her pack. She was losing pressure fast, the dial spinning down. She had a few minutes of flight capacity left and almost no pressure for thrust. The board was not going to get Lucy back to the ship.

"I'm sorry I messed up. I—"

"No, you didn't." Diego unstrapped her pack and slid it from her shoulders.

"Diego, what are you—?"

He pushed her onto his board.

The magnetic couplers locked in her boots.

"Have to get you out of here," he said. He whipped off his pack and slipped it over her shoulders. He connected the fittings.

A series of roars sent nearby birds scattering from their perches. *About a half mile out*, Diego thought, adjusting the fittings and settings. *And coming fast.*

"Oh God, it's them!" Lucy cried.

The flying gear was all set. Diego grabbed her by the shoulders. "Your board's ruined, so you're taking mine."

Lucy nodded. "No! What about you?"

"There's not enough power in my pack to fly us both, so you need to get help."

"But they're coming! And you—"

"I'll be fine," Diego said. He checked her pack. "I've got enough to fly up to that cliff face. I can wait there. Got it?"

"Okay," she said, still breathing hard.

"You can do this."

Lucy wiped her eyes and nodded.

Diego slipped on Lucy's pack and connected the cables and hoses. He glanced at the dial on his glove. Not good.

"Diego . . . ," Lucy said, seeing the worry on his face.

"It's okay," he said.

"You're lying," Lucy said.

"Listen," he said anxiously. "We are going to get out of this alive. You're an Emerson, and Emersons don't fail, remember? Fly just above the tree line. And no faster than twenty-five on the speed dial. Understand?"

"Got it."

"Okay, Emerson, time to go!" He smiled as bravely as he could.

She nodded, but then her eyes seemed to widen. Diego heard something behind them. Breathing. He turned . . .

HUNTSMAN
Creatures by BLACKHEART

He'd grabbed her board and started running when a second allosaurus burst through the bushes at his side.

Its neck lunged, its jaws snapping inches from his face.

Diego sprinted, felt its giant footsteps pounding the earth right behind him.

He fired up the board and, in one smooth motion, threw it out in front of him while pumping the actuators in his gloves. He jumped on the board as it accelerated. He could feel the breath of the allosaurus on his back, the roar growing louder as his board struggled to climb higher.

Diego flew skyward, but the board didn't have enough power left to clear the waterfall, and he crashed into the cliff face, tumbling down onto a ledge. He gripped his shoulder. It burned in slicing waves of pain that made his fingers tingle and his neck seize up. The beasts began to throw their massive bodies against the wall, trying to dislodge him.

"Is that all you've got?" Diego shouted down at them. He staggered and fell to his knees. A large chunk of rock

dislodged beside him, tumbling down. Diego threw himself against the wall, out of breath, his shoulder screaming, his vision getting blurry.

But then the creatures stopped pounding. As if they were connected by the same brain, they reared back on their hind legs and roared toward the sky.

A shadow fell over Diego, and he looked up to see a massive shape flying overhead.

CHAPTER TWELVE

The *Magellan*

The massive airship could not fully be seen from where Diego lay. He traced the thick ropes that connected to one of the cranes on the ship's undercarriage. He saw the name across the side, next to one of the large propellers pushing them forward.

Magellan.

He'd been rescued by his best friend and the Mapmakers of the Vastlantic.

"Greetings, Diego," said the girl beside him as the canoe arced over the jungle. She looked a few years older than him. "I'm Dusty. This is my associate Kiyoshi. You've got one very dislocated shoulder here."

"*Konnichiwa*, Diego san," Kiyoshi said, bowing.

Diego tried to nod to him but was overwhelmed by burning pain. The edges of the world looked hazy. Craning his neck, he spied the *John Curtis* growing in the distance, but even that simple motion made everything start to swim. He closed his eyes, grimacing.

"Hang in there, D," Petey said. "We got here as soon as we could."

"It's probably best if I just fix this now, okay?" Diego felt Dusty's hands on his elbow and back. "Petey, hold his other arm steady, okay?"

"Sure," Petey said.

"Dusty," Kiyoshi said, "I'm not sure this is wise until we are on solid ground."

"What do you mean?" Diego mumbled.

"Relax, Kiyoshi," Dusty said. "No time like the present! Keep your eyes closed, Diego, and count to three with me. One . . ."

"Two . . . ," they said together.

Dusty shoved Diego's shoulder back into place.

His world went white with pain. After a second, he screamed in agony. Despite the razor-hot burning up and down his side, he could move his shoulder again.

"There you go," Dusty said, rubbing her hand over his head. "All systems back online."

"Thanks," Diego said weakly.

The canoe came to rest on the beach, scattering a flock of

curious, pigeon-size dinosaurs.

Petey helped Diego out of the canoe, and then he turned to his rescuers.

"Thanks," Diego groaned.

"Don't mention it," Dusty said. "Though you really would have been done for without us."

"Yeah, I guess so," Diego said.

"Relax," Dusty said. "Just giving you a hard time."

"*Subarashii!*" Kiyoshi said, turning his attention to the robots standing nearby. "What creations are these?"

"They came with us," Diego said. "I built the red one."

"You are a *masuta* of metal servants?" Kiyoshi said, bowing.

"He honors your skill," Dusty explained. "It's his way."

Footsteps crunched in the sand behind them. Diego turned to find Lucy, Gaston, and Paige running up the beach alongside the captain.

"You're alive!" Lucy said, throwing her arms around Diego. He froze for a second, grimacing, overcome by pain, but then gently hugged her back with his good arm. Her forehead, arm, and hand were all bandaged up.

"Are you okay?" he asked.

She pulled back and glanced sheepishly at her bandages. "I got all the way to the beach. But then I had a little trouble with the landing."

"You'll get it next time," Diego said.

"Dusty! Kiyoshi!" A voice called down from the *Magellan*

with a rough Scottish accent. "If you two are done making friends, get back on board. We have work to do."

"Well, you heard the man," Dusty said. "Nice not really meeting you all. Gotta run." She and Kiyoshi stepped back into the canoe, and it began to rise.

"Thank you," Lucy called after them.

Dusty tipped her hat. "Take better care of your boyfriend, Steam Timer. I did it for *him*, not you."

"He's not my—we're friends!" Lucy shouted.

"Let's get you inside," Gaston said, motioning to Diego. "That shoulder needs ice."

Petey helped Diego stumble his way back aboard the *John Curtis*. His vision was still dim, his balance off. He was aware of two figures standing on deck, guiding the *Magellan* directly over the *John Curtis*.

The captain checked in on Diego once he was lying in bed. "The Mapmaker did good work with your shoulder," he said. "You have a couple bruised ribs. You are lucky that is all. Allosauruses are not to be trifled with."

"I'm sorry," Diego said.

"Small words," the captain said. "Apologies are meaningless when you're dead." He handed Diego a cup of green medicine. "Take this for the swelling."

It tasted like sour licorice and burned the back of his throat, but it soothed his pain almost immediately.

Gaston came in with the ice pack. "Here." He wrapped Diego's arm in a sling and affixed the ice pack under the strap.

"You'll have to take it easy for a few days," the captain said. "But understand that you are still expected to do your duties. When you are back on your feet, we will talk of today's mutiny, and punishment."

The captain and Gaston left, their footsteps fading down the deck. And Paige erupted. "What were you thinking, breaking the captain's orders? You nearly got Lucy killed!"

"Paige," Lucy said. "Calm down. It was my fault. I panicked and flew down that stream, and I'm the one who ran into trouble with the allosaurus."

"Yeah, right after that reckless fool took you out of sight of the ship!" Paige shouted, turning her glare on Lucy. "You two got stupid! And you almost ended up dead."

"Paige," Petey said. "Come on. . . ."

Paige whirled toward him. "Shut up!" Then back to Lucy. "I *told* you we should never have hung around with these crazy little boys—especially that one!" Paige locked eyes with Diego. "You ever do anything to hurt this girl, Ribera, and I'll finish you!" She stormed out.

"What's her problem anyway?" Petey said. "And why is she mad at *me*? I didn't do a thing!"

"Petey . . . ," Lucy said. "Don't be insufferable!"

"No, really," Diego said. "What's her deal? It's like everything I do pisses her off." He threw his hands up as he spoke, setting off a fresh wave of throbbing pain in his shoulder.

"Paige was scared. She's looking out for me."

"If that's looking out for you, I'd hate to see her when

she's actually mad," Petey said.

"I don't understand how you could be friends with someone who is always so . . . difficult," Diego said.

Lucy's eyes narrowed. "You don't know anything about her. Give her a break. Paige's parents both work days and nights. She was practically raised by her older brother. These days, between me and the Breakers . . . that's about all she's got."

"The Breakers," Petey said. "I've heard of it. Tough place, right?"

"The toughest," Diego said. "That's the old broken chocolate factory on the border of Old Chicago where the Mid-Time black neighborhoods are. It's where blacks and whites don't mix, let alone Steamers and Mids. It's a rough place, and only the best skaters go there."

"And the toughest kids," Lucy said. "Paige and her brother skated the Breakers to stay out of trouble. So before you say anything else stupid, cut her some slack."

"Man," Diego said, "I didn't know."

"I wish she'd told us about that," Petey said. "She never wants to talk about herself, or to us at all really."

"Well, I still don't get why she's up in my face about what happened," Diego said. "I mean, you're fine. It's not like we got hurt."

"Didn't you listen to a word I said?" Lucy snapped. "It's so obvious why she's mad at you! She thinks you almost got us— me killed." She threw open the door and stormed out.

"What's with her?" Diego said.

"I have no idea," Petey said.

The door had barely closed when it slapped back open and the captain stepped in, another man behind him.

"I brought the man to whom you owe your life," the captain said. "Meet Captain Wallace of the *Magellan*, leader of the Mapmakers of the Vastlantic."

"Glad to see you're in one piece," Wallace said, shaking Diego's hand.

"Thank you for saving me," Diego said.

"Lucky for you, we decided to search the area when Captain Boleslavich failed to meet at the rendezvous," Wallace said. "We had new information to give to your captain about Magnus's location. That said, it was pure luck finding you on this island, so far off course. We were passing within miles of here when my first mate spotted that blond comet bursting out of the jungle through the spyglass."

M Bettson © 2016

"Lucy."

"Yeah, that's the one. We came in for a closer look, and she gave us word about you," he said, adjusting his gloves. "Now that our business is done, we should be off before we give the Aeternum any reason to suspect we've broken our code."

"What code is that?" Diego asked.

"Diego." The captain shot him a piercing look.

"Sorry, Captain Balsamic, I—" Diego slapped a hand over his mouth.

"Balsamic!" Wallace bellowed, bursting into laughter.

"It was an accident, sir," Diego stammered. "I just—I had trouble with your name this one time and I . . . I mispronounced it."

The captain looked like he might explode.

"Well, of course you did," Wallace said. "I still try to avoid saying our good captain's name for fear of tripping over it. And I don't mind the question. The Mapmakers' guild has sworn to be politically neutral, and we're willing to sell maps to anyone for the right price. That said, I like to do what I can for those who I believe are in the right, your captain being one of them. The Aeternum have their eyes on us, though, at all times." He turned to the captain. "Shall we?"

The two walked out. "Balsamic!" Diego heard Wallace say as they walked up the deck. "That's priceless."

The air hummed with the sound of the *Magellan*'s engines warming up. Petey helped Diego to the back deck to watch the takeoff.

MARC GAZONNA © 2016

Once airborne, the *Magellan's* cranes began lifting netted cargo off the deck of the *John Curtis*, including many of the cargo containers from Navy Pier.

"Looks like they traded supplies for information," Petey said, pointing to piles of equipment on the deck.

Diego noticed Paige and Lucy down on the deck. Ajax and Gaston stood nearby, talking to someone dressed in a deerskin shirt and pants, and wearing high boots. "Who's that?" Diego wondered.

"That . . . ," Petey said, "is the new love of my life. She's Captain Wallace's first mate, Clementine Van Jensen, the deadliest shot in the West. I've read about her."

"Clem!" Kiyoshi called down from the *Magellan.* Diego saw a few much younger faces beside Kiyoshi. "Time to go!"

Clementine hugged Ajax and Gaston.

"Good luck with the new recruits," Gaston said, glancing up at the kids with Kiyoshi.

"Ha," Clem laughed. "They'll be easy compared to the saplings you've got on board."

"Man," Petey said. "I wish I was one of those recruits. Training with the Mapmakers would be the best."

Clementine strode to Captain Wallace. "Time to get moving, sir, if we're going to get these medical supplies to the people in Texas."

Captain Wallace shook hands with the captain. "I hope you find your ships in Volcambria. If the *Dauntless* and the *Valiant* survived, I'm certain they'll be there. And if not, send word, and I know what to do."

The captain nodded and clapped Wallace on the shoulder. "You are certain of your spies' information?"

Wallace's face darkened. "I know you have to ask, old friend, but one of my best men lost his life gathering that intel."

The captain nodded. "His life will not have been given in vain. I swear it."

The captains exchanged salutes, and Wallace and Clementine grabbed on to the last cargo net, rising with it up to the *Magellan*. Once they were on board, the ship banked away from the *John Curtis*.

As the *Magellan* shrank on the horizon, Diego felt an ache inside. Texas was a long way from New Chicago, but it was still in the direction of home. Diego missed his room, his street, his family.

He took a deep breath, trying to fight back the fear inside him. The farther he traveled, the harder it became to see how he would get back home.

CHAPTER THIRTEEN

The Captain

O nce the *Magellan* had disappeared in the distance, Diego and Petey headed for the bridge.

They found the captain standing on the bridge balcony taking a sextant reading. Without a word, he stepped around them and entered the bridge. Diego and Petey followed.

"The repairs are complete," the captain announced.

Inside, Lucy was at the wheel, with Paige at her side. Diego found that he couldn't look at them, though, and had to step over by the windows and gaze out at the sea. At first, he felt angry at them, but as he gripped the railing, his head still aching, he realized that he was embarrassed about messing up and still felt guilty for putting Lucy in danger.

"Supplies are stowed," the captain said. "The robots are aboard the barge. Lucy, prepare to take us out of the cove and get us back on course."

"Yes, sir." Lucy throttled up the engines. The ship rumbled as the steam engine roared to life.

Diego watched the jungle island receding.

"Well done," the captain said as Lucy guided the *John Curtis* out. "If only such keen decision making had been on display earlier."

"Yes, sir," Lucy said, blushing.

"Paige," the captain said, "gather Gaston and Ajax and tell them they are to help you with dinner. Take Petey with you. Lucy, after I've finished talking with this one, I'll take over and you may join the others. Diego, outside with me."

Diego waited until Paige had left, avoiding any chance of making eye contact with her, and then followed the captain out onto the deck.

"Your actions back on the beach," the captain said. He stared out at the water without saying more.

"I—I'm sorry, sir," Diego said. "I lost track of where we were. It was a mistake."

The captain had pulled out his pocket watch. He glanced from it to Diego, almost like he was waiting for Diego to continue.

"Um, it's been hard since my dad was taken," Diego said.

"I'm sure it has been," the captain said.

"And I don't know. Flying on that beach was one of the first times I've felt happy in over a week. I guess I didn't want it to stop."

"Spoken like a thirteen-year-old boy," the captain said. "But there are no boys on my ship. The next time you disobey my orders, I'll have you flogged, or marooned."

"I promise," Diego said. "I'll follow your orders, sir."

The captain looked at his watch for another moment, his breaths deep like the giant steam bellows. "Go find the others. They'll be on the aft deck."

Diego followed the sounds of his friends' voices. They were gathered along the aft railing. He paused by the wall, not joining them yet. Paige was there. When she spied Diego, she crossed her arms and scowled.

Ajax and Petey wore heavy leather harnesses and were hooked onto the rails with thick ropes. Paige held a gaffing hook, and Gaston stood by, armed with two enormous guns.

"Nice and slow," Ajax said to Petey, cranking the reel on a long fishing rod. "And give it a little action."

"Like this?" Petey said, bouncing his rod.

"Just like that," Ajax said. "Make that bait do a little dance. Like it's something special. So that big fish has to take a bite."

"What's with the guns?" Diego asked, walking over.

"The defiant explorer returns," Gaston said. "You never can be too careful fishing in the Vastlantic. Sometimes the fish you drag up look tempting to one of the larger, more dangerous creatures, and you end up with an eight-ton carnivore in your face."

"Hey!" Petey said. "I think I've got one!" His rod started to bend. He reeled in the line, straining his legs against the railing.

"Keep it steady," Ajax said. "Don't reel too fast."

"It feels like . . . a big one." Petey struggled to hang on to the reel as it tugged and bowed.

All at once the rod snapped back to straight. If it hadn't been for the harness, Petey would have been thrown all the way to the wall. Below, the water splashed violently.

Gaston peered over the railing. "There's a big shadow down there. I think a young mosasaur thanks you for the snack."

Diego heard footsteps behind him.

"Lucy!" Gaston called. "Come see, we've got a mosasaur right off the stern."

"I'm sure I can see him quite well from here," Lucy said, stopping many feet back from the railing.

"Ah well, your loss," Gaston said. "It's gone anyway." He turned to Paige. "Where were we, before everyone arrived and interrupted?"

"You were yapping on about planes or something," Paige said.

"Oh right, yes. I often fly planes for the captain. I could take you for a ride sometime."

Paige rolled her eyes. "I'll keep that in mind."

"I hope you do. Also—"

"What kind of airplanes do you fly?" Lucy asked.

"All manner of aircraft, mademoiselle: seaplanes, cargo, and fighter planes for the Vanguard," Gaston said. "I have six Aeternum kills to my name."

"I'm a pilot, too," Diego said. "Going to be taking my civilian pilot's test soon. Probably once this rescue mission is over."

"Well, aren't you the fortunate son," Gaston said. "I don't have a mother in the air corps. She was only a maid in New Orleans."

"But you said your father was important," Lucy said.

"He was," Gaston said. "He worked as a cartographer for the emperor Napoléon Bonaparte and mapped the Louisiana Purchase in 1800. He met my mother in New Orleans, and that's where they made their home after the Time Collision."

"Sounds like you had a fortunate upbringing as well," Diego said.

"Does it, now?" The usual playfulness left Gaston's voice. "Which part? You mean when my parents, my sister, and my little brother all died of yellow fever when I was seven? A pirate's life is the only way I'm ever going to see the skies, Ribera."

"Sorry," Diego said.

Paige huffed, ignoring Diego altogether.

"Ooh, got another one!" Petey said, gritting his teeth. "Feels strong . . ."

"Here, Petey, let me help this time." Ajax slid over and added his cyborg arm to the effort. Petey reeled as fast as he could.

"It's a big one!" Gaston said, peering over the side. "Let me tell the captain to slow down." He stepped to a voice pipe on the wall and called the bridge.

The ship slowed to an idle.

There was a thunderous splash from below. Diego watched as a fat, silver fish leaped out of the water, struggling against the line.

"Here . . . it . . . comes," Ajax said. He and Petey pulled with all their strength, the rod nearly breaking. As the fish came alongside, Ajax hoisted it up effortlessly with his piston-driven arm. He released the great fish, and it slapped onto the deck, flopping wildly.

Ajax knelt and pressed his knee into the side of the fish. He pried the hook out of its mouth, leaving a thin line of blood on the deck.

"What do we have?" The captain joined them, looking curious, but when he saw the fish, he froze. "I don't believe it."

"It's a tuna, right, Captain?" Gaston said.

"It looks like a yellowfin," Petey said, "but that's impossible. They're only in the Pan Pacific."

"Ahi," the captain whispered. He crouched and ran his fingers down the glistening scales. "Ajax, throw her back."

"Wait, why?" Petey said, still out of breath. "We spent all our energy getting that thing up on deck!"

"I thought the whole point of fishing was to catch fish?" Paige said. "I could make a mean dinner with them fillets."

The captain stood. "We have many new provisions from

the Mapmakers. You can make something else."

"But, Captain," Petey said. "It looks perfect."

"Before the Time Collision, humans took from the world without restraint or thought," the captain said. "They used up every resource until the fate of the planet was doomed. I will not be part of making that same mistake again."

"It's only one fish, sir," Petey said.

The captain turned to leave. "I'll be in my quarters."

Ajax threw the tuna overboard.

That night, the captain didn't join them for dinner.

"I'll take him a tray," Diego said. He wanted to get away from the galley anyway, where Paige was making a point of talking to Lucy and Gaston and *not* to him.

"You can take him this," Ajax said, emerging from the kitchen with a tray prepared.

"Thanks." Diego got up and took the tray. As he turned to leave, Ajax's hand fell on his shoulder.

"It's not for me to say what happened back there on that island, or who is to blame, but it doesn't make sense to hold it against Paige. She's just looking out for Lucy."

Diego saw Lucy over Ajax's shoulder, struggling to balance the stack of dishes she was clearing and Paige rushing over to help her.

"I know you feel like she's always picking a fight," Ajax continued, "but you might try talking to her sometime."

Diego nodded. "Maybe tomorrow."

"Good. Now, take that to the captain before it gets cold."

Diego headed topside, moving slowly, as it was hard to balance the tray with his injured arm in a sling. He checked the bridge first. When the captain wasn't there, Diego made his way across the dark deck, a cool evening breeze on his face. Stars glittered in the sky. Distantly, some giant creature called across the water in a deep, haunting hum.

Diego knocked on the captain's door, but there was no answer. Maybe he was down in the engine room. He thought about leaving the plate outside the door but worried that seabirds or pteranodons might go after it. He tried the knob and found the door unlocked. As Diego stepped in, he considered that the captain would not approve of him entering.

Diego crossed the cabin as quietly as he could. The captain's quarters were large, the walls paneled in dark wood, and lined with photos. The pictures were all similar: groups of men and women standing outside the bridge, arms around one another. The captain's crews over the years, Diego guessed. So many different faces . . . only Ajax was the same. Diego wondered if the others had been lost to battles with the Aeternum over the years, and if it was possible to leave the captain's service any other way.

The room was lit only by an amber cone of light from the desk lamp. Diego moved a half-empty bottle of vodka and placed the tray by the captain's head. The captain snored lightly. *Drunk*, Diego guessed. He found the cap for the vodka bottle, replaced it, and put the bottle on a small table by the couch.

Diego turned to go, but something thumped to the floor. The captain coughed and shifted his head from one arm to the other. Diego spotted what had fallen: a small sculpture. He picked it up. It was a wood carving of a yellowfin tuna, like the one they'd pulled from the sea. This one was more comically drawn, with a big eye and a smile, like a toy. Diego found a name carved in the side: Natalia.

My Elana & Ahi December 14, 2213

Diego spied a picture frame lying on the desk. A photo of a beautiful young woman in a maroon dress, standing next to a much younger Boleslavich. He was trim, wearing a dark naval officer's uniform. There was no gray in his hair or mustache. The woman's pregnant belly pressed out against her dress. There was a handwritten inscription at the bottom:

My Elana & Ahi
December 14, 2213

The captain was an Elder. Elana was his wife, and Ahi . . . the sculpture. His *daughter, Natalia?*

Diego noticed now that the nearest desk drawer was open. Maybe that would be a good place to put this carving until the captain sobered up. He slid the drawer open a little more. There were more photos inside, a stack of unframed snapshots. Diego wondered if he could risk taking a closer look—

The captain's hand shot out and gripped his wrist like a steel trap.

"Ow!" Diego yelped. The grip was so tight that he dropped the carving, right into the mashed potatoes on the plate he'd brought up.

"Who gave you permission to come in here?" The captain peered at Diego with half-closed, bloodshot eyes.

"Nobody, we just— I thought you might be hungry, so I—"

"Leave at once!" he roared, lurching back in his chair.

"Yes, Captain." Diego stumbled and hurried out of the

room. As he closed the door, he heard crashing sounds from behind him.

Diego rushed down the deck. He never should have gone in there. Maybe Paige was right. Maybe he was reckless. The captain was going to maroon him for sure.

As he neared the galley door, a peal of laughter caught Diego's attention. He stopped and peered through a porthole.

The rest of the crew had gathered around the old boiler fireplace, even Daphne. Petey stood at the center of the group, doing an impression of a vicious creature, maybe a dinosaur. Everyone was cracking up, Ajax laughing in singular, cannon-like bursts that shook the porthole glass.

Diego watched them, feeling more alone than ever. *Go join them*, he thought. But other than by Petey, and maybe Daphne . . . he knew he wouldn't be welcome.

He slipped away from the porthole. He went back to their cabin, but he didn't want to stay there either. So he grabbed the old computer tablet from the desk, along with a small set of tools, and shoved them into his backpack. He lit a lantern and headed back out into the dark.

CHAPTER FOURTEEN

Diego and Lucy

"Hey, Redford." Diego studied the cool metal surface of the robot's face. Sometimes, especially in dark shadows like now, Redford's headlamps nearly looked like eyes and the steel bumpers like a mouth.

Diego had wired a simple camera system into the head-lamps, which in turn attached to a television display in the operator's chair, in the hope that one day his dad would be able to make electronic systems work again. If that ever happened, they could give Redford, and all the Ribera bots, basic artificial programming, but the problem had stumped every engineer the world over. For some reason, even the most innovative designs for electromagnetic shielding failed. Even

Santiago, with the Maker's Sight on his side, hadn't been able to figure it out.

"Maybe someday, pal."

A gust of wind whistled through Redford's joints. Diego noticed fleets of clouds galloping across the sky. He'd planned to camp out on the deck, but instead he climbed up into Redford's storage compartment. He held his lantern through the doorway and peered into the space. Maybe this would do fine for tonight.

Diego knew he couldn't get the computer tablet to work on a permanent basis, but perhaps he could get it repaired enough. If he could find an Elder modulating fuse somewhere on board, that might get it operating for a minute or two before the next electromagnetic spike. Maybe tomorrow, if he was lucky, he could power up its solar cells, and then he'd get a quick turn on an old video game or something before the circuitry shorted out. Santiago had achieved flashes of success with such devices back in his workshop, but it never lasted long.

Diego relaxed and let his hands tell him what to do. He tried not to think—about the dull ache in his shoulder, the sling on his arm, or the nagging worries about his friends, his home, or his father—and just get lost in the trails of wires and circuit boards, spinning drives, and screws.

Diego's eyes fluttered open to daylight filtering through the gap in the doorway. He'd fallen asleep at the table, his cheek resting on the tablet, which had etched red lines on his face.

He sat up, shivered, and realized that he was soaked. And nauseated. The barge pitched up and down violently. Rain hammered on the metal walls of the compartment, rivulets of water seeping down the insides.

Diego stowed the tablet and tools in his backpack, then started back toward the *John Curtis*. The sky and the sea were welded together in slate gray, the wind howling. Waves crashed over the front of the barge, sending sheets of water across the deck. The *John Curtis* pitched up over heavy swells, crashing down the other side in explosions of sea spray. He slipped on the deck, having to grip the piles of debris.

Diego was soaked to the bone in moments. He'd clambered halfway across the barge when he looked ahead and squinted in disbelief.

The rope bridge was gone.

The tethers connecting the ships seemed to be holding, but there was no way to cross the furious water between them.

Diego looked around for another solution. Just then a wave caught the barge and tossed it sideways. It slammed into the side of the *John Curtis*. Diego was thrown to the deck. Burning pain bloomed in his injured shoulder, and for a moment he nearly blacked out. The sling soaked up water, the strap catching for a moment on a rivet.

He rolled across the cold, wet metal, losing track of up and down. He reached wildly for anything to grab on to.

His hand grazed the frayed edge of a tarp flapping in the

wind. He reached for it as his legs flew free of the side of the barge. His fingers closed around the soaked fabric, and he dragged himself back onto the deck. He staggered to his feet, breathless.

A distant sound reached his ears over the waves and wind. Voices. Diego caught sight of two figures on the back deck of the *John Curtis*: Petey and Paige, huddling beneath ponchos, securing the cargo latches.

"Hey!" Diego called. "Guys, over here!"

But they turned and made their way back toward the door.

He inched as far across the deck as he dared, gripping the frayed tarp, fighting to stay upright as sheets of water ran over his feet. "HEY!"

Petey was stepping through the door. . . .

Paige turned. She tugged on Petey's poncho, and the two ran over to the edge of the deck.

Petey put his hands around his mouth. "What are you doing over there?" he shouted.

"I can't get back!" Diego replied, pointing to the empty space where the bridge had been.

"You have to jump!" Paige shouted over the roaring storm.

Diego watched as the barge and the *John Curtis* swayed closer and farther from each other. There were moments when it might be possible, when the barge rose up and the *John Curtis* ducked low, when he might be able to leap for the railing. His shoulder still throbbed. He'd have to grab the railing with one hand.

He waited until they crested a wave, and then he stepped away from the equipment, only to slip again, falling on his hip. He twisted to avoid hitting his shoulder, sliding farther. Had they not just crested a wave, he might have been swept overboard, but the barge tipped downward, and Diego was able to stumble back and grab the tarp again.

"Hold on!" Petey called. Diego saw him unclipping one of the fishermen's harnesses. He tied a rope to it, and then he and Paige hurled it toward him. Diego caught the wet leather straps, one of the metal buckles slapping him in the eye.

The barge lurched close to the ship for a moment. "Take my bag!" Diego called, and threw his backpack as hard as he could. It spiraled through the rain, and Paige grabbed it.

"Now come on!" Petey called.

Diego slipped on the harness and readied himself. He watched the gap between the barge and the ship, waiting . . .

Now!

He lunged and stretched as far as he could. His fingers brushed the hull, so close, but the boat lurched away from him, and he was falling. Paige reached for him, helpless. And then he was under the waves.

The world became a gray, frigid blur—salt stinging his eyes. Diego flailed for something to hold on to, but there was only water and foam tossing him around. He couldn't tell which way was up or down. His chest hurt, his breath wanting to escape. Cold everywhere.

But then the harness straps cinched tight, and Diego felt

himself being tugged. An icy moment later he burst out of the water. He dangled in the air and slammed against the side of the ship again. Through salt-stung eyes, he saw Petey and Paige straining to haul him up. Lucy had joined them.

"Faster!" Lucy shouted.

The rust-streaked side of the barge swayed toward them again, sure to crush him between the two hulls.

The harness pulled him higher. Diego rose a few more feet and pulled his legs up into a crouch as the two boats smacked together, their sides scraping.

There was the railing. He reached for it. . . .

Hands locked around his wrists, dragging him up. He got his elbows over the railing and gasped for breath as they dragged him onto the deck.

"There he is, our prize catch of the day!" Petey said, clapping him on the back. But the worry on Petey's face showed how close it had been.

Diego coughed up seawater. "Thanks."

"What on earth were you doing over there?" Lucy asked as they guided him into the common room.

"I wanted some quiet, to work on stuff," Diego said.

"When you weren't in the bunk room last night," Petey said, "we assumed you were down in the engine room again. Man, D, that was close."

"Too close," Paige echoed. "Again."

Diego glanced at Paige, anger flaring, but he remembered what Ajax had said. "Thanks for saving me."

They helped Diego to a spot by the boiler. He huddled close to it, feeling the heat seeping through his damp clothes.

"Mr. Ribera," the captain said, arriving from the deck. "What were you doing on the barge?"

"Repairing some equipment," Diego said, shivering. "I meant to come back last night, but I fell asleep while I worked."

The captain leered down at him, taking big, grumbling breaths.

His fist shot out to his side and punched the side of the boiler. The echo rang in their ears. "You have disobeyed me too often," he snarled, rubbing his fist with the other hand. There was blood on his knuckles. "I should throw you overboard NOW and be done with it!" He turned toward Diego.

"Captain, no!" Petey shouted.

Diego fell back on his elbows, the captain looming over him.

Ajax's metal arm shot between them, smoke puffing from its piston, holding the captain back. "That's enough, Captain," Ajax said. "You're right, but remember, we still need a crew."

The captain stood up and straightened his coat, his eyes never leaving Diego.

"How much longer will this storm last?" Petey asked.

"It's a flash squall," Gaston said, entering behind the captain. "Very strong, but usually less than a day." He walked over and ruffled Diego's hair. "You are lucky you weren't swept away, *petit frère*."

Diego shook free of his hand but was too tired to comment.

"Lucy," the captain said, "I need you back on the bridge. Gaston, to the engine room with Ajax. Petey, Paige, get Ribera sorted out, then take him to the lower compartments."

He pointed at Diego. "You monitor the hull for flooding, and you stay there until the storm is through. I don't want to see you again until the sky is blue."

Diego huddled as close to the fire as he could get. The shivering was finally subsiding, and he could feel his fingers and toes again.

"Man, D . . . ," Petey said, taking Diego's soaked blanket away and giving him a dry one.

"How could I have known there was going to be a storm?" Diego said.

"Yeah, but still," Petey said. "Not even a day goes by when you're not in danger."

Paige returned from the kitchen and handed Diego a mug of hot tea. She didn't say anything, but Diego could feel her exchanging a look with Petey.

"I know what you're all thinking," Diego said, "but you don't know the whole story."

"And what story is that?" Petey asked.

Diego lowered his voice and told them about his run-in with the captain the night before.

"Wow, Balsamic had a family, huh?" Petey said. "But why didn't you come tell us last night?"

"I just . . . I needed to be alone is all."

"So, what were you working on out there?"

"Just this." Diego pulled the tablet from his bag.

"Why would you waste your time with that?" Paige wondered.

"Paige," Petey warned.

"Back off, Kowalski," Paige said. "Everybody knows those stupid things don't work. Or are you saying that mumbo jumbo of yours fixed it?"

Diego considered telling them about the weirdness when he'd found the tablet, the vision of the octopus-shaped piece, the *transporting*, but he didn't want to risk another fight with Paige.

"It's been on my mind," Diego said. He held out the tablet for them to see. Paige took it and flipped it around.

"Wow, that's actually in pretty great shape," Petey said.

"It might even work for a minute, before a magnetic-field spike fries it. The battery's dead, so I'm going to put it out in the sun later and see if it charges up."

Paige ran her finger over the glass and tapped the power button.

Suddenly, the screen flashed to life, and words appeared:

Hello, Diego, my name is _____

"Whoa, what did you do?" Diego asked, jumping to his feet.

"Nothing! You said it didn't have any power."

"How does it know your name?" Petey asked.

"I don't know," Diego said.

The screen went dark again.

"Um," Diego said. "That shouldn't have happened. It . . . it doesn't even have all the parts it needs." He pressed the power button again. Nothing.

"Did you do that . . . thing you talked about to fix it?" Petey asked.

"Yeah."

"Has anything weird ever happened before when you did?"

Diego wondered again if he could explain it to them, but he wanted to learn more on his own first. "No," he said, and then tried to change the subject. "Maybe it has some kind of voice recognition feature or something."

"But you said it doesn't have any power," Paige said.

Diego shook his head. "I know." He slipped the tablet into his backpack. "We should probably get to our jobs." He jumped up and down a few times to try to get the blood flowing. "Hey, thanks again for saving me."

"Sure thing, D," Petey said.

"Yeah," Paige said. "I never leave a friend behind."

"So . . . that means we're friends?"

Paige allowed a half smile. "Sorta."

The storm lasted through the day and night, finally subsiding before dawn. Diego woke to find the ocean as smooth as glass. The clouds had thinned to damp puffs, like chains of cotton balls, the sun sneaking through in pale rays.

"We should reach Volcambria by late in the day," the captain informed them at breakfast.

"Where exactly is Volcambria?" Diego asked Petey, who was consulting a half-folded navigation chart while he ate his oatmeal.

Petey spun the map around and pointed. "It's part of an island chain called the Islands of the Great Eastern Wall that used to be the east coast of the United States. The islands that lie along the major shipping routes have been charted and mapped, but Volcambria is up *here*, in the uncharted region."

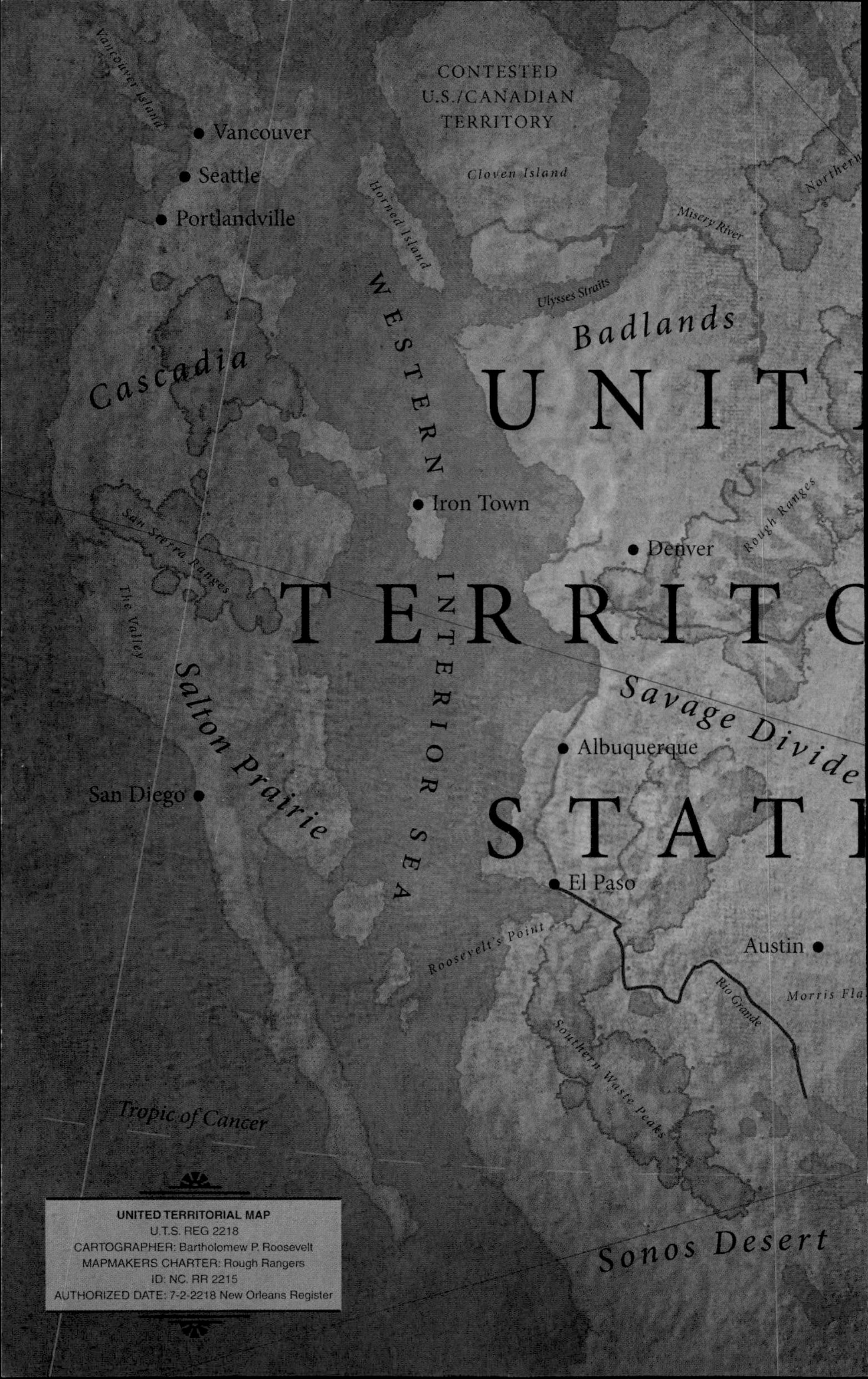

Vancouver Island

CONTESTED
U.S./CANADIAN
TERRITORY

Cloven Island

● Vancouver

Northern

● Seattle

Misery River

● Portlandville

Horned Island

W
E
S
T
E
R
N

Ulysses Straits

Badlands

Cascadia

UNIT

San Sierra Ranges

Iron Town

Rough Ranges

● Denver

The Valley

TERRITO

I
N
T
E
R
I
O
R

Savage Divide

Salton Prairie

● Albuquerque

San Diego ●

S
E
A

STATI

● El Paso

Roosevelt's Point

Austin ●

Rio Grande

Southern Waste Peaks

Mortis Fla

Tropic of Cancer

Sonos Desert

UNITED TERRITORIAL MAP
U.T.S. REG 2218
CARTOGRAPHER: Bartholomew P. Roosevelt
MAPMAKERS CHARTER: Rough Rangers
ID: NC. RR 2215
AUTHORIZED DATE: 7-2-2218 New Orleans Register

CONTESTED
U.S./CANADIAN
TERRITORY

Canadian Province

hunder Coast

Québec •

Montreal •

Superior Bay

Georgian Bay

nneapolis

Isle of Mastodon

Yorktown (New York) •

NORTH
VASTLANTIC
OCEAN

• New Chicago

Mississippi River

RIAL

Quiet Island

River

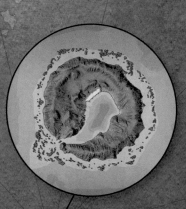

• New Orleans

ISLANDS OF THE GREAT EASTERN WALL

◎ **VOLCAMBRIA**

CUBAHNA

GULF OF
MEXICO

Cayman Sea

After breakfast, the captain assigned Diego to sit on the prow of the ship and depth sound, like the old mariners did in the days before sonar and radar. Diego lowered a weighted rope every few minutes, read the depth by how many feet of the marked rope were wet, and reported the reading back to Gaston, who was piloting. Petey was inside charting their course. Lucy sat high above in the crow's nest. She'd been trained to watch for changes in the ocean's color as an indicator of depth and also for breaking waves, which might signal reefs or rocks. The storm had blown them off course, so they were traversing a shallow stretch of sunken islands that the captain had always taken care to avoid in the past.

"It's over ten fathoms," Diego called.

"Aye," Gaston said. "I think we're through it. What do you say, Lucy?"

"Clear and deep," she reported.

"You're welcome to return to the engine room, *petit frère*," Gaston said. "I'm sure you miss the grease and diesel, and it no doubt misses you."

"Sounds better than listening to you," Diego grumbled, but not loud enough that Gaston could hear. He coiled the rope and gathered up the tablet, which had been charging in the sun beside him.

"What you got there, Ribera?" Lucy called down to him.

"Just this," he said, holding up the tablet. The sun flashed in his eyes and he blinked hard looking up at her. He couldn't be sure, but it looked like Lucy was wearing a pirate's hat.

"Paige told me about that. Can I see?"

"Sure." Diego returned the rope to its compartment, slung his backpack over both shoulders, and then made his way to the top of the bridge and climbed the rigging up to the crow's nest.

Lucy opened the floor hatch for him. "Whoa," he said as he stood, taking in the view.

"This is epic," Diego said.

"It hasn't gotten old, even as my behind's gone numb sitting up here."

Diego smiled and handed her the tablet. He studied the black leather tricorn hat that shielded her face from the sun.

"I like your new hat. You look like a real pirate."

"Gaston gave it to me, said it belonged to an actual buccaneer who sailed with the captain."

"Ah, I see. Well, it suits you nicely."

Lucy smiled. "Of course, it does get hot after a while," she said, taking it off. She turned the tablet over in her hands. "I've never seen a computer up close before. I'm forbidden from interacting with any technology from Elder or Mid Time. It doesn't seem so dangerous to me. Paige told me this did something strange—"

The screen flashed to life again.

Hello. Is this Petey or Daphne or Paige or
Captain or Lucy or Ajax or the French Toad?

"It's like it knows everyone on the ship," Lucy said. "Does French Toad mean Gaston?"

"Maybe."

"You programmed it to say that, didn't you?"

"It was the least I could do, since he always calls me *petit frère*."

"That just means 'small brother,'" Lucy said. "It's not

nearly as bad as French Toad."

"Maybe I'll change it," Diego said. "I programmed it to respond to the crew, but it doesn't know who's holding it."

"It seems to know that it's *not* you, though."

"It might be using this." Diego pointed to the small camera lens above its screen. "Or it might be able to sense variations in touch." He picked up her hand gently by her fingers and held his palm next to hers. "See? Pretty different. Color, size, lines." Diego hadn't realized how filthy his hands were, but also there was something electric about having their hands touching, just side by side.

But Lucy was already pulling hers away and flipping her hands over. "If my mother could see this," she said, examining her chipped fingernails. "A pirate's hands are *not* ladylike."

"You look tough," Diego said. "Seaworthy."

Lucy eyed him. "That makes me sound like a hag."

"That's not . . . I didn't—"

She play-punched his shoulder. "Relax, Ribera. I'm not *always* giving you a go."

A silence passed between them.

"So tell me," Lucy said, "why is this thing working? Based on everything I've ever heard my dad or Georgie say, it shouldn't be."

Diego shrugged. "I put a revolving pulse disruptor fuse in it. I was thinking that would allow it to run for short intervals, like my dad's old Sony Walkman, and then shut down if there's a magnetic-field spike."

Lucy raised an eyebrow at him. "I'm afraid I don't speak—what did Paige call it . . . geek. Especially not the Mid-Time brand."

"Ah."

"You got that was humor, right?"

"I did," Diego said, smiling.

"Good. You know," Lucy said, "back in London I go to an all-girls Traditionalist school. So, talking to Mid-Time geeks is never an option. Talking with boys of any kind is more or less frowned upon, let alone a Mid-Time boy. That would be scandalous."

"Like me?"

"Especially you."

"What's a Traditionalist?"

"You might call it an elite class of British Steam Timers. We're not like your True Believers. We don't stringently reject and wish to separate from the other time classes, but we do value a strict adherence to our time culture."

"It sounds hard, living like that, keeping all the other times out."

Lucy shrugged. "Actually, it's terribly easy, as long as you aren't prone to curiosity, or a conscience. I suffer from both, though I'd never let Mum and Dad know that. They think it's not only a privilege, but a destiny. Or something. Father goes on and on."

"Yeah, I can imagine that. It's a wonder your parents let

you go to our museum school, where you'd certainly mix with other time cultures and races."

"Well, it's only recently that my parents released me and my older brother Archie from homeschooling. Father said that a popular city official criticized him as an elitist and separatist. Having his children attend New Chicago's public school would go a long way to bolstering the Emerson reputation. 'And *everyone knows Emersons are pillars of high society*,'" she said in an exaggerated snobby voice.

Lucy typed into the tablet.

My name is Lucy Abigail Emerson.

The tablet typed back:

Are you a different Lucy? I know Lucy "Dino-slayer" Emerson.

Lucy eyed him. "You're clever."

"It's your gravity board name," Diego said. "I can change it if you want."

"You can leave it. Though I'd feel terrible if I'd actually killed that young dinosaur."

"I'm sure she will be fine."

Suddenly, the tablet blacked out.

"What happened?" Lucy asked.

"It still needs one more piece to make it stable," Diego said. "The Sight showed me what it is, but what I saw seems impossible."

"What do you mean, the Sight *showed* you?"

Diego flipped the tablet in his hands. "What I told you all in the engine room . . . there's more to it than that." Diego paused. He looked at Lucy and found her gazing right at him. He wasn't sure if he should tell her, but when he looked into Lucy's eyes, he knew he wanted to trust her. "It's more than seeing an image in my head," he continued. "It's an ability, a power . . . my father called it the Maker's Sight. It lets me see how to fix machines. I see it like a series of images, almost like flashes of camera snapshots. And then I know how it should go."

"My father would call that witchcraft," Lucy said.

"Would you?" Diego asked.

Lucy shrugged. "I'd say any power that could help us to save our families is a blessing. Perhaps there's more to you than the reckless fool that Paige thinks you are." She smiled.

"At least we know now that I can school you on a gravity board."

"In your dreams, Ribera."

They laughed together for a second, and then Diego couldn't think of a single thing to say. Instead, he turned and gazed out at the water.

"You know your mother is a hero of mine," Lucy said.

"You mentioned that."

"Many Traditionalist girls long for more than our society

maps out for us. Your mother broke free of our stuffy rule book."

"She had to make my grandparents pretty angry to do it," Diego said.

"How remarkable it would be to have that chance," Lucy said. "You know, London has Mid-Time and Elder sections, too. Sometimes Georgie and I would sneak off to the Mid-Time airfield to watch the planes. If Mother ever found out about that . . ."

"They're amazing, aren't they?" Diego said. "Airplanes? The way they own the sky."

"Well, riding the gravity board was like the best of both worlds, skating and flying. It was a dream come true—until those allosauruses."

"You'd love flying in a plane."

Lucy laughed to herself, and then turned to look at Diego. "Can I ask you something?"

"Um, sure."

"Back in school, that degenerate hooligan. He called you something, a name I've heard some Traditionalists whisper back home: clock mongrel. What does it mean?"

"It's something no decent person would ever say. But it's the kind of thing you hear True Believers say all the time." Diego folded his arms. "It means a filthy, half-breed dog of two different times. Before predator fighting was made illegal, they used to breed prehistoric dogs with modern ones to create a nasty new breed to bet on in the dinosaurs' fighting pits. Clock mongrel was the name pit bosses gave those pitiful creatures."

"That's despicable," Lucy said. "I'm sorry."

"Don't be. I know you don't believe that."

Lucy shook her head. "Of course not, or I wouldn't be friends with someone like Paige or a . . . Spanish boy?"

"Me?" Diego said. "No, I'm Filipino, well, half anyway."

"But isn't Ribera a Spanish name?" Lucy asked. "Wait, the Philippines were ruled by Spain for a while, weren't they?"

"Yeah. My dad speaks English, Tagalog—that's the native language—and Spanish. But my mom's Irish, so I'm mixed, like this world."

"Oh," Lucy said.

"*Mestizo* is the word for someone who's half Spanish and half native Filipino. When I was a baby, my dad called me his little *halo-halo*. That's the Tagalog name of a Filipino dessert of mixed ingredients."

"You'd be quite the novelty in my neighborhood back home." Lucy elbowed him, and as she did, a little pendant slipped out of the collar of her shirt.

"What is that?" Diego asked, pointing to it.

"Oh, this." Lucy held it up on the tip of her thumb. "I found this little knickknack the other day on the barge. It was pretty, so I made a pendant out of it."

Diego gaped at it. "Can I have it for a second?"

Lucy unclasped the necklace and handed it to Diego. "What is it?" she asked.

"This . . ." Diego couldn't believe it. He held the object in his palm and ran his finger over it. It was a small piece of electronics in the shape of an octopus. "This is it! I saw this exact thing, in a vision."

"A vision?" Lucy said. "Like your Sight?"

"I'm not sure," Diego said. Seeing the object made the hairs prickle on the back of his neck. "Just a sec."

He closed his eyes and focused, trying the Sight, but all he saw in his mind was the object itself. The charm didn't look like any technology he'd ever seen. Its metal felt strange, almost like skin. He tried again. A tiny spark of brilliant blue energy crackled beneath the surface of the object and surged into Diego's fingertips. The jolt made his arm tremble.

This time, a single image formed in his mind. Diego opened his eyes. "No way," he said. "That's impossible."

"What?" Lucy asked.

"It—this piece . . . it calls itself a Kavohn processor." Diego flipped over the tablet and popped off the back.

"It—what do you mean, 'it calls itself'? You know what it does?" Lucy asked.

Diego got his battery-powered soldering kit from his backpack. He carefully attached the octopus-shaped processor to the circuitry inside the tablet, then powered it up.

The tablet delivered an audio message: *"Foreign processor accepted. Molecular stabilizer configuring. Proto-field engaged in five seconds."*

"Your pendant—this Kavohn thing—was the missing key to the tablet," Diego said.

"How is that possible?" Lucy said.

Diego had no idea. He didn't know where it had come from or even what it was, but the Sight had somehow awoken it, and it showed him the possibility of something. He rubbed his fingers where the tendril of blue energy had touched his skin. It still tingled. He watched a numerical countdown on the screen, dropping from five to zero.

Then the screen went black, and blue energy lines pulsed across it. The tablet spoke, the energy lines dancing as sound waves.

"*Hello, Diego. Hello, Lucy. It is nice to meet you. My name is . . . default settings vocal interface.*" It paused. "*But Diego may give me a name . . .*"

"I can't believe it," Diego said. And then he wondered. He looked at Redford. Could it possibly work?

Then his eye caught something in the distance, far beyond Redford. Something streaking below the clouds, glinting in the morning sun.

"Oh no," Diego said.

MARC GABBANA © 2016

CHAPTER FIFTEEN

Monsters of Sea and Air

For a second after Lucy sounded the alarm, they stood frozen, watching the plane streak toward them, the whine of its engine increasing like a buzzing bee.

"I don't suppose it's friendly," Lucy said.

"Nope." Diego had already recognized the plane: a Japanese World War II torpedo plane, the same as he'd seen in his history books. A single torpedo hung beneath its fuselage. As it closed in, he could see its Aeternum colors.

But that isn't possible . . . is it?

"Let's move!" Lucy said.

Below, they heard shouts. Ajax and Paige made their way to the forward guns.

The air sizzled, and bullets sprayed from the plane.

"Get down!" Lucy grabbed Diego, and they both dropped to the floor as bullets strafed the crow's nest and the bridge below, digging into wood and clanging off metal.

"Go!" Diego shouted. They yanked open the hatch and scrambled down the rigging. "Get to the bridge!"

Gunfire roared from the front of the ship. Diego saw Ajax swiveling the forward gun, while Paige fed a heavy belt of bullets into it. The plane arced and wove while completing its turn and lined up to attack again.

Diego and Lucy jumped to the deck and dived through the door into the bridge as the next rain of bullets pelted the hull. The firing sound retreated down the side of the ship.

The captain jumped up and craned to see out the side window. "He's targeting the steam engine."

"Should we man the rear guns?" Lucy asked.

"Gaston is already there," the captain said.

They heard the rear gun roar to life. The ship rattled from both ends to the pulsing of gunfire.

"Put us into evasive maneuvers!" the captain ordered Lucy.

"Yes, sir." Lucy bit her lip and raced to the wheel.

The captain stepped to the control banks at the back of the bridge and began throwing levers. "I'm shutting down the steam engine and redirecting power to the diesel. Diego! I need you to do a purge of the boiler. It's armor plated, but if there's a rupture at full pressure, it could blow the ship."

"Got it!" Diego shouted, lunging for the lever.

MARC GABBANA

M. Betts © 2016

The plane screamed around. The front gun kept pounding, but the back gun ceased.

"Diego, help Gaston reload!"

"On my way." He met Lucy's eye, hoping she could hear his thought: *Good luck.*

Diego sprinted down the deck, his body taut like coiled wire, wondering when the next round of bullets would come. He heard the buzzing of the plane but couldn't pause to find it in the sky.

He heard barking and found Daphne at his heels. "Go, girl! Get out of here!"

Daphne yipped and stayed with him, looking thrilled by their game.

The plane's engines grew louder. Diego glanced over his shoulder and spotted the plane heading directly toward him over the water. Its guns blazed, bullets strafing the waves. He dived behind Gaston and the protective plating of the gun as the bullets riddled the steam engine.

"I could have used you two minutes ago!" Gaston said, jumping back to the gun sights. "Feed that ammo!" He opened fire, the gun roaring and bucking. Diego grabbed the magazine and loaded it into the cannon's side feeder. He wheeled, bullets chasing the plane. There was a shriek of metal as Gaston tore a large hole through one of its wings. The plane dipped, righted, but then flew on with a shimmy in its gait.

"Nice shot!" Diego said.

A grinding of metal from below. Diego peered over the

side, down the back of the ship. The paddle wheel slowed to a stop, rising from the water as it did and then folding flat against itself like an accordion.

"Are we switching to the propeller?" Diego shouted over the roar of the plane and gunfire.

"*Oui!*" Gaston said, lining up the gun for another shot. "Need the speed and maneuverability."

"But won't that attract mosasaurs or something worse?" Diego wondered, gazing into the deep blue around them.

"Last time I checked, mosasaurs don't shoot bullets, *petit frère!*"

"Stop calling me that!" Diego shouted.

Gaston grinned. "Give me a reason." He pumped another round of lead into the air but then stopped firing and slapped the gun. "Out of range. Why's that plane flying away—is he breaking off the attack?"

Diego squinted into the distance. The plane seemed to be spiraling downward.

"Maybe your shot to the wing was enough."

The plane straightened out, heading straight at them. The torpedo dropped from beneath its belly and slid into the water.

"Wishful thinking," Gaston said.

Diego watched the trail of white bubbles rocketing toward them.

"We need the anti-torpedo mines," Gaston said. He stepped from the gun.

Diego grabbed his arm. "You stay and fire! Where are the mines?"

"*Merde*, Diego! Do you not remember your training?" Gaston frowned. "Those armored compartments!" He pointed across the aft deck.

Diego sprinted toward them, only to have Ajax arrive at the lockers ahead of him. He was covered in sweat, a long smear of blood on his shoulder.

"Were you hit?" Diego asked.

"Seems that way," Ajax said. He flipped the latches and yanked open the locker, revealing three giant steel barrels painted bright yellow. "I'll get these two," he said, squatting and lifting a barrel over each shoulder, then standing with a heavy grunt. He nodded at the third one. "You," he said, and raced back up the deck.

Diego lugged the giant barrel out of the locker and kicked the door shut. He tried to lift it, as Ajax had done, but could barely budge it off the ground. Instead, he tipped it on its side and rolled it up the deck, joining Ajax by the catapult-style mine launcher.

"How's it going, Paige?" Ajax called toward the bow.

Diego saw Paige crouched behind the gun, arms flexed, spraying bullets. "I could get used to this!" she shouted.

"I'll load these two," Ajax explained to Diego. "You load that one, and when I tell you, pull the arming pin!" There were six catapults built into either side of the deck.

"I thought two mines were enough to stop a torpedo?"

Diego asked, lugging the barrel into place.

"That's a big torpedo," Ajax said, lifting a barrel overhead.

Diego struggled to get the mine into place while watching the trail of bubbles grow.

He heard Ajax counting to himself. "Thirteen . . . twelve . . . eleven . . . Diego, pull the arming pin!"

Paige stopped firing. "Guys!" she shouted. "He brought a friend!"

Diego whirled and saw a second plane drop out of the clouds. Diego knew the style: a Japanese Zero fighter. It joined with the other, and both opened fire.

"FIRE!" shouted Ajax.

Diego pulled the arming pin and jumped back. Ajax released the launchers, and the two torpedo mines hurtled into the water, converging on the streaking torpedo . . .

BLAM!

Water exploded upward.

"Yes!" Diego shouted.

"By blood to bones . . . I'll see you in hell!" Ajax shouted.

With its one torpedo spent, the plane banked hard and came back around, putting them right in its crosshairs. Ajax stood in plain view, unflinching.

"What are you doing? Take cover!" Diego shouted.

Ajax chuckled, the booming notes echoing off the deck. "There's more than one way to catch a fox, boy. Sometimes you need to draw him to the henhouse. Ready, Paige?"

"Hell yeah!"

D. Yatomi

Donald Yatomi © 2015

"Why does she get to have all the fun?" Gaston shouted. He unloaded a heavy stream at the second plane but stopped when it turned in retreat and banked up into the clouds.

"Yeah!" Paige said, dancing across the deck.

"Paige!" The captain stepped out of the bridge.

"Yes, sir!" Paige froze, her smile fading.

The captain stared her down. "Well done."

"Thank you, sir."

A small explosion tore through the rear deck near the back piston arm. An alarm blared.

"Paige! Gaston!" the captain called. "Stay at your posts! Ajax, Diego, Lucy, and Petey, put out that fire!"

"Where are these planes coming from?" Lucy called as they raced to the hoses.

"Aeternum scavenger ships sometimes raid the Caribbean settlements," Ajax said. "These look to me like long-range scouts."

They dragged out the hoses, and Ajax hit the valves. Diego braced himself as water pumped onto the flames.

"Here he comes!" Paige pointed, and they saw the Zero drop out of the clouds and mark them before disappearing again.

"Captain, that sneaky bastard is up to something!" Gaston said. "He must be—"

Bullets tore into the armor plating of the bridge, seemingly coming out of nowhere.

"Take cover!" the captain shouted.

Diego dropped his hose and sprinted for the rear deck, his friends beside him. He ducked and turned to see the plane streaking past, but its engine sounded strange, more like a muffled whirring.

"That plane has switched to an induction engine!" Gaston said through the voice pipe.

It was by them in an instant—Gaston's fury of bullets barely missing it—and then back up in the clouds.

"What are induction engines?" Petey asked.

"Somehow, that plane has been modified to switch to a twenty-second-century compression engine," Ajax said. "It makes it virtually silent, and much faster, but it goes through its fuel faster."

"What does that mean for us?" Lucy asked.

"It means he'd like us dead as soon as possible!"

The deck shook as the captain fired up the locomotive engine, disengaging the diesel propellers and switching back to the paddle wheel. The water churned behind the boat as the wheel spun to life, only to slam to a grinding halt, sending a wicked shudder through the ship that rattled every joint.

"What happened?" Diego asked, scrambling to the railing alongside Ajax.

Ajax peered over the side, then rushed to the aft deck voice pipe. "Sir!" Ajax called. "One of the backup fuel tanks exploded, taking out the starboard-side drive crank. The paddle wheel is dead."

The captain cursed in Russian on the other end of the

voice pipe. The ship shook again as he reengaged the propellers. "Lucy!" the captain called. "Get back to the bridge! Petey, assist Paige! Ajax, back to the guns! Diego, to the crow's nest to spot for that plane."

Ajax stopped Diego and secured a pistol in his belt. Diego thanked him and climbed atop the bridge. He hauled himself up the rigging, back into the bullet-riddled crow's nest. The boat sped through the calm seas, the propellers creating a wide wake behind them. Far in the distance, Diego saw a spine of islands, no more than silhouettes. The Great Eastern Wall, he guessed.

Where was that plane?

"Anything?" Ajax called to Diego.

"Not yet!" Diego called. He squinted but saw nothing in the clouds. . . .

"Hey, *petit frère!*" Gaston called.

"What?" Diego said.

"Make sure you hang on tight up there! A strong gust of wind could—" But Gaston didn't finish.

They all heard it at the same time. That strange engine sound in the sky.

Diego whirled, looking in all directions.

"There!" Paige shouted, pointing straight up.

Diego craned his neck, and there was the plane, diving hard right at them. Its guns blazed. Gaston barely got off a shot before he had to dive away, bullets riddling his position.

The plane banked hard and circled around the ship. Paige

unloaded, but the plane was too fast. It came so close to the crow's nest that Diego could see the pilot, light reflecting off his goggles. Diego scrambled for the pistol that Ajax had given him, but by the time he had it out of his belt, the fighter was already past and attacking the back deck again, this time causing Ajax to leap away.

"Are they okay?" Lucy called up over the voice pipe.

Diego squinted through the smoke and saw Ajax and Gaston ducking behind stacks of cargo. "Yeah, everyone's fine, but our back cannons are gone!"

"Diego, get down below and help Ajax and Gaston!" the captain shouted through the voice pipe.

"Got it!" Diego threw open the hatch and started down the rigging. He had only gone a few lengths when he turned and saw the plane banking, coming at them head-on.

"Come on!" Paige shouted, firing.

The plane fired back. A blur of bullets. Paige clipped its wing, but only until her gun sparked and smoked . . . and exploded, sending Petey and Paige careening backward into the wall.

"Guys!" Diego shouted. He leaped from the rigging, collapsing into a roll on top of the bridge, and then scrambled down two decks through the smoke to his fallen friends.

"I'm okay," Paige said, coughing and getting to her feet. "I tagged that sucka, but he'll be coming for us."

"Petey . . ." Diego knelt beside him and slapped his friend's face gently.

Petey coughed and doubled over, at the same time holding up a hand to fend off Diego. "I'm good."

Daphne scuttled over and licked Petey's face.

"*Dieu merci!*" Gaston and Ajax sprinted over to them. "They live!" He threw his arms around Paige and kissed the top of her head.

"What is *with* you?" Paige shouted, pushing him away.

"Nothing, I—" Gaston swept off his hat and kicked at the deck. "I thought you were lost, *belle.*"

"Paige!" Lucy ran out and hugged her friend.

"Status of the cannons?" the captain called from the wheel.

Ajax looked to the front gun. "We've lost all three, sir. Gaston and I can—"

Engines again. Coming in fast.

"Our friend is back!" Paige shouted.

Diego spied the Zero coming from the other side. Its guns blazed, strafing the hull.

"Watch out, Captain!" Lucy shouted.

The Zero arced overhead, and the captain popped up again.

"Ajax, Gaston, break out the small arms from the armory!"

"I can help!" Paige shouted.

"You've done enough; get inside!" Gaston shouted.

"I'm not taking orders from you!"

"Come with me," Ajax said. "We'll get rifles from the weapons locker."

"Paige, be careful," Gaston said.

"You don't need to worry about me, I—"

An explosion rocked the side of the ship. Everyone ducked for cover.

The Zero swooped by overhead.

"That little bugger is going to be the end of us!" Petey shouted.

"Ajax, arm everyone and take positions for cover!" the captain shouted. "Aim for the fuel supply . . . or the cockpit."

Gaston nodded tersely. "Yes, sir."

"Sir," Ajax said. They turned and headed for the armory.

"What else can we do?" Lucy asked the captain.

"Get inside and get down, until they return with the guns," the captain said. "A prayer to your god of choice might also be helpful."

"I don't think rifles will pack enough punch to stop that plane," Lucy said.

That's what they needed, Diego thought. Stronger weapons. *Maybe a weapon that had a stronger punch.*

Diego pulled off his backpack and whipped out the computer tablet. He touched his hand to the screen, and the tablet turned on. He concentrated, but at first nothing came . . . then there was a flicker. He focused his thoughts on the octopus-shaped device inside the tablet. *Show me what you're capable of.*

"What are you doing?" Lucy asked.

"I'm not even sure, just . . ." He turned back to the tablet.

"Kavohn processor, are you programmed for self-preservation?"

"Yes," the computer voice answered, "but accessing those protocols requires you to initiate my full systems, and as I stated before, Diego, only you can initiate this processor's operations."

"How do I do that?"

"You must give me a name," the computer said.

"Your name is Redford."

"Redford," the computer paused. "Please stand by."

Diego placed his hand on the pad.

"Recognizing . . . welcome, Diego Logan Ribera," the computer said. "Administrator access granted."

"Unlock AI functionality. I initialize you as Redford Ribera."

"Authorization accepted. Please stand by. Full systems activation will be complete in five minutes." The screen began to flash.

"What are you doing?" Petey asked as Diego stowed the tablet back in his bag.

"I might have found a way out of this mess. Petey, come with me." He turned to the captain. "Sir, I need to go and—"

"Go, then, Ribera!" the captain shouted. "Apparently you follow orders when it pleases you."

The Zero came around for another pass.

"Whatever we're doing, let's hurry up and do it!" Petey said.

Diego and Petey sprinted across the deck, heads down, as explosions rocked their eardrums and bullets singed the air, clipping the bridge and bow.

Gaston and Ajax reemerged and fired back.

"Are we heading to the barge?" Petey called as they ran, bullets stinging the deck around them. "Because there's still no bridge!"

"I know!" Diego said. He grabbed the railing and threw his legs over, standing on the outer edge, the sea pounding below.

"Oh man oh man oh man," Petey said, climbing out to join him.

The ship rocked and reeled. Diego gripped the railing. "When the barge gets close . . . ," he said, measuring the gap of water.

The whirring of the plane got louder in their ears.

"We're easy targets here!" Petey said.

"Get ready." The barge rose up, drifting closer. "Now, Petey!" Diego jumped. Falling through space, circling his arms. The barge bucked, seemed like it might ebb away from them again—

But they landed hard on its deck, pitching onto their knees. Diego hit his sore shoulder against the side of a metal container, and it lit up in pain. He forced himself to his feet, sprinting for Redford.

"Undo the restraints!" Diego shouted to Petey. "Then fire up the boilers and get in the operator's seat."

"What are *you* gonna do?" Petey said.

"What I'm meant to do," Diego said. "I think."

"Okay . . . ," Petey said.

The boys clambered up onto Redford's shoulders, where Petey took the cockpit and started throwing ignition switches and twisting pressure dials. Diego dropped to his knees and ducked beneath the control panel behind Redford's head. He searched among the different-colored wires, selecting two and connecting them to the back of tablet.

Redford shuddered as his boiler chugged to life. The tablet was still booting up.

Redford lurched forward, getting up onto his knees.

"Petey!" Diego called, barely slapping the interface panel closed.

"I thought I'd get him ready!" Petey called.

"No, that's good! Just . . ." Diego glanced to the sky.

Redford bucked, and, all at once, the engine and the tablet sputtered and shut down.

"What happened?" Petey called down.

"I don't know!" Diego said. It was as if the circuits had surged and fried, like all the complex electrical systems did in this world. "That fuse I installed should have allowed it to work for a little longer!" The special piece from Lucy . . . the Sight had showed him.

"Well, it worked for one thing!" Petey pointed to the sky.

The Zero was heading their way. Its guns opened fire on Redford.

Diego and Petey ducked as bullets and chunks of metal rained around them. The bullets tore at Redford's arms, legs, and chest plating, but he was so massive that the damage was minimal.

The plane shot overhead, Gaston and Ajax chasing it with bullets to no avail.

There was a clanking, and Redford's engines coughed back to life. His headlamps lit up.

"There we go!" Diego shouted. "Petey. Get out!"

Petey and Diego leaped down onto heaps of scrap metal, but as Petey rolled to the deck and took cover, Diego slid down the front side of the pile and ran to where he could address Redford directly. And also be seen by the Zero.

It banked, coming straight at them. . . .

"Redford!" he shouted. "Protect yourself and your friends!"

The robot's lights flared, and he groaned to his feet.

MARC GABBANA © 2016

Petey scrambled up the heap to Diego's side. "You did it, D! You . . ." A shadow fell over them.

Redford spun and his head lowered, like he was looking down at the two boys.

Diego felt a tinge of fear as the giant machine loomed over them.

"Does he . . . know us? Know we're friends?"

Diego nodded. "I think he does."

He waved at Redford and gave him a thumbs-up. "Good job, buddy!"

Redford stared down at them . . . then blasted a puff of thick white steam in reply.

CHAPTER SIXTEEN

Volcambria

"This is unreal," Paige said.

"That is what we thought when we discovered this place," the captain said. "The island is the tip of a dormant volcano. It is surrounded by coral reefs, and in turn by this unnatural wall of wrecked ships, planes, vehicles, and machines reaped from across time."

"But why is all this here?" Lucy wondered.

"One of the many unsolved mysteries of this strange island. It has been our home for many years, but we've only scratched the surface of its many secrets. That graveyard of ships and machines, as best we can tell, is some . . . strange consequence of the Time Collision."

MARC GABBANA
A. SERRANO
© 2017

"He is a wonder," the captain said, looking at Redford, joining Diego and his friends at the bow of the ship.

"Yeah," Diego agreed.

"You must tell me how you accomplished it."

"I, um . . . was fiddling around with that tablet, you know, to keep my mind off my dad." Diego talked carefully, avoiding mention of the Maker's Sight. "Then I realized that Lucy's charm might be Elder technology. I had a hunch it was an advanced harmonic magnetic stabilizer. And I was right."

"That is impressive," the captain said with a sigh. "I am an Elder. That trinket Lucy wore looked like no piece of technology that I've seen. The smallest harmonic stabilizers I ever saw were the size of watermelons and could never have protected a computer, even an antique like your tablet."

"Weird," Diego said. The captain had confirmed what Diego sensed down deep—if that charm wasn't Elder tech, it was something else. But what? And who built it?

"It only makes your creation all the more astonishing," the captain said. "That is why when we get to the base, I want you to remove the tablet."

"What?" Diego said. "No way."

"We do not know what that technology is," the captain said. "It could be dangerous in ways we don't even realize."

Diego shook his head. "It would be like killing him." Out of the corner of his eye, Diego noticed that he'd caught his friends' attention, and they were turning toward the conversation.

"That may be," the captain said. "But this is an order."

Diego looked at Redford. He took a deep breath and turned to face the captain. "Redford saved your life, your ship, your whole crew. You're asking me to kill one of my friends, and I won't do it."

The captain stiffened, getting ready to shout.

Paige joined Diego. "Sir, if it wasn't for Redford, we'd be goners," she said.

Petey stepped up next to her. "I saw Diego build that robot, sir. It's always been special to him, and after today, it's special to us. He's like family."

"Do you share this opinion, Ms. Emerson?"

"Aye," Lucy said. "Redford's part of the crew, sir."

"A robot on my crew . . . ," the captain grumbled, but then he turned and shouted up to Redford. "And what say you, my big friend? Will you sail under my command?"

Redford slowly turned his head back toward the bow and blew out a plume of white steam.

"That's how he says yes, sir," Diego said.

The captain exhaled slowly. "Fine, then."

"Woo-hoo!" Petey shouted, slapping a high five with Diego and then with the girls.

"You've proven yourself today," the captain said to Diego. "And earned a reprieve from punishment for your past transgressions. We will discuss Redford later."

Redford led the vessels around a bend, and the captain pointed ahead. "Welcome to Arkhipov Castle, stronghold of the Vanguard."

"Blimey," Lucy said. "This place is wicked."

"It is good to be home," the captain said. "Now we can—"

The captain stopped, staring hard at the empty piers. He stormed inside.

"What's with him?" Petey wondered.

"The docks are empty," Ajax said, bowing his head. "We had three other ships in our fleet: a tugboat called the *Intrepid*; a gunboat, the *Valiant*; and the *Dauntless*, a World War II destroyer. All were badly damaged in a battle with the Aeternum off the coast of Newfoundland. Most of the crew of the *John Curtis* transferred to those boats to help with repairs, but then a flash storm separated us. We hadn't heard from them, but they knew to sail to our base. The captain expected to find them waiting for us."

"We hoped for the best," Gaston said, "but . . . it seems our people are gone."

"Do the Aeternum have them?" Lucy said.

"We cannot know," Ajax said. He sighed and headed inside.

"I think they were also supposed to be part of our rescue mission," Petey said. "Not sure how we're going to pull this off with just these three pirates and us."

"We don't know the captain's plan yet," Diego said, trying to keep up a thread of hope. "I'm sure he had a backup plan in case his other ships hadn't returned."

Still, he couldn't escape the sinking feeling at seeing those empty docks, and the worry that even after coming all this way, finding his father was only more impossible than before.

Diego spent the next hour helping to unload and secure the cargo. Redford did most of the lifting, transferring storage containers onto the flatbed cars of a narrow-gauge train that ran the length of the main dock. When they were finished, Diego drove Seahorse and led Redford to the hangar near the castle where the robots would stay.

"You'll be okay here," Diego said.

Redford looked around but didn't reply.

"I'll come visit you. Okay?"

Redford puffed steam. *Fine.*

Diego caught up with everyone and boarded an old-fashioned trolley that would take them up to the castle. Ajax and the captain went the other way with the train of cargo.

"Why is the castle called Arge-pop?" Paige asked, looking up at the looming structure.

"Arkhipov," Petey corrected. "I'm betting it was a Russian king, or a general."

"That's pretty good, Monsieur Petey," Gaston said. "Vasili Arkhipov was actually a lesser-known Russian commander, but he saved the old world from nuclear destruction in the year 1962. Back then, there was this standoff between . . . I think it was Cubahna and—"

"The Cuban Missile Crisis," Petey said.

"Cuba? You mean the Spanish colony?" Lucy asked.

"Yeah," Petey said, "but after that. The old United States of America and Russia, which was called the Soviet Union, were enemies and nearly went to war."

The trolley entered a cave, plunging them into darkness.

"Commander Arkhipov refused to launch a nuclear torpedo against the Americans," Gaston said. "The captain says he saved the world from war and yet no one really knew of him, so he is honored here."

"The captain built this castle, right?" Diego said, studying the walls. "But then why does part of it look ancient?"

"You have sharp eyes, Ribera. The stone base and rear sections of the castle are different from the rest. They were here when our captain discovered this place. He built Arkhipov on the old ruins."

A loud grinding of gears prevented the conversation from continuing. The trolley had reached the castle. As everyone gazed around in awe, Lucy leaned against Diego's shoulder.

The trolley slipped through a tunnel into a massive cave. The walls glistened with seawater, and the ceiling was covered in stalactites. The trolley lurched to a stop on a metal platform. With a hiss and a grinding of gears, the platform began to rise toward a high ledge. The platform clanged to a stop at the ledge, and the trolley proceeded toward daylight, and the front doors of the castle.

As the light fell on them, Lucy shifted away. She stared straight ahead, almost like she was intentionally *not* looking at Diego.

The trolley pulled to a stop before the great stone building.

"This way," Gaston said.

They entered through enormous oak doors and into a great main hall. Huge wooden pillars towered around them, made of bound-together, full-grown tree trunks that were collared at the top, bottom, and center by black iron braces. The floor was made of large planks of worn, scarred wood and covered with a vast Oriental rug. At the back of the hall beyond a bonsai tree, a grand wooden staircase split left and right up to three floors.

"Over there is the common room and the library," Gaston said, pointing to ornately carved entryways to their left. "To the right are the dining hall and the kitchen. And past that is a hallway that leads to operations, the telegraph room, maintenance, and the darkroom."

Petey paused in the center of the echoing hall. "Hey, what's this?"

Diego saw him pointing to an inscription on the wall by the library.

"Is that Latin?" Lucy asked, joining him. "Let's see . . . remember . . . the, um . . ."

"'Remember, upon the conduct of each depends the fate of all.'" The captain had joined them.

"What's that supposed to mean?" Diego asked.

"That we shall live and die by each other's actions," the captain said. "This is more important than ever for you, my newest crew members, with the *Intrepid, Valiant,* and *Dauntless* lost." He slapped Diego and Lucy on the backs and spoke to everyone. "Gaston will show you to your rooms. Then I expect you to meet me in the map room in one hour."

They walked up the grand wooden stairs, their steps echoing into the dark recesses of the cavernous room. To either side, brass and black metal latticework housed Victorian-era elevators. Paige whispered something to Lucy, while Diego and Petey craned their necks this way and that to see the elaborate stonework and the many hallways leading in countless directions.

"Boys' rooms are that way," Gaston said when they reached the top of the stairs. "Take any one you want. You will find assorted clothes in the drawers and closets from past crewmembers. Please use them. The girls, too." He motioned Diego and Petey off in one direction while he continued with Lucy and Paige in the other.

But they hadn't taken two steps before Paige stopped and looked at Gaston, hands on her hips. "Excuse me?"

Gaston laughed. "Oh, I wanted to see you safely through this gloomy castle and—"

"I'm sure we can manage," Paige said. She pushed him gently. "You'd best be heading in *that* direction."

Petey and Diego started down the hall on their own. The corridor was empty, dimly lit. The doors were identical, and so were the rooms inside. Eventually the boys picked one, collapsing onto twin beds. Beside each bed was a military-style footlocker, a set of drawers, a desk and chair, a bookcase, and a gas lamp on the wall. There was a single closet in which hung two naval uniforms similar to the ones on the *John Curtis*.

Diego flopped down on the bed. Petey did the same. He stared at the ceiling, his body still feeling like it was swaying on the waves.

"Who do you think this is?" Petey asked. Diego found him with a picture of a young man holding hands with a pretty girl. An older couple stood behind them, looking on.

"One of the lost soldiers, I bet," Diego said.

Petey nodded. "I never thought I'd say this, but I miss my parents."

"Me too," Diego said.

"You know . . . I didn't want to be here," Petey said.

"Yeah, and I'm sorry—"

"But now, I'm glad I am."

Diego looked at his friend. "Me too, Petey." He stared at the ceiling and smiled, but it didn't last very long.

"How is your room?" Petey asked as Paige served up sandwiches.

"Sterile," Lucy said, "but quiet, and it doesn't smell like gunpowder and gasoline."

"Ours feels like barracks," Diego said.

"Same here," Paige said. "I know these guys are supposed to be pirates, but they feel more like military. This place is like a base."

"I was thinking that, too," Diego said.

"If they were real pirates," Lucy said, "wouldn't they be in alliance *with* the Aeternum, rather than against them?"

"Yeah," Petey agreed. "And I know they're getting paid for this, but it doesn't seem like they care about money. Doesn't it feel like they're fighting for something else?"

"It does," Lucy said.

"Guys," Diego said. "Isn't the fact that these guys are soldiers a good thing? I mean, I told you about that photo of Balsamic. He's a decorated war veteran."

"Yeah," Paige said, "but I'd bet blood to bones that they're not telling us everything."

"That's what's been worrying me," Lucy said. "I couldn't quite put my finger on it."

"Hold on a sec," Diego said. "Paige, did you say 'blood to bones'?"

"It's something Ajax always says. Like while we were trying to shoot down that Zero, he said"—Paige imitated Ajax's low, monotone voice—"'By *blood to bones* . . . I'll see you in hell!' What of it?"

"I heard him say that too," Diego said, "but that's weird."

"Why?" Lucy asked.

"Because I heard my mom say something like that," Diego remembered. "Before she fired at the Aeternum agents in New Chicago."

"Well, she was in the military," Lucy said. "Perhaps it was a common phrase during the Chronos War."

"Maybe," Diego said, but that seemed like quite a coincidence. He thought of his dad's capture—Magnus and Balthus had known him. Siobhan had said that they'd worked together in the past. This was another connection, albeit a small one, between two more of the people involved.

The four joined up with the rest of the crew in the map room, sunlight filtering through the windows. Everyone stood around a wide, heavy table. It was covered in charts, but atop the papers lay one giant map, expertly sketched. It was marked with the seal of the Mapmakers of the Vastlantic and signed with over twenty names.

"Here," the captain said, laying a thick finger on the map where he had placed three small model ships. "This is where Magnus is located and where he's taken your people."

"Yorktown?" Petey asked, reading the name above the small cluster of islands at the northern reach of the Islands of the Great Eastern Wall.

"What is left of the former city of New York," the captain said. "We believe that Magnus is attempting to restore an underwater Elder power station. This is why he needed your family members."

"My father and brother will never agree to help him," Lucy said.

"Why would he want to do that?" Diego asked.

"This is no ordinary generator," the captain said. "The reactor is capable of producing a kind of power that would allow Magnus to control the world, to make it to his liking."

Diego looked up at the captain, expecting him to continue, but he didn't. Diego glanced at Petey, who raised his eyebrows like the same question was on his mind: what kind of power *was* this?

But when the captain spoke again, he moved on. "According to Wallace's spies, the Aeternum are making runs for supplies while Magnus works. He will have six weeks before the Vastlantic summer storms begin. At that point, Magnus will either have to ride out the summer in Yorktown or rejoin his forces in the European territories. We estimate that Magnus will need five weeks to finish the repairs."

"If he is on schedule, he'll depart before the storms," Gaston added.

"This is not much time for us to find and train new recruits," Ajax said.

"No," the captain said. "But if we time our raid right, we can defeat Magnus and rescue our people with a small force."

"How small?" Paige said.

"Fourteen years ago, Magnus attacked New Chicago with six warships and thirty planes, only to be turned away by a handful of well-trained children not much older than yourselves. One fighter plane with an untested, sixteen-year-old girl at the controls single-handedly destroyed a third of his air squadron and two of his ships."

Diego found Lucy looking at him with a smile. He felt his face getting red. It was always weird to hear the woman who made him meals and nattered at him to get his homework done spoken of in such a heroic way.

"Numbers alone do not determine victory," the captain continued. "Courage, determination, and a superior plan win the day. Now, get some rest, and in the morning I will show you how Magnus can be defeated."

"This mission sounds crazy," Petey said as they walked back to their room.

Diego agreed, and yet, the thought of his mother beating

bigger odds filled him with courage. "We've come this far, haven't we?"

"I guess."

The two readied for bed, then chatted for a while. Eventually, Diego heard Petey's breathing settle down to a slow, even rhythm, and soon he was asleep as well.

Only to bolt awake moments later. Diego sat up, breathing hard. He'd had it again.

The dream.

Fly.

The gravity board, Dad disappearing, the girl, the chase through New Chicago to the clock tower, and then everything exploding around him.

But something had been different this time. Even worse. When Diego had looked down at the crowd, he'd seen Paige, Lucy, and Petey there. And then when things fell apart, he lost them too, along with everyone else.

Diego sat there, breathing deeply, reminding himself that it had only been a dream. When he realized that sleep would not be returning anytime soon, he got up and headed to the kitchen. Maybe Siobhan's trick of warm milk would help.

He was outside the kitchen door when he heard voices: Gaston, Lucy, and Paige. He was about to enter when the door swung open and Paige and Gaston walked out together, both smiling. Paige was holding a sextant.

"Where you two off to?" Diego asked.

"Gaston is taking me out on the balcony to teach me how

to take a reading of the moon with the sextant," Paige said.

"Oh right, a moonlight training session. Is that what they call that on the South side?" Diego asked, chuckling.

"Oh, you're so funny, Ribera," Paige said, crossing her arms. "I thought all you North-side pansies were supposed to have good manners. Didn't your mommy and daddy teach you anything?"

"They taught me how to take a joke, something that you can't seem to do."

"Yeah, well, you need to learn to respect your elders, fool," Paige snapped.

"She does have a point, *petit frère*," Gaston said.

"I *respect* my elders, Paige, but you aren't my elder. You don't count. . . . You're only a little older than me. Do you know what respecting your elders even means?"

"How can *you* talk about respect? You mean like the respect you showed your father when you yelled at him at that power plant—telling him off? And how you didn't want to be like him? Was that the kind of *respecting* you're talking about?"

Diego felt the heat rise in his face. Words locked in his throat.

"Come along, Paige, the moon and stars await," Gaston said, pulling on her arm. Paige hesitated, but said nothing and left.

Diego stood there frozen for a second, then rushed into the kitchen.

Lucy looked up from the counter where she was sipping a mug of tea. "Hey—"

"You told her about my dad!" Diego shouted. "The fight—what I said!"

Lucy's eyes went wide. "Diego, wait. . . ."

"Dammit, Lucy! How could you do that? I mean . . . I didn't tell anyone else. I trusted you!"

"I—"

"Forget it." Diego walked out.

"Diego, wait!" Lucy called, but Diego didn't stop. He ran through the great hall, down the stairs, and straight out of the castle.

He hurried through the dark, fists clenched, muttering to himself. He'd thought she was someone he could trust. But clearly he'd been wrong. That was the last time he went telling anything important to some traitorous girl.

Diego emerged on the beach. Waves lapped at the sand. Moonlight dappled the water. A symphony of insects harmonized from the trees, in all directions. He trudged down to the water's edge and kicked at the little waves. Then something caught his eye. He turned to see a giant silhouette sitting a little ways up the beach.

"Redford," Diego said, walking toward him.

Redford's big head turned, and he offered a short puff of steam.

HUNTSMAN
A. Bettm... © 2015

"Why aren't you in the hangar, buddy?" Diego asked.

Redford nodded to the sand beneath him.

Diego crouched down beside him. "Oh, good eye. That's pretty cool." He traced his finger across the markings in the sand. "A lot of sea animals build nests like these to protect their young. Maybe tonight's the night . . . you can never

tell with Mother Nature."

Redford turned toward the castle, and Diego heard footsteps padding quietly on the sand.

"You two want some company?"

Diego turned away from Lucy. "What do you want?"

"A chance to explain myself."

"What's there to explain? You told Paige about the fight I had with my dad. I didn't tell anyone about that—not Petey, not my mom. I thought I could trust you."

"Yes," Lucy admitted, her voice barely above a whisper, "but . . . you can. I mean, yes, I did tell Paige, but it wasn't like that. She's my best friend; we talk about everything, and I didn't think. . . . I know that doesn't make it proper, Diego, but it was because I was telling Paige how you were different from what either of us thought. How you and I were actually a lot alike and how we both didn't agree with what our fathers wanted of us. . . . That's how it came up. You have to believe me."

"Oh yeah, I believe you. I believe you were gossiping with your friend, and you told her something I never wanted anyone to know about."

"Diego . . ."

"You said we were friends," Diego said, "but . . . you're a liar. A real friend wouldn't have told anyone my secret. And . . . we are nothing alike. At least I had the courage to tell my dad what I thought about what he wanted for me. But you, you're a fake. You act all tough . . . a secret rebel who dresses up and skateboards when her daddy isn't looking. But you're a coward. You run and hide from telling him who you are or what you want."

"That's—ugh! Stop being such a jerk!" Lucy stomped the sand, and tears glistened in her eyes. "If you really think that, then you're the one who's been lying this whole time, acting like a good and decent boy when really you're self-centered and cruel."

Lucy stomped off hurriedly, but then stopped and turned around. "I thought you were an amazing boy, and I told Paige what happened with your dad because I wanted her to see that she was wrong about you. To like you too, and to know that . . . you're a kid with the same kind of problems. But I was wrong—you are exactly what she said you'd be."

This time, she didn't turn back.

He sat there, stunned. Part of him wanted to run after her and apologize, while another part of him never wanted to see her again.

There was a creaking of gears, and Redford crouched, looking at Diego.

"What?" Diego said. "Did you hear what she said? Man, she's a piece of work. She—"

Redford nudged Diego onto his side with his finger.

"Hey," Diego said, getting to his feet. "What's your problem?"

Redford extended his finger again, this time pushing Diego backward. He stumbled into the waves.

"You—"

Redford pushed him again, and this time he toppled into the water on his butt.

"Redford!" Diego jumped up, shivering. "Okay, so I was harsh with her, but come on—"

Another push. This time, Diego didn't go down, but he

splashed out up to his knees, the spray soaking him further.

"Okay, fine, I get it. Stop, okay?"

Redford nodded. He turned around and began carving his finger through the sand.

"What are you doing?" Diego asked, shaking as he trudged out of the water. Redford had etched wide lines into the sand. Diego couldn't make out the shape, so he swung up the side of Redford's leg until he could stand on his hip. From here, he could easily make out the words Redford had written:

CHAPTER SEVENTEEN

Turtles and Tactics

Petey and Diego woke the next morning to clothes landing on their beds and Gaston standing in the doorway. "I had to guess at the sizes," he said. "Captain wants us on the beach in ten minutes. You can grab food on your way past the kitchen."

"Ten minutes?" Petey asked, rubbing his head. "Why didn't you wake us sooner?"

"I thought it best if you came down after the others, to avoid any fireworks in the dining hall," Gaston said. He smiled at Diego. "*Petit frère* knows what I mean."

"What gives?" Petey asked.

"I'll tell you on the way."

They dressed in the training clothes and headed downstairs, grabbing muffins from the kitchen. As they hurried down to the beach, Diego explained the short version of his fight with Lucy.

"Man, some best friend you are," Petey said. "You told Lucy about your fight with your old man but you couldn't tell me?"

"Jeez, Petey, I'm sorry. It was embarrassing, and I felt terrible about it. It's not that I didn't want to tell you. I hadn't told anyone, not even my mom, but then it slipped out when me and Lucy were hanging out." But he had also felt something . . . different about Lucy.

Petey nodded. "I guess I'm cool with it. But you know you can tell me anything, right?"

"I know," Diego said. "I won't make that mistake again."

Petey slapped him on the shoulder. "Hey, who knows? Maybe she'll be over it?"

But when they arrived at the beach, Lucy and Paige turned their backs to the boys.

They were lined up along with Gaston and Redford. Seahorse was parked by Redford, and behind the captain was an old World War II navy seaplane.

"You two are late," the captain said.

Diego glanced at Gaston, but he was standing there, casually looking forward.

"Sorry, sir," Petey said. "It won't happen again."

"Twenty push-ups," the captain ordered. "Now."

Diego and Petey dropped to the sand.

"Not just them," the captain said. "All of you. You are a unit. If one of you is late, you are all late."

"Fools," Paige muttered as she and Lucy also dropped to the sand. "You can use your knees," Paige said to Lucy, showing her how. "You'll get stronger, stronger than these two for sure."

"As strong as you, I reckon," Lucy said, straining between push-ups. "Maybe stronger."

"That's my girl!" Paige then proceeded to whip off her twenty in the traditional style. Both girls finished before Diego and Petey.

When they stood up to get in line, Diego and Petey had to move down to the end. There was only a narrow strip of sand left beside the water.

"Hey," Petey said to Paige, "can you guys give us a little space?"

Paige glanced over coldly. "He can get his feet wet."

"It's fine," Diego said, stepping into the ankle-deep water.

"There will not be time for us to find new recruits and train them before Magnus leaves Yorktown. This mission will be up to us," the captain said. "So, I have a task for each of you."

"What's the plan, sir?" Gaston asked.

As Diego listened, his breath shortened. It was one thing to find yourself in trouble; it was quite another to *plan on* getting into trouble, to know that danger was coming. He could see it on Petey's face, and Lucy's, maybe a glimpse on Paige's, too.

When the captain finished outlining the strategy, he stood aside and pointed down the beach. "There is an antiaircraft gun tower two miles ahead. You will begin every day by running to it and back. When you return, you will swim out to the safety nets and back. Then Gaston will drill you in combat on the beach, Ajax will educate in weapons at the range, and I will teach you tactical theory in the map room. Every day after lunch, you will train at your specific mission duties. Remember: the only way we will succeed is if you work hard, and"—his icy stare fell on Diego and then Lucy—"together. Now *run*."

They took off down the beach, their boots digging in the soft sand. Diego was surprised to see Redford bounding along behind them. Diego heard a bark. Daphne sat in the big robot's operating chair. Watching.

"At least someone's having fun," Petey said, already out of breath.

Diego was nearly seeing spots after the run, feeling like he would never catch his breath. And they'd barely returned before Gaston was ushering them into the water. They took off their boots, dove out past the waves, then swam across the harbor. Diego's arms burned, and his legs began to ache. He'd never swum so far. He didn't think he would even make it to shore, but he kept checking on Petey, who looked at him with the same worried expression, and somehow they pushed each other onward.

After a brief rest to dry off in the sun, Diego joined Ajax

and the captain at Seahorse, while everyone else went to work on their pieces of the rescue plan.

"You must be able to drive this bot faster and more precisely than ever before, as well as master its deep-water maneuvering capabilities," the captain said as they loaded inside. "We will have precious little time during the rescue, and there will be no margin for error."

They spent the rest of the morning practicing diving and breaching, and after a quick respite to wolf down a sandwich, everyone reconvened on the beach for combat training.

Diego noticed Gaston and Paige laughing as they returned from their training, Gaston saying something quietly that led Paige to push him away, grinning.

He also noticed Lucy stalking back to the beach with Petey talking to her, but whatever he was saying, she didn't want to hear it.

"Sparring," Gaston said, stepping in front of them with two sets of boxing gloves. "We will learn how to punch and how to be punched."

"Don't we want to *not* be punched?" Petey asked.

"That is preferable," Gaston said, "but not always possible. Sometimes you must absorb a blow in order to deliver your own. Paige and I will demonstrate."

"You sure you're up for that?" Paige said, taking the gloves with a smile.

"More than sure, *belle*."

Paige slipped on the gloves and adopted a sparring

position: knees bent, gloves up to protect her face. She and Gaston danced around the square drawn in the sand, ducking, feinting, trading blows. Some of the hits sounded hard enough that Diego imagined he would have been flat on his back, but both combatants shook it off.

"Nice," Gaston said. "As you can see, the key is to maintain your balance and composure. Lose your cool, and you'll end up KO'd. Now, who will fight first?"

"Ribera and Emerson," the captain ordered, pointing at them both.

"What?" Diego said.

"You're joking," Lucy said, pursing her lips.

But Diego didn't want to risk earning the captain's wrath, so he took the gloves and slipped them on. Lucy did the same.

Gaston demonstrated a defensive position, with their hands protecting their faces.

"Now, move," he said. "And look for a weakness."

Diego's hands felt clammy in the gloves. He started to move on his toes, and though it was the last thing he wanted to do, he gathered up the nerve to look Lucy in the eye.

She glared at him from behind her gloves, moving left and right. She dipped toward him, then darted back. "Come on, Ribera, or did you already take your best shot last night?"

"Knock him out cold, Luce!" Paige called.

"Look, about what I said," Diego said, moving in a circle with her.

Lucy's eyes narrowed.

"I think we need to talk about this."

Lucy didn't respond. She kept darting around, gloves high, her brow sheened with sweat.

Finally, Diego stopped and dropped his hands. "Come on already, Lucy, would you say someth—"

Diego stumbled down to his knee, his whole face throbbing.

Lucy's shadow fell over him. "I win," she said, and dropped the gloves beside him. "Not so much of a coward after all."

"Yeah, girl!" Paige shouted.

"Oh, *petit frère*," Gaston said, clucking his teeth. "Rule number one, never drop your guard."

Diego pushed himself up. Petey grabbed his arm. "You okay, buddy?"

"Yeah," Diego said. He turned to say something to Lucy, but she was sitting next to Ajax, with both Paige and Gaston tending to her.

"Let her cool off," the captain said. "But then you will fix this problem."

"Yes, sir," Diego said.

That night, they ate at one end of a long, empty table in the cavernous dining hall. Aside from exchanging a few comments with Petey, Diego was mostly quiet, unable to keep himself from listening to Lucy, Paige, and Gaston as they laughed their way through dinner.

When the meal was finished, Petey and Gaston stayed to help Paige clean up the kitchen. Diego waited until Lucy was leaving the dining hall, then followed her.

"Hey," he called. "Lucy, can we talk?"

Lucy slowed but didn't stop walking. "Not really," she said over her shoulder.

"Captain's orders," Diego said.

"Oh, please."

"I'm serious. He said we have to straighten out our problem."

"Ha," Lucy said. "We don't have a problem. We have you being an insufferable cad."

She walked away again, so Diego grabbed her hand.

"Come on, can we . . . can we *please* talk about this outside?"

Lucy looked at him coldly, then at their hands. She pulled hers away, but slowly, so that her fingers slid across his palm. Diego flinched at the sensation.

"Fine," she said.

They walked out onto the balcony. Diego kept going, down the steps to the beach.

"Where are you going?" Lucy asked.

"Away from everybody. I don't want Gaston or Paige coming by." In truth, that was only part of the reason.

Lucy huffed, but then she joined him.

They walked out onto the moonlit sand, the ocean calm and glassy, like a second starry sky. Diego walked with his hands in his pockets. Every now and then, one of them would stumble in the sand and their shoulders would brush against each other's. Neither of them said anything about it.

Diego scanned the shadows at the edge of the beach, looking for what he'd seen before.

"I don't feel like going any farther," Lucy said.

"Just a little more," Diego said, spying the spot up ahead. "Trust me."

"You're being weird," Lucy said, but she slipped off her shoes and left them behind as they walked. She caught Diego noticing. "What? I like the sand between my toes, and my mother will never know." She nodded to his feet. "You should try it."

Diego smiled. "Okay." He kicked off his shoes and flexed his toes in the cool sand. "Yeah, that's pretty good."

"Like getting a foot massage with every step," Lucy said.

"Now I'm picturing a beach made of hands," Diego said.

"Ew," Lucy said, and pushed him gently on the shoulder. "Don't ruin it."

"Sorry." They were nearing the spot. He led her up into the shadows beneath the palms and waited for Lucy to join him. When she was into the shadows, he held out his hand. "Stop there."

"Stop bossing me around," Lucy said. She looked around and noticed their familiar surroundings. "If we're here to resume our fight, then I'm going back."

"You can't move now," Diego said. "Now hold still and close your eyes."

"I will not."

"Trust me."

"Why would I do that?"

"Because I'm sorry, and there's something here for you to see."

"I can't see very well if my eyes are closed," Lucy said, almost smiling. "Fine."

Diego gently placed his hands on her feet.

"What exactly are you doing?"

"Keep your eyes closed." He glanced down at the sand as he let go of her. "Now, don't move or you might hurt them. Okay . . . open your eyes."

In the sand at Lucy's feet, there was a quiet, shuffling sound, and then Lucy gasped.

In moments, so many of the tiny turtles were shuffling out of the sand that the spot looked alive. They scrambled over Lucy's feet and around her ankles, making their way instinctively toward the sea.

"Oh . . . they are the most adorable things ever." Lucy knelt down, watching their little flippers churning the sand. She ran a finger over the back of one of their papery shells.

"Now watch. Keep still," Diego said, and he closed his eyes and spread his arms. He pictured the turtles, their little faces, their shiny eyes. . . .

"Blimey," Lucy whispered. All the turtles had formed a perfect ring around Lucy, gazing at her, their little heads bobbing up and down.

"Diego, are you . . . are you doing this?"

"Yes." Diego opened his eyes and saw that the little beings had responded.

"You did that . . . ," Lucy said, "with the Maker's Sight?"

Diego nodded.

"Why?"

"I think you know why."

Lucy looked at him and crossed her arms expectantly.

"I, um, I thought about what you said and why you told Paige about what happened with me and my dad . . . and I get it. And I . . . I know I shouldn't have said that about you being a coward. I mean, I didn't have the guts to tell my mom or Petey what happened that day with my dad. You're not a coward, and you're not fake. . . . You're doing what you have to do. And I don't know what it must feel like to be in your place. So, um, I'm sorry." With that, the turtles returned to their journey toward the water.

Lucy sighed. "You feel alone, and sometimes . . . you feel trapped." She nestled into an empty spot among the migrating baby turtles. "But having someone to talk to makes it feel like you're not on your own, and that makes it tolerable. I shouldn't have told Paige, and she shouldn't have said what she did."

"Well, I was riding her pretty bad about Gaston," Diego said.

"Right. Well, you should know better now than to mess with that one."

"Lesson learned."

Lucy nodded, looking at the turtles. "You knew those turtles would be there, didn't you?"

"Redford and I spotted the mounds in the sand last night, and all day I thought about showing them to you. That you would think it was neat."

"So, all day you were thinking about how to apologize to me," Lucy said. "How did you do it? I mean, with these turtles. Are you *talking* to them?"

"No, not talking. It's more like I can send them a thought, feeling, or images, and they seem to . . . act on it. It's like hypnosis, I think. Back in New Chicago, something happened with Daphne that gave me the idea. I wasn't totally sure it would work. But when I brought you here, I calmed my mind and started to think over and over how . . . nice it was to be near this girl," Diego said. "And I guess they *felt* it and came to be near you."

Lucy looked away, holding back a smile, her face flushed. "This power . . . being able to send your thoughts to other animals, is that a normal part of the Sight?"

"I don't know. My dad never told me that it was something the Sight could do," Diego said. "It's no big deal."

"I'm not sure I believe you," she said. "If you can do that to animals, does that mean you could do that to a person?"

"I don't know. I never thought about it. That would be kinda wrong, though, wouldn't it?"

"Yes, it would."

"So," Diego said. "Am I forgiven, or what?"

Lucy punched him in the arm. "Perhaps."

"Ouch!" Diego winced. She'd hit his sore shoulder. "Yeah, well, you sure don't punch—"

"Don't say 'like a girl' or I'm leaving."

Diego smiled.

"Good—oh . . ." Lucy's brow wrinkled with concern. "Yikes, did you bump your nose when you fell this afternoon?"

"What?" Diego felt his upper lip. His finger came away with a smear of blood. "Oh, I guess," he said. "Maybe it's a delayed reaction to your punch."

Lucy smiled. "Thought you were made of tougher stuff than that, Ribera."

He doubled over, put his hand over his mouth, and coughed, so hard that it brought spots to his vision. When he sat up, he could feel fresh blood trickling from his nose.

"Diego?"

"I'm fine."

"Okay, come here, you." Lucy pulled on his arm. "You are not well."

She turned him sideways and started to pull him backward.

"What are you doing?" Diego asked.

"Just relax. I've mended my brothers' bloody noses plenty of times, and Mother will not tolerate the stains, so I've learned a thing or two." She laid his head back in her lap and pinched his nose.

"Does that hurt?" Lucy asked.

"No," Diego said, his voice high and nasally. Lucy smiled.

"We have to hold it like this for about two minutes, and the flow should stop."

Diego found himself looking up at Lucy and noticing

more than ever how pretty she was. The thought freaked him
out because he almost told her. Her eyes sparkling in the light
off the water, the moonlight catching her cinnamon freckles,
the curve of her nose. But then Diego realized that he was
staring up at her dumbly.

"How many bloody noses have you fixed?" he asked.

"Five or six," Lucy said. "My father would never approve
of your long hair," she said, gently running a finger across
his forehead to brush his hair aside. "Then again, he wouldn't
approve of Paige or Balsamic or pretty much any single thing
that's happened."

"He'll approve when you rescue him," Diego said.

"He might pass out from shock at the sight of me," Lucy said. "That will sure make it harder to rescue him." She laughed for a second, but it died away. "Or he'll get us all captured again while he's busy lecturing me."

"I'll let him know to watch out for your right hook," Diego said.

"Oh, will you, now?" Lucy made a fist above Diego.

He reached up and grabbed it as if to stop her. Their hands stayed there, weightless for a moment, fingers intertwined.

"Okay." Lucy pulled away, releasing Diego's nose. "The bleeding should be stopped, and we should get back."

Diego sat up, his heart pumping like he'd sprinted or landed an impossible trick on his gravity board.

"Are you okay to walk back?" Lucy said, already on her feet.

Diego stood, dizzy for a moment, but steadied. He wiped at his nose. Dry. "I'm good."

Lucy held out her hand. "Come on then, slowpoke."

Diego slid around to the other side of her and took her hand.

As they walked, Diego glanced at his other hand, the one she'd meant to grab. He'd had it closed this whole time, since his coughing fit. After a quick look, he flicked his arm behind him and wiped his hand on his pants.

He heard the lightest sound of something landing in the sand.

As they trudged toward the castle, Diego thought back to the moment he'd coughed, to the splitting pain he'd felt. He still tasted the blood and felt the raw, empty space. And he wondered if he was learning the real price of the Maker's Sight.

CHAPTER EIGHTEEN

An Oath Before
the Storm

Diego and his friends were drying off from their swim the next morning, and as they caught their breath, Redford and Daphne played on the beach. Redford picked up a large log and threw it twenty yards. Daphne chased after it, but only when she reached it did she seem to realize that there was no way she could pick it up. She looked around, found a stick more her size, and dropped it at Redford's feet, tail wagging. Redford bent to pick it up but couldn't get his giant fingers around it. Instead, he held out his hand, and Daphne sprang into it. He placed her up in her favorite perch, in his operating chair.

"Bonjour, crew," Gaston said, arriving behind them. "The

rest of training is postponed. Captain wants you to meet him and Ajax out past the gun tower. Here's a map." He handed the paper to Petey, and the four looked it over.

"That's a few miles away," Petey said, still breathing hard from their workout.

"Are you expecting us to run there?" Paige asked.

Before Gaston could answer, Redford's hands thumped to the ground on either side of them. Diego looked up at him. "I think Red's going to give us a lift," he said.

"Well, that seems like cheating," Gaston said, "but the captain does want you there on the double."

Redford scooped them up and started jogging down the beach in giant, loping strides. Daphne yipped with delight from her perch.

"This is how we should always travel," Lucy said, the wind blowing her wet hair. She and Diego sat on one shoulder while Paige and Petey sat on the other.

Diego shared a glance with Lucy. She gave him a slight smile that seemed to acknowledge the night before but also say that today it was back to business.

"Okay, Redford, there's the gun tower," Petey said. "There should be a road over there." He pointed up off the beach.

Redford vaulted through dense bushes and vines and emerged on the wide road. It was a straight, two-mile strip with lights on either side.

"This isn't a road," Diego said. "It's a runway." Up ahead, there were enormous hangar doors built into the imposing sheer rock walls of the Volcambrian crater.

Redford reached it in a minute. The kids slid off by his arms.

"What is this place?" Paige asked.

"A hangar," Diego said. The place seemed familiar to him, though he wasn't sure why. He started toward the giant doors.

"Hey, D," Petey said. "Gaston said to wait for the captain."

"I know," Diego said, but he kept walking. This runway was enormous. He could picture the giant cargo planes that might have once taken off and landed here. And those doors . . . he walked into the shadow of the crater wall, studying them and wondering what was inside. "I am waiting," he added to Gaston, "just in here."

"I wouldn't mind getting out of the sun," Lucy said.

Diego gripped the side of the door and pulled, but it wouldn't budge. "Hey, Redford," he called. "Give us a hand?"

Redford tromped over. With a puff of steam and a grinding of gears, he pulled open the doors. Diego stepped into the shadows, Lucy right behind him.

Inside the hangar, the air was cool and dank, with a sweet earthen smell. Lights hanging on cords from the high ceiling cast a dim glow over the cavernous space. Diego peered between rows of machines, his footfalls echoing off the dust-covered metal surfaces.

"This place is stunning," Lucy said.

"There have to be hundreds of vehicles," Petey said. "I mean, this is one heck of an arsenal."

Diego kept staring at a Japanese Zero. It had its original paint scheme and markings, but this one had also been altered, like the one that had attacked them. He glanced at a Minotaur robot and its disassembled weaponry at its feet. It was an Elder weapon from the Argentinian civil war.

"Your eyes don't deceive you." The voice echoed through the hangar. The captain and Ajax approached.

Diego looked back at the arsenal. "My dad built these."

"Your father is a brilliant engineer and inventor," the captain said, "and he is a man of great courage but . . . he sought a different path to serve our common purpose. Before he made machines to rebuild the world, and toys

D. Yatomi

for amusement, he was the master of technology that could destroy."

"And what about those planes that attacked us?"

"Yes, but he didn't build these weapons *for* the Aeternum. It was to destroy them. The ones that attacked us were once Vanguard planes. But all this," he said, gesturing to everything in the hangar, "was long before his life in New Chicago, before he was a husband and a father. It was part of a different time for all of us." The captain turned and raised his voice. "Ajax, a little more light."

Gears began to grind, and steam pumps hissed. The hangar doors slid open and flooded the room with daylight.

"Is this really it?" Lucy exclaimed, pulling herself up to the cockpit.

"British Hawker Sea Fury," Diego said in awe, "the kind my mother flew."

"It's like the *Skywolf* she flew for the Silver Squadron of New Chicago's air corps when they fought the Aeternum at Dusable Harbor," Lucy said, climbing up onto the wing and slipping into the seat. "The girl who shot down nine enemy planes."

"A Steam Timer like you," the captain said. "And not much older at the time."

"Watch out," Lucy called down with a smile, and imitated opening fire on Diego with the plane's twin guns.

Diego pretended to grab his chest.

"Oh." Lucy ducked out of sight for a moment. "Oi, Ribera, look at this!"

"Lucy . . . ," Diego began.

"Those are your parents' initials, right?" she said.

"Yeah but . . ." He was staring at her hair. "Where did you find that?"

"It was stuck over here in the side of the panel. Why?"

"It's my mother's missing chopstick. She carries the other one as a good luck charm," Diego said. The sight of it caused a soft pain in his chest as he thought of his mom and home, both so far away. And yet here she was, and this plane that was nearly identical to her own.

"Oh." Lucy reached up to take out the chopstick. "Sorry, I had no idea."

"No." Diego stopped her hand. "Keep it. She'd want us to have her with us. We're going to need her luck."

"Thank you."

Diego smiled, and yet inside he was rocking back and forth like he was out at sea. He dropped to the floor and returned to the captain. Everyone had arrived, along with Gaston.

"Yes, Diego," the captain said before Diego could even ask what was on his mind. "Your mother flew in that plane. She was here, for training, along with your father and your uncle Arden."

Diego gazed around at the weaponry. "They were here. . . . You knew them. You fought together."

"Your parents were and always have been part of the Vanguard family. Though it has been many years since your father and I have walked the same path. But they are why we took this mission," the captain said. "That and . . . other reasons."

"Why didn't you tell me before now?" Diego asked.

"You needed to earn your place as a part of the crew first," the captain said. "But now you've risked your life to bring your loved ones home, and you deserve to know the truth."

"I have a bad feeling about what you're going to tell us," Paige said.

"As well you should. Diego, your father built this arsenal when he was full of a different purpose."

Diego remembered Magnus's words back at the power plant. "What purpose?"

"Long ago, your father believed as I once did—as Magnus and Balthus still do—that the Time Collision could be reversed. *Unmade.* That the old world could be brought back."

"How would that even be possible?" Lucy asked.

"There are machines," the captain said, "scattered across this world, called Quantum Reactors. They are twenty-third-century creations. Many cities from that time had these reactors, though it is not known how many came through the Collision. But what is known, what your father and I, along with Magnus and Balthus and the rest of our team, discovered, was that restarting four of these reactors would provide the power necessary to change the world back. To undo the Collision and restore time to its previous order."

"You all worked together," Diego said. "You and the enemy."

"We weren't enemies then," the captain said. "We were men of the Dark Years, thrown into a world of chaos and violence. We fought together under the Union flag to end the

Chronos War, but we were still men who remembered our old worlds, our old homes, and dreamed of nothing but getting home. We called ourselves the Time Crusaders."

"But my dad loves this world," Diego said. "He always talks about how much hope he has for the future."

"He feels that way *now*, as do we all," the captain said. "But as I said, this was before. The loss of our homes and our families was still fresh in our minds and hearts, and the world around us was chaos. We were determined to regain control of these reactors, which meant taking back the cities and rescuing the technology from those who were busy destroying one another." He pointed to the fighter planes and tanks. "Your father restored weapons like these for that purpose."

"But how come you didn't succeed," Paige said, looking around, "even with all these weapons?"

"That's just it—we did," the captain said. "The first city we took back was Rome. We secured the Quantum Reactor, restarted it, and only then did we learn the terrible price to be paid for our arrogance."

Diego suddenly felt like he knew what the captain was going to say next. Like he'd known it for years, a cold, hollow fear that had been freezing deep inside him.

"I suppose it should have been obvious," the captain said. "But to change the world back meant returning to a timeline before any of you were ever born or existed. We turned on the reactor, only to watch a child who was among our group disintegrate before our eyes. And that was just the beginning." The captain's voice lowered. "All throughout the city. Every child . . ."

He snapped his fingers. The sound echoed in the hollow silence.

"That's horrible," Lucy said. "How could you not have known that would happen?"

"We were deceived," the captain said. "An Elder scientist had convinced us that by recalibrating the reactor's energy field in a certain way, we could restore the old world and still maintain the current timeline without causing a paradoxical collapse."

"A para-what?" Paige said.

"It doesn't matter," Ajax said. "That bastard lied to us. And now he and his general are out to finish the job."

"Balthus was the scientist," Diego said, remembering the man from the power plant. "Wasn't he?"

"A traitor," Ajax said.

"How could you have worked with them?" Diego asked. "Why did you trust them?"

"At the time, we had no reason not to. We thought we were all searching for the same thing. After the Time Collision, it was Balthus who found us, united us. Magnus Vorenus was already with him. He was a great warrior and general, and very convincing. Balthus's science seemed to back it up. And you have to understand. We *wanted* it to be true. All of us had lost so much. We wanted so badly to believe."

"You became enemies after that," Diego said.

The captain nodded. "Once we knew the cost—what returning to our old world would do—we could not in good conscience put our own suffering before that of millions of innocent children and their families. So we decided: what was made would stay made. But Magnus didn't agree. He wanted his family back, his *world*. Those who fight with him dismiss all this as an abomination."

"Does that go for this world's children?" Lucy asked.

"To him, you are an irrelevant mistake, nothing more. And so we fought. Soon after the reactor in Rome was destroyed, the Chronos War ended, and the Dark Years drew to a close. Magnus was defeated, but it was only a matter of time before he reemerged stronger and more determined. We retreated to this place and built our army to defeat him, to stop him before he could find other reactors. Sure enough, he returned, leading a band of raiders he named the Aeternum. He plagued New Chicago, but then, after a crushing defeat in Dusable Harbor, he disappeared. We'd won, or so we thought. As the Dark Times receded and the world found order, we heard rumors of his activities, but for years it was as if he'd vanished. Your father and mother had fallen in love and wanted to get on actually *living* in this world."

The captain took out his pocket watch and wound it. "The Aeternum returned, of course, with vast armies and a navy. Now they've taken cities in the European territories and have their eyes set on the Americas. To the rest of the world, the

Aeternum seem no different from any other force bent on conquest."

"But Magnus is still only after the reactors," Diego said.

"And if he succeeds," Petey said, "every child in this world will die."

"I don't get it," Paige said. "Why keep this a secret? Why not tell everyone? If the world were united against Magnus, there's no way he'd win."

"Perhaps," the captain said. "And yet, we cannot be sure how many new followers would join Magnus's ranks. There are still many in this world who might want what Magnus could offer: a way back.

"Our hope is that the more time goes by, the more people will find peace and prosperity here in the post-Collision world, and the better humanity will be," the captain said. "People will look toward the future, not the past. You young ones are all the proof Santiago, myself, and the rest of our band ever needed in order to know that we are in the right."

"This is why my father and brother, and Santiago and the other engineers, were taken, isn't it?" Lucy said, biting her lip.

"Yes. They are needed to restart the Quantum Reactors," the captain said. "We can only assume that Magnus has found a reactor in Yorktown. This fight has long been in your family, Diego, and now it continues." He reached toward the tarp covering the nearby plane. "Your father might be the most talented engineer this world has ever seen, but he's also likely the world's deadliest weapons designer as well."

He pulled the tarp free.

Diego knew the plane. "My uncle Arden's fighter." He thought of the picture on his wall, of his parents and uncle standing beside it looking young and fierce, and the one showing Uncle Arden next to his T-28. . . . But the plane was different now.

"What did this?" Diego asked, running his hand over the strange shredding pattern in the armor.

"A multiphase fragmentation gun. One of your father's most sophisticated inventions, and well beyond the reach of any twenty-third-century science. But Magnus stole it while it was in transit to protect London, and then it was used by the Aeternum in the Battle of Dusable Harbor. It took all your mother's and your uncle's skill to defeat it, but it cost your uncle his life."

Diego turned and faced the captain. "This is why my

father swore never to make weapons."

"He could never forgive himself for his role in Arden's death, as well as those of many others."

A silence fell over the group. Diego didn't know what to say.

"The truth is hard," the captain said, "and I'm sure you wish your father had told you before now."

"You know what?" Diego said. "I get it. Maybe I'm glad I didn't know that until now."

"It sure would have made doing homework seem pointless," Petey said.

"I'm glad to have told you," the captain said. "I will leave you now to decide how you feel about our mission. You have done well with your training and the tests of mettle so far. But this test is about your beliefs. If you choose to commit to the Vanguard, join us in the map room at sundown."

The captain left with Gaston and Ajax, shutting the hangar doors.

"Let's talk outside," Diego said, looking around. "This place has ghosts."

He led the way down to the beach. They sat at the edge of the surf, Redford flicking logs down the beach for Daphne to run after.

Diego thought of the octopus-shaped device that was inside Redford and how the captain had wondered at its potential danger before. He now understood the captain's fear. If discovered and replicated, these devices could be used to reactivate the complex weapons and computer systems of middle and future times.

"So," Petey said, "what do you say, D?"

But Diego couldn't answer. "I need to walk for a minute," he said, and left the group without another word.

"Diego?" Lucy called.

He saw her getting up to follow but held out his hand. "Just give me a sec."

He trudged off down the sand, his eyes hot, his throat tight. He wasn't sure why this feeling washed over him now, of all times.

Something splashed beside him. He looked up to see Redford trailing along in the surf. "Go back with the others," he said.

Redford blew a short puff of steam. *Nope.*

"Okay, fine, then," Diego said. He took a few more steps and stopped. His shoulders sagged, and he looked to the sky as tears came.

Redford's heavy finger gently touched his shoulder.

Diego didn't want to speak, but then the words tumbled out. "He was trying to tell me, Redford. He wanted me to understand why it was so important for him not to make weapons . . . and I didn't understand. I didn't want to. . . ." He buried his face in his hands.

Redford bent over, dipping his shoulder. Seeing this, Diego climbed up and opened his interface panel. Words flashed on the tablet's screen:

You still love him.

And he loves you.

Diego wiped his eyes. "You make it sound so simple."

Redford puffed steam, as if to say: *That's because it is.*

Diego closed his panel and patted Redford on the back of the head. "Thanks, friend." He hopped down to the sand. "Come on."

They headed back to the others.

"Are you all right?" Lucy asked.

"Yeah," Diego said. "So . . . are we in?"

"We're in," Petey said. Lucy and Paige nodded.

"Then let's go."

"We're ready," Diego said, standing tall across the table from the captain, Gaston, and Ajax, "to do what must be done."

The captain nodded. With a deep breath, he reached beneath the table and produced an old map. It showed the world as it had been known a few years after the Time Collision, with many islands, continents, and stretches of ocean still unexplored. Across the top, scrawled in thick black letters, were the words:

What is made stays made.

There was more text on the side, a series of lines, and then beneath that, a long list of names, each signature made by a different hand. Diego saw many names he didn't know, but some he did: Santiago, Siobhan, Arthur Huston, the captain and his men, the Mapmakers.

"Look there," Lucy said, pointing halfway down: Her Majesty Queen Victoria.

"And there," Petey said, pointing to Bartholomew Roosevelt.

The captain pointed to the text above the names. "This is the oath of the Vanguard. Speak it out loud, and join our cause in full."

They spoke the oath together:

"What is made stays made.
We fight together and for each other till the very end.
To the very last.
We've come far and will go farther still.
I pledge my life, my blood, and my bones to this end.
To keep this world—until it turns no more, this is my oath."

As they finished, Diego felt an electric surge inside, a power joining them together. He felt stronger and bolder. Ready.

"Who are you to have come so far?" he called, a gleam in his eyes. "To go farther still! Name yourselves as Vanguard!"

"Not just as the Vanguard," Lucy said, drawing all eyes. "We are our own family within yours. We name ourselves . . . Rangers. The Rangers of the Vastlantic!"

The captain looked at her blankly.

"Sir, you and your men founded the Vanguard. But we

four . . . we had to venture across the untamed sea, face certain death, to earn our place in your family. We deserve our own name beneath yours."

The captain held her gaze for a moment longer, seemingly holding back traces of a smile.

"Rangers," he said finally.

"Yes." Lucy stood tall, head up. Diego had to hand it to her. She had the most guts of them all.

"Very well, *Rangers*," the captain said, "Name yourselves!"

Diego felt goose bumps break out on his arms. "Diego Ribera!"

"Petey Kowalski!"

"Paige Jordan!"

"Lucy Emerson! We are of London and New Chicago,

and we pledge our loyalty to the Vanguard, defenders of this world!"

"Are the Rangers of the Vastlantic prepared to do what must be done?" the captain asked. He raised his sword.

"We are!" they answered in unison.

"Do the Rangers understand the responsibility before them and all that comes with it?"

"We do!"

"Do the Rangers swear by their blood and by their bones to hold these words true?"

"We do!" The four friends clasped hands.

"Rangers, welcome to the fight."

CHAPTER NINETEEN

What the World Can Be

I n the weeks that followed, the Rangers of the Vanguard trained long and hard. They grew stronger, sharper, and more disciplined. In the hot sun on the beaches of Volcambria, they practiced fighting. One day, Petey even bested Paige, who was by far the most experienced, nearly a blue belt in jujitsu back home. Around the grounds, the jungle, and the castle, they played a combat game called Catch, Escape, or Disable, each of them taking a turn as the enemy and stalking one another in the shadows. They learned to read their environment for advantage and escape, to utilize what was around them for attack and defense.

Out on the runway, Ajax taught them about weaponry

from the twentieth, twenty-first, and even twenty-third centuries. The concussive hand cannons were Diego's favorite. Designed by his dad, they used antigravity technology similar to his gravity board.

He found that he was skilled at boxing and good at hiding, yet not quite up to Lucy's skill at tactics or Petey's resourcefulness when needing to make do with their surroundings. Unless of course they were near any weaponry, which Diego handled the best, even modifying a couple of pieces of machinery.

During their time with the pirates, Diego's friends had earned the respect of the captain and his crew. And although things had been better between him and the captain since the attack at sea, Diego never felt like the captain believed in him. This seemed particularly obvious during their boxing rounds. In the ring, the captain would constantly remind him to focus and criticize his choice of tactics no matter whom he fought or how he did.

One morning in the fourth week, they drew straws, and Diego ended up in the ring with Gaston. The captain, watching from a bench nearby, sighed and shook his head.

Diego caught this out of the corner of his eye, renewing his frustration. The old Russian had already made up his mind that Diego would lose the fight.

"You know that boy is gonna whip you like he always does," Paige said. "You're too young, too short, and Gaston's—too fine."

"Fine? Really?" Diego said as Ajax finished wrapping his hands.

"Maybe," Paige said.

"Don't underestimate our boy, Ms. Jordan," Ajax said. "I was as small as young Ribera once, and all I needed was focus to win against most foes."

Paige, Petey, and Diego looked at Ajax skeptically.

"Cyborg—please, you were never that small!"

"It's true. Sparring is all about being calm and focused," Ajax said.

"I am focused on him," Diego said.

"But you're always focused on the one power punch, a knockout," Ajax said. He laced Diego's gloves. "And that makes you easy to read—predictable. Gaston turns it against you."

"Yeah, D," Petey said, "you're stronger than he thinks. You gotta outsmart him."

Paige let out a sigh and put her hand on Diego's shoulder. "Maybe there's something I can do."

As Diego stepped into the ring, Paige sidled over next to Gaston, who was on the far side dancing in place, knocking his gloves together, a sheen of sweat on him from going rounds with Petey and Lucy.

"Hey there, *monsieur*," Paige said with a mischievous smile. She leaned into his ear and whispered something.

Gaston grinned. "Well, we already know how the *petit frère* will fare, so why don't I just take that now?" He leaned toward her like he was going to kiss her cheek, but Paige shoved him away.

"Not until it's over."

"What are you talking about?" Petey asked as Paige returned.

"I told Gaston that the winner of this match gets a kiss from one of the girls," Paige said.

"Paige!" Lucy gasped.

"I wish it could be both," Gaston said with a chuckle. "Sadly for you, only one lovely lady will get to know the thrill of these lips."

"Eww," Petey said.

Diego's eyes met Lucy's, but she looked away.

Gaston tapped him on the shoulder. Diego snapped back and saw him grinning. "Let's get this over with quick, okay, lover boy?"

"How about I flatten your face?" Diego said, and he threw a punch, but Gaston was out of the way well before it arrived, blocking with one arm and jabbing Diego in the ribs with the other. Diego stumbled.

"So predictable," Gaston said, knocking his gloves together.

Diego staggered back, stepped one way, darted the other, and threw a left hook—

Gaston was ready, and Diego's punch had barely arrived before Gaston's glove was right in his face.

Diego tumbled over, his jaw howling.

"Aha," Gaston said, grinning at Paige. "Now, on to the lips!"

"Get up, Diego," Petey urged.

Diego jumped up and took a step toward Gaston—but stopped. "Hey!"

"Oh ho, look who wants the other lip fattened," Gaston said. "After all, you won't be needing them."

Diego stood his ground. He realized that, in spite of all Gaston's *petit frère* comments, being shorter than Gaston might give him the advantage.

Gaston motioned with his gloves. "What are you waiting for?"

Diego thought about the lessons they'd learned the last couple of weeks. About what Ajax had said once about fighting a larger opponent. "When you fight the bigger man, he'll always underestimate you because you're small," he'd said. "And he'll always fight from the outside, where his reach is strong, so you've got to draw him in close where he doesn't like to fight, where your size and speed are more effective."

It was all about being calm, Diego realized. All about being still in the face of the attack. About *seeing* the next step. That was what Gaston always did . . . he was counterpunching. He'd let Diego try to punch him, and as soon as Diego swung, he'd be exposed, and Gaston would let him have it.

"Looks like I'm waiting for the *poulet*," Diego said, still not moving. "Who'd want to kiss that beak anyway?"

"Oh." Gaston clicked his tongue against the roof of his

mouth. "My *petit frère*, do you think you can beat me with insults?" He raised his gloves and edged toward Diego.

Diego stepped in, close enough to be an easy target. He faked like he was going to punch but at the last second held back. Gaston reacted, feinting and then swinging. Diego moved even closer. He slipped under Gaston's swing and stepped in, blocking the direction that Gaston always went to. For a half second, Gaston looked confused as he found himself within Diego's range. Diego heard the taller boy gasp for the first time. Ajax's words came back to him: *Stay in close going upstairs then downstairs; working combinations to the body keeps him off balance.*

Diego stared in disbelief.

"Way to go, D!" Petey shouted.

Redford steamed in delight, raising his arm to the sky.

Diego smiled and realized he'd been holding his breath.
His hands were shaking inside his gloves. So much for being
calm. But he nodded and turned toward Lucy.

"So . . . ," he started to say—

But hands grabbed him by the shoulders.

"I didn't say which girl was going to give the kiss," Paige said with a devious smile. "And, boy, do you need a shower."

Lucy's face was bright red as she laughed into her hand.

"Ribera," Gaston said, staggering to his feet and rubbing his head, "that one belonged to me."

"Not today it didn't," Paige said. "And my kisses belong to *me*."

"Yowch," Petey said under his breath.

"Well, well." The captain joined them, unsmiling. "Ribera, in the ring you are prone to anger and are easily distracted. You choose terrible tactics that cause you to fail repeatedly."

"But—" Diego said.

"But . . . I did not see that boy in the ring today. I saw a glimpse of the warrior to be." He put a hand on Diego's shoulder. "A young man who found a way to prevail against a stronger adversary."

"A lucky swing," Gaston said, wiping at his mouth.

"Gaston," the captain said. "The boy has earned a respite from your tongue."

"Aye, Captain."

"I have new jobs for all of you today," the captain said. "The end is approaching, and we have many preparations to make."

Lucy and Paige were ordered to replenish the munitions on the *John Curtis*, while the captain sent Petey and Diego out across the bay to retrieve a list of spare engine parts from the ship's graveyard.

"That was some KO," Petey said as they sat on Redford's shoulder. Daphne was scurrying back and forth across Redford's head and operating chair, barking whenever a gull or pteranodon circled near.

"Settle down, girl," Diego said, petting her, but she darted by as another winged creature came within range.

Diego turned back to Petey. "Thanks. It's a relief to shut

Gaston up for once."

Redford left the bay and crossed the emerald waters
between huge piles of ships and airplanes lying on the out-
croppings of coral, almost as if they'd been placed there.

Redford blew a plume of steam.

"Yes, Redford. It is very beautiful here."

"And dangerous," Petey said, peering down at the water.

"An elasmosaurus," Petey said. "You can tell by the elongated neck." He turned back to Diego. "Say, how do you know what Redford is saying?"

"I feel like I understand him. But I'm guessing, really."

Petey narrowed his eyes, then leaned over and opened the interface panel. "*This is very beautiful,*" he read off the tablet. "That was a pretty accurate guess."

Diego shrugged. Was he understanding Redford now? He still felt a dull ache in his mouth. There was so much he didn't get. He thought about telling Petey about his newest discovery, about Daphne, the turtles, and losing the tooth.

He scanned the wrecks instead. "That looks like the one the captain was talking about."

Redford let them off on the deck of a nearby ship, then began salvaging parts from the wreck's engine.

"So tell me," Petey said, "what was it like?"

"What?" Diego asked, though he was already blushing.

"Come on. That was your first kiss, right?"

"You know it was," Diego said. "But it wasn't exactly a kiss. More like an attack on my face. Her lips were, like, strong."

"Strong?"

"Like, made of iron. If I hadn't had a fat lip already, she might have given me one."

They both laughed.

Diego turned away, wanting to change the conversation topic, and spied something in the distance.

"Petey, check it out. See that little boat out there?"

The boat was marooned on a rock, hanging off it at a cock-eyed angle. It had a long, sleek hull that came to a sharp point, and its low, stubby cockpit was dotted with antenna. Small machine guns were mounted at the bow and stern.

"World War II patrol torpedo boat," Petey said. "They were called PT boats."

"Do you see what's on the deck?"

Petey shaded his eyes. "Are those what I think they are?"

"When Redford's done, we'll check it out before we head back."

Redford filled his small barge with engine parts, and the two boys climbed back aboard. After a quick visit to the PT boat, they climbed onto Redford's shoulders for the return journey to the bay.

A short time later, they reached the *John Curtis*.

"Check it out," Petey said, pointing at the ship's new changes.

"Wow," Diego said. "Those reconfigurations and that paint job. Might be enough to throw off the Aeternum and give us the element of surprise. Brilliant work, sir!" he called up to the captain as they pulled up alongside.

"It was a group effort," he said. "You found the parts I requested." He looked over their haul and pointed to two metal cylinders. "You know those are useless if they're empty."

"If they were empty," Diego said, "I wouldn't have brought them back."

"What are they?" Lucy asked, joining the captain.

"Just something to make our odds of winning a little better," Diego said.

"I'd say those were Mark 18 torpedo launch tubes taken from a torpedo boat in the ship's graveyard, and if Diego is correct, each launcher carries a standard US Navy Mark 18 torpedo," the captain said.

"Exactly, sir," Diego said. "I'll have those torpedoes ready for battle."

"Good work," the captain said. "Now, let's get these parts on board and see about getting our new launchers mounted and prepped for the mission."

Redford lowered the boys to the deck. As Redford loaded the supplies onto the *John Curtis,* they watched Ajax operate Seahorse, carefully lowering the Kingfisher seaplane to a newly installed platform mounted on the back deck of the ship.

"Is that a new airplane catapult, sir?" Diego asked.

"Steam powered," the captain said. "All the changes make us look like a Yorktown salvage ship, including the reengineered paddle wheels to operate from the side. Our seaplane will appear to be for search and rescue."

"Until they're close enough to spot that modified front end, and the Vought F4U Corsair engine that Redford and I installed," Diego said.

"Ajax's side cannons will give them a fright, too," Petey said.

"With the way I fly," Gaston said, "by the time they see our modifications, it will be too late." His voice was muddled by his swollen nose. "What about you, Ms. Lucy? I saw you checking out the plane before. Would you like to learn how to fly?"

Lucy didn't respond.

"Gaston," the captain said. "We should head back to the castle."

Ajax arrived on deck, his shirt splattered with oily liquid.

"What happened to you?" Petey asked.

"One of Seahorse's hydraulic hoses came loose," he said, pulling off his shirt and turning to get a rag. Lucy was the first to see Ajax as he turned away, and she gasped. Then they all saw the scars. Crisscrossing patterns of them covered Ajax's back, jagged and deep.

"They are surprising, at first, I know," Ajax said, turning to face them.

"Are they . . . ?" Paige asked. "I mean . . ."

"Yes, but don't trouble yourself," Ajax said. "It was a long time ago, back when I was all man and not part machine, and yet not a man at all. The world I came from saw me as property. I was born in Jackson, Mississippi, and sold to a tobacco plantation in North Carolina. But I escaped and took a new name from my birthplace, and from the man that set to make me free: Abraham. Became Abraham Jackson, but folks just called me Ajax for short. I wore the Union blue of the Fifty-Fourth Massachusetts Infantry, fighting to free my brothers and sisters, and to ensure that children, that *you*, would never feel the pain of a whip on your back. But then the Time Collision brought me here, and I learned what true freedom could be." He stood and started working with the pressure gauges on the plane catapult.

"I'm sorry for *that* time, but this world isn't free, Ajax," Paige said. "We've still got scars on the inside. My parents still struggle, still face people who hate us because of the color of our skin."

"But you don't have to hate back." Ajax shook his head. "And at least you and your parents came into this world . . . as people. You are too young even to know how good you have it. As slaves, we were forbidden to learn to read. But in this time, there is no punishment . . . and no shame in wanting to read. And here I was, a free man learning from a Mid-Time schoolteacher who taught little kids. The captain put me in a school where the students there were older folks like me. Peoples of all colors and times . . . it was a privilege. And now I've read your Mid-Time books about the great changes, the leaders like Martin Luther King Jr. and Mahatma Gandhi, people who didn't have to raise a gun to change the world for the better. They fought, but in a new way. A better way. And now, here, after the Time Collision, we all have a chance like we never had before. You know your history, but you are no longer bound to it."

"I still feel like we are," Paige said. Ajax strode over to Paige, whose gaze had dropped.

"Yes," Ajax said. With his human hand, he lifted up her chin so her face caught the light. "But no one has to be. You

have the freedom to choose a better way."

Listening, Diego understood something he hadn't before. The captain and his men weren't just fighting to keep the children of this world alive, to "make the best of it" in this new world. They truly believed that this world was a chance that humanity would otherwise have never had. "We can literally make our own future," Diego said.

"Yes," Ajax said. "You are not resigned to the march of time that leads to the wasteland of the Elders. No matter what this world throws at you, you are truly free. Don't ever forget that."

"Did you lose your arm in the war?" Diego asked.

"I lost more than my arm," Ajax said. "And it was the war against Magnus that got me this beauty here." Ajax held up his arm. "But fighting for this world was worth it." Ajax tipped his hat and turned back to check on the catapult.

"This world is a second chance." The captain arrived behind them.

He gazed off the back deck as the sun set across the harbor. The kids joined him. Ajax kept working. Light painted the clouds in orchid hues. Birds chirped and darted over the treetops. The captain glanced at Petey. His eyes were shut, the orange light bathing his face.

"Gaston and Ajax have been through a lot," the captain said. "I have asked so much sacrifice of them. Most of my men have paid with their lives. They have all been like sons and daughters to me, and yet still I believe as Ajax does."

"Sir . . . ," Diego said. Now seemed as good a time as any.

"What happened to your family?"

The captain sighed. "They died long ago, before the Time Collision. My soldiers are my family now."

"And us," Lucy said.

"We should head back to the castle," the captain said. "You all need a good night's sleep. Tomorrow we will make our final preparations."

CHAPTER TWENTY

Games of War
and Jubilation

The next morning, Diego was up and on the beach with the sunrise, in line with everyone else. After sprints and exercises, they huddled with the captain and reviewed their mission, the captain diagramming each team's position in the sand. Afterward, they split into their pairs and spent the whole day running their routines, again and again in the hot sun.

Hours later, Diego caught up with the captain walking along the beach.

"You did well," the captain said as Diego walked by his side. "We are ready."

"Captain," Diego said, "I have a request—a favor, really.

Would you mind if I went back to the hangar? There's something I'd like to work on. It's a surprise, sort of. For my friends. Because we are leaving in two days, I wanted to ask if we could have tomorrow to ourselves."

"That will be fine. You've earned it. But on the condition that Gaston is allowed to join you."

"Oh, um, sure."

"Gaston has never had friends his own age. You and your Rangers are the first. Have your day, but your evening . . . that belongs to me."

"Yes, sir!"

Diego headed down to the beach and got a lift from Redford over to the hangar. Inside, he sent Redford in search of a spare airplane wing. Diego found a supply cart and started making his way through the hangar, collecting the parts he'd need for his project.

He was passing the Sea Fury when he heard a rustling sound.

Lucy popped up out of the cockpit. "Oh, hey," she said, and climbed down.

"What are you doing here?" Diego asked.

"Ah, nothing, just had some free time." She jumped to the floor with a book under her arm.

"What's that?"

"Nothing." She glanced toward the doors. "I should get back to the castle."

"Sure," Diego said. He pointed at the book she held. The

leather binding looked familiar. "Isn't that the flight manual for the Sea Fury?"

"Oh, um," Lucy held it out. "Yeah, but . . ."

"Lucy, I saw how excited you were about the plane the other day."

"Okay . . . here's the truth. When I turned twelve, one of Georgie's friends took me up in a Tiger Moth. He was a pilot with the RAF. It was so amazing! And he let me fly for a few minutes, and I still dream of it every day. Ever since then I've wanted to be a pilot. Not that it's really possible for someone like me."

"That's what I dream of being, too," Diego said. "And why isn't it possible? There have been a lot of amazing female pilots. Amelia Earhart . . ."

"Harriet Quimby," Lucy continued, "Jackie Cochran, and of course your mother, but . . ." Lucy's face fell. "That's not the life I'm meant for."

"Why not?" Diego said. "Remember what Ajax said? This is a different world."

"Not so different," Lucy said. "My father is a Traditionalist to the core. He has my life mapped out. He even has suitors in mind for when I come of age."

"Suitors? You mean like . . . a husband?"

Lucy nodded.

"That's . . . that's awful," Diego said. "Your dad has no right to do that. To decide your future for you."

"Victorian values aren't like your Mid-Timers'," Lucy said.

"There are expectations and obligations to the honor of my family. A marriage to the right family, possibly a noble one, would ensure the Emersons' place in the British kingdom."

"You mean your *father's* place," Diego said.

Lucy sat up straight. "Yes, for him, but for my mother and brothers, too."

"Yeah, but there has been open trade and travel to England for the last sixteen years," Diego said. "From what I've read, London is like my city. It has the same time-divided cultures and all the same problems that we do."

Lucy shrugged. "That doesn't make a difference for me."

Diego could tell that she didn't want to discuss her future any further. "Well, I think if you want to fly, you should."

"Thanks. What are you up to?"

"I'm gathering parts for something. Want to help me?"

"I'm supposed to get back. Gaston and Paige are in the library. There's only so much of Gaston's flirting that she can take before she loses it. I have to make sure we're all in one piece for the mission." She smiled. "Especially after what you did to him yesterday."

Diego smiled back. "Can I at least walk you out?"

"That would be very proper of you," she said with a curtsy.

They walked quietly through the gloom. Diego couldn't think of what to say next. He was still eyeing the machinery around him for the last few parts he needed.

Lucy gasped. "Oh, would you look at that."

"Oh yeah," Diego said. "That's a—"

"1929 Blower Bentley," Lucy finished for him.

"I'm impressed."

"As you should be," Lucy said. She ran her finger over the dusty hood. "I've seen this car around London, and I adore it. Georgie's favorite is the Aston Martin DB5, but it's the Bentley for me."

"That biplane is pretty cool, too," Diego said. "It's too bad it's so wrecked. The Bentley's been stripped of a lot of parts, too. It would be great if we could fix them up."

Lucy breathed deeply. "Do you really think you could do that?"

"Anything's possible, although that thing is in pretty rough shape."

"Pity that," Lucy said. "Here I thought you were going to charge into the challenge like an Emerson." She stepped toward the door. "Off to rescue Paige."

Diego saluted her. She smiled and saluted back.

Diego made his way to the machine shop, his mind buzzing with ideas, and found that Redford was hard at work. Redford had separated the aluminum sheeting from an old airplane wing they'd found and laid the pieces next to the milling machines and saws.

"Nice job, buddy," Diego said. "We're going to use that to make a present for my friends."

Redford blew a puff of steam.

Diego cocked his head. "What do you mean, there's a present for me?"

Redford nodded to the table near the saw. Diego spied a small device resting there.

"It looks like an old camera," Diego said, picking it up. "It even has film . . . wow. But how am I going to make the pictures?"

Redford made a noise like a croak.

"Really? Well, I guess that makes sense. It's like Volcambria is the most amazing scrap yard ever."

Redford puffed again.

"Okay, we'll try it later, but let's get started on this wing."

Diego worked tirelessly. After a while his shoulders and fingers ached. When he looked up to take a break, he noticed the light had changed. Outside it was night. *Just a little longer,* he thought.

The next time he looked up, the project was finished, and a faint purple light filtered through the hangar doors.

Diego staggered toward it, his body tingling with exhaustion. He stepped out into the cool, predawn world. He rubbed his head. "Redford," he called over his shoulder. "We worked all night."

Redford puffed, *Obviously.*

"It wasn't obvious to me! I thought it was, like, midnight or something. I'm starving."

Diego made his way back to the castle through the deep jungle shadows. Purple land crabs skittered out of his way and into their sand burrows. The air smelled sweet, damp, and the bay was nearly as smooth as glass. Distant clouds on the horizon had begun to glow a deep pink. Diego felt like he was the last person in the world.

His footsteps echoed in the silent castle. He reached the galley and found a plate of food still out on the table. A pair of mice scampered from it. His dinner.

He took the plate and pushed through the kitchen door, only to find the captain standing over the central table. He glanced up. "Well, you are in one piece. . . . Good."

Diego yawned.

"Is your surprise ready?"

Diego rubbed his head. "Yeah, though I barely remember the last few hours. What are you doing?"

"A surprise of my own." Boleslavich wore oven mitts. With a spatula, he slid small, circular cakes from a skillet onto plates. They smelled sweet and tangy. "*Syrniki*," he said, "though the cheese we received from New Chicago cannot match that of my homeland. Here, eat."

He pushed a plate toward Diego, then added a slice of bread and a boiled egg.

"Delicious," Diego said through a mouthful of the warm cake.

"I like to make them on the morning before a departure."

Diego felt a twinge of nervousness. Working all night had kept his mind off what they were about to do. He wondered if he would even have slept had he come back.

He ate fast, his *syrniki* finished in moments. "That was great," he said.

The captain was still busy at the stove. "The others should be up soon."

Diego slugged a cup of coffee. He hated the bitter taste but was certain he'd need the energy. "Can you tell them to meet me in the hangar after breakfast?"

The captain nodded, his hands busy preparing the food. "Thanks."

Diego headed back to the hangar and checked over his work. All seemed ready. He threw a tarp over it and then sat down against the saw table leg. He thought he'd rest for a second. . . .

"Hey, D, wake up!"

His eyes fluttered open to see Petey, Paige, Lucy, and Gaston standing over him.

"This is where you spent the night?" Gaston asked.

"Mmm . . . I . . ." Diego got to his feet. He tried to rub the sleep from his eyes, but he was still so tired. "Okay, I have something to show you guys. Redford?"

Redford had been standing by the tarp since Diego had sat down, waiting patiently. He pulled it back and revealed Diego's all-night project.

"Whoa!" Petey exclaimed.

"Are those what I think they are?" Gaston asked.

"Yeah," Diego said. "Tomorrow, destiny owns us. But today, let's ride."

"I'm game," Paige said.

Lucy beamed at him.

"All right, let's do this." And they took off.

"These handle amazing!" Petey shouted over the wind.

"Genius!" Lucy called.

"Slamming!" Paige shouted.

A. Baltimore © 2017

"Now watch this!" Diego called. He switched on his dad's Walkman from his pocket and affixed it to a chest strap. A cord hung there, and he plugged it into the bright yellow device. When he tapped the screen and pushed a big green button, music began to blare from two small speakers mounted to the tops of his backpack straps.

"That's sick!" Petey shouted.

They spent the day skimming across the island, turning its every feature into a giant skate park. The hours passed in a blur of screaming wind and laughs. They dropped in over waterfalls, snatched guavas from a tree and ate them in flight, played hide-and-seek in the ship graveyard, and for long stretches, thought of nothing other than board, air, and speed.

Later, breathless, their voices raw, they flew to the highest peak on the caldera rim and admired the view of the lush island and the endless sea. "It looks like Neverland," Lucy said, her face serene in the sun.

"This whole world is Neverland," Petey said.

"We all know that story, don't we?" Paige realized. "No matter what time we're from."

"But we will all be growing up tomorrow," Petey said.

Diego didn't want to think about that. "Hey," he said, pointing down the coast. "We haven't explored there yet."

He led them down the mountainside to a small strip of white sand, the inner rim of a shallow cove, its turquoise water protected by a coral reef.

The five sat together and watched the sun fall to the sea.

As its orange belly dipped beneath the horizon, the silhouettes of dorsal fins sliced through the water beyond the reef.

Petey lay back, lacing his fingers behind his head. Paige whispered something in Gaston's ear, and the two shared a laugh. Diego suddenly felt very aware of Lucy sitting next to him. His heart was speeding up, like this was some kind of moment, and yet what could he say?

Diego jumped when he felt her fingers creep over his. Lucy folded her fingers into his. There was only a narrow space between them. None of their friends could see. Their hands stayed that way as the sun sank and dipped out of sight, leaving a cool, lavender world. Flocks of feathered pink clouds paraded across the sky.

Finally, Lucy pulled her hand back. She was the first to stand. "We should get back. We're Lost Boys no longer. Tomorrow we are Rangers."

"Let's take a photo," Diego said. He pulled out the camera. "I think this thing will work."

"All right, everyone in." Diego held the camera out as everyone leaned in close. "I can't get us all in the frame. Maybe if we duck . . ."

"You all stand at the water's edge," Gaston said, taking the camera. "I'll take the photo."

"But then you won't be in it," Paige said.

"I'm not one of your Rangers." He smiled when he said it, but Diego thought he heard a note of disappointment. "Say *fromage*," Gaston said.

"How did we look?" Diego asked as he took back the camera.

Gaston nodded. "You look like a band of heroes."

"Let's get going!" Petey said, shooting up into the sky. "Last one back has to clear the dining table!"

They flew through the deepening dark, back to the castle. They were quiet as they walked inside, making occasional jokes, but the laughter died away quickly.

"You're back!" the captain called from the library. "Hurry to your rooms and change. I'll expect you down here at the top of the hour!"

"What's he talking about?" Diego wondered as they climbed the stairs.

"It's a Vanguard tradition," Gaston said with a knowing smile.

Diego and Petey returned to their room to find strange outfits on their beds.

Diego was slipping on his tuxedo coat when there was a knock at the door and Gaston popped in. "How are we doing?"

"Can you help me with this?" Diego asked as he fumbled with his tie.

"You know, I once had a little brother," Gaston said. "He was shorter than me, like you, and funny. He was a tough kid, but he didn't have the right hook you have. I teased him all the time."

Diego expected Gaston to continue, but he didn't. "Did you give him a hard time like you do to me?"

"Of course." Gaston almost smiled, but not quite. "You two are my brothers now," he said. "And it will be my honor to fight beside you."

"You too," Diego said as Gaston finished the tie. Then he reached up and messed up Diego's freshly combed hair.

"Jerk," Diego said.

"My pleasure," Gaston said.

Downstairs they found that the captain and Ajax had dressed up as well—the captain in a black Russian naval uniform and polished black knee-high boots, his beard trimmed and hair combed back; Ajax in his Union blue dress uniform with sash. He had replaced his giant mechanical arm with a smaller one that was polished to a mirror finish.

The two had prepared a huge meal, many courses that spanned the different regions of the new world. Diego smelled the tangy spices of India and the sweet marinades of Cubahna, even the tantalizing aroma of roasted Italian beef from New Chicago.

Everything was laid out on fine, antique silver plates. The captain had set up a Victrola that played vinyl records of classics like Mozart and Vivaldi.

"Holy crow!" Petey said as Lucy and Paige walked through the large oak-framed door leading into the dining room.

"This is my parents' music," Lucy said. The men turned to see Paige and Lucy dressed in sassy, elegant dresses from the Roaring Twenties, with delicate jeweled and feathered headbands. Lucy wore a pearl necklace; Paige, a ruby pendant.

Diego jumped to his feet and moved to slide out Lucy's chair. Gaston did the same for Paige.

"Why, thank you," Lucy said.

"Sure," Diego said. He was struck by the long line from her ear to her shoulder, the way her cheeks lifted when she smiled, the glimmer playing between her eyes and her necklace.

They sat and found that their glasses included a small amount of wine.

"A toast," the captain said.

Everyone raised a glass.

"May the world stay made. And may we prevail."

"Hear, hear!" Gaston called.

When they were finished eating, the captain put on a new record with faster, peppier music. "We shall dance!" he said.

Diego stared into his plate. He didn't dance.

Ajax and Paige took to the floor, alongside the captain and Lucy.

"Here goes nothing," Petey said as the first song ended. He took Paige's hand from Ajax, while Gaston and Lucy began to dance.

"Dang, Petey," Paige said as the song began, "this isn't some kind of polka!" She stepped back and rubbed at her foot.

"My mom said you can polka to anything," Petey said.

"It's all I know."

"Not everything," Paige said.

Ajax had put on a new record, and when the next song began, Paige froze.

"What is it, Paige?" Lucy said.

"This is one of my daddy's favorite songs." She quickly composed herself, walked to the captain, and held out her hand. The captain bowed, and the two took the floor.

"You dance wonderfully, Ms. Jordan," the captain said.

"And you, Captain, are dashing in uniform," Paige said. "I used to stand on my father's feet when I was a little girl and dance with him to this song. It's Nat King Cole—"

"'Unforgettable,'" the captain said. "It's a lovely song."

"You know, sir . . . you would've made a great father."

Diego was impressed that Paige would speak to the captain that frankly.

"My daughter would've been around your age, Ms. Jordan, and it would've honored me . . . if she had turned out to be anything like you."

"Thank you, sir," Paige said.

As the dance partners drifted apart and the room became silent, Diego thought he might get out of it. But then the captain chose another song, and Lucy tapped Diego on the shoulder.

"Mr. Ribera," she said, curtsying. "Since you are the only gentleman who has yet to ask me to dance . . . it falls on me to ask you. I know how improper that is, but I do hope you'll forgive me, and do me the honor."

"Do I have to?"

"Oh, come on," Paige called as she spun by with Gaston. "Man up and dance already!"

Diego blushed red as he got to his feet and took Lucy's hand. "What do I do?" he asked.

"The other hand goes here," she said, pulling it toward her waist. "And then you move your feet like this." She shuffled her feet, and Diego tried to keep his in rhythm . . . and stepped on her toes.

"I should stop," he said, pulling away. She held him back and looked into Diego's eyes as she leaned down and slipped off her heels.

"Now you'll have to be careful." Lucy pulled him in closer and smiled.

Diego smiled back. "Okay, I'm sorry in advance about your toes."

"Shush," she said, and leaned close against him. Diego felt her cheek against his, and smelled her hair, and tried his best not to make them fall over.

They made slow circles around the floor. "I knew you'd get the hang of it," she said. Then she spoke so close to his ear that Diego felt the warmth of her breath. "Be careful in York-town, okay? Think before you act, you daredevil."

Diego smiled, but fought nervous tremors. "I will. You too, Lucy. Do you still have my mother's chopstick?"

"Yeah," she said.

"Good. It will bring you luck."

They didn't speak again, just danced, until the song ended and the needle scratched.

PART THREE
Until It Turns No More

In the end, it's not the years in your life that count. It's the life in your years.

CHAPTER TWENTY-ONE

Where All Paths Lead

Diego woke to the sound of the paddle wheel churning rhythmically and the occasional *whump* of the bow against a wave. For a moment, he didn't know where he was, but then he smelled the brine of the open ocean and heard Petey's sleeping breaths above him.

They'd boarded the *John Curtis* the night before after dinner. The captain had said they'd all sleep better if they were already in motion, and they had a long way to go.

Diego lay there for a moment, fear brewing in his belly. He thought about the night before, about dancing with Lucy, about her voice in his ear, her cheek against his.

Sleep would not come, so Diego slipped out of bed,

dressed, and headed for the galley. He smelled bacon and coffee and thought of his last good morning at home, before all this began.

He found Paige in the galley, sitting alone at the long table. She sipped tea and stared into the boiler, the light from the flames flickering on her face.

"Hey." Diego sat beside her and filled a mug with coffee.

Paige eyed him and his mug. "You're too young for coffee. It's going to make you jittery."

"We're too young for a lot of things, but that isn't stopping us." He sipped and puckered. "And it can't make me any more jittery than I already am."

"You and me both." Paige wrapped both hands around her mug and held it close to her face, letting the steam filter over her.

"Of course you're not worried. You're tough as iron," Diego said.

"Ha! When you live past Ninety-Ninth and Washtenaw, you learn how to put on a tough face. You have to be hard 'cause all you got is yourself and your family to watch your back."

"Lucy is family?"

"She's my girl."

"You know I would never do anything to hurt her—"

"He'd say the same thing."

"Who?"

"My big brother, Alejandro. We called him Ali for short. Truckloads of courage, unbreakable heart, never thought anything through, he just . . . *did*. That was my Ali's way." Paige started slicing up an apple and offered Diego some. "And *you* are just like him. Do you know the Breakers factory down where Old Chicago meets the black neighborhoods? That's where I met Lucy."

"Really?" Diego knew the place, but not that Lucy had ever been anywhere near there.

"See, when Steam Timers need to get downtown quick, they take the Dan Ryan waterway, and that takes you past the Breakers. One day I was skating with my crew, and guess who shows up at the fence watching us . . . pretty little Victorian doll all trussed up in some dress. She was on her way home with her mom in a broken taxi boat.

"Her mom was arguing with the boat driver, not minding Lucy, and so this fearless, delicate little bird wanders away from her momma and up onto the Breakers blacktop."

"That place is . . ."

"Yeah, you know it. It's no place for a Steam-Timing British white girl. Anyways, she's watching my brother and me skate, and she calls us over. I'm thinking, 'Is this girl for real?' and I say, 'What you want, *shante vanilla*? You shouldn't be coming around here.' And Princess Goldilocks says"—Paige mimicked Lucy's accent—"'My brother and I learned to ride the wheeled planks back in London with some East End bruisers. I got quite good, but you appear to be even better. I'd wager that with proper instruction, I'd be great, maybe better than you. Would you teach me?' Can you believe that?"

Diego laughed, just imagining the scene.

"She was all fearless and proud like the queen of England herself come to visit, and if she was terrified to talk to us, you couldn't tell. Even though we were probably the first black people she ever talked to." Paige smiled, remembering it. "But dang, the courage in this girl! My brother and I laughed—we couldn't believe it. Then Margaret Emerson comes up and says, 'Get away from my daughter, you street savages!' That's when it went bad.

"This older boy, real tough thug—T-boz. Well, he comes up and starts yelling at Margaret and Lucy to leave, then shoves Margaret."

Paige snapped her fingers.

"Without thinking, Alejandro grabs T-boz and puts him to the ground so Lucy and her mom could get away. Afterward, my brother let T-boz go."

Paige stopped, and for a moment, Diego didn't think she would go on. "T-boz doesn't take to being disrespected on his turf and in front of his crew. It made him look weak. So he stood up and got in Ali's face, and it might have gone real wrong right there if a police boat hadn't come over when they spotted Margaret and Lucy on the Breakers property. T-boz bolted. Lucy's momma tried to give my brother some money for helping them. Can you imagine? Ali politely said no, and those policemen picked 'em up and brought them home.

"Next day," Paige went on, "a little kid up and steals my skateboard and runs into that ruined chocolate factory. I told

Ali to let it go, but he wouldn't. So he runs in there . . . and T-boz and a bunch of his boys were waiting for him." Paige got up and poured herself a mug of coffee. "Alejandro would've been seventeen this year. Now my momma and daddy just have me."

"Paige . . . I'm sorry."

She sat back down, clutching her mug with both hands. "A few weeks after, I ran into Margaret and Lucy while I was skating near the dinosaur meat markets at Dusable Harbor. She called me over to thank me for what my brother did. Told me she'd read about what happened to him in the papers and said she was sorry. Margaret told me that she and Lucy went to the market every day after her homeschooling and that if I wanted to . . . maybe I could skate with Lucy while they were there. That was after school started last semester. Lucy and I have been friends ever since."

"I don't know what to say," Diego said.

"You're not supposed to say anything. . . . You're supposed to be smarter than Ali was. That's what you can be. Don't hurt my girl and don't get yourself killed tomorrow. That's what you can do for me. Deal?"

"Deal. And hey, be careful out there too, and don't distract Gaston."

"Whatevs, Ribera."

Diego leaned over and hugged Paige. She was stiff as a board, but after a moment, she hugged him back.

"I gotta get breakfast plated."

"You want help?"

"Nope."

Diego finished his coffee and stepped out onto the deck. The sun had crested the misty horizon and bathed his face.

"There he is." Diego turned and saw Petey and Lucy coming his way. "We thought you might have pulled another all-nighter."

"Nah."

Petey and Lucy leaned on either side of him.

"This time tomorrow we'll be in Yorktown," Lucy said.

"Yeah," Diego said. He wanted to add something else, but nothing came. The future hung there between them, getting closer.

CHAPTER TWENTY-TWO

The Battle at Yorktown

D iego stood in the crow's nest, staring into the inky pre-dawn. In front of them was a small island, its surface splattered with bone-white droppings from pteranodons and pterosaurs. It was called Jersey Devil Island, and it stood directly between the *John Curtis* and the distant skyline of Yorktown, keeping them out of sight.

His dad was close. Diego could feel it.

Less than four miles ahead, beneath the waves, his father was being held in an underwater power station that, if activated, would wipe him and every child of this world from existence. They had no idea how far Magnus and Balthus had gotten in their efforts to repair and restart the Quantum Reactor. They might be days away, still. Or only hours.

But Diego was near his father again, with a chance to save him.

He climbed down and joined the others in the galley. Ajax and the captain had laid out weapons for each of them.

"These are concussive hand cannons," the captain said, running his hand over the table. "CHCs. They work using an antigravitational field, like your boards. A half pull of the trigger will stun a three-hundred-pound man. A full pull will make sure your target never rises again.

"These are air corps 9mm P26s for you two," the captain said, handing the two pistols to Paige and Gaston. "Waterproof.

"Check your watches with mine," the captain said, holding out his wrist. After they checked their times, he turned to Lucy. "You're in command now, Miss Emerson. Mr. Kowalski, you are navigator and first mate. I don't need to remind you that this ship is a part of my family."

"We'll take care of her, sir," Lucy said.

"Gaston, Paige, report to the Kingfisher and await my launch order. Your mission is to take out the battleship in Yorktown Harbor."

"Aye, sir," Gaston said.

"Ajax, Diego, and I will be in Seahorse and make for the reactor. We will all be in contact via these radio devices that Diego has constructed." The captain motioned to a set of handheld phones connected to small speakers. Diego had found a way to refurbish and pulse shield individual two-way radio units for each person to wear. He and Redford had found enough walkie-talkies inside some of the ships in the wreckage surrounding Volcambria. It amazed him how much of the derelict technology rusting away in those scrap piles was salvageable. He wasn't sure how well the communication system would work over these distances and, like his Walkman, the disruptor fuses he'd placed inside them would overheat and have to reset every few minutes, but their tests yesterday had indicated that they would work.

The captain took a deep breath. "You've been tested in battle. You've been trained, your skills honed. Your minds are sharp, and our purpose is true. Do not falter, and do not fail each other." With a quick nod, he turned and marched out.

The rest of them stood there, the air heavy and silent.

"Good luck," Diego said to Petey, and those words flew from one to another, and they hugged and shook hands.

The captain's voice sounded over the pipe line. "Everyone report to your battle station."

Diego breathed deeply. "Let's do this."

Moments later, the Kingfisher hummed across the waves and lifted into the sky. Diego settled into his seat in Seahorse, and Ajax sealed the outer hatch and the intake valves.

As they descended into the blue depths, Diego saw the *John Curtis*'s engines spin to life, churning the water and startling the great shadow of a nearby archelon.

"This is the captain, over," Lucy said on the radio system. "We're moving into position."

Boleslavich chuckled. "Now she's the captain."

"This is Kingfisher, over," Gaston said, his voice crackling with static. "We're in the air and proceeding to target. The sun should be at our backs when we hit Yorktown."

"Godspeed to you both," Boleslavich said over his radio. "And Gaston, remember, that Aeternum battleship has two ready-launch fighter planes. Destroy that ship before they launch."

"Petey's headed to the crow's nest with the spyglass," Lucy said. "Captain, out."

"Here comes the sun," Gaston said over the radio. "And away we go."

Diego focused on piloting Seahorse around the rocky skirts of Jersey Devil Island. They cleared its shallow flanks, and the seafloor dropped away to a sandy shelf lit in cool blues. Lights shimmered in the murky distance, forming concentric circles.

"Turning off the exterior lights," Ajax said. They'd been essential for navigating around the Devil, but now their primary concern was stealth.

Diego brought them down to the shelf. Not far to their left, the world dropped away into fathomless darkness. The light was dim down here, but there was still enough filtered sun to give the rippled sand a ghostly shimmer. Schools of thick gray fish, enormous mantas, and a small basking shark all moved slowly out of Seahorse's way.

"Hopefully they won't decide that we're food," Ajax said.

The undersea world was as beautiful as anything Diego had ever seen, but he kept his focus straight ahead. It seemed like hours passed in the ten minutes it took for them to close on their glowing target. There were teeth of rock here and there in the sand, and Diego maneuvered from one to the other, hoping it shielded their approach.

"How are we doing up there?" the captain said into his radio.

"*John Curtis* holding steady," Lucy said.

"No sign of activity from here," Petey added.

"This is Kingfisher," Gaston said. "We are bearing true toward the target. All clear and—wait a minute."

Silence.

"What is it?" the captain asked.

"We've got a bogey," Paige said, her voice tight. "Trying to identify . . ."

"It's an Aeternum Me 109. He's pulling up alongside us . . . ," Gaston said.

Diego could hear him and Paige conversing tensely but couldn't make out their words.

"What's happening?" the captain asked.

"What's up, Mr. Enemy Pilot!" they heard Paige call. "Yep, don't mind me, we just—"

They heard a gun cocking . . . then the radio went dead.

"Paige . . . Gaston?" Diego said.

There was no reply.

"I think the fuses reset," Diego said. "It might be a few minutes before—"

"It's okay," the captain said. "Gaston is a seasoned and

skilled fighter pilot. They can handle one Aeternum fighter. Now, our focus needs to be here."

He pointed out the window, and Diego narrowly missed an outcropping of rock. "Sorry."

"There she is," the captain said.

"Is my dad down there?" Diego asked.

"He and Lucy's father were brought to fix the nuclear ignition sequencer. It's inside the dome of that power station."

Which meant they were close.

"That cable car is a good sign. It's here, so that means *they* are still there. According to Wallace's spies, it should be Magnus and only a few men. We'll dock at that second set of air locks, on the other side," the captain said.

Diego brought them to the far side of the structure, stopped Seahorse, and powered down its engines to silence. High above, he could see the bellies of the two Aeternum warships bobbing on the surface.

He flexed his fingers on the controls. Now they had to wait. Once Gaston and Paige launched their attack, it should draw off the warships.

"If that attack plane took them out," Ajax said, "this will all be for nothing."

The captain activated his radio. "Kingfisher, come in. Status? Kingfisher, over."

All they heard was the hiss of silence.

"Could be the radio's acting up," Diego said again. "At this depth, maybe—"

"This is Kingfisher, back on the air!" Paige shouted over the radio. "That plane we encountered bought our disguise and peeled off—so we're cool. About to break through the clouds here and . . . Oh my God, is that New York? It doesn't look like any of the pictures in our books!"

"We're clearing the city and sighted the battleship."

The speakers exploded with the sound of metal being torn apart.

"Holy crap, it followed us . . . the 109! We—" Her voice was interrupted by the chatter of machine gun fire. Distantly, they heard Gaston cursing in French.

And then the crackle of silence.

"Lucy, Petey, keep the radio silent until there is anything to report or until we've reestablished contact with the Kingfisher. Seahorse over and out," the captain said.

"Understood, Seahorse, *Curtis* over and out."

The captain checked his watch. "We can't wait any longer."

"But sir," Ajax said. "Those ships are still there."

"It's now or never. The longer we wait, the greater the risk of being discovered. Diego, if you please."

Diego docked at the air lock and peered into the darkened corridor beyond its thick doors but didn't see signs of anyone walking around. *Dad,* he thought. *I'm right here.*

"Hand me your gun," the captain said. Diego did, and the captain checked it and handed it back to him. "According to the schematics from Wallace's spies, your father, Magnus, and the others will be three floors down in the NIS launch chamber. We'll find them, take out the Aeternum, and bring our people out."

He and Ajax unbuckled from their seats and checked their weapons. "Seal this door behind us," the captain said. "If we don't return in thirty minutes, no matter what, you are to leave and return to the *John Curtis*, and all of you are to retreat immediately for Volcambria."

"Yes, sir." Diego wanted to go, but he knew he was the least trained for a fight. And someone had to guard Seahorse. Still, he hated the idea of waiting behind.

The captain opened the door and stepped into the corridor. "Diego, if we don't make it back in time, we're not coming back at all . . . and you will follow orders."

"Yes." Diego felt a lump in his throat as he said it.

The captain would succeed. Of course he would.

The two men took off down the passage.

Diego sealed the door, powered down the robot, and waited. He stared at the clock. Each minute seemed to take forever.

Suddenly, a deep thud reached them through the water, knocking Seahorse sideways. Diego fired up the stabilizers and checked the Seahorse's air lock for water breach.

"Torpedo impact!" Petey said, breaking radio silence.

"Paige and Gaston must have succeeded!" Lucy sounded relieved.

"Captain . . . anyone there?" Paige shouted. Then they heard the roar of Paige's guns. "Die, you son of a—"

Diego glanced out Seahorse's window. The sound of the radio might attract attention. He turned it down as low as it would go, but he couldn't bring himself to turn it off.

"Three o'clock!" Gaston shouted. "Coming out of the smoke!"

"Paige...we're here!" Lucy called over the radio. "Gaston!"

"Captain," Paige said, "if you can hear me—be advised the battleship is not destroyed! Repeat, the battleship is not destroyed! We were spotted and fired on, and the Aeternum

moved ships in to protect—"

"Paige, this is Diego! Say again, what is your status?"

"If anyone can hear us, we hit an Aeternum tanker ship . . .
got fighters on us . . . and . . ."

"Paige!" Lucy screamed. "Why won't she answer?"

"Lucy, it's no use," Diego said. "We can hear their broadcasts when they talk, but their radio must be damaged. They don't seem to hear us."

"I can see one of the gunships over the station leaving," Petey said.

Diego looked up. Both Aeternum engines spun, creating storms of bubbles. One of the ships slid forward, leaving massive wakes behind it.

"It's going, all right," Diego said. The chaos of bubbles and waves had subsided. One of the ships was gone, but the other still idled up there. Not leaving. "Crap."

The Kingfisher's transmission burst across the speakers. "Gaston, where's that fighter?" Paige shouted.

"He's in the clouds!" Gaston shouted. "But . . . we've got bigger problems!"

"Two more fighters!" Paige shouted. "Coming in at nine o'clock! Right! Bank right! We need to throw them off!"

"Anyone, if you . . . we're clear now and heading home."
They heard what sounded like crying. "Hang on, Gaston. . . ."

The radio went dead.

"Lucy," Diego said, "the captain went for our families. Sit tight and wait for the Kingfisher. Seahorse over and out."

"Copy that."

Silence.

They were late.

Diego sat there in the deep blue, trying not to freak out. He'd been afraid to try his radio again. He'd been lucky not to have been discovered already.

The minutes had crept by so slowly in the silent darkness, and yet now it had been ten minutes since the captain said they'd be back.

Something had gone wrong.

The captain had been clear: Diego was supposed to leave.

And yet . . . his dad, his friends, Lucy's family.

He couldn't go. He *wouldn't*.

Just then he heard something outside. He jumped up and peered out of the air lock. A lone figure approached from the station. He wore a hooded cloak and held a CHC pistol like Diego's. When he passed by a light, Diego saw that it was Balthus, stepping into the air lock.

Diego jumped back, gripping his pistol and aiming it at the door. He would shoot. He would have to . . .

But the door didn't open. Diego stepped back and saw

that Balthus had opened a control panel on the wall. *That's the panel to the lights.* He was going to engage the emergency floodlights, making Diego temporarily blind in the darkened bot. *Very clever.* He looked around. What could he do? Then he remembered the camera in his utility belt.

Diego hurried to the master override controls, reset the lights, and quickly pulled out his camera. He wound up the timer for the auto flash, attached it to the controls, and set the timer. Then he dashed back across the cockpit and hid behind the dive suits that were hanging in an equipment closet set in the wall.

The emergency lights blazed to life. Diego blinked hard, letting his eyes adjust. He heard the door open, and Balthus stepped in.

"Come now," Balthus whispered, "come out. I know you're in here. I'd hate to hurt you, too."

Diego shut his eyes so they would readjust. *Three . . . two . . . one . . .*

All the lights went out.

"What?" Balthus said. Diego's camera started to beep. He heard Balthus turn and step toward the sound. The camera shot a picture, emitting a series of sharp flashes. "Aah!"

Now! Diego popped out, aimed at Balthus's silhouette, and fired. The shot rang out, deafening in Seahorse's tight command compartment. Balthus staggered but didn't fall. His cloak vibrated violently but then settled down. *That cloak! The material absorbed the blast—*

Diego pulled down the dive suits between them and lunged for the air lock. Balthus raised his gun at him, but paused as Diego passed into the light of the air lock.

"Diego!" Balthus shouted.

Diego tore down the hall as thundering footsteps pounded behind him, and found himself in a huge cargo bay. It was full of shipping containers and high stacks of equipment and supplies, the space dimly lit by suspended globes. He ran down an aisle and ducked into an open container then fought to control his frantic breathing. His heart was beating so loud he was sure that Balthus could hear it.

"Come out, boy!" Balthus shouted, his voice echoing in the cavernous space. "We have your friends, the Russian and the cyborg. You want to see your dad, don't you?"

Diego pressed himself against the cold metal.

"I know what the Russian told you," Balthus said. Diego heard his boots echoing on the metal floor. "We aim to change the world back, it's true, but it won't be like he thinks. I can protect you. Keep you and your family alive and together. The power of the Quantum Reactors can do much more than simply change the world back."

Diego tried not to listen. He looked around for something to help him escape. The container was empty except for piles of random junk: useless circuit boards and gears, an open box piled high with valves. There were tools scattered around the floor. A stack of cans . . .

"There's so *much* we could do with the help of men like your father, and young men like you."

Diego's eyes settled on the cans. He crawled a few feet and inspected their labels. Paint, mineral spirits. One of the cans on the bottom contained machine oil.

"Don't try my patience." Balthus's footsteps echoed closer.

Diego slid out the can of oil from the stack an inch at a time, the other cans wobbling. He grabbed a screwdriver from nearby and started prying open the can. The screwdriver kept slipping, but then he got it.

He scrambled forward and dumped the oil in a swirling pattern outside the container, and it slowly spread into a wide pool. Then he stepped out of the container, tossing the screwdriver. It clanged off the wall and floor.

Balthus's footsteps slowed. He rounded the corner, a dark silhouette in the dim light. Diego aimed his gun at Balthus's chest, steadying it as best he could.

Balthus smiled and walked slowly toward him. "Come now, Diego. Put down your weapon. You're a smart boy. You know it won't work on my cloak."

"No," Diego said. "I want my people." *Come on . . . just a few more steps.*

As Balthus stepped out onto the oil, Diego raised the gun higher to aim at Balthus's face.

Looking down at the unconscious foe, Diego nearly cried out in disbelief. He'd done it! He took Balthus's gun, checked that it was loaded, and slipped it beneath his shirt. Diego grabbed a pile of rags from inside the container, and tied Balthus's arms and legs. He stood over him another moment, breathing hard. But he had to keep moving. Paige said they'd missed the battleship, and now it was coming. Time was short.

Diego followed the corridor, staying near the wall, and reached the opening to a massive chamber. He peered around the corner, his fingers clammy as he gripped his gun. When he saw the scene below, his breath stopped in his throat.

Diego saw his father, the sword tip at his throat, and Santiago's eyes tracked up and found him in the shadows, almost like he sensed his presence.

"Diego! Run!" Santiago shouted.

Magnus yanked Santiago's head back and raised the sword. "Well, the gods have delivered unto me a gift!"

"No!" Diego shouted, sprinting down the gantry to the

main floor, gun raised. He barely saw the bodies he passed, but he knew they were men from the Arlington station, men who'd worked with his father, and the horror of it all made him feel like, if he stopped moving, he would collapse, vomit. No. He had to keep going.

He moved forward, not noticing the cloak that Magnus wore . . . exactly like Balthus's.

Diego extended his arm, aiming the gun. Magnus hit Santiago in the head with the hilt of his sword and tossed him aside. Diego fired, but Magnus swept his cloak, and it absorbed the blast. He lunged, and before Diego could react, Magnus shoved him in the chest, sending him sprawling to the ground. Diego lost the gun. It skittered across the floor, and Magnus kicked it over the side of the platform. He stood over Diego, pinning him down with his boot.

"Welcome, young Ribera," Magnus said. "Now, what have you done to my chief scientist? I hope for your sake that he is unharmed."

Diego couldn't respond, the pain crippling him.

"We'll find out soon enough. This disruption by your captain has set us back considerably. I should kill you all, but it pleases me to hurt you instead. Santiago," Magnus barked. "It's time to input the activation code on the NIS."

"I'll never do it," Santiago said. He pushed himself back up to his feet, keeping a wary eye on the tip of Magnus's sword.

"Won't you?" Magnus lowered his sword and pressed the tip against Diego's abdomen. "Do it. Your boy is brave, but I'll show you what he's really made of."

"No!"

"Your captain and your child came to save you," Magnus said. "Ironic, don't you think, that if you'd given Boleslavich the weapon he asked you for all those years ago, your son's life would not be in danger now. But now you stand on the edge of giving me the means to destroy him in order that I may have back . . . my own."

"At the cost of countless millions."

Magnus didn't reply. He raised the sword to strike Diego.

"Fine. You win, Magnus." Santiago tapped at the computer console.

"Ignition codes accepted. Nuclear ignition sequencer activated."

"Good." Magnus withdrew his sword but leaned over Diego and put his boot against his throat. "For a *mistake,* you're quite the little soldier, aren't you? Your father probably never bothered to mention that he once swore an oath to me to help restore the world, only to break it for the love of a girl. Just so they could make you—another child that has no right to be."

Magnus pushed down harder. Diego grabbed at his neck, spots appearing in his vision. He squirmed, trying to get free. . . .

And as he did so, he felt a sharp pain in his back.

Balthus's gun.

"Let him go!" Santiago shouted.

Magnus twisted, raising his sword at Santiago. "Easy. Another step toward me and your boy dies."

Diego strained to reach his belt. He fiddled to get the gun free, felt it slip into his fingers.

"Hey, Magnus, here's *your* mistake!"

Magnus landed in a heap on the floor, right in front of the captain, who had just staggered to his feet.

"Diego," Santiago said.

Diego rolled over and pushed to his knees. He looked to the captain, now standing across the gantry, and to his father.

"You disobeyed my orders," the captain said.

"Yes, sir," Diego said, and he fell into his father's arms.

CHAPTER TWENTY-THREE

Fury and Love

Diego had imagined it, more times than he would ever have admitted. His father's arms around him again.

"My son," Santiago said. "How is this possible?"

"I had to find you," Diego said, fighting back tears.

"It's okay. It's all okay, now."

Diego nodded into his shoulder.

"Diego." He looked up to see the captain rubbing his head and slowly walking across the gantry toward them.

"I'm sorry, sir, but I—"

"What's done is done, Ranger, and I'm glad for it," the captain said.

"Alex," Santiago said, and the two men embraced.

"We'll speak of the past another day," the captain said. "For now, we have work to do."

"Captain, what happened? You and Ajax were gone way past the designated return time."

"We had the element of surprise," the captain said. "But we arrived to find Magnus executing some of your people. So we chose to intervene. Ajax and I were able to dispatch Magnus's men, but those accursed cloaks gave Magnus and Balthus the advantage."

"Your companion fought valiantly," George Emerson said, crossing the gantry with Georgie, "but the weapons proved no match against their cloak shields. The general subdued them with those concussive guns. I wish I could say the same for the engineers. That heartless savage butchered them."

"What about him?" Diego asked, pointing at Magnus.

"He's alive. The cloak dampened the blow but knocked him out," the captain said. On the main floor, Ajax was being helped back to his feet by the surviving engineers. Free of Magnus's sword pinned through his mechanized arm, he walked over and held the blade above the prone general. "I can end it here, sir."

At first, the captain didn't answer, and the engineers nearest Ajax backed away.

The station shuddered again.

"We will leave the general to this place," the captain said. "It is not long for this world. And enough blood has been spilled." The captain looked at the ragged survivors from New Chicago. They were beaten and thin. "Ajax, get those engineers back to Seahorse and wait for us there. The three of us will stay with the Emersons and deal with the crisis here."

"Captain," Diego said. "The Kingfisher sent an urgent message. The battleship wasn't destroyed. It's on its way here. If we're going to do something, sir, we better do it fast!"

"We must shut down this reactor now and return to the surface!"

Santiago shook his head. "I can't. The controls are locked. Nothing can stop the ignition sequence. We have to get off this platform before the reactor ignites and sends its power shooting toward the surface."

"What if that happens?" Diego said.

"Since this is the only station projecting the quantum energy stream, there will not be enough energy to create the field around the planet. But the energy will form a bubble around this station, likely about twenty miles across. It will only last ten or fifteen seconds, but that will be enough . . ."

"Enough time to kill every child inside its radius," Diego finished.

"Well then, we'd better hurry out of here—" George began, before an explosion rattled the reactor station down to its bolts.

"What was that?" Santiago shouted.

Water began to spring from wall joints, from seams and doorways, spraying in all directions.

"Kingfisher! *Curtis*! Report!" the captain shouted into his radio.

"This is Petey, sir! We are in a bad way up here. Taking heavy fire." Explosions and gunfire drowned out Petey's voice.

"Petey, report!" the captain shouted. But only static came through the radio. The station rattled again.

"Captain! Lucy, over. We've engaged one of the Aeternum gunships—getting hit hard! The Kingfisher is in—dogfighting three fighters and—Petey, get down!"

"My God," George said, horrified. "Is that my Lucy? You brought *Lucy* into this?"

"She came with me, sir," Diego said.

"Diego! Are you there?" Lucy's voice again, heavily garbled.

"Why you . . . little clock mongrel!" George shouted. "How dare you bring—"

Santiago's fist landed just above George's chin. George spun and crumpled to the floor. "You won't insult my son after he and his friends saved our lives!"

George staggered to his feet, his hair tousled, rubbing his jaw, but his hands quickly raised to fists. "You'll pay for that."

"That's enough!" The captain stepped between them. "I need you both to stop this reactor from blowing. And so do your children."

"Of course," Santiago said.

"Lucy, hang on," the captain said. "We are on our way!"

But they were only answered with silence.

"Get her out of here," George said, spitting blood. "If she's on a ship, tell her to go far away, at full throttle."

"They are pitched in battle, and they aren't going anywhere," the captain said.

"And at full speed, that ship will not escape the quantum blast radius in time," Santiago said. "We have to stop this reactor now." Santiago took a deep breath, surveying the water spraying in around him. "This place will be flooded before we could come up with any kind of work-around to subvert that computer."

Diego thought about what they'd seen from Seahorse. "What about the array?" he said. "If we blow up the antennae array, would that stop the bubble from being created?"

Santiago's brow wrinkled in thought. "If the reactor couldn't transmit, the failsafe protocols would funnel all the quantum energy back into the earth. Diego, that's it!"

"We'll need to find the systems to disable the array," George said.

"No time," the captain said. "But I have the means to destroy it on my ship. Let's go."

"Wait, what about—" Diego turned.

Magnus was gone.

"*Warning: Reactor ignition in forty-four minutes.*"

"Leave Magnus to this accursed place," the captain said. "Santiago, take point."

As they started up the gantry, another vicious explosion rocked the station. Water sloshed in the corners, and a new alarm began to sound. The locomotive engines roared to life, and the reactor began to lower itself down into the shaft, huge, watertight doors closing above it.

They rushed down the corridor, through the storage area, and back to the air lock. As they ran, Diego glanced back to where he'd left Balthus. Balthus was gone. Santiago heard pounding on the door of a storage compartment near the air lock and opened it to find Ajax and the others locked inside.

"The general was waiting for us," Ajax said.

They reached Seahorse to find the door open. The captain ducked in first and roared with frustration.

"Magnus!" the captain said. Diego stepped in, his boots crunching on shards of broken glass. He saw the captain picking up one of the metal panels that had covered the dashboard. Circuits had been pulled out, wires dangling here and there, levers yanked free, and control banks smashed.

"Santiago, can this be repaired?" the captain asked.

Diego saw his dad studying the controls. Santiago put his hands on the console and closed his eyes, his brow wrinkling. So many things he wanted to ask his dad about . . . that he finally *could*. Once they were out of trouble.

"Can you fix it?" he asked.

"Yes," Santiago said. "I can." He turned to George, Georgie, and Ajax. "But only with your help."

"This had better work," George said.

"Get this done," the captain said, then turned, yanked the

ax free, and ran out through the air lock.

"Boleslavich!" Santiago called after him, but the captain's boot steps had already faded.

"I'm going to get the captain," Diego said.

"Diego, no, you—"

"I'm not leaving him behind!" Diego shouted.

Santiago stared at him . . . but then nodded. "Do you have your gun?"

Diego pulled it from his belt. "Yeah."

Santiago checked his watch. "Fifteen minutes. If we're going to make it, you have to be back."

Diego raced through the station, splashing through the watery passageways, trying to remember how the layout had looked from outside.

Finally, he rounded a corner and arrived where he'd been hoping to, only the sight that greeted him was hard to comprehend.

It was the second air lock, but it was larger and configured differently from the other. There was a large chamber; the back wall was made entirely of glass. The captain stood before a single glass-and-steel door at its center. Beside him, a set of tall brass levers protruded from the floor.

Magnus stood on the other side of the glass, inside the underwater cable car's connecting air lock. Behind him, Diego could just make out the unconscious form of Balthus. The captain and Magnus glared at each other, their faces a few feet apart, separated by glass and ocean.

"Sir," Diego said.

The captain looked over his shoulder, spied Diego, and then turned back to Magnus in his cage. The men's eyes were locked. "I hot-wired the cable brake before he could get away," the captain said. He pressed a button on the wall, activating the wall-mounted speaker system.

"You have me, old friend," Magnus said. For the first time, Diego heard a note of uncertainty in his voice. "Pull me back in and let's settle this man-to-man. No weapons, you and me."

"Don't do it!" Diego shouted. "Captain, come with me. We only have a few minutes!"

The captain took a deep breath.

Magnus shook his head and clicked his tongue like he was scolding a child. "Yes, Captain, leave like the coward you are, like last time. Run from your mistakes rather than answer for them." He looked at Diego. "He'll abandon you someday, when you no longer . . . serve his purpose. Just ask your father."

"How dare you," the captain said.

"How dare *you*?" Magnus said. "How can you train these children and send them off to die for . . . *this*?" He raised his arms to the sea around him. "This obscenity of a world."

"This is my home!" Diego shouted.

"And what about MY home?" Magnus slammed the glass with both hands, his voice distorting the intercom. "What about my children? My wife?"

"We all lost people, Magnus."

"No! I didn't lose them, Alex. They were taken from me."

The station computer crackled over passageway speakers, cutting in and out. "*You now have th . . . ty-two min . . . eactor ignition. Evacuate . . . mediately.*"

"Captain," Diego pleaded. "Please."

"Go, Diego," the captain said.

"No, you—"

"Magnus is right. We both have sins. And we will both pay for them. Together. Go!"

"I won't!" Diego crossed his arms, shaking. The frigid water was over his knees now.

"You will, Diego! I am ending this—"

"Elana Ekaterina Boleslavich!" Magnus shouted. "Born Elana Ekaterina Marapova in Moscow. You two met at the National Academy of Sciences, in the Ukraine. You had a daughter that you named Natalia Aleksandra Boleslavich. She would be . . . Ah, but you don't know. . . . She *is* seventeen years old. And she's as lovely as Elana is."

The captain slammed the ax against the floor. "Stop your treacherous lying!"

"Not lies, Aleksandr." Magnus smiled. "Your wife and daughter are alive. And I have them."

"No . . . it's not possible, it can't be."

"I'll prove it with a word, a nickname that only you and Elana could know: Ahi."

"No," the captain said.

Magnus grinned. "Now you believe me, don't you? Release me, Captain, and you may find them. You and I can fight another day. I swear on my honor I will not harm them."

"Your honor," the captain muttered, but Diego could see the way he was shaking, could hear the defeat in his voice.

"Find me again and face me alone. Defeat me and they are yours. You have my word." Magnus bowed.

The captain fell to his knees. Around them, alarms blew more urgently. Diego could see the tears in the captain's eyes, the anguish scarring his face.

"Come on, Captain," Diego said. "He's lying. Don't let him. We need to go—"

"Ahhh!" The captain lurched to his feet and swung the ax with lethal force.

It slammed the glass, embedding in the door. When the captain wrenched it away, water sprayed them.

"Balthus did it, didn't he?" he asked Magnus. "My God, he really did it." He dropped the ax. Diego went to him, pulling his arm.

"Captain! We have to go!" The water was rising fast.

"It's no use, boy," Magnus said. "He knows it's true."

The captain stood, his shoulders slumped, and grasped the brake lever.

"Captain, no," Diego said.

He pulled the lever. The cable wheels groaned as they began to spin, and the sea trolley slipped away from the air lock. As it disappeared into the black water, Magnus gazed back at Diego and the captain, and saluted them with a smile.

Diego struggled to stay upright. The water was swirling near his chest. He grabbed the captain and dragged him away from the glass. He still didn't budge, and Diego slipped and submerged completely, the frigid cold all around him.

Icy darkness, his muscles failing.

Then strong arms yanked him up, and the captain pulled him, striding back through the passageways. They struggled against the water until they reached Seahorse. Ajax let them in through the air lock, and they collapsed to the floor.

"Diego! Finally," Santiago said.

"Did you get it to work?" Diego gasped.

"We've got something rigged," Santiago said. He glanced at the captain. "Magnus?"

The captain shook his head.

"Another time," Santiago said. "Ajax, uncouple us."

They detached from the domed structure, backing away and then lifting. They'd barely made it to a safe distance when the dome imploded, rocking Seahorse violently. Santiago kept a tight hold of the controls and righted them.

"Is that the *John Curtis*?" Santiago asked, pointing to the surface.

"That's it," the captain said.

"But the array," Diego said. "We can't leave—we need to destroy it before—"

"Seahorse is unarmed," Santiago said. "We need something to blow it up with."

The captain checked his watch. "Twenty minutes. I have

two torpedoes aboard my ship."

Santiago glanced at Diego and then turned back to the controls. "Time is tight. I hope whatever is going on topside isn't as bad as it seems."

"We'll have to act fast," the captain said. "Everyone, gather your weapons and be prepared to disembark."

As they neared the surface, the water churned from explosions, and the trails of bullets penetrated the blue.

Seahorse rose fast, breaking the waves beside the John Curtis. They were immediately strafed by bullets. And something struck them and exploded, causing alarms to go off and water to seep in.

Diego raced to the top hatch. He waited for a pause in the clanging of bullets, then popped open the hatch and peered out. Plane engines growled overhead, and Diego looked up to see the Kingfisher wrapped in a spiraling dogfight with a German 109 and a Japanese Zero. He switched on his radio, and it vibrated with the sound of throbbing machine guns.

"Petey, release the smoke bombs!" Diego heard Lucy shout.

Seahorse came alongside the John Curtis while Diego grabbed the tether line and tensed, readying to jump over.

"Lucy, this is the captain," Diego heard over the radio. "Power down. We are going to tie on to the ship."

"Do it fast, sir!" Lucy replied. "We lost that gunship under cover of smoke, but they are out there."

"Holy crap! Enemy ship behind us!" Petey shouted. "I repeat, enemy ship! Break off, break off!"

Diego spun and saw the *Vengeance* bearing down on them.

Petey dove for safety just as the *Vengeance* fired on the *John Curtis.*

"Petey!" Diego screamed.

"Break off, Captain!" Lucy shouted. "Submerge while I draw that enemy ship away."

The *John Curtis* accelerated and began to pull away.

"Wait!" Diego called, but Seahorse was already starting to lower. Diego looked back at Petey lying on the deck . . . and he lunged out of Seahorse, slamming into the side of the *John Curtis* and barely grasping the deck rail. He hauled himself up and bolted toward Petey.

"Are you all right?" Diego asked, sliding down beside him.

"I'm all right," Petey groaned, pulling himself up to a sitting position. Diego helped move him to the wall.

"The gunship is closing!" Diego shouted toward the bridge.

"Lucy," the captain said over the radio. "Do you still have the torpedoes?"

"We only have one, Captain!" Lucy replied. "Petey and I used the other to destroy the first gunship."

"Use the one you have against the *Vengeance*!" the captain said.

"Yes, sir!"

"Sir, what about the reactor station?" Diego asked.

The radio hissed, but for a moment, no one spoke. Diego was about to ask again when the captain replied, "Diego, we'll rig up a mine or some other form of explosive device to take out the station."

Diego and Petey sprinted for the torpedo tubes mounted on the aft deck.

"Just need another moment to line up the boat," Lucy called through the voice tube.

The *John Curtis* eased out of a turn, straightened out, and slowed. Diego watched as the *Vengeance* angled to aim its big side guns at them.

"Are the torpedoes armed?" Lucy asked as Petey flipped the switches.

"Aye, aye, captain!"

"Now, fire!" Lucy ordered.

Diego slammed the release lever, and the torpedo hurtled out into the water, carving a triangle of foam in the sea.

"Come on . . . ," Diego said.

The *Vengeance* started to turn hard, but too late. The torpedo struck it broadside in an explosion of water and fire.

"Yes!" Petey and Diego high-fived as the *Vengeance* broke apart and its smoking hull slipped beneath the waves.

They watched as the Kingfisher dived from the clouds. It flew erratically and landed hard, skipping across the waves like a stone and leaving a spray of water. Moments later, Seahorse pulled up alongside the ship. Lucy slowed the ship to stop. Diego and Petey ran over and tied Seahorse to the ship, and its passengers disembarked.

"Where's my daughter?" George demanded, scanning the decks.

"She's busy piloting the ship," the captain said. "The fact that we are all alive should prove her excellence. For the moment, Mr. Emerson, you and your boy please take the others below. Ajax, man the aft guns with me."

"There's Paige!" Petey said, pointing to where she was emerging onto the wing of the Kingfisher. But any joy in seeing her alive was cut short as Paige pulled Gaston out onto the wing. He was covered in blood and oil, and he wasn't moving. Paige unholstered her pistol and pointed it at the sky and started firing.

"Incoming!" Ajax called.

The Me 109 hurtled out of the sky, bearing down on Paige. Ajax and the captain chased it with streams of bullets but couldn't slow its attack.

The plane, nearly on top of Paige, burst into a fireball, debris shooting in all directions. Another plane raced overhead.

"Is that . . . ," Diego said.

"*Skywolf!*" the captain called.

Mom! Diego watched as Siobhan brought the *Skywolf* around in a wide arc. She buzzed by the deck, saluting them, and her eyes caught sight of Santiago on the deck. Then she turned away and raced skyward to engage the last

two fighter planes.

"Let's get Paige and Gaston aboard," the captain said. "And then—"

He was cut off by the deep explosions of massive guns and the whistling of incoming fire.

Huge shells exploded, barely missing them.

"There!" Petey shouted, pointing toward Jersey Devil Island. The island sat about four miles from where they were, and past it they saw the huge Aeternum battleship rounding

the coast, swinging into position, lining up its guns.

"We need to move!" Diego shouted.

"Too late," the captain said. "He's got us dead to rights."

Diego watched as the giant guns took aim, their sinister black chambers gleaming in the sun. . . .

But a new buzzing reached their ears. Streaks of molten cannon fire rained down from the clouds, strafing the battleship. Smoke, fires erupted, and the battleship burst into flames.

A huge shadow emerged from the clouds in the distance.

"The *Magellan!*" Diego shouted. He high-fived Petey, then turned to find Lucy—she was right there and threw her arms around him.

"That is a sight for sore eyes," the captain said, waving his hat to the *Magellan* in the distance. "Now, everyone at the ready!"

Diego turned back to the ocean and his smile faded.

The *John Curtis* pulled up alongside the Kingfisher. Ajax and Petey climbed down and carried Gaston up. He hung limp between them, his pilot's suit stained with blood.

They laid him on the deck. His body was still, lifeless. Paige came up the ladder right behind them and dropped to her knees beside him. Paige was dirty and bloodstained, her clothes still dripping wet. Her tears flowed freely as she cradled his head while the captain knelt at his side.

"Paige . . ." The captain placed his arm around her.

"He was shot—but there was no way to come down, sir," Paige said. "Couldn't land . . . couldn't shake 'em." Paige wiped her eyes. "It took all his strength to keep us in the air, moving, fighting—living. He said he had to save me." Paige sobbed and held Gaston tightly against her. "It's not fair," she whispered. "I should've . . ." Her tears fell on Gaston's still face.

After a moment, Diego and Petey stepped forward and each put a hand on her shoulder. She spun and fell into them, her body wracked with sadness. She screamed into Petey's chest, and he wrapped his arms around her.

The captain took Gaston in his arms and held him. "You've

been a son to me, Gaston Le Baptiste. Godspeed you to the distant shores."

Diego looked at Gaston. Silent. He'd always seemed older and so irritating, but he looked young and innocent now, except for the blood crusted on the side of his head. "Bye, *frère.*"

Outside, another cannon explosion rocked the ship. Bullets pinged the walls.

Paige wiped her eyes and looked up toward the skies. "Payback."

"Ajax is at the rear guns," Petey said. "I bet he could use some help. Let's go give those bastards hell."

Paige straightened up and nodded. "With pleasure." She glanced back at Gaston. "Mission's not over," she said. "Not for us."

"The *Magellan* may have what we need," Diego heard Santiago saying. He was standing by the captain, watching the airship approach.

"They're still about ten miles out," the captain said. "At their speed and against this headwind, they'll be here in seven minutes."

Santiago glanced at his watch. "Not good. We've got less than twelve minutes. That's not enough time to bring explosives down to Seahorse and get back to the station in time." He glanced at Diego, then at the *Skywolf*, which had just touched down on the barge. He turned back to the captain. "Aleksandr, fashion four mines together with a timer. That should be strong enough, then I'll take it back down, attach it with Seahorse, and get clear."

"I've only low-yield torpedo mines aboard the ship," the captain said flatly.

Santiago held the captain's gaze for a long moment and nodded. "You and I know that they'll have to be enough."

"Dad, no! That's too dangerous."

"No, Santiago," the captain said. "Stay here with your boy. I should be the one. Let me take the bomb. You stay here with Diego."

"I'm sorry, old friend. Seahorse's controls were damaged nearly beyond repair. There is no way to engage the autopilot,

and I'm the only one who knows how to operate the make-shift controls," Santiago said, shaking his head. "It has to be me. So please, the bomb."

The captain looked at Santiago and nodded. "Good luck, old friend."

"And to you, Aleksandr."

"Diego," Santiago said, "go help your captain. I need that device. Hurry now, son. I'll have to drop that bomb and get clear of the blast—so no time to lose."

"Okay," Diego said, and he followed the captain, but he paused at the hatch and turned to see Santiago approaching Lucy, who had come down to the aft deck to look for her family.

They stayed like that for just long enough that Diego started to worry.

Diego saw tears at the edges of Lucy's eyes.

"Diego!" the captain called from the stairwell. "Let's go!"

"One sec!" Diego turned to follow, but then he saw his mother climbing aboard the *John Curtis* with Ajax, who had retrieved her with a longboat. "Mom!" He waved. She was up onto the deck when a flash of movement distracted her. Diego saw it, too.

Santiago was getting into Seahorse, untying the tether and pushing the bot away from the *John Curtis*. But where was he going?

"Dad, what are you doing?" Diego yelled. Instinct took over, his feet moving on their own. His eyes locked with his mom's, and then she was running, too.

They reached the rail together.

Diego stepped back, pulling free of his mom, and activated his radio. "Dad!" he called into the static.

"Diego," Santiago's voice crackled. "Be strong, son . . . follow your own path."

"Dad, wait!" The radio crackled. "Come back!"

"How . . . can I?" he asked, knowing there would be no answer.

"Santi . . . ," Siobhan whispered.

"Dad." Diego stared at the radio.

Silence.

A geyser of water shot skyward. Massive waves rippled out of the epicenter, crashing over the sides of the *John Curtis* and swamping the decks. The water bubbled and roiled with huge, foam-topped waves.

Diego toppled to his back. He reached for the railing, only to be thrown back the other way by the waves emanating out of the disturbance. Diego collided with Ajax, hit the wall, then finally got his feet underneath him and lunged for the railing. He pulled himself up and looked over the side.

"Dad!" Diego shouted, scanning the water helplessly. He had to come back. Had to . . .

Something glimmered beneath the waves. Diego leaned up on his toes. There was a light, deep beneath the blue, glowing brighter. Through the watery blur Diego saw lines, glinting metal, glassy reflections . . . Seahorse's canopy!

But as the light grew brighter, Diego saw that this was something else. Buildings, shining in sunlight, somehow beneath the waves, like he was looking through a window at a city, a vast, futuristic metropolis. It had majestic towers, arcing monorail tracks, everything sleek and—for a moment the image crystalized into monuments of glass and steel that pierced the surface of the water . . .

And then it was gone. A shimmering flicker. Diego blinked and shook his head. What had he just seen? Had the explosion caused it, or had his mind been playing tricks on him? And yet, it hardly mattered. It hadn't been Seahorse. Hadn't been his dad. The water was dark again, unknowable and cold, no sign of life beneath its surface.

CHAPTER TWENTY-FOUR

Path and the Promise

Diego can see it: he stands with his father, leaning against the railing on the roof of a towering skyscraper. As the sun sets, buildings cast long shadows over the city, and pulsing gas lamps flicker to life, rimming the dark sea. The ocean breeze caresses his face, bringing its salt-and-diesel smell.

"When I was your age," Santiago says, "this building was called the Sears Tower. It was the tallest in the world, and in my time, that was an accomplishment of great importance.

"As time passed," Santiago says, "another tower was built in a different part of the world, one even bigger and grander

than this. And then another."

"Who built the biggest tower?" Diego asks. "Was it the Elders? Their towers on the other side of the city dwarf this one."

Santiago smiles at Diego. "The tallest building hasn't been built yet, son. . . . Can you imagine it, though? Taller than the Elders', taller than anything ever imagined before. Perhaps even so tall that it would touch the rim of the sky. Close your eyes."

Diego does.

"Can you see it? Can you see what it would need?"

Diego imagines a great structure. "Lots of men, and robots," he says, "and so much glass and steel and hard work. It would take years to build, but"—the form grows in his mind's eye—"it would be so beautiful!"

Santiago's hand falls on Diego's shoulder. "Yes, it certainly is." Diego glances up and sees that his father's eyes are closed now, too. "And more amazing than anything I ever imagined. Do you want it to be real?" Santiago asks. "This tower of yours."

"Definitely."

"Open your eyes."

Diego looks around, but there is still only the setting sun across the city below. "For a moment I thought it might be here," he says.

"It's *here*," Santiago says. He touches Diego's forehead. "This is where it lives. Its promise." He touches Diego's chest. "And here is where you'll find your path." Santiago smiles.

"Follow it through to the end, no matter what. This is what is in the heart of every man or woman who has ever built a tower, or conquered a mountain, or changed the world."

"Do you ever miss the world you came from?" he asks his dad. "Some people think it was better."

Santiago sighs. "Sometimes I miss a street corner, or a restaurant. There were these hot dogs from Portillo's that, oh man . . ." He laughs. "But, no. The only world I want to live in is this one, because you and your mother are in it. That was my world. But here, this is *ours*."

Diego's eyes opened. The dark bled away, and the warmth of light poured through the window in their room. He was in Arkhipov Castle. It was dawn.

He was surprised he'd slept. Yesterday had seemed like it would never end. Dad . . . every time he thought of it, the sight of Seahorse submerging, the fleeting glimpse of the future made by the quantum explosion. He kept telling himself it was impossible, that his dad couldn't be gone. But he was.

So Diego could live.

But now Diego had to live without him.

"Hey, D." Petey stood nearby, lacing up his boots. "You had a good dream, it sounded like." He spoke carefully. "I got back from the shower, and as I was getting dressed, you said something in your sleep. 'It would touch the stars.'"

"Yeah," Diego said. It had felt so real, being there on the building top with his father. He wanted to go there again.

Diego sat up. "What are our duties?"

"The captain is showing the Emersons around the island. Ajax is unloading gear. There's going to be a ceremony later tonight."

"Oh, right," Diego said.

"Balsamic says we have the day free. What do you want to do?"

Diego got dressed. "Actually, Petey, I've got something in mind."

"Sure, whatever you want."

"I've got a project I want to do, over in the hangar. Feel like joining me and Redford?"

"That sounds great."

When they finished hours later, Diego heard his mother and Lucy over by Sea Fury, talking about flying. The captain and the Emersons were discussing various machines. Diego sent Redford and Petey looking for fuel. Wiping his hands on a grimy rag, he joined his mom.

"I can't believe you flew so well when you were sixteen," Lucy was saying. She glanced over her shoulder, toward the sound of her father's voice, and lowered her own. "How in the world did you convince your parents to let you become a pilot?"

"I didn't tell them until it was too late." Siobhan turned and opened her arms. "Diego." As he moved in for a hug, he saw his mom trying to keep up a smile.

Diego hugged her hard.

"What have you been up to?" she said, her lips against his hair.

"A little project. You guys want to see?"

"Actually, the captain wants me to explain some of Santiago's designs to the engineers. Best as I can anyway. I'll catch up with you later."

"Captain Ribera . . ." Lucy's face had gotten pink.

"What is it, darling?"

"I, um, I found this, in your old trainer plane. I believe this belongs to you."

"My other lucky chopstick. I thought it was lost. Thank you." Her eyes welled up. "Santi gave me these before my first mission, and said they would bring me luck."

Diego put his arm around her. "They did, Mom."

Siobhan nodded. She hugged Diego fiercely. "Show me your new machine later, okay?" She turned back to Lucy. "This one belongs to you now, young warrior. It's your lucky battle charm." She placed it in Lucy's hand and closed the girl's fingers around it. "May it keep you safe."

Lucy and Diego headed back to the shop. "Petey told me you finally got some sleep," she said.

"Yeah." Diego didn't want her to ask anything more about how he was doing, and she didn't. "Okay," he said as they rounded the corner, "Redford, Petey . . . here we come!"

"Diego, it's magnificent!"

"I never could have done it without Petey and Redford," Diego said.

"We were essential," Petey said, except he was shaking his head side to side.

"And what, pray tell, is this?" George Emerson had walked over to them.

"Diego made it," Lucy said, her smile fading. "He's an amazing builder, just like his father."

Diego tensed. He wondered if George would dare speak ill of Santiago given the circumstances.

"An impressive toy," George said. "Perhaps the flying circus is in your future."

Diego pictured his dad hitting George in the mouth and smiled. "Actually, it's not for me," Diego said.

"Either way," George said. "I came to find you, Lucy. We'll rejoin the other engineers now. Come along."

"I'd rather stay here," Lucy said.

"Young lady, bite your tongue and bow your head! This foolish adventure has earned you no right to be insolent."

Diego saw Lucy's fists balled tight. He wondered if she'd stage a full revolt.

But she gave Diego an apologetic glance. "Yes, Daddy," she said in her iciest tone, and walked away.

"Man," Diego said, pretending to wipe sweat from his brow. "That guy's a real—"

Redford blew a puff of steam.

Diego smiled. "You said it, Redford."

"What did he say?" Petey asked.

"He told me I'm not allowed to repeat it."

"Whoa, Redford!" Petey shouted, and slapped a high five on his metal leg. "You've been spending too much time with Paige!"

Diego laughed. It didn't last long, but it felt good.

At dusk, everyone gathered in the map room. All the windows and doors had been thrown open wide. A chilly breeze whispered around them, laced with the smell of salt. They stood around the large map table. Two maps were laid out, and atop them stood two brass candlesticks. One candle was lit, the other was not. Once everyone had arrived, they looked to the captain.

"We stand together at this day's end to wish our fallen comrades safe passage as they cross over to distant, unknown shores. May they find peace knowing that the world they fought for remains and that we will honor their sacrifices."

The captain held out an arrow to Siobhan and Diego. "For a husband, father, and comrade."

Siobhan nodded for Diego to take it.

The captain held out another arrow. "For our brother in arms, second pilot, navigator, and deck officer who had no equal."

Captain Wallace stepped forward and took the lit candle from the table. He led everyone outside to the balcony, where Ajax waited, holding a large bow.

HUNTSMAN

As the flaming arrow sailed into the dark, Captain Boleslavich spoke softly: "We all come from the fire. We burn bright, each of us an ember sent high, to shine our light as long as we can." The falling flame arced downward and winked out against the midnight-blue water.

The captain lit the second arrow and handed it to Ajax. He let it go with a sharp snap of the bow. It hissed as it traveled and joined the other at the bottom of the cove.

They stepped back inside. The captain lit the second candle with the first and blew out the first one.

"Diego," the captain said. "Come here."

Diego stepped closer, and the captain motioned to the map before him. It was newly drawn.

"Please read the inscription at the top," the captain said.

Diego looked it over for a moment, then read:

"*A world to be found. A world to be made.*
And what is made shall never be unmade.
We fight together. We fight for each other.
To the very last, till the very end.
We've come far and will go farther still.
So say the Rangers of the Vastlantic."

As Diego read, the words burned into his heart. This was his mission now, too. His fight.

"Diego," the captain said. "You and your friends are hereby recognized by the Vanguard as our own. This map belongs to you as a reminder of your vow."

"There's no title on this map. Why?"

"It is your map of the world, and it is up to you, the Rangers, to fill in the blank spaces as you find your way in it."

He picked up a quill and dipped it into a small ink jar. "In memory of the fallen at Yorktown, we hereby dedicate ourselves anew." He handed the pen to Diego and motioned to a corner of the map.

One by one, they all signed.

"Thank you, sir," Paige said.

"All right," George suddenly burst out. "I've had enough of this . . . indoctrination!" He grasped at Lucy's wrist as she held the quill to sign. "You may fight for what is right, Captain Boleslavich, but you shamelessly bend the lives of those too young to know otherwise to your will. And I won't have it for my daughter! She will not be one of your so-called *Rangers*. She is a child and a proper young lady, made for a decent and honorable life. You will not take those things from her."

"Father," Lucy protested. "I was not *made* to be anything except me! And this is what I want!"

"Nonsense! What do you know of what you want? This man, these *boys*, have been filling your head with foolishness. Thank heavens I found you in time. The sooner we're away from this, the better." George took Lucy by the arm. "Captain," he said, calming his voice, "we support your cause, but we will not be party to it with our blood."

"You may not have a choice," the captain said. "All this was only the beginning." The captain saluted Lucy.

"That's enough theatrics," George said. "Come, Lucy."

But Lucy yanked her arm free.

"Lucy. Now."

Lucy looked at her feet, then at her friends. Her eyes were red and full of tears. She leaned toward Paige and whispered something into her ear. Then her eyes found Diego again.

He almost called to her, almost held out his hand.

But Lucy turned away and stepped to her father's side.

Diego watched her go, feeling his fragile resolve slipping. His heart sank as she left the room. He nearly ran after her, but his mother's hand fell on his shoulder. "Two brave souls such as you are bound to meet again." Then she leaned to his ear and whispered, "We'll make sure of it."

With the ceremony completed, the Vanguard and the Mapmakers talked tactics. Wallace planned to bring the engineers and the Emersons back on the *Magellan* first thing in the morning, and also to update Magistrate Huston. The captain, Ajax, and Siobhan were forming a plan to find Magnus. It was all interesting, but Diego couldn't pay attention.

"Hey."

Diego turned to find Paige beside him. "What?"

"Message from Lucy. She told me to tell you to meet her at turtle beach, wherever that is."

Diego nodded. "When? Now?"

"No, fool. After lights-out. So don't fall asleep or nothing."

"I won't."

CHAPTER TWENTY-FIVE

One Destiny Divided

Diego sat in the sand looking up at the stars. He heard Lucy's footsteps approaching, but when he turned, he was surprised by what he saw.

"I know," she said with a shrug. She wore the same proper Victorian dress she'd had on when they'd left on their adventure. "But it will be bad enough if Father catches me out here, and even worse if I'm still in"—she mocked him with a deep, stern voice—"'*those outrageous and highly inappropriate pirate uniforms!*'"

"Your buccaneer's hat probably pushed him over the edge." Diego laughed, but only for a moment. "I can't believe you're leaving in the morning."

"Yeah." She didn't add anything else.

Somewhere in the distance, a pteranodon called.

"Where will you go?" Diego asked.

"Back to New Chicago for a month or so, until the summer storm season passes. And then off to merry olde London."

"Taken back to prison, more like," Diego said.

"That's not fair."

"Couldn't you stay longer?" Diego asked.

"Father's had enough of New Chicago." She took his hand.

Diego sighed. "He's being a real jerk."

"Careful," Lucy said. "The old Lucy Emerson would box your ears for that kind of comment."

"Sorry."

"It's okay. I always knew this was how he would feel. Silly me to ever hope that he might be able to change."

"He has no idea how amazing his daughter really is," Diego said. He gave her hand a squeeze. She laughed and leaned into his shoulder. But her laugh faded quickly.

They heard a clanking sound from down the beach. Redford stood in the breakwater, gazing out at the moonlit waves.

"What will be next for you?" Lucy asked.

"Petey, Paige, and I are staying for another week with my mom. We'll help repair the *John Curtis*, and then . . . it's back to school for the rest of the year, I guess. Mom might let me train with the Mapmakers for the summer. Petey and Paige are going to ask their parents about it, too."

"You won't be joining the captain and Ajax?"

"They are leaving for a long while. Once their repairs are done, they're setting sail to find new recruits and to search for information about where Magnus might be holding the captain's wife and daughter."

Lucy's fingers intertwined with his. The waves shushed against the sand in a slow, steady rhythm.

"Diego, I have something to tell you."

"What?" Diego asked.

"Do you remember back in Yorktown, before your father took Seahorse, he said something to me?"

"Yes."

Tears spilled from Lucy's eyes. "Everything was so chaotic, I didn't have time to think about what he meant. . . . I'm sorry."

"You don't have to be," Diego said. "What did he say?"

"He said, 'Tell Diego to always remember who he is to me, and to his mother.' That sometimes you forget that. And then he said, 'Tell him and his mother that what I do today, I do for them. And that I love them.'"

"Thanks for telling me." He pushed through all his complicated thoughts and tried to voice something that he'd been putting together in his head over the last day. "I think I understand now what my father has been doing all these years. He was still fighting the war, but his weapons were happiness, dignity, and prosperity. Every city, or outpost, or family that he helped with his steam-converter technology was a victory against Magnus. The more people who believe in this future, who feel that they belong here, who are happy, the fewer who will want to join Magnus and change it back. And once we're home, I'll try to continue my father's work, for the city and for the Vanguard. I'm going to keep that going. Who knows? It might end up being me that works on your father's steam converters."

"Well, that should be fun. They're as sturdy as his beliefs." Lucy sighed. "Seriously, though, I'm envious of your future. Mine sounds like death."

"Then don't go," Diego said. "Tell him no."

"I know you don't approve, and believe me, neither do I. But you don't have the right to defy my father's wishes, and neither do I."

"Don't you?" Diego said.

"No." Lucy shuffled away on the sand. "I can't."

"But why not? After all we've been through?"

"Because it's not just about me!"

"Then I'll kidnap you."

This made a smile crack Lucy's armor. "Like you even could."

"I'm sorry. I just feel like you have a right to be happy, to choose your own path."

"That's a very American thing to say," Lucy said. "Always only concerned with yourself."

"Yeah, but *you* aren't from *their* time, and I'm sorry, but . . . they're not from ours," Diego pleaded. "You're a Ranger of the Vastlantic!"

"I know who I am," Lucy said. "I mean, you don't get to . . . Ugh! Why did I even come out here? I wanted to say a proper good-bye, but leave it to you to make everything confusing!"

A series of splashes distracted them.

"Oh great," Lucy said. "Now Redford's coming to watch us fight again."

She got to her feet, gathering her boots under her arm and her dress in her other hand. "I'm going back. Tomorrow's going to be a long day and—"

"Lucy, wait!" Diego said. He jumped to his feet. "I made the flying car for you."

"What?"

"The Bentley plane car . . . it's for you, for when you become a pilot. So that you have a plane unlike any in history. All your own, even more special than *Skywolf*."

Lucy's lip quivered. "No one's ever done anything that nice for me. How is it that you can be so infuriating and so sweet all at the same time?"

"It's my special talent."

Lucy laughed. "Does anyone else know?"

"Not even Petey."

"Good. No one can ever know." She took a deep breath. "I cannot accept your gift. As much as I want to, doing so would shame my father and embarrass my family. But I do accept it." She put a hand over her heart. "Here."

Diego didn't know what to say. "I wish you could take it."

"I know." Lucy wiped at her eyes. "Okay, I'm going to bed now, though I doubt I'll sleep. Listen, tomorrow morning, I'll present myself accordingly, and we will say good-bye with a handshake and a thank-you. Please accept it graciously and act like a gentleman. If you're a true friend, you won't make it hard for me, okay?"

"Okay."

"No, promise."

Diego swallowed. "I promise."

"Good." Lucy paused, her eyes taking in the ocean. "Good night, Diego. I will think of you all the time." She made a little shrug, wiped her eyes, and left.

Diego watched her go, wanting to run after her, grab her arm, ask her to stay longer, but he didn't, for her sake.

Redford puffed steam.

"Yes," Diego said, wiping at his eyes, "she was crying but, no, we weren't fighting. Or, at least, not at the end."

Redford put a hand on his hip.

"I'm serious! Don't throw me in the water again! I was trying to do something nice."

Redford puffed again, and his hand lowered to the sand. Diego stepped up on it, and Redford raised him to his shoulder. Diego climbed onto the cockpit chair. Daphne was there, and he scooped her into his arms. She barked in the direction of the lone figure disappearing into the shadows beneath the palms.

"Yeah, Daph," Diego said, rubbing her head. "I'm going to miss her, too."

The next morning, though he'd barely slept, Diego remembered to do as he was told. Lucy, looking radiant in a white dress, said good-bye to each of them, her father allowing her this one last respite.

Ajax gave her a wooden carving of the *John Curtis*. The captain reminded her that she would always be part of the Vanguard. Petey gave her a salute and called her "Captain Emerson." Siobhan hugged her and told her to be proud of her strength. She and Paige hugged the longest, promising to write to each other.

When she got to Diego, he extended his hand. When Lucy put her hand in his, a small, surprised expression crossed her face. But she continued shaking his hand.

"Good-bye . . . ," Diego said.

"Good-bye, Mr. Ribera. Do stay out of trouble."

"Safe travels, Ms. Emerson."

For a moment, it seemed Lucy would say something else, but instead she curtsied and returned to her father's side.

Diego stood with Paige and Petey as the Emersons joined Captain Wallace on the platform. Diego watched Lucy rise up, away from them. She watched him back.

"I saw that," Paige said in his ear. "What did you put in her hand?"

"Oh," Diego said, reaching into his pocket. "One of these."

As the *Magellan* faded into the puffy clouds, Diego felt certain of one thing: he would see Lucy again.

Their adventures together were far from over.

CHAPTER TWENTY-SIX

A Dream Changed

A week later, the *John Curtis* steamed into New Chicago Harbor. Diego knew he was home when he saw the first silhouettes of the immense walking cranes through the mist on the horizon. After so many weeks on the open sea, it was a shock to smell the acrid tinge of diesel fuel, that slight undercurrent of sewage that said *home*.

He stood beside Siobhan at the prow. Diego ran his finger over the railing, its surface chipped and splintered by bullets. He sighed. It had been a great adventure, but they'd all sustained damage.

"I can't believe we're back," he said.

"Neither can I." She put an arm around him and squeezed.

MARC GARDANA

A. Baltz © 2011

"Sometime after we're home, I have a few words for you about how you took off across the world without telling me."

"Sorry," Diego said.

"I only wish I'd been with you."

Diego's spirits fell. His dad should be with them now. That had been the point of leaving in the first place.

"What is it?" Siobhan asked.

"I feel like I failed," Diego said. "I was supposed to save Dad."

"You did," Siobhan said. "But after that, your father made his own choices, and he saved you."

"I know."

"And I know something else," Siobhan said. "He was never prouder of you."

Another squadron flew overhead, this time flanking the *John Curtis*, so low that Diego and Siobhan could see the pilots.

Ahead, they could hear the clanging of the harbor. Fingers of steam rose off the city as it woke to this lovely spring day.

The *John Curtis* released the barge carrying Redford and the *Skywolf* to a city tug near Navy Pier. As they rode past the pier, Diego pointed out where he'd been shot at, and where they'd found Redford.

"See, these are the parts a mother doesn't want to hear," Siobhan said.

The pier was packed with people, and so were the sides of the canal. Hundreds, stretching all the way to their building. Diego stood with Petey and Paige, and when the crowd spotted them, a huge cheer erupted. Confetti sprinkled through the air. Diego waved back, and the shouting only increased.

"Guess word of our adventure got back before we did!" Petey shouted over the cheering, soaking it all in.

"They honor your heroism," the captain said, arriving beside them. He rested a hand on Diego's shoulder. "And your sacrifice. They don't know the whole story, of course. But they know enough, for now."

The crowd in front of Marina Towers threatened to spill over into the canal. As the *John Curtis* tied off at the dock, Diego turned to the captain and Ajax. "Thank you, Captain Boleslavich."

"Finally you honor my family name. Maybe there's hope for you."

"Thanks for not throwing me overboard."

"We were honored to fight by your side," the captain said.

"Agreed," Ajax said.

The captain looked at him squarely. "Do not dwell on the loss of your father," he said. "Remember his life, and the life he gave you." He pushed Diego gently away. "Now go enjoy this moment. We will soon have more work to do."

"Thanks, Captain," Diego said. He shook hands with Ajax as Petey and Paige said their good-byes, and then the three made their way through the cheering crowd.

They stopped for pictures, slapped hands, and it took

them nearly a half hour to get all the way inside and safely into the elevator.

"Lucy's bumming she missed that," Petey said.

"Are you kidding?" Paige said. "She would have *hated* all that informality. It would have been so fun to watch!"

Diego smiled, but it made his heart ache. He wondered where she was. Close enough to hear that crowd? Or locked away in her family's apartment in Old Chicago? She deserved this as much as they did.

The elevator clanked to a halt, and Diego was surprised to find they'd stopped at the workshop. "Why here?" Diego asked, hesitant to be in his father's space so soon.

"It's a parade!" Petey shouted, running ahead with Paige.

Diego stepped out with Siobhan. "What are they talking about?" he asked.

"The people deserve a show from their heroes," Siobhan said. "Magistrate Huston had the canal cleared all the way from here to City Hall. Everyone is waiting to salute you." She patted Diego's shoulder. "I want you to make the memories for a new dream."

Before Diego could ask what she meant, Siobhan gave him a gentle shove into the shop. "Fly," she said.

Diego turned back, trying to hide his surprise. She could

never have known about his dream. And yet . . .

He found Petey and Paige already putting on their steam packs and gloves. The five gravity boards, Diego's and the four he'd made, were lying on the workbench.

"I had Ajax send them ahead," Siobhan said.

Diego stepped to his board and then ran a finger over Lucy's. It would have been perfect if she'd been here.

He noticed Paige looking at Gaston's board. She smiled. "They'll be with us, you know?"

Diego took a deep breath and nodded. "Definitely."

After he strapped on his pack, he slid the photo of the four friends out of his pocket. He folded it so that it was a narrow rectangle, only showing Lucy, and then he slipped it in the strap of his glove.

"Ready?" Petey called. "First one to the clock tower wins!"

He grabbed his board and leaped out the window. Paige followed.

Diego waited a moment. Just to give them a head start. He wanted it to be fair, after all.

Lucy wouldn't have needed one.

Then he fired up his Walkman, sprinted for the window with his board in front of him, and dived out into the morning sun, headfirst.

The crowd in City Hall Plaza was bigger than anywhere else, cheering, waving, the magistrate standing at a podium decorated with bunting.

And for a moment, Diego felt a dash of worry, remembering his dream: the people disappearing, the world falling apart. He glanced up at the face of the clock in the tower, and

as he did, the minute hand moved. . . .

But not backward. And the screams from below were only of joy. And the air and the sun and the sky stayed made.

The clock moved as it should, as it *would*, as long as he and his friends kept their vow and continued on their path.

Forward.

Epilogue

He woke in a fog of pain, the world distant. When he tried to move, he felt only a stinging sensation and distance, as if his limbs were miles away. *Broken bones*, he thought, *internal bleeding, my spine . . .*

Blinking away pinpricks of light, he saw the blazing sun, and beneath that a strange, vast world unlike any he'd ever known.

But there was more pressing business now. Horses and riders. Thirty or more. Approaching fast. The seven in front, however, were distinct. Those weren't horses they rode. The shape was different.

He tried to stand, to face them, but collapsed.

Their leader motioned to one of the horse riders, an Asian girl, maybe fourteen. She dismounted and joined the leader.

He spoke urgently to her in a foreign tongue, then gave her a rough push forward. She stumbled, righted herself, and cast an annoyed glance back.

The clothing looked familiar. Somewhere in the highlands of the continent. Tibetan, Mongolian maybe.

"Hello," she said in halting English.

"Hi," he said. "You speak English."

The girl nodded.

"Who are you?" he asked.

She bit her lip and glanced over her shoulder. This was probably not information she was supposed to give. "Song," she said.

Their leader shouted at her in their strange tongue.

"He will speak to you now." Song stepped back, and the leader approached, ax drawn.

"Thor Rammuelson," the leader said. He lowered his ax and pressed, saying more in his ancient Norwegian tongue.

"He wants your name," Song said. "And to know where you come from, and why you are here."

The stranger felt the edge digging into his ribs. The slightest pressure would break the skin. "The where is very far," he said. "The why I cannot say, but my name is . . . Santiago Ribera and I'm from a place called New Chicago."

Acknowledgments

When my son, Dylan, was a young boy, we'd often play together for hours on end drawing pictures and creating things with his toy Legos. Our imaginations at play. One afternoon my son had fashioned a robot from random Lego parts and bricks in his collection but had fallen short in completing the robot's head. Undeterred, he grabbed a toy tractor from his farming play set and taped it atop the robot's shoulders to make its head. He proudly presented me his *tractor-bot*. In looking at it, the spark of an idea took hold, and I painted what would be the first image for *Timeless*. That evening when I put Dylan to bed, he asked me to make up an adventure about his robot that included the two of us. Years later, that bedtime story would become . . . *Timeless*.

There were many folks who helped me bring this epic adventure to life. I want to start off by thanking my friend Kevyn Lee Wallace, who inspired me to have the courage to follow my dreams and create this story. Special thanks to Philip Metschan, who was my sounding board on our daily commute to Pixar. As my carpooling partner and office mate he had no escape from my story-obsessed mind. His patience in reading my drafts and providing feedback and his help in making visual sense of the *Timeless* world was invaluable. To Greg Dykstra, resident dinosaur expert and sculptor at Pixar, who gave me great information and was patient with my endless questions. Thanks to Jessica Coville, Mark Burstein, and Adrienne Fedak Ranft for reading my evolving drafts and helping me whip my story into shape. Thanks to Iain Morris, whose brilliant eye and design sensibilities helped me bring the early *Timeless* artwork out into the light. I want to thank master artists and storytellers James Gurney and Iain McCaig for their inspiration, encouragement, friendship, and darn good advice they gave me along the way.

Like the fellowship in Tolkien's epic saga, *Timeless* would have never made it to the journey's end without its own fellowship. My thanks to Steve Tzirlin, who, with Brooklyn Weaver, saw what *Timeless* could be, and to Michelle Kroes. And thanks to my agents at the Gernert Co., Will Roberts and Seth Fishman, who at times was equal parts Gandalf and Samwise lending advice as both an author and an agent as I traveled unfamiliar lands. Together they helped *Timeless* find its way.

I want to thank everyone involved at HarperCollins. To Katherine Tegen, for believing in my story and artwork, and to Ben Rosenthal—I couldn't have asked for a better editor to brave the unknown in making the kind of book I wanted to make. It was uncharted territory for both of us, and we came out on the other side wiser and stronger for the adventures ahead. Huge thanks to Kevin Emerson and Amy Ryan, along with Carla Weise and Jason Cook, for helping me make the book read and look as fantastic as possible. I also want to thank Alana Whitman and Ann Dye in marketing, and publicist Stephanie Hoover. Thanks to assistant editor Mabel Hsu, production editor Kathryn Silsand, production manager Allison Brown, and copy editors Andrea Curley and Maya Myers.

Growing up I loved classic adventure and science-fiction stories like *Treasure Island* and *Twenty Thousand Leagues Under the Sea*. My favorite versions of these stories were illustrated by the Golden Age of American illustrators, such as N. C. Wyeth and Howard Pyle. I'd always dreamed of making an adventure like the ones I cherished as a boy. I loved creating stories and artwork, and my career in animation and film design was born out of my passion for visual storytelling. In creating *Timeless*, I wanted to make something epic in scope, something forged from my experiences and artistic vision. I wanted to create a book that read like a movie. The creation of the art of *Timeless* was a tremendous undertaking that was both as ambitious and complex as any film that I helped make. I'm thankful for having good friends who contributed their time and talents in helping me bring the visual story to life.

Thanks to Pippa Morris, who managed to keep me

organized and on track in the preproduction phase of creating the art. To Adam Clement, Merle McGregor, Mark Burstein, Llisa Demetrios, Carl Halberg, Ed Knapp, and John Andrew Miller, whose help at this stage was invaluable.

Special thanks to Bruce Mitchell, costume designer and fabricator extraordinaire, who created a functional costume prop for Ajax's arm, and to Isaac C. Singleton Jr., who modeled it for me in costume to better paint the character. Thanks to the artists who created the original models and sculptures for the *Timeless* world that helped in the creation of the final paintings: Philip Metschan, Rachelle Danielle, Robert E. Barnes, John Duncan, Dan Whitton, Kurt Kaufman, Frank Zeng, Karel Charles Murray, and Lucas Aceituno and Alison Kellom. To the amazing artist and sculptor Dan Jones of Tinkerbots, who allowed me to feature one of his fantastic vehicles in one of the paintings.

Warm thanks to my Rangers: Dylan, Emelia, Drew, and Shawna. Thanks to my captain and cast of characters: John B., Sterling, Brian, Leilani, Justine, Octavio, Chris, Nozomi, Leslie, Nicole, and Anaida; and the Kohlman, the Morris, the Barnes, the Merck, and the Burstein families, along with all the folks who toiled in costumes during the hot summer days to help me create the characters in the paintings.

My deepest gratitude to my artist friends who helped me by contributing additional design and paintings that brought the world to life: Brynn Metheney, Marc Gabbana, Noah Klocek, Tang Heng, Noëlle Triaureau, Josh Viers, Robert Chew,

Wade Huntsman, Wendell Dalit, Naveen Selvanathan, Brian Matyas, Armand Serrano, John Nevarez, Yoriko Ito, Paul Lasaine, Randy Gaul, D.J. Welch, Karla Ortiz, Colin Fix, and Iain McCaig.

I want to thank all my friends and colleagues who supported me through this journey. To my parents for their love and support, and to my friend Johnny May, who reminded me to take care of myself as I pushed myself relentlessly this last year.

And finally, I want to thank my wife, Sharon, and my son, Dylan. You two were my pillars of strength and my well of inspiration that fueled the vision. Your love, patience, and unending support made it all possible. Thank you both for giving me the adventure of a lifetime.